"Mind the duck!

Mary's warning ⟨...⟩ turned her head towar⟨...⟩ to do the exact opposit⟨...⟩ ⟨...⟩ ᵤₕₑ path.

"Aargh!" cried Beι ⟨...⟩ was sent sprawling to the ground.

A loud, angry "Quack! Quack!" was followed by a flurry of wings and feathers as the slightly stunned duck half flew and half staggered to the sanctuary provided by the river.

"I did tell her to watch out for the duck," Mary muttered in her own defense as they rushed to help Betty to her feet.

Penny and Doris took an arm each as Mary reached to retrieve Betty's handbag. It had landed precariously close to the edge of the river, and the dastardly duck was snuffling at it before Mary seized it and handed it back to Betty.

"Mary!" cried Betty. "Grab that envelope!"

Swiveling, Mary saw a large brown envelope and stooped for it before it could fall into the water. "Got it!" she yelled, waving it in the air. Unfortunately, the envelope being upside down, the contents spilled onto the ground around her, luckily missing going into the river. She bent down to pick them up and was surprised to discover they were all newspaper cuttings.

A Wing and a Prayer

by

M. W. Arnold

Broken Wings, Book 1

A Wing and a Prayer

Cover Art by *The Wild Rose Press, Inc.*

The Wild Rose Press, Inc.
PO Box 708
Adams Basin, NY 14410-0708
Visit us at www.thewildrosepress.com

Publishing History
First Vintage Rose Edition, 2020
Trade Paperback ISBN 978-1-5092-3301-4
Digital ISBN 978-1-5092-3302-1

Broken Wings, Book 1
Published in the United States of America

Dedication

For my ever-patient Lady Wife, Christine.
I couldn't have done this without
your belief, encouragement, and patience.
Keep doing what you're doing.

Acknowledgments

I'll start off with my wonderful, patient editor, Nan Swanson. Thanks for taking me through everything I needed to get this book to a state where it was ready to be published. I don't know how you do it. To the rest of the Rose Garden team, my thanks for letting me in and making me feel so welcome.

For the unwavering support they've shown me over the last couple of (difficult) years, I'd be remiss if I didn't single out the ladies (and gentlemen) of the Romantic Novelist's Association. So many of you have been there for me I can't individually name you, as there wouldn't be enough room. However, thanks go to Elaine Everest, for suggesting this as a genre I could write in, Sue Moorcroft and Erin Green for your unending encouragement, and all those in the Birmingham Chapter and the Belmont Belles: I love you all (Don't tell my Lady Wife)! This is a wonderful society, and if you're an aspiring writer, you couldn't do better than to get on its New Writer's Scheme. Some of the best writers I know are graduates of this process.

To the Air Transport Auxiliary Association, thanks for fielding my questions.

To everyone else who encouraged me with this project, thank you very much!

And to you, the reader, thank you so, so much for buying a copy of *A Wing and a Prayer*. I'd like to think you enjoyed reading it as much as I did writing it. Reviews are everything to writers so, if you'd be so kind, please do leave a review.

Prologue

January 1942

The frost was hard upon the airfield as the ground crew watched the Tiger Moth pull up sharply to avoid a spinney of oak trees. It was a near-run thing, and if the pilot hadn't gunned the engine to hop over at the last second, the biplane would have ploughed into the treetops. Nonetheless they could plainly see branches, torn off by the near miss, caught up in the tailskid as the biplane rocked from side to side, the engine now coughing as the pilot struggled to maintain control.

Leaning forward on their bikes, their anxiety only grew as they could see the pilot's head lolling back and forth. From where they were, they had the best view of the approach, and they all held their breath as the biplane's wheels touched down with considerable force, bouncing the aircraft ten feet back into the air.

The port wing dipped alarmingly toward the grass airfield, the pilot correcting only just in time. With the engine pitch whining, the pilot pushed the control stick forward and the wheels hit the ground, bounced once, twice before reluctantly settling on the runway, the tailskid leaving behind the branches it had collected.

As it was the last aircraft due to land that day, which was fortunate as the frost had formed early that evening, the ground crew was keen to pull her back to the flight line. If luck was on their side and there were no problems, they'd be in the pub by half four, any later and the Friday crowd would have drunk the best beer. Wartime shortages were nothing new, but the hard-working engineers resented missing out on the fresh barrels old Bert always managed to get in on a Friday afternoon.

Spurred into action by the erratic landing, the sergeant pulled out his binoculars and put them to his eyes. What he saw pushed him into more frenzied action. Jumping on his bike and yelling for someone to get the doctor, *now!* he pedaled furiously toward where the diminutive biplane had eventually rolled to a halt, coming to rest in the drainage ditch, along the end of the grass runway. The ditch had claimed many an unwary pilot.

From a haven of peace in war-torn southern England, all now became semi-organized chaos as men sprang to help. One jumped onto the running board of a waiting ambulance, startling a gently dozing driver and prodding him to drive over to the idling biplane. Everyone else followed their sergeant as quickly as they could. Whoever the pilot was, he or she was in severe trouble.

The pilot's flailing arm reached for and failed to make contact with the ignition before flopping down onto her lap and knocking a blue thermos flask to the cockpit floor.

Reaching the plane, the sergeant switched the engine off, ignoring the blood that coated his fingers from where the pilot's head had crashed into the instrument panel. After giving her an urgent shake when she failed to respond to his desperate shouts of

"Miss!" he pulled the neck of her flying suit aside and placed his fingers against the side of her neck. Nothing. Nevertheless, he placed the fingers of his other hand in the same place, waited a few more desperate seconds, and then took them away. As gently as he could, he leant the pilot's head back against the headrest and slumped down on the lower wing, looking up only when the ambulance screamed to a halt.

Placing a hand on the doctor's shoulder as he made to climb up, he shook his head. "Don't bother, Doc. She's gone."

The deathly quiet was broken by a woman's heartbreaking scream of anguish.

Chapter One

May 1942

"Penelope!"

Nobody bellowed quite like her father, Penny Blake knew well, though the sound didn't make her shiver with fear. The days when she'd been wary, let alone respectful of him, were long gone. With a resigned sigh she stood up, for she recognized what that particular bellow indicated: displeasure.

"Now what am I supposed to have done," she muttered, putting down the copy of *Flight International* magazine she'd been reading. Sliding her feet into her slippers, Penny made her way downstairs to where her father was waiting for her in his study.

The door was open, and standing behind his beloved green leather wing-backed chair was the man in question. If this had been a silent melodramatic movie, he'd be twirling a handlebar moustache. As it wasn't, he merely looked like he was about to blow steam out of his ears, he'd turned so red.

"There you are," he told her in what, considering the volume he'd been using moments before, was a commendably restrained voice. "Would you care to explain this?" he asked, waving a magazine back and forth in front of her face.

Standing before him, her hands deep in her

dressing gown pockets, Penny waited for him to stop wafting the magazine as if it were a rabid fan, so she could see what had got his dander up this time. As far as she knew, she hadn't been caught dancing on any tables at clubs lately, nor had she been photographed out with a young man her father deemed unsuitable. That by itself was difficult to avoid, as she couldn't think of anyone she knew whom her father did deem worthy of courting his eldest. Those he'd once considered—she believed he'd given up that particular method of keeping her out of trouble—were, in her opinion, one short step away from being total imbeciles.

In the end, she had to reach up and grab the magazine so she could see what he was on about. She hadn't realized the picture had been taken. She loved it and made a mental note to track down a print.

"I thought I'd banned you from flying," her father stated. "And now I see this on the cover of *The Tatler*. Not only had you crashed, but a bloody photographer was there to record the whole ruddy thing. Don't get me wrong. I'm glad you didn't die, but here"—he jabbed a finger at the magazine, right into Penny's grime-smeared yet beaming face as she stepped from the cockpit of a biplane that had lost its undercarriage—"you're smiling away as if nothing has happened. Don't you have any sense of what you could have done to the family name?"

Things had been building up for months, probably years if she was honest with herself. With those words, plus what she'd earlier read in *The Times*, she believed the time had come to make her final break from what hadn't felt like home for way too long. Someone else might have taken his words as an attempt at reconciliation, but not Penny.

Penny folded the magazine and put it in her pocket, then carefully arranged her features into what she hoped was a blank, a face that showed her father she cared as little for him nowadays as he obviously cared for her. "Firstly, Father, you cannot ban me from flying. I own my own plane. The one in that picture was a friend's, and I can and will fly whenever I can."

She stopped speaking as the expression on her father's face suddenly resembled the mouse that got the cheese. "Ah, now that's where you're wrong. I've checked with the police, and as a civilian, you should not be flying. I don't even want to know where you got the fuel from. So unless you want to be arrested, I suggest you start listening to me. Understand?"

This was something Penny had hoped he wouldn't figure out. A banker by trade, his only concern since Penny's mother had died was keeping the good name of the family spotless—though she'd never been able to get a clear answer to why. She had a feeling something in his past had caused his thinking toward his family to become skewed. The kind and loving father she remembered from her past had perished with his wife.

She'd been flying ever since she'd persuaded her father to pay for flying lessons, and so far as he'd been concerned, his little lady could do no wrong. That was before his beloved Sarah had passed. After that, purely coincidentally so far as Penny was concerned, her name started appearing regularly in various magazines, especially the *Penny Post* and *The Sketch*. He'd put up with them at first, even the accompanying pictures and by-lines. However, the prettier she'd grown, the more titillating had been the headlines, and that had been when he'd tried to ban her from flying in the hope the magazines would find somebody new to salivate over.

"You're right, Father," she eventually said and saw the look of triumph appear on his face, which was swiftly wiped away by what she told him next. "However, you won't have to worry about me for much longer."

Turning his back on his daughter, her father lit his pipe and blew out a cloud of blueish, stale-smelling smoke before venturing to ask, "Oh, and what do you think you can do?"

"Something I wasn't able to before the war, but now I can."

"And what, pray, is that?"

"I'm leaving home. I'm joining the ATA."

Now she had his attention, and he turned back to face her, looking puzzled. The look didn't suit him, as he prided himself on being someone who knew a lot about everything, all of which added up to he knew a lot about nothing Penny considered worthwhile.

"What, when it's at home, is the ATA?"

Oh, what asking that had cost him; she could see in the way his mouth opened and closed before he'd been able to get the words out that he hadn't wanted to ask.

"The Air Transport Auxiliary, Father. They're looking for women volunteers. I'm going to deliver planes all around the UK."

From the amount of snorting that issued from his mouth and nose, Penny didn't think she could have said anything that would have surprised him more. After a minute or two of blustering, he appeared to be ready to speak again. She had to rack her memory for when she'd last seen that face, and when it came to her, she almost took a step back in surprise. She remembered the expression from happier times, times when her mother was still around, as it involved love. Love. Now, that was a word she hadn't associated with her father in a long, long time, so she wasn't sure quite how much she should trust it. At the least, she'd listen to what he had to say.

"You've a cousin, a cousin in Canada. I've been in correspondence with him, and he has a son about your age—well, thirty-two—who's seen your picture and, despite all your shenanigans, is prepared to marry you. He's a good, hard-working man, never been in any bother in his life."

Had he really suggested that? Suggested that she marry someone she didn't know anything about just because he had a good name? Penny carefully looked at her father and could see clearly he actually meant what he said. It had been just another game. So much for love. To keep, in his opinion anyway, the family name in good stead, he would marry his daughter off to someone he'd never known and send her off to the other side of the world. Upon that thought, it hit her: if he couldn't control her, rein her in, then having her out of reach of all the newspapers and gossip-mongering magazines would be accomplishing the same thing. No one around to worry about, no one around to besmirch the name.

Her father had been watching her face, and as she'd learned to read him, so had he her. "Well?"

There could be only one answer. "No." Penny then turned her back and slowly, determinedly, walked back upstairs to pack.

The last words she heard from her father were,

"You walk out of my house, and you'll never be welcome here again!"

With her back to her father, she fought the tears threatening to burst forth, determined to remain strong, and won. Despite the pain, this was the right thing to do, both for herself and for her country. By making this decision, she was turning her back on her family, on her younger sister, whom she would miss even though they rarely agreed on anything. What caused the most pain was not being able to tell her in person why she was leaving. She hoped she'd understand one day and that her boarding school would, as soon as they received it, give her sister the letter she would write before leaving her childhood home for good.

In her bedroom, she stayed long enough to write that letter in which she poured her heart out to her sister, begging her to understand and to forgive her. Finished, she put it into a suitcase, to be mailed later, and grabbed her bank book, as many clothes as she could fit into a couple of suitcases. She included her flying clothes, her all-important flying license, and her log book, then stuffed the week-old acceptance letter from the ATA into her coat pocket and walked out of her room and back down the stairs.

Her father was where she had left him, both hands still gripping the rear of his chair as if his life depended upon it. Resisting the strong urge to throw her arms around his neck and implore him to love her as he once had, Penny strode past the cold study and opened the front door.

Without looking back, as to do so would irreparably damage what was left of her heart, she closed the door behind her and walked out toward the next chapter of her life, toward a place where she hoped to find a home and a new family. Who knew, perhaps love!

Chapter Two

July 1942

"Shut the bloody door!"

"Really," Penny tutted as she kicked it shut and shook her unruly brown hair from beneath her flying helmet, sending beads of rain splattering around the small wooden hut.

As she unzipped her Sidcot flying suit, revealing a non-regulation and decidedly off-white, heavy woolen pullover, Penny offered up a silent prayer to whichever god was on duty that day to take pity on her. It had been raining cats and dogs at Hamble airfield all day. Now, approaching dusk, she was pig-sick of it. If Thelma told her she'd have to come back tomorrow to re-take her test, again, she'd give good odds she wouldn't be responsible for her actions.

It'd been a long and cold Tuesday, most of it spent waiting in this heatless, forsaken place that served as their flight line hut, biding her time until First Officer Thelma Aston could spare the time to take her up in a Tiger Moth. She'd only arrived the previous Friday, and they'd had to cut short her flight yesterday due to the weather taking an even bigger turn for the worse and forcing them to land after they'd been up for only ten minutes. Today hadn't started out any better, and when a couple of pilots had called in sick, Thelma had informed her that she'd have to wait, as aircraft deliveries took precedence over everything else. Since they were shorthanded, Penny'd be pitching in. The aircraft being Spitfires, she hadn't argued, and with the aid of a friendly dispatch rider speeding her back to the factory, both deliveries had taken barely two hours. Her own flying experiences meant she fully understood the need to recover from "numb-bum syndrome," so she'd not bothered Thelma to take her up until she'd been back for half an hour.

Hanging up her flying suit to dry on the peg next to her locker, Penny sat down to pull off her flying boots, weary to her bones.

"Care for a hand?"

Penny glanced up into the round, cheery face of a very well covered woman she hadn't noticed who, from the accent, appeared to be an American. Beside her was a large leather suitcase, which looked a little out of place next to a battered gray carpetbag, a flying helmet placed on top. The lady took off a black leather glove and held out her hand.

"Doris Winter."

Due to the teeming rain she'd just flown in, Penny's boots seemed to have shrunk onto her feet. If she was going to fly alongside this Doris for the Air Transport Auxiliary, she may as well start on the right foot. Or the left, depending upon which she got off first.

"Penny Blake."

They shook hands, and Doris turned her back on Penny, motioning for her to extend a leg. Taking the one proffered and clamping it between her legs, Doris took the booted foot and with surprisingly little effort for such a slight-looking woman (she'd undone her thick white fur coat before bending over, and Penny had seen that underneath it she was wearing a bright red—and unless she were much mistaken, cashmere—jumper that clung to some very obvious curves) pulled it off in one go. The second boot took two tugs but was off in short order too.

"Phew, thanks for that, Doris," Penny said, wiping her brow and pulling off her thick socks.

"Pleasure, sweety," Doris replied in that delicious accent, retaking her seat. "Can't have been a lot of fun up there."

"Oh, I don't know," Penny replied, toweling her hair dry and then pulling a clean pair of stockings on. "So long as I can fly, I don't really mind what the weather's like."

"Rather you than me." Doris shuddered. "I don't really do rain."

"You may have to get used to it," cut in the imposing figure sitting next to Doris. "It doesn't tend to do much else over here, and this is supposed to be summer!"

Doris let out what could only be described as a guffaw and clapped her hand on her companion's shoulder. "You'll have to forgive Mary. I've only known her since the train journey here, but she has a certain—how do you Brits put it?—wit. She's an acquired taste."

"Have not! I mean, am not!" Mary answered, not helping matters.

"Ha!" Doris laughed. "See what I mean?"

"If you don't mind my asking," Penny began, straightening her seams, "what's a Yank doing in the ATA?"

Doris's face took on the expression of someone who had been waiting for this very question. "You know, you're the first person to ask me that. Neither at Liverpool nor at Luton were they curious. You really want to know?" Upon looking around, her audience were unashamedly staring at her, waiting upon what she said next. "Fair enough. There's been talk back in the States of setting something up that does the same job as this ATA, but I can't wait that long. Someone dear to me died for a cause he believed in, and I see no reason why I should wait any longer for something that may or may not come to pass. Hitler's evil, and I want to do my share. Besides," she added after a short pause and with a twinkle in her eye, "you can't get fish and chips in my home town like you guys get here. New York City's the best city in the world, but I'd walk across the Atlantic for a serving of yours."

Further repartee was brought to a halt by a loud cough.

"If you've all quite finished!" First Officer Thelma Aston was leant back against her desk, an expression of wry amusement upon her face. "May we get back to business? If the two of you," she pointed at Doris and Mary, "would mind getting to your feet? We may be a civilian service. However, a little respect wouldn't go amiss."

Perhaps not as fast as Thelma would have liked, the two newcomers got to their feet. Their stance, with some leeway, could be described as respectful. From the frown on her forehead, accompanied by a slight shake of the head after waiting for a few seconds, Thelma realized this was the best she was going to get, and when Penny joined them, she allowed a small, a very small, smile to leak onto her lips.

"Penny Blake," she read rather unnecessarily from the piece of paper in her hand, before turning her gaze to where Penny was investigating the state of her nails. "You'll be pleased to hear you've passed, and as from this moment, I'm certifying you as operational. Report for a familiarization flight of the area tomorrow morning at nine a.m. You'll go on your first delivery flight Thursday morning. However," she said raising her voice to be heard above the congratulations that Doris and Mary were piling upon Penny, "if we need you—really need you, mind—then you may be utilized tomorrow afternoon."

Too happy and relieved to bristle at her superior's slightly brusque manner, Penny contented herself with, "Yes, ma'am," and promptly sat back down, a wide smile upon her face.

"As for you two…" Thelma turned her attention to her newcomers, both of whom made efforts to add a little more respect to their posture. "It's too late in the day and the weather's too bad to take either of you up, so report back here for nine in the morning as well, and we'll get around to taking you both up."

Doris raised her hand.

"It's not school, Miss Winter. You don't have to put up your hand to ask a question, though I do appreciate it. Now, what is it?"

Doris pointed to the paperwork with her name on it upon Thelma's desk. "I take it you've seen my logbooks?" A nod came in response. "Well, you can see that I've been flying for about five years now, and I've over six hundred hours to my name."

"Your point, Miss Winter?" Thelma inquired.

Penny could see Doris was doing her best to rein in her impatience.

"My point, ma'am, is that I'm surprised I need to have anyone check out my flying."

Thelma rolled her eyes before replying, "Miss Winter, as I'm sure you've heard many a time since you came to this country, we are at war. Everything is checked, even in the ATA, and that includes such things as flying credentials. So yes, you will have your flying test with me, hopefully tomorrow, time and weather permitting."

"But we've already been checked out by the people at Hatfield," Mary couldn't help moaning.

"Satisfying the people at Hatfield is one thing, satisfying me quite another. Their main concern is that you can fly without hurting yourself, mine is to make sure you don't hurt anyone else, especially me. To that end, you will go up to prove to me you can indeed fly. Tomorrow morning, ladies, bright and early. Understood?"

Both Doris and Mary snapped slightly closer to military attention and replied clearly and somewhat more loudly than the size of the hut merited, "Yes, ma'am!"

Their reply seemed to satisfy Thelma, as she allowed a less scary smile to grace her lips before laying Penny's report on her desk. Folding her arms, she once more addressed Doris and Mary. "Have either of you been assigned a place to stay?" Both shook their heads. "Bugger," Thelma swore and swiftly turned around to snatch up the receiver of her phone. Dialing, she waited, then waited, then waited a few moments more before slamming the phone down. "Bloody

Dorothy must have gone already."

"Who's Dorothy?" Penny asked, getting to her feet and pulling on her ATA jacket so she was all clad in navy blue.

"No, I don't think you've met her either, have you," Thelma replied, shaking her head. "Dorothy's in charge of all administration on base, and that includes arranging billets for our pilots."

"So where does that leave us?" asked Mary, wringing her hands as she noticed the worried look on Thelma's face.

"Well..." Thelma drew out the word, rubbing her chin and looking around the hut. "I guess you could bed down here for the night?"

Mary looked like it'd been suggested she take tea without milk. "Here! On the floor?"

"It'd be an adventure," suggested Doris, though Penny was certain she was only joking. However, as Thelma hadn't immediately discounted the idea, she thought she might be taking it seriously.

"May I make a suggestion?" Penny spoke into the silence and went ahead when no one objected. "There're spare rooms at the house I live in, and I'm sure Betty—she owns the house," she added for the two prospective lodgers' benefit, "won't mind another couple of guests, at least for the evening. What do you say, girls?"

"I'm game," was the immediate response from Doris, who pumped Penny's hand vigorously again.

"I don't suppose I'd be allowed to go into London to book into the Savoy, would I?" Mary asked. The look of incredulity on Thelma's face showed what she thought of that particular idea, so Mary turned back to face Penny. "I'd be delighted to accept, Penny, thank you."

Thelma let out a sigh of relief. "Yes, thank you for this, Penny. Please thank Betty for me when you see her, too. You've solved an awkward situation. I'd hope Dorothy has something arranged, but as she's obviously decided to bugger off without telling anyone… I'll be having words with her tomorrow," she finished, not troubling to keep the scowl of annoyance from her face. "So unless there's anything else?"

Penny, Doris, and Mary all shook their heads.

"In that case, I'll wish you a good night and will see you all tomorrow morning," Thelma finished before grabbing her hat, handbag, and gas mask case and striding out of the hut, leaving behind three women who were suddenly unsure about what to do now.

After several seconds' awkward silence, Mary spoke first.

"Penny, thanks awfully for putting us up tonight. I hope it won't get you into trouble with your friend."

"Betty? No, she's the sweetest soul I've ever come across. She wasn't meant to be my landlady when I arrived last week either, but—shall we put it this way—Dorothy doesn't seem to be the most reliable of sorts. I've only ever seen her once, and that was when I signed the multitude of forms when I first arrived, though she disappeared before we came to the matter of accommodation. She rarely seems to be around when she's needed, from what I understand, and whilst Thelma was phoning around trying to track her down, in walked Betty, who promptly offered to put me up. We hit it off over the weekend, and on Monday she spoke to Dorothy and told her she'd be very happy for me to stay with her permanently. Thelma told me earlier everything's now been arranged."

"As easy as that?" Mary asked, obviously not quite believing what she'd heard.

Penny shrugged. "As easy as that. Remember what Thelma said? We're not a military force, though the ATA does have certain similarities. However, it does mean it's easier, when it's needed, to bend certain guidelines. And so long as we're safely billeted, that's the main thing."

"And you don't think she'll have a problem with a couple of freeloaders?" Doris threw in.

"I'm not sure what a freeloader is, but there really are plenty of rooms," Penny stated after a few seconds, enough for the other two to catch on she was sidetracking the question.

Doris persisted. "We won't be chucked out in the middle of the night?"

Penny could only shrug. "To be perfectly honest, I can only say you'll have a roof over your heads tonight. Betty's away at her parents' and said she won't be back until the wee hours, so you should be safe until morning."

Doris let out a shrill burst of laughter. "That'll do me, honey," and matched actions to words by getting to her feet and hoisting her carpetbag over one shoulder, grabbing the handle of her suitcase with the other. "Shall we go?"

Mary too got to her feet and buttoned up her coat—tweed, Penny noted—and then surprised them all by asking, "Where can we get a taxi?"

"Um...taxi?" queried Penny.

Doris let go of her case and linked her arm through

one of Mary's. "Honey, I don't think there're any taxis on an airbase. She's got a point, though, Pen. How do we get to your place?"

Penny poked her head out the door and was pleased to note it had stopped raining. "We walk," she informed them. "It's only just over a mile." Then she took note of the size of Doris's case and the two cases clustered at Mary's feet and decided otherwise. "On the other hand, give me a few minutes, and I'll see if I can whistle up something from the MT flight."

"MT flight?" Mary queried as Penny was about to step through the door.

"Mechanical Transport," explained Penny and then hurried out.

Mary turned to Doris after the door had shut. "That's not much clearer," she admitted.

"Nor for me," agreed Doris, "but I think it means she's gone to borrow a car."

"That's okay, then," smiled Mary and lowered herself onto a seat to wait.

****

"And this is the cottage," Penny told them as they pulled up outside a two-storied red brick house with twin windows projecting out of the slated roof, a hint of further rooms hiding under the eaves. It looked much too large to let itself be called a mere cottage.

Doris whispered loud and long, "When you said cottage, I was wondering how it'd fit four grown women…" She paused and stretched her neck back so as to look upward at where twin chimneys groped majestically for the skies. "But now I can see." She turned to look up at Penny. "I think you need to think about renaming it, though," she added, indicating the sign in neat white letters nailed to the front gate.

Penny jumped with reasonable ease from the cab of the lorry in which she'd persuaded a friendly driver to chauffeur them, and offered a hand to Doris and Mary as they shuffled with somewhat less grace after her.

"I don't think Betty would agree," she told them as they made their way to the lorry's tailgate and took back their luggage from the driver, who'd hopped into the rear. "She's very fond of the place and the name. It used to belong to her parents, so The Old Lockkeeper's Cottage it'll stay." She turned her attention to their driver. "Thanks, Harry."

"At your service, ma'am," he offered, with a touch to his forage cap and a very cheeky grin. "See you at The Victory later?"

Penny glanced over at her new housemates and, as she suspected, could see only weariness in their eyes and the postures of their bodies, likely from the traveling. "Not tonight, Harry, but thanks again."

With one more wave, he was back in his cab and the lorry was on its way.

Doris and Mary also waved their taxi service goodbye and then turned back to scrutinize the cottage again. "It really is something else," added Mary, and then asked, "Is it really a lockkeeper's cottage?"

Penny took up a piece of Mary's baggage and shoved open the gate with her foot. "To be honest, no. That's the River Hamble, not a canal, but I think it suits it anyway. Come on, let's get inside and put your baggage away, and we can talk over some tea. I don't know about either of you, but I could do with a cuppa."

Ten minutes later, Doris and Mary sat around a large, well-used oak table in the kitchen whilst Penny put the kettle on to boil. "I'm afraid there's no fresh milk until tomorrow morning. It'll have to be black."

"Black's fine," replied Mary.

"I'll take anything you can offer right now," said Doris, adding, "How're you for sugar?"

Penny lifted the lid off a blue-striped sugar dish. "Looks like we're out of that, too."

"Doesn't matter. Sorry, I've only been in England since the weekend, and I keep forgetting about rationing."

"You'll get used to it," Penny told her whilst adding a couple of teaspoons of tea leaves to a teapot and pouring in the boiling water from the kettle. "We'll get your ration cards sorted out tomorrow, and then we can get you both registered."

"Registered?" asked Doris.

"I guess no one's explained the rationing system to you," stated Penny, to which Doris could only nod. "In a nutshell, each person gets a book of coupons in which, when you make a purchase, it's marked up against your ration for that week. You register in a shop of your choice. I'll take you to our local store as soon as you get your book, and that's where you have to get your food from."

A frown formed on Doris's brow. "Doesn't sound like much fun. So what's included?"

"The basics, like milk, sugar, butter, and meat," put in Mary. "Thanks," she added as Penny poured the tea through a strainer for her. "Just don't ask or dwell on how much or, should I say, *little* you get. It's been enough of a shock for me lately, so heaven knows what it'll be like for you Yanks."

"I don't think I'd take a bet if I were you," Doris

agreed with a slight shudder. "I've got quite a sweet tooth."

"I'm afraid it's likely to take you quite a while to get used to it," granted Penny, taking her seat after finishing with the tea. "But I wouldn't be too worried. We're a bit out in the sticks here, though Betty tells me she's good friends with the farmer just down the road. Betty also grows her own veg and apparently always gets a good harvest of potatoes, carrots, and runner beans, which she swaps with him for extra meat, butter, and milk."

"What about cheese?" interrupted Mary. "I'm very partial to a bit of cheddar."

"There," Penny answered, "you'll have to work with your ration like the rest of us. I'm partial to cheese myself. However, Betty told me there aren't any farmers in the area who make it. Sorry, Mary."

Whether it was the bad news about the cheese or simply the long day catching up with her, Mary picked up her tea, blew on it, settled back into her chair, let out a slight shudder, and didn't reply.

"Speaking of food," Penny said, "are you both hungry?"

This made Mary perk up enough to nod, whilst Doris's stomach chose that moment to let out a loud rumble.

"I'll take that as a yes, then." Penny laughed, getting to her feet and placing her empty cup in the butler's sink. "I'm afraid I'm not much of a cook, though I am trying to improve, so how do you feel about fish and chips? My treat!"

Doris vigorously shook her head. "I won't hear of it. After your kind offer to put us up, the least I can do

23

is pay for dinner." Matching actions to words, she reached down, pulled out her purse, and before Penny or Mary could say otherwise, slapped a £5 note on the table.

Eyes bulging, Penny reached forward and gently pushed the crisp white note away with a finger. "You haven't got anything smaller? I think if we turned up at the chippy with this, they'd think we wanted to buy the place!"

"Really?" asked Doris. She then opened her purse again and had a rummage. "I've got five of those five-pound notes and about twelve pounds in pound notes. Will that help?" she asked, looking up to where both Penny and Mary were staring at her with some stupefaction.

"What the hell, Doris?" Mary said, her eyes nearly bulging out of their sockets. "Are you trying to tell me what you said on the train is true?"

Doris had, by now, a look on her face that was a mixture of annoyance and confusion. Before she could say anything, Penny asked, "What did you say, and what's it got to do with all this money? You didn't rob a bank, did you?"

Fortunately, Doris picked up that Penny wasn't serious and let out a small laugh. "No, I'm just a lonely millionairess."

Chapter Three

A loud, persistent ringing in Penny's ears was making it difficult to keep her eyes closed, while a bright light was doing its best to burn through her eyelids. Annoyed, she turned onto her back and stretched. She'd have to accept the fact that, again, six in the morning had come around. She threw the blankets back, fumbled with cold fingers to turn off the alarm clock, dragged her dressing gown from the end of the bed, and threw it on against the morning chill. With her feet tucked into slippers, Penny padded out of her room and across the landing toward the bathroom. These were times she missed the comfort of her family home the most.

A quick wash later, she'd changed into her regulation ATA uniform (which made her feel like an overgrown Girl Guide) and traipsed downstairs to the kitchen. It'd been a very long night, and what with being declared operational, a shudder of what she hoped was excitement swept through her. She suspected it'd be a while before she had enough energy for another late-night gossip session, let alone a proper night out.

Doris had insisted upon paying for their fish-and-chip supper, and once she'd been successfully coaxed inside the shop, it turned out she hated the smell of vinegar. She'd gone crazy. After they'd quieted her down, she'd told them that though you could get fish and chips in New York, the choices weren't as wide as they were here. Penny and Mary informed her fish wasn't on the ration, and then they'd had to talk her out of buying everything on the menu, eventually having to remind her that it wasn't done to flaunt money around in wartime England. Fortunately, she hadn't taken their admonishments the wrong way and soon calmed down enough to settle on a large cod and chips, with a bottle of Guinness chaser for all.

On the short walk home, Penny and Mary had to be very careful to keep their own vinegar-splashed suppers separate from Doris's, something she was constantly at pains to inform them. Upon getting back to the cottage, everyone had set to with gusto, and the food had disappeared in a remarkably short period of time. Doris had pronounced it a complete success and the best thing she'd eaten since she'd disembarked at Liverpool. Indeed, the other two had to convince her it wouldn't be a good idea to have fish and chips every night, if for no other reason than their waistlines, as they might not be able to get into the cockpits of the aircraft they hoped to fly if they carried on this way. Doris complained this was a real shame, which prompted a silly conversation as to how they could convince the aircraft manufacturers to make cockpits for the larger lady. Not that any of them believed they were of that persuasion, though Mary remained unconvinced she had anything but child-bearing hips. Neither of the other two could honestly deny this, though both reassured her that they wished they both had a few more curves, even Doris, who Penny thought had a figure to die for.

Doris had insisted they buy some Guinness, as she

thought it was all English people drank. Luckily, she'd loved the *black stuff* and had finished hers well before she'd finished her food. Guinness, Penny and Mary had been happy to inform her, she could have more than once a week. Doris had to be persuaded out of putting in a standing order for a crate to be delivered once a week. This had led to the two of them talking Doris into telling them her story, especially the millionairess part. An enthralling, tragic, yet inspiring tale soon followed.

"The best way to describe how my family saw me would be as a rebel. I rebelled against the constant dinner parties that Mom and Pop were always holding, against the stream of so-called eligible young men they kept sending my way, against my two sisters always sucking up to everyone in sight. You name it, I rebelled against it. The final straw was my eloping on the day I graduated from college to marry a young man none of my relatives knew anything about."

"You didn't!" exclaimed Penny.

"Not even your sisters?" Mary asked.

"What? Trust those two with something so personal?" Doris snorted. "Not on your life. They'd turn on each other for a buck."

"How nice," Penny stated, tongue firmly in cheek, taking a sip from her glass of Guinness. "That can't have made a happy household."

"It wasn't," Doris simply agreed, shaking her head.

Mary leant forward, her elbows on the table. "You were saying you eloped."

Doris slid down in her seat and allowed a smile that spoke of fond, precious memories. "I'd met him at a college party. His name was Donald. You know those Hollywood moments, where the girl sees the boy across the crowded dance floor, the couples parting like the Red Sea before them until they stand nose to nose. We barely exchanged names before he swept me around the floor in the most romantic waltz I'd ever known. I knew in that moment he was the one for me, that we'd be together forever. And I couldn't dance back then!"

Penny scratched her head as Doris paused, afloat in moments of the past. "What was so wrong with him you couldn't tell your parents?"

Doris was so lost in her memories it took a few seconds for her to realize Penny had spoken. "What was wrong with him? Nothing. Everything, if you listened to my parents."

Mary picked up on the past tense Doris used and glanced at her ring finger. "You're not wearing a wedding ring. What happened?" she prompted.

Doris took her ring finger between the thumb and forefinger of her right hand and tenderly rubbed where a wedding band would be. After some slight hesitation, she reached up and pulled out a gold chain from around her neck, on it a simple, glittering golden band. A tight smile that spoke volumes of the pain she still felt was etched upon her face; unnoticed, a single tear leaked from an eye.

"This is the ring he gave me on our wedding day in the summer of thirty-eight. He was the son of a simple farmer, very poor compared to my family, but he had a heart of gold to match this ring. I think that's what my parents really objected to. Either way, they refused to meet him, let alone attend our wedding."

"What about your sisters?" Penny asked.

"Ha!" An ironic laugh escaped Doris's lips, with more than a bitter flavor to it. "Oh, they were totally on my parents' side. They'd grown so enamored of the family money by then I think they'd do anything not to lose it."

"So what happened to Donald?" Mary had to know.

Doris paused in her story, bringing the ring to her lips before tucking it away and finishing off her Guinness. "I suppose you can put it down to the impulsiveness of youth. He'd always been a keen flyer, and he was the first one to take me up in this old biplane of his. He loved it to death, even though I swear only a prayer held it together. If my parents had ever met him, though, they'd have found he was a very passionate man, about a lot of things. Passion got him, in the end."

"They'd never even met him!" Penny exclaimed, unable to keep the shock from her voice.

"What happened?" asked Mary, whisper quiet, nearly falling off the edge of her chair as she leant forward, her glass halfway to her lips and forgotten.

"The fool volunteered for the Nationalist Air Force in the Spanish Civil War."

"Really!" Penny half-yelled out and then clamped her hand to her mouth at her sudden outburst.

"They were so desperate by that time I think they'd have taken anyone who could glide. I had one letter after he'd been there for around a month. Then the next one I had was from his commander to tell me he'd been shot down and killed. Some marriage, eh?" Doris finished with a shrug. "I never even had a body to bury, and just his old biplane to remember him by."

With much shuffling and scraping of chairs, Penny and Mary enveloped their new friend in a huge, loving hug; none of them were aware of the tears streaming down each of their faces.

"What did your parents do when they found out? I assume you told them?" asked Mary, after a few minutes.

Wiping her eyes and nose with her handkerchief, Doris nodded. "After I'd spent six months doing nothing but crying, yes, I turned up on their doorstep."

"They didn't refuse to see you, surely?" put in Penny fearfully.

"Not quite, Pen. We had a...a discussion, of sorts. It certainly wasn't a happy reunion. My father let me into the house just long enough so I could give him my news, and then he told me he never wanted to see me again. I'd never been the favorite, but that was still hard to take."

"No!" Penny and Mary exclaimed loudly as one.

Doris finished Penny's Guinness to give her extra time to pull herself together. "Afraid so. Apparently the shame I'd brought to the family was too much to allow me back into its bosom. However, before he kicked me out of his life, he told me he would give me an allowance of ten thousand dollars a year and the deeds to the family apartment overlooking Central Park."

"What's Central Park?" asked Penny, Mary appearing to have been struck dumb upon hearing of the cash.

"It's a huge park literally in the center of New York, hence the name."

"That's...nice?"

"Very nice," Doris answered, summoning up a smile.

"And that explains the cash earlier," added Mary,

managing to find her voice.

****

Penny was brought out of her reverie by the sight of Betty, fully dressed for the day in her uniform, waiting for her at the foot of the stairs.

"Good morning," Betty said, her voice slightly more clipped than usual. "Is there anything you want to tell me?"

Caught slightly unawares, Penny ran a hand through her hair. She'd forgotten about Betty coming back in the early hours.

"About our new guests?" Betty added a hint.

Penny greeted her with a hug. "Yes, about the, um, girls. Sorry. I hope you don't mind. They only arrived yesterday afternoon, and Dorothy wasn't around to fix them up—you know what she's like—and I couldn't let them sleep in the flight line hut!" She looked up from under her lashes at Betty, taking advantage of the other woman being a good few inches taller than her. "I am sorry, Betty, but they're good girls."

Betty didn't look quite convinced. "How can you be sure? You've known them less than a day!"

"I know," Penny conceded, "but you know that feeling you get when something feels right? I got that as soon as I met them, and, well, I simply couldn't leave them to freeze in that hut."

A small smile creased Betty's face. "No, I don't suppose you could."

"You'll like them too," enthused Penny, now convinced her friend had calmed down, "as soon as you meet them."

Betty turned her head as the sound of out-of-tune singing rang out from upstairs. "I've kind of met the

31

American girl, a rather unusual meeting, I admit."

Penny was intrigued to hear more. "Go on."

"Let's just say she was carrying her towel instead of, ahem, wearing it as she came out of the bathroom."

"She wasn't!"

Betty added, turning back to face Penny, "She may not be very tall, but wow, with a bust like that, she's going to be very popular with the men."

Penny's hands flew to her mouth so she didn't burst out laughing. She'd seen who had crept up behind her friend.

"That's real kind of you, Betty," said Doris from the second step up, causing Betty to turn swiftly and go a bright beetroot red. She reached out and put her hand on Betty's shoulder. "Don't you fret. I imagine I was quite a shock."

"Somewhat," she agreed, reaching down and rubbing an ankle through her stockings. "But whoever left their suitcase in the lounge is in trouble."

However, before she could assure Doris that Betty hadn't a malicious bone in her body, a timid voice from the top of the stairs piped up. "That would be mine, I'm afraid." Mary was gripping the banister and looking like she'd rather be anywhere else. "I'm so sorry. I completely forgot about that one."

Betty let her genuine smile out. "Forget it, no real harm done. Why don't you come down, and we'll have some breakfast." She turned her head to face Doris again. "Then you can introduce yourselves properly."

Safely sat around the kitchen table, a boiled egg in front of each of them, Penny made the introductions, and then everyone tucked in.

"That was delicious," stated Mary, placing her

spoon down next to her eggcup, "but you really shouldn't have wasted one of your eggs on me."

Betty smiled back at her. "Don't worry, I didn't. We always have plenty of eggs. I keep chickens."

"What!" yelled Mary, pushing her chair back with a loud squealing noise and leaping to kneel upon it. "Where?" she asked looking around with wide, wild eyes.

"Not in here, obviously," Penny answered, struggling to keep a straight face. "Betty keeps them out the back, next to the vegetable garden. Why? What's wrong?"

Wiping her forehead on her sleeve, Mary, still glancing worriedly around, slowly sat back down before looking at the other girls with a very sheepish expression. "Sorry. It's just that I'm a little afraid of chickens. It's those scaly feet of theirs," she added with a shudder.

To lighten the mood, Doris turned to Betty and said, "By the way, I owe you a couple of light ales. We ran out of Guinness," she added.

"Do I really want to know?" Betty asked of Penny and Mary.

"We had a little chin-wag last night and got a bit thirsty," Penny replied, not going into any more detail. Betty caught the wink that Penny threw her, though.

Betty glanced at her watch and exclaimed, "Heavens! It's eight thirty! We need to get a move on or we'll be late, and that's not a good idea. I assume you two are due to have your flight tests today?" she said to Doris and Mary, knowing how things worked at the airfield. "Did you pass your test yesterday, Penny?"

"I've got a familiarization-of-the-area flight today,

though Thelma did say she'd use me if she needs to."

Betty got to her feet and clapped her hands together. "Well, if everyone's got everything they need, we'd better not keep Thelma waiting."

"I'll just go and move my suitcase," Mary told them, scuttling from her seat.

After nearly a minute, Mary hadn't reappeared, so Penny was about to shout out when the sound of breaking glass came from the lounge.

"Bugger!" cursed Mary's voice. "I'm so sorry, Betty," Mary added, coming back into the kitchen, a silver picture frame carefully balanced in her hands. She put it on the table.

"What the hell have you done?" Betty shouted upon seeing the frame, jumping to her feet so quickly she knocked her chair over. "My poor Eleanor," she uttered, snatching the frame and holding it to her chest.

Doris got up and moved to put her arms around her. "We can get you a new frame, Betty. It'll be all right. I'm sure Mary's very sorry."

Mary was the picture of anguish, having heard Betty's cry and now seeing how she was behaving, rocking back and forth with the frame clutched to her as if she'd never let it go. "I am," she agreed. "I truly am. I'm so sorry, Betty. I fell over my case and threw out my hands to stop myself from falling, and..." She ran out of words.

Seeing how upset Betty was, Doris asked, hoping to distract her, "Who is she? Someone special?"

When Betty answered, she spoke so softly the words barely escaped her mouth. "Very. Her name's Eleanor, and she was my twin sister. She was killed last August."

Chapter Four

Third Officer Herbert Lawrence shivered and, for the fourth time since arriving, consulted his wrist watch. He'd been huddled on the front step of his Aunt Stone's cottage, coat buttoned up to his chin, since the brisk walk from the train station at five in the morning, and despite it being cold enough to freeze the balls off a brass monkey, he didn't want to wake up his aunt by knocking.

Leaning back against the front door, Herbert took out a packet of Players and, with numb fingers, lit up and took a long drag. His aunt, Ruth, hated cigarette smoke and never allowed anyone to light up inside her cottage, so catching a smoke now was a good idea. Stretching out his six-foot frame, Herbert did his best to ignore the early morning frost he'd melted with his coat-covered bottom. He pulled out her last letter. In their infrequent correspondence, Ruth told him she could now grow enough vegetables to barter for extra bacon and butter with the local farmers. She'd also learned to kill and butcher the rabbits and chickens she kept.

He must have fallen asleep, as the next thing he knew, the door was pulled open and he fell backward into the hall.

"Herbert!"

Looming above him was a vision he hoped

M. W. Arnold

wouldn't be seared onto his mind. Thanking small mercies that the morning sun didn't rise through the kitchen windows, he scrambled to his feet. "Hi, Aunty…um…surprise!" he said, kissing her quickly on the cheek and trying not to stare at the white chiffon negligee she was wearing.

"I'll say! Come in, come in," she invited, stepping back and shutting the door after he'd grabbed his kitbag and brought it in. "Put the kettle on whilst I throw on some clothes."

Ten minutes later, the kettle had boiled on the gas cooker and the tea had been made. Hoping he wasn't being presumptuous, Herbert had slung his kitbag in the front parlor and made himself at home at the kitchen table. Feet propped up on a chair, he was sipping his tea when Ruth walked in, resplendent in a ditzy floral tea dress. Bobby, her trusty black-and-white spaniel, trailed behind her into the room, flopped down beneath Herbert's chair, and fell asleep.

"Great guard dog you've got there, Aunty," he remarked.

Ruth glanced down at her softly snoring dog and gave him a fuss behind the ears, which only prompted him to snore louder.

Herbert laughed.

"You've known him all his life, Herbert. The only time you'll ever see him raise a paw in anger will be if he thinks anyone wants to harm me."

Herbert reached down and also ruffled the dog's ears.

"So, to what do I owe this honor? I don't think we've seen each other since you joined the ATA. They're treating you well, I presume?"

"Yes, thanks, Aunty," he replied. "The food's pretty bland, but that's the same everywhere these days. I'm here for the next month at least, as they need a taxi driver until all the women pilots are up to speed."

"And let me guess," Ruth went on shrewdly. "You'd like a nice, comfortable place to stay?"

Herbert had the grace to look sheepish.

Ruth didn't bother waiting for an answer. She put her empty cup down, rose to her feet, and kissed the top of his head. "You know you're always welcome. Go put your things in your old room. You know where I keep the bedding."

"That's wonderful, Aunt Ruth," he cried, jumping to his feet and enveloping her in a bear hug. "I don't have to be in work until tomorrow, so would it be awfully cheeky if I went and had a few hours shuteye?" Herbert matched actions to words by loosening his tie and undoing the top two buttons of his shirt.

"Well, as I can't have you falling asleep at the table, perhaps you'd better. I'm going to be working from home today, so no snoring." Herbert pretended to look offended, but Ruth wasn't having any of it and swatted him playfully around the top of his head. "Off with you, before I change my mind."

"Thanks, Aunty," he said, deciding not to tease her anymore. He grabbed his kitbag and dragged it and himself upstairs.

"Do you want any toast?" she yelled at his retreating back.

He popped his head around the corner of the landing. "Maybe later," he answered before disappearing toward his bedroom.

Left alone, Ruth cut two slices of bread from the

national loaf, placed them under the grill, and went to the cold box in her cellar to check the state of her butter supply. The secret to half enjoying this hybrid excuse for bread, she'd rapidly discovered, was lashings of butter. Opening the lid, she found to her disappointment that she was very low and barely had enough for the slices she was grilling. She'd have to see if she had enough carrots free to barter for a re-supply. Perhaps not their best use, but as homemade butter was so much better than what the ration provided, so worth it. Thanking God for her foresight to have been on good terms with all the local farmers from long before the war, Ruth rushed upstairs before her toast burnt and placed the barely adequate pat of butter on the table.

Sitting in her front parlor, she watched the mist dancing over the surface of the river and waved to her nearest neighbor, Betty Palmer, as she trudged slowly along the river bank toward her cottage. Betty—that wasn't a happy story. She'd known her for a very long time and tended to think of her as the sister she'd never had. That had made it all the more painful when she'd been unable to help her in her most desperate time.

Running the town newspaper, she had a responsibility to investigate and report what affected the town of Hamble and to be as impartial as possible. When that news was the most…"personal" was the right word…to come along since the repurposing of the airfield, it had made it very difficult to keep her impartiality. Reporting the facts was one thing. However, Betty had come to her home begging for help to find answers, and she hadn't been able to assist her. She felt like she'd let her friend down, badly.

Since then, though they'd been convivial to each

other, things hadn't been the same. The times when they spent a pleasant evening sitting outside sharing some elderflower wine or down The Victory over a nice glass of white were now a fading, sad memory.

Herbert broke into her melancholy thoughts by unexpectedly placing a hand on her shoulder, causing her to jump and spill the remainder of her tea onto the table.

"Don't do that, Herbert!" she told him, getting a cloth from the sink. "I thought you'd gone to bed."

"How many times, Aunty—please call me Lawrence!" he said from the chair he'd taken. "Decided I wasn't tired," he added to explain his presence.

Ruth filled a glass with water from the tap and came back to sit down next to him, shaking her head. "You know I can't do that, Herbert. My sister, bless her soul, named you after our grandfather, and that's who you'll always be to me. If you prefer using your surname as your first, that's also your choice, but I won't change."

His Aunt Ruth was now the only person he knew who still persisted in calling him by his given name, and though a little annoyed, he decided to let the subject drop.

"Fair enough. So how're things in the wide world of the reporter?"

Ruth shrugged. "Nothing much, to be honest. About all that's happened lately is the news that Hamble's going to be an all-women flying station for the ATA."

"Apart from yours truly," Lawrence pointed out, doffing a hat he wasn't wearing.

"But you said you'd only be here for the next

month or two."

"Ah," he began, tapping the side of his nose, "if the pickings are rich, I may try and wrangle a longer stint."

"Firstly, my lad," Ruth started, "make sure you see—or try to see, I should say—Dorothy in admin to let her know I've told you it's okay to stay here. That way she won't have the bother of finding you somewhere, and I'll get paid for the dubious pleasure of your company."

"And secondly?" Lawrence prompted, sneaking his fingers across the table toward the glass of water and having his knuckles rapped for the trouble.

"Secondly, when was the last time you kept a girlfriend longer than a month? Haven't you tired yet of playing on the deaf-in-one-ear routine? It's wartime, and there are many men much worse off than you."

"I suppose you're right," he conceded and then pantomimed a yawn of epic proportions and got back to his feet. "Maybe I'm tired after all. I'm going back to bed. See you later," he added, kissing her on the forehead and heading back upstairs.

Ruth could be right, he thought after closing his bedroom door and flinging himself on top of the blankets. He'd been deaf in his left ear since an uncle, who definitely wasn't a favorite, had swatted him around the head for breaking his kitchen window with a golf ball. The best stroke he'd ever made, he maintained to this day, and he swore the injury was the real reason he'd never got his handicap below eighteen.

She was right, though. He had used his deafness as a ploy to get the girls to go out with him. Not something he was proud of these days. He also wasn't having any luck in uniform, as the women he met thought he was in a cushy number when they realized he was in the Air Transport Auxiliary and not the Royal Navy or Air Force and soon broke up with him.

He couldn't blame them, really. The civilian population had no idea the dangers they faced each day as they flew in unarmed aircraft that didn't even have the benefit of a radio. There were regulations about the last time of day they were allowed to land, what kind of weather they could take off and fly in; both could and had been ignored for the needs of the frontline stations. Not to mention the danger of being caught by a German aircraft and shot down. They weren't even tutored in evasive maneuvers, or how to fly by instruments.

The thought made him sigh, and he decided to risk a quick cigarette. Rising smoothly and as quietly as he could, he opened the window. If the ladies only knew the truth about him!

Chapter Five

As they walked to work, neither Penny, Doris, nor Mary said a word, but trailed in Betty's wake. As for Betty, she neither slowed her pace nor quickened it, and this made Penny hope Betty wasn't actually angry at them.

Her choice of words to describe her sister's death had been...interesting. When Penny had moved in at the end of last week, the picture had immediately grabbed her attention, being the only one on show. Betty didn't seem to be one for knick-knacks about the place, and upon being asked about it, she'd shrugged, muttered, "Sister," and said she felt like a walk. She persuaded Penny to join her along the riverbank. In hindsight, it'd been a none too subtle way of changing the subject.

Now, here she was, again trudging along the riverbank teeming with ducks, moorhens, and swans, this time in the direction of Hamble airfield, Doris and Mary by her side. No one was saying anything, and all three pairs of eyes were set on the slumped shoulders of Betty as she made a steady pace about ten feet in front of them.

As they came to the right turn at The Victory pub that would put them on to the road to the airfield, Doris blurted out, "Did you know about any of this?"

A heron burst out of the hedgerow and startled

Penny so much that only Mary's quick action in grabbing hold of her arm stopped her from stumbling and falling into the river.

"Thanks, Mary," she said, wiping a hand across her brow and happily accepting her arm as they set off up the road. Doris took up station on her other side. "To answer you, she told me her sister had died. She certainly never mentioned anything about her being killed."

"Shouldn't we talk to her?" Doris asked.

"You do it," Mary advised. "She doesn't like me very much," she added looking very downcast.

That was when Betty stopped, shook her head, and turned to face the other three, who halted a few feet away from her.

"Here and now's not the time to talk about this— and Mary, don't worry. You took me by surprise, and I just...blurted out the truth, the truth I've been keeping to myself these past months."

"But you said she'd been killed?" Mary queried, unable to stop the question they were all wondering about.

Betty took a look around as if to make sure no one could overhear her. Apart from a ginger cat that stalked past them on its way down to the river and a heron that called loudly as it passed overhead, they were on their own. The town of Hamble was a quiet place of only a few thousand souls, and being near the river early in the morning, they were very unlikely to be overheard by anyone.

"I shouldn't have put it that way." Betty shook her head.

Mary seemed to have the bit between her teeth.

"No smoke without fires," she mumbled.

Betty heard her, though, and for a second, it looked like she might be about to share what she thought. However, a Puss Moth passing low overhead was enough to change her mind.

"We'll talk tonight, I promise," she added.

"But what if we're billeted someplace else?" Doris asked, glancing back over her shoulder in the direction of the cottage she'd already fallen in love with.

A smile spread over Betty's lips as she walked the few paces back to the group and linked her arm through Doris's free one. "Well, as I'd likely get two others dumped on me at some point, refugees or unfortunates who've been bombed out, I may as well take in you pair of reprobates whilst I still have a choice."

Mary beamed over at her. "You mean that? Even after I've done my best to first cripple you, then send things flying?"

"I'll take the chance," Betty told her with a smile. "So what do you say? Want to room with us?"

Mary looked at Doris and both nodded. "If you'll have us, we'll be very happy to take you up on your offer."

"That's settled then," Betty agreed. "I'll find Dorothy and sort everything out so it's all official."

"Presuming you can find her," put in Penny.

"Very true."

****

Two hours later, a rather frustrated Doris heaved herself out of the rear cockpit of the Tiger Moth biplane she'd just taken up for her test flight, jumped down to the grass, and waited for Thelma. To say she was frustrated was to put it mildly. Things hadn't been helped when she'd been in the operations hut that morning and seen the list of who was flying what. Seeing those immortal words Spitfire and Hurricane chalked up had been enough to make her mouth salivate, and here she was back in these infernal biplanes!

After what seemed an eternity, Thelma finally trotted over to where Doris had been leaning, none too nonchalantly, against the lower wing. "Well? Satisfied?"

"With your flying, Ms. Winter? Yes," Thelma told her, jotting another note on her clipboard and then tucking it under her arm. "With your attitude, not quite so much."

Doris took off her flying helmet. "My attitude?"

"Yes, your attitude. Let me put it this way. We may not be a military unit, Ms. Winter, but to operate to full efficiency, we need to show at least a modicum of discipline. I will make a few, only a few, allowances for your being American, but don't try us too much. You signed a contract, which means if the circumstances are severe enough, we can terminate that contract. Do we understand each other?"

Swallowing her first instinct to argue back, Doris settled for a respectful, "Yes, ma'am."

"Thank you, Doris. Now, so far as your flying's concerned, there's not much I can teach you about Moths, so take this over to Ops," she handed her a note, "and they'll add you to the roster. So long as you don't have any problems with navigational familiarization flights this afternoon, you'll be joining Penny and the other girls on delivery flights Friday."

Delighted though she was, Doris was still a little

surprised she'd be operational so soon. It must have showed on her face.

"Yes. If circumstances allowed, we'd give you more time to get used to things and the area, but it doesn't. We need everyone we can get, for reasons I can't explain. Now, trot over to Ops and send your friend…" Thelma consulted her clipboard, "…Ms. Whitworth-Baines over."

"I think she prefers to be called Mary," Doris offered.

"I would too, with that mouthful," Thelma muttered, revealing a dry sense of humor. "Oh, can you and Penny meet me in the mess after this flight? I'll bring Mary along with me if she has any problems, otherwise I'll tell her to meet me there."

****

Doris dangled her fork in front of her eyes and let the unidentifiable mess drip slowly back onto her plate. "Would someone please explain to me just what this is supposed to be? 'Cause it sure as all hell doesn't taste like anything I've had before."

"I've learned it's best to eat with your eyes closed. It helps numb the taste buds," advised Penny as she shoveled in one forkful after another.

Mary had shoved her plate away and was instead making do with a cup of tea and bread and butter. "I wouldn't begin to guess what this is *supposed* to be! Though," she added as an afterthought, "personally, I can tell you that quail is very overrated."

"Let me put it another way, Doris," added Penny between mouthfuls. "We're all down for one more familiarization flight this afternoon before we knock off, so close your eyes, open your mouth, and—look out, stomach, here it comes." Suiting action to words, she proceeded to demolish the rest of her stew before sitting back with a smack of her lips and staring around at the incredulous looks upon her friends' faces. "Think of it like this—it's fuel for your stomach. You need that as much as planes need petrol."

Though her face said she didn't believe her, Doris took a deep breath and managed to get half of her plateful down before she pushed it away, unable to eat anymore. "That'll have to do," she said, swallowing again to make sure everything she'd consumed stayed down.

Before Penny and Doris managed to persuade Mary to also eat up, they were distracted by Betty pulling out a chair and putting down her own plate and cup of tea to sit next to Mary.

"I hear you both passed your tests," she began, taking a sip of her tea as Mary and Doris both nodded. "I managed to track Dorothy down, and all the paperwork's been arranged. You're staying with me." Though hardly surprising, Betty was rather annoyed that no one expressed their thanks. "Don't anyone rush to thank me for providing a nice, clean, warm roof over your heads, then," she muttered, slouching back into her chair.

Doris remembered her manners. "We're sorry, Betty. Mary and I are very, very grateful to you, really! The thing is, we're trying to persuade Mary here to eat this—we think it's stew—so she'll have something in her stomach whilst flying this afternoon. But," and here she threw an evil stare at Mary, who stubbornly sat with her arms crossed in defiance, "she's being pigheaded."

"No, I'm not!" denied Mary vehemently. "I just

47

know what I like."

"You may have to reassess your stance, my love," advised Betty, now putting away her stew with gusto. "We manage to eat pretty good back home, but whilst on base, it doesn't change that much from this. If you're here for an early flight, there's a good chance you'll get powdered egg, but don't hold out too much hope for anything else that would excite your taste buds. If I were you, I'd shovel it down, follow it up with a cup of this builder's tea they serve, and hope to keep it down. After a couple of weeks you'll be used to it and won't give it a second thought."

With a look that patently said, *I don't believe you, but you're probably right*, Mary proceeded to tentatively eat her stew. Or rather, she did her best to feed it straight down her throat so she didn't have to taste it.

Whatever worked, Betty thought, and then did her best to take Mary's mind off what she was doing. "Tell me where you got your uniform, Mary," she asked, reaching out and running a hand appreciatively down a sleeve. "It doesn't look like the Bosten Reed…"

"That's Austin Reed," corrected Penny.

"Sorry, Austin Reed, we're wearing."

On first glance, they were the same, but if you looked closer and then felt the material, the differences were there. Subtle, but there. The fabric was softer, with more give to it, and a finer cut. "Where did you get this?" Penny asked.

Between spoonfuls of stew—and judging by the rate she was putting it in her mouth, Mary had decided to go with the quicker-you-can-get-it-down-the-less-you'll-taste-it route—she looked up into Betty's eyes to say, "After I'd seen what the lady who interviewed me was wearing, and especially after she told me where she sent everyone to get their uniform, I decided my family's tailor in Savile Row would do a better job. I must say," she paused to admire her own jacket, "they do seem to have done an awfully good job, don't you think?"

Penny and Doris exchanged glances that clearly said they weren't sure if they'd been insulted or not. Penny surreptitiously stroked her uniform beneath the table and felt a moment's pang of jealousy before remembering she wasn't in the ATA to show off but to do a job, and a stained uniform from Austin Reed would look exactly like one from Savile Row...from a distance. And it would be less expensive to clean.

"There, finished." Mary laid down her spoon and immediately drank down the rest of her tea and, before anyone could stop her, Betty's also. Betty stared with some dismay at her disappearing refreshment.

"Someone looks like they needed that," Betty grumbled, getting to her feet for a refill.

Realizing what she'd done, Mary slapped down the now empty cup and looked sheepishly at her friends. "Oh, dear, I think I've upset her again."

As Betty sat back down, she patted Mary on the back to show there were no hard feelings, this time keeping a finger through the handle of her cup.

A moment later, a spanner was thrown in the works by the arrival of Thelma, who took the remaining seat at the table. To the surprise of Penny, Doris, and Mary, Betty immediately got to her feet, picked up her tea and plate of bread and jam and addressed, it seemed, all bar Thelma at the table with, "I've got to get back to work, ladies. I'll see you at home later."

Penny noticed that as Betty left the room, Thelma sighed and turned to her own bowl of stew. "Care to tell us what that's all about, Thelma?"

"So the three of you are all set for your first deliveries tomorrow, then?"

"Looking forward to it," answered Doris, though she raised an eyebrow at Penny, as Thelma had ignored the question.

Mary wasn't so backward in coming forward, though. "What just happened between you and Betty, Thelma?"

Awkward silence reigned as Mary leant toward Thelma, fixing her emerald green eyes on her with a stare that could melt iron.

Doris didn't miss this. "I wouldn't play poker with this one, Thelma."

"More like baccarat, dear," Mary advised, still not taking her eyes from where Thelma had broken into a sweat.

Finally, Thelma gave up and blinked. "Okay, okay. Just stop staring at me like that. I think I've got a headache coming on."

Whilst Thelma closed her eyes and rubbed her knuckles at her temples, Mary turned her face away and whispered to Penny, "Thank Christ for that. I don't think I could have kept my eyes open for another second!"

"Do you really play baccarat?" Doris asked. "Everyone I know plays poker."

"My family never let me play poker. They said only a certain class of people played poker."

"What kind of people would that be?" Doris asked,

intrigued to know where this conversation was going.

"You really want to know?"

"Oh, I do, Mary, I do," Doris assured her.

"On your head be it," Mary told her. "Americans."

"Pardon?" replied Doris, nearly choking on her tea.

"You heard me. My parents believe poker is the common person's card game, and hence, that's why they only allowed me to play baccarat."

"Well," Doris told her with a gleam in her eye, "I guess I'll just have to educate you some, won't I."

Mary matched Doris's grin.

Thelma had taken this opportunity to finish up her sandwich and tea and had gotten to her feet. "Much as I'd love to stay for a chat, I must get back to work as well."

Mary, newly reminded of what had been happening before she'd been sidetracked, stood up to block her path. "Oh, no, you don't, First Officer Aston. Please, sit back down. What's up between you and Betty?"

"You're not going to let it go, are you?" Thelma took her seat with a sigh of resignation. "And call me Thelma, please."

Mary merely stared at her, waiting for an answer.

"Well, you asked. You all know that Betty's sister's dead?"

"She told us this morning she was killed," Penny amended.

Thelma looked around before answering. "I was there the day she died, and I will say it did look suspicious."

"Suspicious. How?" Mary pressed.

"She'd been aloft in a Tiger Moth, and you both know how far up those can go." Everyone nodded in agreement. "I was with the doctor who attended her. When we got there, she was lying on the ground and her lips were a terrible shade of blue. Not one of my best decisions."

"Blue?" took up Doris. "It can't be hypoxia, since the Moth can't get high enough for anyone to die from oxygen starvation. The only other thing I know of that will turn someone's lips blue upon death is poisoning."

"But surely this all came up when they did an autopsy?" asked Doris.

Thelma snorted. "What autopsy?"

Mary's mouth dropped open. "You mean they didn't do an autopsy? Why ever not?"

"Who knows." Thelma shrugged. "That's what Betty asked, and all they told her—fobbed her off with, more like—was rubbish about how, in wartime, accidents happen, and then something about she died from lack of oxygen."

"But that's preposterous!" Penny uttered through clenched teeth.

"All true," agreed Thelma, "but what could she do? Everything was signed and sealed and locked away. She threatened to involve the police, and the coroner all but laughed in her face. So far as the authorities are concerned, that was the end of the story."

"Poor Betty," said Penny with heart. "That explains why she thinks she was killed, but why's she got a problem with you, Thelma? You couldn't have done anything to save her."

Thelma looked around the sparsely crowded mess before letting out a sigh. "You'd find out, at some point, we're not on the best of terms, so I'll let you know why. I couldn't do anything to save Betty's sister, but I was due to take up that Moth, and when I got called away, she somehow, despite not being in the ATA, took it up instead of me." Thelma sighed again. "So far as Betty's concerned, it should have been me who was killed instead of her sister."

Chapter Six

Whilst in most of Europe July could be counted upon to be pretty much the definition of summer, sunny, it appeared Hampshire had a different idea. One minute, the birds were on the wing, flitting this way and that, enjoying the warm sun on their bodies and the profusion of midges brought out by the promise of a beautiful day. The next, a bank of dark, evil-looking clouds had swooped in and chosen the airfield over which to settle. Flying was curtailed.

Thelma put the phone down and turned to where everyone was gathered. Times like this made her glad that by the end of the week she'd only have female pilots. Presently there were three men as well as her four female pilots, and according to the orders she'd seen that morning, another three were to come over the next few weeks. Looking around the flight line hut, things were pretty crowded, and heaven only knew what it'd be like when they had their full complement.

"That was Jane," she informed them, leaning back against the desk and waiting for everyone to give her their attention.

"Who?" asked Doris, being naturally nosy.

Thelma answered before anyone else. "That, Doris, was Flight Captain—and your, for want of a better word, boss—Jane Howell. She wanted us to know she's heard from the Met office, and this foul weather's in for the rest of the day, so sorry, all flying's cancelled."

"Thelma."

"Yes, Lawrence?"

"What about the two Spitfires that Henley's expecting today? From what I understand, they really need them after the other day's rhubarb."

"I'm Doris," the American said, holding out her hand.

"Lawrence," he said by reply, shaking her firmly by the hand. "Herbert Lawrence."

"Sorry to interrupt, but Mary and I turned up only yesterday and haven't met anyone else apart from Thelma, Penny, and Betty."

"Ahem." Thelma coughed to regain their attention. "As pleasant as this is, Doris, once I finish, you'll have all the time you wish for introductions."

Doris went bright red. "Oh, yes. Sorry about that."

Thelma turned to where Lawrence was awaiting his answer regarding the Spitfires. "Henley knows the situation, and as they've been stood down for the next five days, they can wait a day. Understood?"

Lawrence nodded.

"And to carry on from there, as all flying is cancelled, consider yourselves off duty. Report back as normal for eight in the morning. Third Officer Winter, you now have as long as you like to talk to Third Officer Lawrence. Dismissed."

Once Thelma had left the hut, its occupants were left in a strange Mexican standoff. However, Penny soon found that Doris wasn't shy in coming forward. "I guess that's Thelma's cue for us to get introduced. Penny..." She patted her friend on the knee, causing her to jump slightly at the unexpected contact. "As you've been here a few days more than either Mary or me, have you met these gentlemen before?"

Penny got to her feet and had just opened her mouth when the men, all except Lawrence, stood as one, pulled their coats on, placed their hats on their heads, and strode out without a word.

"I guess that leaves me," stated Lawrence. "I won't make excuses for those gentlemen."

Doris huffed. "So-called *gentlemen*."

"So let's call them idiots," Lawrence continued. "At least we won't have to put up with them for much longer." He got to his feet and moved to stand next to Penny before inclining his head toward Mary.

"Mary Whitworth-Baines," she answered, getting to her feet and standing next to Penny while indicating Doris should join them. "And the last of our trio is our American cousin Doris Winter."

"American?" Lawrence looked over at Doris, now on the other side of Penny. "Ma'am, Herbert Lawrence at your service. But please, call me Lawrence. I can't stand being called Herbert. It's so old-fashioned. Only my aunt insists upon calling me that."

Doris shook the hand he offered. "I presume you had a good chat with Penny when she arrived, then?"

Both Penny and Lawrence shrugged their shoulders. "The Friday she arrived was much like today, though they were still hoping for the weather to clear, so they didn't send us home. I don't know if you've noticed, but there's not a lot to do here when there's no flying. Little hint, bring a book in. So yes, we had a bit of a chat, more about where the next cup of tea would be coming from than anything else. I must say, Penny, you and your friends certainly brighten up the place!"

"Thank you, Lawrence, I think." Penny beamed in pleasure whilst simultaneously blushing.

"To save a bit of time, ladies, I'm a bachelor, only because I've never met the right lady." Penny swore his gaze flicked once more over Doris as he said the words. "In my mid-thirties, broken and slightly bewildered. Deaf in my left ear," he added, tapping said ear. "We may see quite a bit of each other out of work too, as I'm living with my aunt Ruth just down the riverbank from Betty's. Also, I'll be here longer than the other chaps as I'm your designated taxi driver for a while. On that note, I too must be off."

Pulling on his raincoat, Lawrence nearly had the door handle ripped from his grip by the force of the wind as he pulled it open. "Wow!" He turned to where the ladies had taken a step back at the unexpected ferocity of the wind. "Watch yourselves. It's a blowy one," he added somewhat unnecessarily.

"He seems nice," suggested Mary, stepping behind Penny before adding, "He certainly seems to like you, Doris." She ducked to avoid the playful swat aimed at her head.

"Whatever," Doris replied, but both Penny and Mary noticed their friend wasn't quite able to meet their eyes. "So, as we've an unexpected afternoon off, what do you two want to do?"

Joining the others in putting on their coats against the storm raging outside, Penny suggested, "I don't know about you, but I fancy a walk down town. I'm sure I noticed a local newspaper office when I came in from the train station, and I fancy seeing if they've got an archive."

"Why do you want to do that?" asked Mary, doing up her last button.

"I want to see if they've got anything on Betty's sister. Let's face it, this doesn't seem the kind of place where much goes on, so there should be something."

Mary looked over at Penny, her head canted to one side in question. "Didn't Betty say she'd talk to us about that tonight?"

Penny couldn't quite look Mary in the eye. "I know," she allowed, hands on hips, "but I like to find out all I can when something interests me."

"I'll join you, Pen," piped up Doris. "If you don't mind, that is?"

"Not at all," she replied.

Mary put her hand on the door "Suit yourselves. I'm going to see Betty and get a front door key off her. I could do with sorting out my room and having a nap."

Penny and Doris looked at each other at hearing this plan. "Good idea. We'll join you."

Hamble wasn't a huge airfield such as the well-known fighter bases like Biggin Hill and Duxford, but it still took them five minutes to battle through the near-horizontal rain until they made it to the ops hut. When Penny pushed the door open, apart from a girl reading an old copy of *The Picture Post* which, to her horror, featured a picture of herself on the cover, the only other occupant was Betty. Fortunately, Doris was already past the girl and had sat next to where Betty stood drinking a cup of tea and staring out the window. Mary joined them, also showing no sign of having noticed the picture. Penny breathed a little easier.

"Penny for them?" Doris asked, poking Betty gently in the ribs to get her attention.

"Oh, hello, you lot," she said, jerking out of her reverie. "I suppose Thelma's stood you down. Are you off back home?"

"Yes," Mary confirmed, "which brings me to why we're here. If you're not going back yet?" she asked and only had a short wait until Betty shook her head. "In that case, could I have a front door key, please? I want to go put my things away and take a nap. Oh," she then remembered, "I hope you don't mind, but I took one of the rooms up in the attic. Is that all right?"

"No problem," Betty assured her. "They haven't been used in an age, so they could probably do with a good airing, but you'd have found that out last night."

"I like having my own space. The manor always seemed crowded, so this suits me fine. Unless either of you two want the room?" she asked Doris and Penny.

"No, thanks, I'm good," Penny told her, whilst Doris contented herself with a shake of her head.

"Well, if that's settled, here…" Betty dug into her handbag. "Take the spare."

"Thank you," Mary said gratefully, putting the key safely away in her purse and moving toward the door. "I'll see you all later, then."

With Mary on her way back home, Betty asked what the other two were going to do.

"We're off for a walk around town," Doris half explained, keeping the part about going to the newspaper archives to herself.

"Don't you want one too, Doris?" Betty said holding up another key. "I've only got the one on me. There are others but, well, they're at home." She shrugged.

Penny had the answer. "It's okay, Betty. I've one,

remember. I'll get a copy made for Doris whilst we're in town."

****

"Any idea why Betty was staring out the window when we left?" Doris asked Penny as, arms linked, they hurried as best they could through the driving rain.

Shoes clicking over the cobbles and with a newspaper held over her head in a futile attempt to shelter, Penny wished she'd kept her flying suit and boots on. If she wouldn't have been drier, at least she'd have been warmer. They'd both stuffed their hats down their coats to avoid them being blown away.

"Not really," Penny admitted, "but I suspect she's been like that most of the day. I doubt our bringing up her dead sister this morning helped."

Each was lost in her own thoughts as they came to the edge of town.

Doris stared around, fighting an urge for her jaw to drop. "Well, it's not New York, but it ain't no ghost town either. Come on, the sooner we find that newspaper place, the quicker we can get home."

"Let's get the key cut first," suggested Penny.

As luck would have it, they quickly found a branch of F. W. Woolworth's, and it only took ten minutes to get the key cut. With aid from a helpful shop assistant, they obtained directions to the *Hamble Gazette*. They walked past a boarded-up pub with a sign nailed to the entrance—"Gone to fight Hitler. Back for teatime." Doris and Penny both grinned upon seeing this typical example of British humor.

"We'll have a pint with you when you get back, my friend," said Penny, raising a non-existent glass to the absent publican.

"My kind of guy," Doris echoed.

As they turned the corner, painted on a low stone wall surrounding a church was an arrow and the words, "To the river."

"That'll be handy if we get lost," remarked Doris, following up with, "Come on, the newspaper place can't be far." She increased her pace.

As Doris expected, Lower Street wasn't a long one at all. "Hey, you call this a street?" she burst out as they walked past a sign for the *Hamble Gazette* next door to a greengrocer. "I don't know what your definition of a street is, but this is…this is so, oh, I don't know…short!"

"I've never been to New York, or anywhere in the USA, but I'd guess that anywhere but London would seem small compared to what you're used to," Penny finished with a laugh.

Doris allowed herself a small smile but still shrugged. "Very true, actually. However, we'll have to go into London so I can compare for myself."

"Deal," agreed Penny, shaking her friend's hand.

"Anyhow, Miss Marple," Doris teased, looking up at a sign, "we've arrived. What now?"

"Miss Marple? I'll have you know I'm twenty-four and have never worn tweed in my life!"

"Enough with the mock outrage," Doris told Penny. "I saw the way your eyes lit up when you heard what Betty thought. You smelled a mystery."

"Was it that obvious?"

Doris leaned in and spoke in a conspiratorial voice. "Only to another Agatha Christie buff."

"So you too think there's more to Eleanor's death than Betty's been told?"

"Much more, but I'm not sure how we'd go about proving it."

Penny hesitated. "Me either, but you saw how upset she was this morning, and she's been very good to me since I got here."

"I'd have to go along with you there. She'd barely met Mary or me, yet she offered us both a roof over our heads. Who knows where we'd have ended up if she hadn't been so gracious. So what do you hope to find from the archives?"

"Who knows?" Penny admitted. "I suppose some background, and we'll have to hope Betty will fill in the blanks tonight."

"Do you think she will?" ventured Doris.

"So long as we don't upset her, but, to be on the safe side, let's make sure we think carefully before saying anything about this escapade to her later."

Penny laid a hand on her friend's shoulder. "As the great Miss Jane Marple said, there is nothing more cruel than talk."

Chapter Seven

Standing before the receptionist's desk in the offices of the *Hamble Gazette*, Penny wondered whether she was betraying Betty's trust. Even if she wasn't, was it the right thing to do? She'd never known Eleanor and had no logical reason why she should be doing this, other than Betty had quickly become a friend and it felt right to see if she could help. She'd had to run away from her family to gain her freedom, but she would never have wished her own sister ill, let alone dead, as overbearing and frankly detestable as she might be.

A cough from the lady behind the desk caught her attention.

"Can I help you? My name is Ruth Stone, and I run this newspaper," the lady behind the desk introduced herself.

Ruth was a smiley-faced lady in her late forties, with tight brown curls down to her neckline. A pencil behind her left ear was precariously balanced alongside her wire-rimmed glasses. Her brown eyes sparkled with curiosity, and Penny could feel herself warming to her already.

So, not the receptionist, as Penny had assumed. "Hello," she said, holding out her hand, "I'm Penny Blake, and this is my friend Doris Winter. We're in the ATA down the road." Walls may have ears, but eyes are made to see, and as they were in uniform, pretending they were something else wouldn't have made sense.

After shaking their hands, Ruth indicated they should take a seat. "I haven't seen you around before, so you must be pretty new. What can I do for you?"

Now it came time to ask, Penny found she'd slightly lost her nerve. Doris jumped in. "We were wondering if you keep an archive of your previous editions?"

"You're American!" Ruth exclaimed, clapping her hands together in delight. "Would you be interested in an interview? I'd love to do a piece on how our cousins see the war, especially since you joined."

"Would you let me think it over, Ruth?" Doris replied after what she considered a suitable thinking time.

"Oh, sure," came the cheerful reply. "You know where to find me when you've made up your mind."

"About this archive," Penny said, having found her voice. The conversation was in danger of swinging off target.

"Yes, yes. Sorry, I tend to flip from one subject to another," Ruth told them, joining her fingers together and leaning back in her chair. The pencil dropped, unnoticed by her, to the floor. "What are you looking for?"

"Any reports or articles you may have done on an Eleanor Palmer. We believe she died in January this year."

At the mention of Betty's sister's name, Ruth leaned forward and transformed from being friendly. She now radiated, if not menace, then a sense of deep personal interest in what had just been said. "That's a rather strange request. I've got to ask where your interest comes from."

"We board with Betty," began Penny, "and we only found out about her sister this morning."

"So why the interest? Did Betty tell you what happened?" Ruth persisted, running a hand through her curls and peering over the top of her glasses.

"Well..." Doris began to say and then had to stop and think how best to proceed. "Well, Betty said one thing about her, and then another...another person we know said another, and we're intrigued to find out what actually happened. Something doesn't seem right when two people so closely involved say different things, especially where a death is concerned." When she'd finished, she glanced over at Penny and raised an eyebrow, hoping her friend would understand her unsaid question and be the one to say it out loud. Now they were here, she felt a little silly.

Penny was also feeling somewhat sheepish and undid a few of her coat buttons to give herself a few seconds to think, not an easy thing as they were both under Ruth's intense scrutiny.

"It's like this," Penny began, squirming slightly under the older lady's unblinking stare. "I love a mystery, and so does Doris," she added, not wanting to be the sole recipient of her wrath if what she was about to say went down like a lead balloon, "and we both feel there's more to Eleanor's death than what Betty's been told. For a start, we don't believe she died of oxygen deprivation. The Tiger Moth simply can't get high enough."

For at least a minute, Ruth Stone studied Penny

and Doris, and you could almost hear the cogs whirring in her brain as she tried to make up her mind if the two strange women in front of her were serious or not. At last, she pushed her chair back and got to her feet.

"Come on," she told them over her shoulder. "Archives are down in the basement. Mind those boxes," she told them, waving a hand at a number of wooden boxes that made accessing the basement a little awkward. "We had a bit of a clear out and haven't figured what to do with all this junk yet." She stopped with a hand on the doorknob. "Now, before I allow you down there, there's something I've got to tell you both. Betty Palmer and I have been friends for a long time. I knew her when she started school, I was there for her when her mother died and for when Eleanor died, too. I despaired of her ever getting through, and I won't see her hurt in any way. Do we understand each other?" she demanded, fixing Penny and Doris with a look that dared them not to take her seriously.

Doris was the first to step forward and offer her a handshake. "I swear, Ruth, though I barely know Betty, I can see how much her loss hurts, and I would never do anything to hurt her. I only want to help, if I can."

"Same here, Ruth," agreed Penny, offering her hand too. "Please believe us."

Ruth took each hand in turn, then opened the door, turned on a light, and led the way down a set of steep, narrow stone steps. Whilst Penny and Doris took off their coats and laid them over the backs of two chairs that stood next to a large wooden desk, Ruth busied herself in rifling through a row of filing cabinets that stood at the back of the cellar. With a resounding thump, she dropped a pile of newspapers on the desk, causing both Penny and Doris to jump in surprise.

"Here you go, girls," she said, wiping her hand across her brow. "These are all the papers that would have anything in that we'd have written about that poor girl. Imagine, she was only twenty-seven. It's not an age for anyone to die." She brought out a watch on a chain from her pocket. "It's nearly half three, and we close at five, so take your time. Have you got a notebook?"

"Knew I'd forgotten something," answered Penny. "How about you?" she asked Doris, who shook her head.

"Never mind," said Ruth. "I'll send Walter down shortly with some tea and a notepad. Make yourselves comfortable and come up and find me, or Walter, if there's anything else you need."

Penny turned in her chair as Ruth started up the stairs. "Thanks for being so kind, Ruth. We really appreciate it."

Ruth paused at the door. "Think nothing of it. Oh, and don't worry if you lose track of time. We can walk home together. I'm actually your next-door neighbor! Well, if you can count fifty-odd yards as next door. My cottage is just around the bend from Betty's. See you soon."

"Ain't that nice?" Doris said when she was sure their host was out of earshot.

Crossing her ankles, Penny leant in toward Doris, casting an eye at where Ruth had left the door ajar, possibly so she could eavesdrop on what they might discuss. It sounded like Doris had something she needed to say.

"Is there a problem?"

"Call me Miss Picky," Doris told her, "but isn't this all a bit too easy?"

Penny couldn't help but laugh. "Too easy? My dear, this is a small country town with a small country newspaper. It's not like we walked into the offices of *The Times* and asked if we could have free rein to look through their files. Doris, she's been very good to two people she doesn't know. Cut her a little slack."

"I suppose it's not *The New York Times* either," she replied, her shoulders relaxing. "Okay, perhaps I was being a little paranoid."

"Anyone down in the hole?" a yell came from the door to the cellar.

Penny looked up and saw a man dressed in gray waistcoat and matching trousers holding a tray in his hands and looking down at them. "You must be Walter," she said, getting to her feet. "Come on down."

"Tea for two and a notepad each, I believe, was the delivery, ladies," he said, placing the tray down in a space Doris had cleared on the table. "And I've managed to scrounge up a few biscuits, too," he added.

"That's so sweet of you," Doris said, smiling up at him and flirtatiously batting her eyelids, then batting them again when it became clear Walter wasn't paying her any attention. Maybe her flirtation muscle needed practice. "Thanks, Walter. We'll be okay now."

He smiled his thanks at Doris and trudged back upstairs, leaving the door open too. It appeared Ruth had left orders to that effect. She couldn't blame her. If she didn't know them, she'd do the same. For a moment, she thought she saw a shadow, a man-shaped shadow, flit across the doorway, and was going to ask Penny if she'd seen anything, only her friend had her back to the door and it would've been a waste of time. Plus, it had happened so quickly Doris wasn't certain she'd actually seen anything. Turning back to the newspapers, she joined her friend in their task.

****

Keeping to the shadows, Ralph Johnson cursed his carelessness. In his desire to hear everything said in the cellar, he'd allowed the American woman to nearly catch a glimpse of him. Too late to think about blackening his face to help him blend into the background. His RAF battle dress would have to suffice, and so long as he was quiet and stuck to the shadows, he should be okay.

A crash from the front office was followed by a curse from Ruth as she told Walter off for bumping into the coat stand and causing it to crash to the floor. Freezing in place, he strained to listen for movement, any movement which could put him in danger of discovery.

He'd followed the two women on his own initiative, there being no opportunity to call His Lordship during the day, after hearing the American mention Eleanor Palmer as they'd walked past the rear of the mess whilst he was snatching a quick cigarette. He'd been briefed to keep an eye and ear out for anyone talking about the late Eleanor. Luck had been on his side when they'd gone into the newspaper office. He'd watched as they'd chatted with that nosy parker Ruth Stone until she'd led them out back and down the cellar. That had left him with a dilemma. Should he stand watch outside or, and this was far riskier, should he try to get into the offices without being seen?

His luck was in, though, and whilst he was

pondering what to do, the man she called her assistant
stepped out front with the teapot and disappeared
around the corner. Before Ralph could change his mind,
he'd nipped in through the door Walter had left open
and managed to conceal himself behind the pile of
boxes near the stairs. After he'd heard the Ruth woman
come back upstairs, he'd waited for her assistant to
come back up after taking down some tea before
creeping out from his hiding place and poking his head
around the open door.

Amateur mistake and something His Lordship
would no doubt have words about, together with certain
repercussions Ralph didn't like to dwell on, if the man
got to hear about it. He'd make certain he didn't. The
scars from the last *reminder* still smarted, and as he was
out on his own initiative, he'd better make certain the
risk was worth it. As it turned out, by moving the boxes
slightly he was able to create a small gap between two.
He then found he could hear what was being said
downstairs well enough. Being careful not to upset the
stack, he settled down to listen.

****

By half four, the pile of discarded newspapers on
the end of the table had grown so it towered over those
yet to be read when Penny finally came across the
edition that bore the headline, "Sister of woman found
dead in Tiger Moth cries murder!"

"Wow!" she said, sitting back into her chair. "Now
that's what I call a headline."

"That's not coffee!" put in Doris, shuddering and
putting down her cup.

"I'm not surprised." Penny looked at her friend in
wonder. "You do know that's the same tea Walter

brought down over an hour ago? It's stewed by now. If you want a cup of coffee around here, you're going to be disappointed, I think. Betty's only got tea, and I don't think you'll find anything but Camp coffee on base. I don't recommend you even try that."

"So where will I get real coffee, then?" Doris looked positively miserable at what Penny told her.

Penny shrugged.

"Sorry." Doris pushed her cup to one side. "Ignore my moans. I'll just have to find some. You've found something?"

"Take a look at this." She handed the newspaper to her friend. "What do you think of that?"

Doris held the paper up and whistled. "Wow! Do you remember seeing anything in your national newspapers when this happened? This was published January twenty-fourth last year."

Penny closed her eyes whilst she thought back, but she had to shake her head as nothing came to mind. "No, nothing I can think of, and not making light of her death at all, but with all the death and destruction that's going on, it's very unlikely to have made even the news of anything other than this paper."

A hand clamped down on Penny's shoulder and she nearly jumped out of her skin.

"Very good reasoning, Penny, isn't it?"

"Ruth! Where the hell did you come from?" Doris exclaimed, as she dragged a chair next to where she sat.

Putting down a fresh pot of tea and three fresh cups, Doris poured and then settled back to take a sip. "I'm afraid it's still not coffee, Doris," she told her as she put her cup down.

Doris's expression was one of amazement. "Just

how did you hear that?"

Tapping the side of her nose, Ruth smiled enigmatically. "A good reporter never reveals her sources."

"Crap," replied Doris. "Spit it out, honey."

"Fair enough. You're a Yank."

Penny and Doris exchanged glances and silently decided that yes, they liked this woman, even if she did have a penchant for teasing. Penny pushed the paper she'd come across to Ruth. "How soon after Eleanor died was this?"

Ruth picked up the paper to refresh her memory. "If I remember rightly, only a couple of days. As I said, I've known Betty for years, and she called me up the previous afternoon, in a right state."

"I can well imagine." Penny shook her head sadly. "What then?"

"Well, she told me she didn't believe the official cause of death, hypoxia, and that she was getting nowhere asking anyone for answers."

"What about the autopsy?" asked Doris.

Ruth snorted in disgust. "What autopsy? 'This is wartime,' the doctor in charge told her. He said there wasn't going to be one and she should just accept her sister was dead."

"I don't imagine that went down very well," Penny ventured.

"You're right," Ruth agreed. "In fact, she made such a nuisance of herself they told her she was taking two weeks' leave, whether she wanted to or not, and then she was to report here to Hamble."

"Hmm. Sounds like someone wanted her out of the way," decided Doris.

"That's what Betty thinks," agreed Ruth.

"And she still hasn't heard anything different?"

"No." Ruth shook her head. "She found out something very interesting before they managed to get her out of Luton, though."

"What was that?" Penny asked, thinking things were getting more and more like a Miss Marple mystery by the minute.

"She managed to check the flying schedule for that day, and Thelma had crossed out her name and entered Betty's instead. Somehow, Eleanor took Betty's place."

"So that's why she blames Thelma," Doris said, letting out a breath she hadn't realized she'd been holding.

Chapter Eight

At the stroke of five, Ruth got up from her chair near the front door, bid a goodnight to Walter, and locked up before heading down to the cellar.

"Walter says, 'Goodnight, Penny,'" she told the surprised young lady, who promptly dropped her pencil.

"Who?"

Doris had to stuff her fingers into her mouth lest she burst out with laughter. Fortunately, their host was understanding. "My—what is it you call them in the States, Doris? I've got it. Cub. He's my cub reporter. That's junior reporter to you and me, Penny. The young man who brought your tea down earlier?"

"Ah." Penny picked up her pencil and drew another newspaper toward her. "Hair that looks in need of a brushing, what could politely be called a thin moustache, and, unless I'm much mistaken, flat feet," she added, enjoying the twin looks of surprise upon Doris and Ruth's faces. "See, I was paying attention," she added smugly.

"I thought you hadn't noticed him!" declared Doris.

"Perhaps I'm a better Miss Marple than you, my dear," she teased.

"I'd say you're a sly one, Miss Marple," Doris said with a laugh.

"It appears you weren't the only one paying attention," Ruth put in, pulling up a chair and making herself comfortable. "I didn't get a minute's work out of him when he got back. In fact, you may have heard a crash a short while ago?" Both Doris and Penny nodded, having nearly left the cellar to investigate the cause. "That was him knocking over the coat stand when I mentioned your name. Honestly, I had such a hard time keeping a straight face whilst telling him off. My dears, I didn't think anyone could go that shade of red. What a picture!"

Doris promptly snorted her gulp of tea back into her cup, which set everyone off laughing once more.

"Poor boy," Penny stammered once she'd dried her eyes. "He seems sweet, in a helpless sort of way," she added, turning her head as the other two both raised their eyebrows.

"If you wish me to speak to him for you..." ventured Ruth.

"Er, no, don't worry yourself, Ruth," she told the older lady hastily. "I can look after myself if needs be."

Doris reached across, took her hand, and patted it. "Sure you can, honey, but we're here to answer any questions you may have."

"Doris!"

"I'm just teasing you, Pen." Nevertheless she made certain only Ruth saw the wink.

Ruth tapped the table to get the two ladies' attention back to the business at hand. "Apart from that headline, have either of you found anything else?"

Penny pushed the paper she'd found toward the editor. "Nothing much more, to be honest. This one has a similar headline, but all the narrative is much the

M. W. Arnold

same as the first article there, stating the facts and what Betty believed, but nothing else. Then there are follow-ups the next week, before the story disappears," she added, slumping back and finishing off her tea.

Ruth picked up the papers Penny indicated and flicked through them before throwing them back onto the pile. She sighed and looked up at her new acquaintances. "I'm sorry. I didn't think you'd find anything. After all, I edited those papers and wrote most of those stories. If you think it's easy getting anything out of the Ministry of Defense or Information these days, think again. After what they gave me had run out, no matter how much I love Betty, I could see dragging out the story wouldn't accomplish anything. I thought if I did, it'd only hurt her more, and I couldn't do that."

"Was she angry at you for that?" Penny asked after a moment's thought.

"A little," Ruth admitted. "She started talking to me again after a week or so."

"Even though you weren't able to find anything else out?"

"Even after that," Ruth agreed. "None of it did anything to change her mind. She still thinks her sister was murdered."

They were all silent with their thoughts for a few minutes before the somber mood was broken by a loud barking coming from upstairs.

"That'll be Bobby wanting to go home," Ruth declared, looking over her shoulder to where, at the top of the stairs, a small black-and-white cocker spaniel stood looking down at them, tail wagging furiously.

"Ladies, meet Bobby. Bobby, stop the barking.

We're the only ones here. Now, go get your leash."

"How did you teach him that trick?" Doris asked Ruth as she let them out and then locked up again.

"Actually," Ruth told them, accepting the leash from Bobby's mouth, "I've no idea where he picked it up, and I've had him since he was a puppy. He's ten now and still the laziest dog I've ever known," she said, but the affectionate way she fondled the dog's ears showed how much she loved her companion.

Nobody noticed the dark shadow of Aircraftman Johnson as he crept out from his hiding place, a frown upon his face as he realized his predicament.

****

"So how long have you run the newspaper?" Doris asked, linking her arm through one of Ruth's, whilst Penny did the same to her other, Bobby leading the way at a very gentle trot.

Despite the gathering dusk, Penny could hear the sadness in Ruth's voice. "Since the end of 1939, when my son joined the Army."

Penny took a deep breath before asking, "I'm sorry if I'm overstepping the mark, Ruth, but what happened?"

Ruth stopped walking, causing Bobby to yelp when he came to the end of his lead. "It's not as bad as that, Penny," she said, though it took her two goes to get the words out. "He's a prisoner. The Germans took him at Dunkirk. He was in the Second Dorsets, and they were part of the rear guard."

Upon hearing this news, both Penny and Doris did the only thing, the natural thing, and threw their arms around Ruth. At their feet, Bobby belied his tag as the world's laziest dog by alternately jumping up and pawing their legs and yapping set to wake the dead. When they finally let her go, Ruth turned her face briefly away so she could wipe the tears from her face.

"Look at me," she sniffed, "you'd think I'd have cried all my tears by now."

Doris pulled her close and held her by the shoulders. "Don't be silly. There's certainly nothing to be sorry for. I'm sure you miss him. Do you hear much?"

"I do, letters and postcards, though it's not a regular thing. I think they're delivered as and when the Germans feel like it. At least that's what it seems like to me," she finished with a bitter laugh. "He's a lieutenant, so he should be okay, I hope."

"Is he married?" Doris asked.

Ruth shook her head. "No. The newspaper was his life. He took it over from his father after he died and used to work all the hours God sends. It's only a small provincial paper, but Hamble has a way of getting under your skin."

The three of them started back down the riverbank. Ruth let Bobby off his leash and a commotion of quacking and barking quickly followed. A family of Mallard ducks waddled out of a bush as quickly as their little legs could carry them and promptly launched themselves into the river, where they quacked their intense displeasure at being so rudely awakened. Their canine alarm clock was powerless to do anything more except stand on the bank and yap at them.

"Don't worry," Ruth said as they strolled past. "He won't jump in—hates getting his paws wet."

"Were you working for the paper before the war came along?" Penny asked, eager to find out more.

"Family business." Ruth shrugged her shoulders.

The determined glint in her eyes and stubbornness in her voice made Penny smile and think here was a woman to admire, someone with determination. She decided to become friends, and not only because she was her next-ish-door neighbor.

"Now it looks like old Hitler isn't going to invade," Penny ventured after there had been silence for a short while, "don't you think it'd be a good idea to put all the signposts back?"

"Can't see it happening," Ruth replied. "It'd look too much like relaxing our vigilance. Why did you ask?"

Penny looked a little sheepish. "Well...I've always had a bit of trouble finding my way around."

Doris dug in her heels, bringing the troupe to a halt. "Hang on! Are you telling me you have trouble navigating?"

Penny looked indignant. "Only on the ground. I've no problems when I'm up in the air."

"Well, that's good to know." Doris laughed.

A few minutes more and they arrived at the Lockkeepers Cottage to find Betty kneeling on the ground, tickling a shamelessly wriggling Bobby as he rolled back and forth before her.

"I wondered where he'd disappeared to," Ruth admitted, joining Betty on the ground, which only set the spaniel into more throes of ecstasy as she joined in with the tickling torture.

A loud crash, followed by a heartfelt, albeit muffled, expletive came from the open attic window of the cottage, then a groan of someone in pain.

"That's coming from Mary's room!" shouted

Betty, scrambling to her feet.

Far from being disappointed at being deprived of his fun, Bobby jumped to his feet and beat all his human companions to the open front door and disappeared up the stairs, yapping away as if he were a puppy and not the lazy dog Ruth had described. Behind him came Betty, closely followed by Doris, and bringing up the rear were Ruth and Penny. The room they caught the dog up in looked like a bomb had hit it. He was lying on the floor with his bottom to the doorway, tail wagging, head resting on his paws, his attention fully focused on the sight before his nose. And what a sight!

Two suitcases lay upturned, their contents spilling out across the floor. A nightstand had toppled sideways, and the plant that had once stood on it now lay on its side, earth spilt onto the floor, the vase fortunately not broken. The worst—or most comical—thing about the whole earthquake zone, though, was the bed, halfway across the floor, upon which lay a mattress. Protruding from beneath the mattress was a stockinged foot which, presumably, belonged to Mary.

Everyone had stopped to stare except for Bobby who, upon spotting it, jumped to his feet and started to lap the foot, eliciting a giggle from their trapped friend before she managed to say, "I hope that's that dog I heard earlier?"

As far as ice-breakers go, it had the desired effect, and everyone started to laugh, apart from the lady herself. "If you've all quite finished, I'd appreciate a hand!"

"Come on," said Betty, wiping her eyes, "let's get her out of there. Everyone to a corner and…heave!"

The four of them made short work of removing the mattress, and a rather disheveled Mary was revealed in all her glory. Her skirt was somewhere around her waist, her blouse had come untucked, and the less said about her normally perfectly pinned blonde hair, the better.

"Thank God for that," she said, breathing a sigh of relief. "I thought I was going to be stuck under there forever."

After helping her straighten her clothes, Betty asked, "Care to explain what happened?"

"It's a little bit embarrassing," she began, obviously reluctant to go into details.

"You mean more embarrassing than showing your knickers and having your foot licked by my dog?" teased Ruth, flicking Mary's petticoat and patting Bobby on the head. "By the way, I'm Ruth. I run the local newspaper."

"Uh-huh," Mary answered, distracted, before trying to explain. "It's like this. I can only sleep with my feet pointing north, so I was trying to move the bedroom around without bothering any of you."

"So how did that work out?" Doris couldn't resist asking, not troubling to keep the grin from her face and nearly causing the others to fall about laughing again.

Mary glanced around before answering, a smile starting to appear on her face now. "Guess I wouldn't make much of a cat burglar."

"Why north?" Betty asked, "And how do you know where north is?"

Mary turned and rummaged under where the bedclothes had been dumped on the mattress. After a few seconds, she held up a small compass. "Silly

M. W. Arnold

childhood thing."

Ruth took a look around the room, then turned back to where she'd noticed Mary watching her. "Do you mind my asking why the attic?"

Mary stared straight ahead, obviously deep in thought, trying to decide what to tell them, before answering.

"You know I said I lived in a manor," she stated, and though she didn't, Ruth kept quiet. "I come from a large, extended family, and to say that no one gets along would be the understatement of the year. All I ever wanted was somewhere quiet. I was fourteen before my parents relented and allowed me to take a suite of rooms up in the attic. Admittedly I only had use of them when I came back from boarding school for holidays, but it was somewhere I could get away from it all. Now I like my peace and quiet."

"Just how posh are you?" asked Doris, looking at her friend in new wonder.

Mary ran a hand through her hair before answering. "Something around thirty-five-ish in line to the throne, I think."

"Are you on speaking turns with the King then?" Penny asked.

She shook her head. "I doubt if he's even aware of who I am. You may slap me down if I get too posh, though—not now!" she yelled, as all three launched themselves at her, knocking her back onto the mattress in a tangle of limbs to the accompaniment of much excited barking.

****

"That dog could snore for England!" Betty stated as Bobby snuffled in his sleep before resuming the snoring. "Honestly, Ruth, I don't know how you've put up with him for so long."

Ruth reached down and turned him over, which made no difference whatsoever. "Joe got him as a pup, and now he's...well, away, having Bobby around is like a part of Joe is still here, and it's not so lonely," she added, a melancholy expression on her face.

Betty refilled her friend's cup and then went into the kitchen to put the kettle on to top up the teapot, so as not to waste the leaves. "I'd forgotten," she said when she walked back into the lounge.

Her friend looked across to where she sat, her cup of tea untouched and a blank expression upon her face. All the same, Ruth shook herself out of her reverie when she realized the other three women were watching her.

"I'm sorry, ladies," she apologized. "It's times like this I miss my old man. Tom wasn't much of a husband, but now Joe's not here too, I miss the company."

Betty smiled again at her friend. "You don't need to wait for an invitation."

Penny clapped her hands together. "Yes! Doris and I have had such a good time with you today."

This got Betty's interest. "You didn't meet on the way back?"

Doris looked at Penny, and Penny looked anywhere but at Betty or Doris, who sighed as she realized she had to explain what they'd been up to. For her part, Betty looked simply curious.

Honesty was the only and right thing to do. "After you told us about your sister, Penny and I couldn't get her out of our heads, and we decided we couldn't wait until this evening to find out more. So we went to search out the local newspaper office, and that's where we came across Ruth. We asked if we could look at the paper's archives to see what it had to say about her…death."

Silence from Betty greeted what Doris had said, and her expression didn't change, either. Before anyone else, Ruth had her say.

"They were completely respectful of your sister, Betty. Please don't be angry with them for curiosity. I think they honestly want to get to the bottom of what happened to her, and after what they've read and heard, they don't believe the official report either."

Both Doris and Penny could only sit and wait for the outcome of their admission and hope for the best. Eventually, a small, wry smile crept upon Betty's face.

"I won't say I'm too happy about what the pair of you did, but I think you acted for the best of reasons, so I can't be angry with you, either."

Both Penny and Doris let out a breath of relief. For her part, Mary had lifted the disapproving expression she'd had upon her face, and Ruth looked reassured.

"However," Betty said, getting to her feet, "if you don't actually mind, I'm going to go and sit by the river until bedtime. I…I don't feel like talking anymore about Eleanor. Do you mind?"

She then carried on, grabbing a cardigan that was hanging from the banister on her way. Before she could open the front door, though, a sharp rapping came from the other side.

Upon opening it, to her surprise there stood a skinny airman under a rain-soaked coat. He quickly shoved a bandaged hand from sight as she spoke. "Yes.

Can I help you?"

"Aircraftsman Ralph Johnson, ma'am. Sorry to disturb you, but I was wondering if I could speak to Doris?"

Not really having a reason to deny him, Betty told him to wait there and she'd go and get her. Within a few minutes, Doris was back with her friends in the lounge.

"That was quick," remarked Mary.

"And rather strange," Doris added.

"What did he want?" put in Penny.

"That's why it's strange," Doris continued. "He began by asking me if I wanted to go for a drink at the local with him. Not only don't I know what a *local* is, but I don't know who he is! All he'd say was his name and that he worked up at the base. Then, when I was trying to let him down gently, he asked how you were, Betty, twice, and when I wouldn't answer, he scowled and took to his heels. Do any of you know him?"

Betty shook her head. "I may have seen him around base, but that's all."

Chapter Nine

Ralph fidgeted under the gaze of Group Captain Evans and for the umpteenth time wished he'd never come across the damned man, let alone become his driver.

He'd foolishly helped with dropping a headless corpse down a well on his first weekend. There'd been a large bonus for that little job. However, since then he'd had him by the short and curlies, and he was now no longer simply a getaway driver for hire. Then the war had come, and he thought he'd be able to use that to get away from the Group Captain, but it appeared the military weren't keen on those with a criminal record, or at least not desperate enough to take them yet. He'd been stuck with his bloody "Lordship," as he liked to call himself, though he was no more nobility than Ralph was king of the moon.

A sharp finger snap brought him back to the here and now. His Lordship had a revolver leveled at his head. "When I ask a question, Johnson, I expect an answer straight away. Clear?" he added, cocking the weapon.

"Yes, your Lordship. My apologies," he responded, inclining his head slightly in a gesture of the respect he'd long ago lost. All the same, he felt it safer to say what he'd done the previous night. "I'd heard her talking with her housemates in the mess, so I took it upon meself to follow them as closely as I could, in case she let something slip."

"This'd better be good, Johnson. Remember what happened the last time you used your own initiative…" Ominously, he left his sentence unfinished.

Ralph swallowed rather uncomfortably and gave the rest of his report as quickly as possible. "The woman called Penny Blake and her Yankee friend, Doris Winter, walked into town. I followed them and they ended up at the offices of the *Hamble Gazette*. I didn't hear anything while they were walking, but I got lucky at the newspaper." Upon hearing this, the Group Captain leant forward. "I managed to sneak in when the front door was left open and hide at the top of the steps to the cellar."

"What did you hear?" His boss was unable to keep the eagerness out of his voice.

Yet again, Ralph cursed his bad judgment at getting involved with this man. Ralph crossed his fingers behind his back. "Though difficult, my Lord, I did hear the two of them were looking for what the paper had to report about the death of the woman."

"And?"

"After I was locked in," Ralph continued, rubbing his sore hand behind his back—he wasn't foolish enough to believe he'd get any sympathy—"I went down to the cellar, and found the papers they'd been looking at on the table. There wasn't anything to learn. The paper only had the facts they'd been provided with."

"You're sure of that? Definitely nothing that could arouse any suspicion?"

Ralph shook his head, hoping he'd be dismissed

soon. "No, sir. I'm sure."

The Group Captain leant back in his chair and contemplated his employee shifting from foot to foot in front of him. Finally, he placed the revolver onto his desk, got to his feet, and stood before Ralph, clapping him on a shoulder.

"Very well. Good work, Johnson—but," he added quickly in case Ralph would be stupid enough to smile, "try to avoid acting on your own initiative. When I want you to do something, then you follow my orders. Is that understood?"

Ralph, knowing a dismissal when he heard one, stamped to attention. His Lordship liked little details like that. "Yes, sir!"

Taking his wallet out of his inside pocket, the Group Captain handed him a five-pound note. "Get yourself a drink, and then get back to camp. I'll be in contact when I need you." He turned back to his desk.

Ralph didn't need a second bidding, and tucking the unexpected note into his trouser pocket, he left by the main door. He didn't notice the elegantly dressed woman who strode into the office and confronted the Group Captain the moment Ralph left.

"Did he find any clues to where my pearls are?" the woman demanded of her husband, her hands set on her hips and a glare emanating from her stunning turquoise eyes.

George Evans went to place his hand over hers, but as often seemed the case lately, as soon as his hand touched her perfectly manicured one, she pulled hers away. He pushed his chair back and joined his wife on the chaise lounge. Here too he was frustrated, as she lay out full length, leaving him no room.

Knowing to keep her waiting for an answer any longer would be foolish, as she had rather a short temper, he told her, "No, nothing, my dear. Don't fret. I'm sure they'll turn up."

"That's what you've been telling me for months now, George, and I still don't have them back. You know what I told you—if I don't have my pearls, you don't have me."

"You'll get them, Virginia," he assured her. Then, recalling their whirlwind marriage the previous year, he asked, "Why don't we go out for some lunch? It's not too late to get a table at the Ritz."

The expression of contempt his wife turned upon him was so cold he half expected to see ice appear on the polished floor. Without another word, she got to her feet and strolled slowly, seductively, back the way she'd come.

Damn those pearls! She was very, very proud of them. They'd been a present, she'd claimed, from a very important film producer. She told this to everyone they met, though she was very careful never to actually reveal his name. Soon enough the pearls and, by default, themselves had become famous. The Group Captain ran his various civilian side businesses from the office and, because he was based at RAF Bentley Priory, was able to spend an inordinate amount of time at home. He'd never gone into exactly what those other interests were before they got married, though considering an apartment in Belgravia was out of the wage bracket of even a Group Captain, Virginia had quickly surmised the main source of his income was on the shady side. Only then had her true colors appeared and he realized he'd been outmaneuvered.

Everyone has to keep records, even ones they'd rather the authorities never found out about, and he'd been naïve enough to trust her with the combination to his safe. When he'd come home from the Ministry of Defense one evening, he'd found her at his desk with all the papers from his various shady deals laid out before her. She knew everything, including where he obtained black market petrol, butter, cuts of meat, tea, and sweets. He'd tried sweet-talking her with promises of silk stockings and other luxury items even she'd not seen since the outbreak of war. He promised holidays once the war was over, cruises around the Mediterranean, everything he could think of, but to no avail. His threats were halfhearted, as he was still so in thrall of her he'd never have found it in his power to raise a finger to her. She then told him he could have his papers back, only he should be aware that she now had copies. Though in public she was still as attentive as ever, she'd never even pretended to be nice to him in private again. It wasn't until later he'd fully comprehended what she'd done; the control of power in the marriage had changed hands.

His wife might think she had him over a barrel, but he couldn't give a damn about her pearls, no matter how famous they were. He was very glad he hadn't left anything in the safe to prove his guilt in the murder of the woman he'd believed was responsible for the theft.

That bloody doctor had overstepped his remit, and it might end up costing him, George Francis Evans, his neck unless he could cover all his tracks.

Chapter Ten

"Mind the duck!"

Mary's warning was a smidgeon too late. Betty turned her head toward the shout just when she needed to do the exact opposite and keep her eyes on the path.

"Aargh!" cried Betty as she was sent sprawling to the ground.

A loud, angry "Quack! Quack!" was followed by a flurry of wings and feathers as the slightly stunned duck half flew and half staggered to the sanctuary provided by the river.

"I did tell her to watch out for the duck," Mary muttered in her own defense as they rushed to help Betty to her feet.

Penny and Doris took an arm each as Mary reached to retrieve Betty's handbag. It had landed precariously close to the edge of the river, and the dastardly duck was snuffling at it before Mary seized it and handed it back to Betty.

"Mary!" cried Betty. "Grab that envelope!"

Swiveling, Mary saw a large brown envelope and stooped for it before it could fall into the water. "Got it!" she yelled, waving it in the air. Unfortunately, the envelope being upside down, the contents spilled onto the ground around her, luckily missing going into the river. She bent down to pick them up and was surprised to discover they were all newspaper cuttings.

M. W. Arnold

"Don't look at them!" Betty demanded, trying to tear herself out of her friends' grasp before Mary could peruse the contents. She failed, as Doris had caught her sleeve in the sling of Betty's handbag, and she was jerked to a halt.

"Betty," Mary began slowly, tucking the clippings back into the envelope after briefly looking at each, "why've you got a bunch of clippings about your sister in your handbag?"

Betty, Penny, and Doris all looked at each other and then at Mary as if she'd lost her mind. To all of them, the answer was obvious, but when she continued to look at them for an answer, Doris gently told her, "Mary, honey, I'm sure she carries them as a reminder."

Betty finally disentangled herself and reached out to take back the envelope, stuffing it back in her bag and holding it close to her chest.

For a few minutes, they walked along in not so companionable silence. Well, not quite silence, as the duck Betty had stumbled into appeared to have taken a disliking to the foursome and proceeded to escort them until they came to the turning on the riverbank that led to the airfield, quacking its displeasure loudly into the brisk morning air. It took a good hundred yards before the annoying noise abated and then finally stopped.

"I don't think you'll need to get a goose guard-fowl after all." Doris elbowed Betty in the ribs, causing her to stop in her tracks and start laughing, which had the same effect on her other companions and broke the awkward silence that had settled like an ominous fog over the morning.

Betty enveloped Doris in a bear hug. "I think you're going to be good for me, my Yankee cousin."

Doris returned the hug with interest. "So long as you don't make a habit of calling me Yankee," and before either could object, Penny and Mary threw their arms around them and they staggered around like a drunken huddle.

Betty, being the meat in the sandwich so to speak, was the first to object. "Getting short of oxygen here, girls!"

After a little sorting out of limbs, the foursome continued on their walk to work, the cold morning air making mist of their breath. "So, Betty," began Penny, "you said you'd talk to us about your sister this morning. As Doris and I didn't find anything at Ruth's paper, do you have anything to prove that she was murdered?"

"Other than it's not possible for a person to die of hypoxia whilst flying a Tiger Moth? Plus, even if that were the case, how was she able to land the damn plane? Shouldn't it have crashed and…" Betty hesitated before concluding what she'd started to say, "…burned? Yet it landed near perfectly, as if she was still in control."

"Damned good questions," agreed Doris.

"But why do you think Thelma's to blame?" Penny asked. "Surely you don't believe she actually killed your sister?"

Betty hung her head but continued to walk. After a few moments, she answered, though Penny had to dig in her heels to bring the procession to a halt and ask her to repeat, as she couldn't make out what she had said.

"Not really, though Thelma was the one who put my name down to fly the Moth that my sister was killed in."

Betty crouched down and put her head in her hands as a realization hit her, hard. Her friends didn't say a word. She needed time to get her head around the idea she'd just been hit with—a change in how she'd thought ever since her sister had died. She'd got so used to blaming Thelma, even though her sensible self knew the outcome was but the result of a series of happenstances, and if Eleanor hadn't needed to get onto the airfield…

"You're right," she whispered and then, a little louder, as if she too needed to hear the words, "You are right." A single sob escaped before she stood up straighter, gathering herself. What came out was more of a confession. "It's my fault she's dead, not Thelma's."

Doris was puzzled. "Why would your sister even be flying, Betty? Was she in the ATA as well?" A lot more was going on here than they'd seen at first sight, and she hoped Betty would lead them out of the dark.

Betty tried to hold all three of her friends' hands at once before giving that up as impossible. "Come on. If we're any later, Jane will have our guts for garters, and you three need to get up in the air. I promise, and this time I mean it—I'll tell you all over lunch. Try to bring a bit of an appetite. The cook mopes if no one eats."

****

"Have I missed anything?" Mary asked, leaning heavily on the back of a chair with one hand whilst her dish of soup wobbled precariously in the other.

Penny took pity on the soup. "Here, give me that. If you spill it, we'll get another hole in the floor, and it's drafty enough in here as it is."

"I heard that!" yelled the cook from behind the

servery before turning on his heel, muttering to himself, and disappearing back into the kitchen.

"Well done, lass," someone shouted from across the other side of the mess, raising his cup of tea to her in salute, and was promptly echoed by the vast majority of everyone present.

"Take a seat, your ladyship." Penny laughed, putting down the soup and pulling out a seat for Mary. "The Oscar may have to wait a while. To answer your question, though, no, you haven't missed anything. We were waiting for you."

"I guess I'd better start, then," Betty told the three and sat back to take a sip of tea before beginning.

"Eleanor, my sister, is—or was…" She paused, took in a deep breath, and went on, "unusual, an acquired taste. In fact, if you're a reader of the society magazines, or certain pages in the newspapers, then there's a good chance you've heard of her. Have you read of a jewel thief by the name of Diamond Lil?"

To her surprise, Doris's hand shot into the air. "Me! I know who you mean," she said excitedly. "I read about her in a magazine called *The Sketch*, on the ship over here. I think it said she specializes in jewelry, especially diamonds. She's never been caught, and I don't think anyone even knows what she looks… Hold your horses! Are you trying to say this Diamond Lil's your sister?"

"Shh," Betty grabbed Doris's hands before her voice got any higher. "No one else knows!"

After allowing her friends to calm down, Betty continued with her story. "I didn't see much of her outside of the, uh, job, but yes, I knew what she did. However, she was my sister. I couldn't turn her in.

Though maybe if I had, she'd still be alive."

Mary placed a hand around Betty's shoulders and kissed her quickly on the cheek. "Don't dwell on that thought. Are you sure this is the right place to tell us?"

"You'll do as I bloody well order you to, my son!" was yelled from behind the kitchen door. "Now get out there and serve that bloody food before I have you up on another charge!" The kitchen door banged open, and Ralph appeared behind the servery, spoon in one hand and a tea towel in the other, his cheeks coloring a nice shade of rouge.

Betty shrugged her shoulders, and Mary left one of her hands rested there. "As good a place as any, so long as we don't talk too loud. I also want to get it over with. Maybe then we can put our heads together. That's if you're all serious about helping me get to the bottom of what really happened?"

"Of course we are," all three proclaimed at once.

"So my sister, she turned up one night begging me to loan her my flying suit the next morning. I didn't ask why, and she didn't tell me much, only that she had to meet someone on base. I woke up the next morning to find she'd already gone and had left me a note on the kitchen table begging me not to come in to work. As she'd also taken my ID card, I'd have got us both in trouble if I'd tried. We looked enough alike for her to get on base with it, and so long as no one asked her to prepare the flight roster… Heck, she could even fly. She wouldn't have any problems taking a Moth up for a spin. Next to the first was a second note, sealed, instructing me to open it only if she wasn't back by midday. Those were the longest four hours of my life, I can tell you."

"Come midday, I didn't wait a moment longer, and tore it open. I wish I'd ignored her instructions," she told them, a haunted expression upon her face. "She was due to meet another fence. Anyway, I ran to the airfield as quickly as I could, and after some confusion at the gates, I managed to get on base, and that's when I heard the ambulance's siren. Something inside me knew Eleanor would be at the center of whatever was happening, and I followed it as quickly as I could to the landing strip. As soon as I saw them carrying a body from the aircraft, I knew.

"What I couldn't understand was what she was doing in the plane. I had a look at the flight roster for that day when I went back a week later, and my name had been penciled in for the flight test. There're only two people who can do that, and the boss, Jane, wasn't on base that day. Thelma was the one who put my name down."

"Eleanor took the plane up so you wouldn't get in trouble, I'd say," stated Doris, "but that doesn't mean Thelma's to blame for her death."

"And Thelma wouldn't have known it wasn't you that morning, would she? Plus, why would she have wanted her dead?" Penny asked, not noticing who had come up behind her.

A cup of tea was placed at the only free space at the table, closely followed by the rest of Thelma.

"Is that the reason you've been so off with me, Betty? You blame me for your sister's death?"

This certainly wasn't the place for this conversation, Penny decided, and was about to speak up and tell her so when they were rudely interrupted by a loud barking from outside.

"That sounds like Bobby!" Betty said, getting to her feet in surprise and running to the door. "What on earth's he doing here?" She leant down to fuss the dog, who was now pawing at the mess door and then, upon seeing Betty's face, started to run around and around in circles, all the time barking his little head off. She knelt down beside him, trying to calm him down. "You know, I haven't known him to behave like this before, to be so boisterous. He's certainly never come onto base before."

Mary joined Betty in trying to calm Bobby down. "Shouldn't he be with Ruth?"

Betty shrugged as the door opened again and Ralph poked his head outside. "Cook wants to know what all the noise's for."

That was when the air raid siren started to wail its haunting melody. People rushed out of the mess as doors all over the base crashed open and people flung themselves into the slit trenches that dotted the edges of buildings. Betty grabbed Bobby and, as fast as she could, ran to a trench, to find it already occupied by her friends and Ralph. Panting, she huddled down as far into the ground as she could, tin helmet crammed down as tightly as possible and clutching Bobby to her breast to prevent him running off. After a minute or so, nothing had happened, and she wasn't the only one whose eyes were now scanning the sky for signs of incoming enemy aircraft.

And that's when all hell broke loose!

A high-pitched whine started behind them, from the north, a direction in which no one's eyes had been looking. Everyone was expecting an attack would come from the south, from the direction of the Solent. Before anyone could even shout a warning, the whine grew to a deafening roar as two single-engine aircraft swept overhead at treetop height, noses pointing toward the airfield. Unable to prevent herself, Betty kept her eyes above the parapet and saw two large black objects, one from beneath the fuselage of each, fall ominously to the ground. There were two massive blasts, mounds of earth were thrown into the air, and Betty's helmet was blown from her head, knocking her onto her back in the trench, her hands still in a vise-like grip on the now whining Bobby. The two enemy fighters were nowhere in sight by the time the noise from the blasts had died down, their pilot's thoughts undoubtedly already turning toward their lunch.

They were lucky, with only Betty being slightly injured in the sneak attack. Apart from a ringing headache, a small cut to her forehead where her helmet had crashed into her as it flew off, and a slight redness around her chin from the strap, the only thing really hurt had been her dignity.

Flight Captain Jane Howell, Betty's commanding officer, stopped by to visit whilst the station doctor patched her up and then insisted she go home for the rest of the day. They'd been very lucky, Jane explained. The two raiders had missed the airfield entirely and had instead blown up an acre of potatoes. They'd probably mistaken this airfield for an operational one and, not wanting to hang around and risk being intercepted by the RAF, had dumped their bombs and run for home. From the headache Betty was nursing, she personally didn't feel the raid had been a failure.

The hero of the hour had to be honored, too, and it seemed nearly the whole of the station's personnel made a point in searching him out.

"Who's a good boy, then?"

"How's old Radar Ears?"

"Maybe we should ask Ruth if we could have him as the base mascot."

"I think he'd be quite happy with some treats, myself," Betty shouted once they got her home, rubbing the dog's ears as he lay on his back, legs akimbo and enjoying being the center of attention.

"Do you think we should tell her she's shouting?" asked Doris, struggling to keep a straight face.

Penny shook her head, doing her best to ignore Mary, who stood in the doorway to the kitchen, having finished making a meat-and-potato pie, and was now laughing so much she had to support herself against the door frame. "Not yet. I'm pretty certain her hearing's back to normal and she's having us on. Aren't you, Betty?"

She got her answer as Betty dissolved into peals of laughter too. The doorbell chose that moment to ring.

"You're a rotter, Betty," Doris told her, getting to her feet and going to answer the door. A few seconds later, she brought an unexpected visitor into the lounge. "Up for some company, Betty?" she asked, showing Thelma into the room.

"I thought we had some unfinished business, Betty," she began, "so I hope you don't mind my coming around." She stood, shifting awkwardly from foot to foot, unwilling to come all the way in.

Leaving a well-fussed Bobby panting on the floor, Betty got to her feet and stood in front of Thelma. "This time yesterday," she said slowly, taking great care to enunciate each word, "if you'd have appeared on my doorstep, I'd have chucked you out on your ear." Thelma went to take a step back but was stopped by Betty reaching forward to take Thelma's hands in hers. "Now, I'm sorry, Thelma. I blamed you for the death of my sister for no good reason. There's nothing else I can say. Will you accept my apology?"

"Of course I will," Thelma told her, pulling her into a hug. "You were grieving, and probably still are. I happened to be in the wrong place."

Betty pulled herself from Thelma's embrace and regarded her for a moment. "Would you stay for dinner and another apology?"

Chapter Eleven

Mary wrenched open the front door a little harder than she'd normally have done, right in the middle of another rap, and Ruth spilled into the hall. Mary barely had enough strength to prevent her from falling.

"Whoops! Sorry about that, Ruth," she told the older woman, steadying her before letting go.

"That's okay," Ruth told her, straightening her skirt. "Hi, everyone," she called. "Pardon the intrusion, but has anyone seen Bobby? I let him out a few minutes before those Nazi buggers made a nuisance of themselves. He was barking his head off, and I haven't seen him since."

In answer to his name, Bobby trotted in from where he'd been asleep on a rug in the lounge and launched himself at his owner.

"There you are!" Ruth bent down to rub the ears of her spaniel. "Where did you get to, you little devil?"

Betty, smiling, knelt down at the other side of the dog and stroked his back. "You've a little hero there, Ruth," she told her somewhat startled friend. "He turned up at the airfield about a minute before our air raid siren sounded, barking his head off as if his life depended upon it! It turned out ours did."

Only then did Ruth notice the plaster on Betty's forehead. "What happened to you?" she asked, reaching out her fingers to gently touch the wound.

Betty placed her fingers over Ruth's. "It's nothing," she dismissed Ruth's concern. "This is my own fault. I was watching the aircraft as they dropped their bombs, and I got caught in the blast. It's only a cut!" She batted her friend's hands away again as she made to perform a closer inspection.

"If she'd had a Lewis gun, she'd have shot the bugger down!" joked Penny, helping Betty and Ruth to their feet.

"Either way, if it hadn't been for old Bobby here, things could've been a whole lot worse. I'm not saying he saved the whole base, but he sure as hell helped."

"Looks like someone's getting treats tonight!" Ruth told her faithful dog, feasting her eyes on him with pride. Clapping her hand to the side of her leg, only then did she spot the other visitor. "Thelma! Is that you?"

As if to show the newly found accord between the two, Thelma came to stand next to Betty and put an arm around her waist as Ruth considered the two of them. "I assume this means you've sorted out your differences?"

"It does," agreed Thelma.

"In that case, unless you're going to chuck me out, I think I can spare some time to hear what brought this about."

"Come on in," Doris advised them. "Maybe if I do the brew, I'll make a cup that's passable."

After being asked to hurry up as they were all dying of thirst, Doris finally brought through a tray with the tea and a plate of scones she'd found in the larder, together with a dish of butter and some homemade raspberry jam.

"I hope you don't mind my bringing in some

nibbles, Betty?" she said, laying the tray on a table.

"Of course not. Damned good idea."

"Anyone else up for fish and chips later?" Doris asked, raising an eyebrow.

"We've created a monster." Penny nudged Mary in the ribs and then, in answer to the raised eyebrows from Betty and Thelma, elaborated. "The first night she was here, Doris treated us to a rather large portion of fish and chips, and I've never seen anyone eat as fast in my life!"

Doris didn't even look contrite at the amazed glances of her friends but licked her lips at the memory as she poured. "It's not my fault. We've the same thing in the States, but there's something about the way you do it over here that puts it into a different league."

"If you're not careful, you won't fit in a cockpit!" Betty couldn't resist teasing her.

"No chance, hon," Doris declared. "I've the kind of constitution where I can eat anything and never put on any weight."

"I think I hate you," decided Thelma. "I've only got to look at anything fattening and it goes straight to my waist. Not," she added, pinching her own trim tummy, "that that's been a problem since rationing came in."

"Well, it's a good thing fish isn't on ration, then," Doris decided with some finality.

"Anyway," prompted Ruth, "whilst Doris plays mother, I want to hear about this wondrous outcome. We get few enough miracles these days, so I'll take all I can get."

"I'm afraid it's not much of a story, certainly not one worthy of putting in your newspaper. It's all these three's fault," Betty waved a hand in the general direction of her house guests, "and their mischievous ways."

"Hey!" Penny protested. "Nosy, if you please."

"They seem to have an ear for a mystery," Betty continued, acknowledging what Penny had suggested with a tip of her head, "even if it's one I was beginning to put behind me."

"You were?" enquired Thelma.

Betty patted her friend's hand. "Or at least I was starting to believe I was. Then these three decide to go all Miss Marple on me and…"

"Not you as well," Mary interrupted. "Next thing, you're going to tell me you've got all the books!"

"They're all on my bedside table," Betty told her, not missing the looks of delight on Penny and Doris's faces. "So these three convinced, or re-convinced me, if that's a word, something very fishy was and is going on." She turned to her friend, and before Thelma could take the cup Doris offered her, took her hand. "I blamed you because you put my name down to fly that morning and my sister took the plane up instead of me. That was wrong, and I'm sorry, again." She paused to gather herself before continuing. "Was I the real target?"

"I think you must be right," Thelma agreed, barely giving it any thought. "I only put your name down to fly with about an hour's notice." Then, her gaze downward, she said, "I…I can give you a reason why someone would want to kill me, though I'd rather not tell anyone just yet. Please, trust me on this," she implored, still not looking up.

Inquisitive glances flitted back and forth between all the friends in the room until, finally, the four others all nodded their agreement.

"Very well," Betty spoke for all of them, "though I will expect you to tell us if it affects any of us. Agreed?"

"Agreed," everyone said in turn.

"Why would you be the target, though?" asked Ruth turning her attention back to Betty.

"I haven't told you everything about my sister," Betty began, and then, at Thelma's raised eyebrow, she remembered Thelma also didn't know about her sister's occupation of choice. "Eleanor was a cat burglar, and a very good one." Somewhat to her surprise, Thelma didn't show any signs of interrupting or asking any questions, so she continued. "Suffice to say, cat burglars have certain needs—they need people with certain skills, and they don't work alone. Perhaps it'll make things clearer, simpler to understand, if I tell you how Eleanor and I grew up."

After pausing for a sip or two of tea and a bite of the scone Doris had kindly made up for her, Betty began her story. Her voice was quiet, a little hesitant, though once Thelma took the hand that didn't have the half-eaten scone in it, she had the strength needed to tell her friends a long-held secret.

"Our father is someone who is, or at least was—I no longer take any notice of what he does—high up in the government, while my mother was only ever interested in status. I can only believe the two of us were an accident, as certainly I have no memory of any affection, or hardly any contact, for that matter, from either of them. When we were five years old, they put us both in an orphanage. I don't know why they waited so long, to be honest." If Betty heard the collective intake of breath, she didn't let it interrupt her. "At least the place was fairly good, though much like every other orphanage in being devoid of any real affection, let alone love. Plus, you have to remember, this wasn't long after we'd just come out of a prolonged financial crisis, so there wasn't much call for adoption at the time. We had only each other to rely on, and that's the way it stayed until the day we left. However, that's not to say the place didn't have its uses."

"I almost hesitate to ask," Ruth couldn't help but say.

"An orphanage is a very good place to learn certain...skills. Eleanor learned how to do what she does...did, very, very well. Or at least she was never caught. A burglar doesn't work alone, especially if they specialize in high-end...merchandise. I never had the balance, sleight of hand, or simple skill to do what she did, so I learned how to pass on what she stole. I believe the term is fence. And I was a bloody good one."

"Are you still a fence?" Mary asked. Despite her scoffing at the Miss Marple fixation of the others, she had been following Betty's story avidly.

"I only ever worked for Eleanor, and now with Eleanor gone, I'm retired from that profession." She addressed Ruth. "This is going to be hard, but you do know you can't use any of what you've just heard."

"I know, I know," she agreed with a resigned sigh. "However, would I be right in thinking you believe you were the real target because of your, let's call it, other profession?"

Penny agreed. "Do you mean someone nefarious, as Miss Marple might say, could be aware of what

Betty did?"

Betty nodded, though with little enthusiasm. "Eleanor was always most, most careful in her *dealings*. Not once did she ever leave a clue, a fingerprint, anything which could have been traced back to her. She was very proud of that. Oh, not that I think any of you would, but the jobs we planned were always targeted at the rich, particularly those whose business dealings were on the shady side."

"That sounds remarkably like a modern day Robin Hood!" piped up Doris, clapping her hands together in delight and then, upon seeing the glum expression upon Betty's face, recalled that at the center of this whole affair was the loss of a sister, a twin sister, and she gathered a more respectable countenance before continuing. "I'm so sorry, Betty. That was very thoughtless of me."

"That's okay," Betty assured her. "I'm perfectly aware of how it sounds, and there is more than a modicum of truth in what you said. Though I don't believe either of us ever described our affairs in such a way, that is what we were doing, I suppose. There is…was, one important difference, though—we kept the proceeds. That's how I managed to buy this place. So, not quite female Robin Hoods after all."

"Still not as good as coffee," Doris chimed in after taking a sip, a look of disgust upon her face.

"Why jewels, though?" Mary asked, ignoring her friend's out-of-place comment, getting more and more interested despite her previous scoffing "Why not cash or, or something else?" she finished a little lamely.

"Don't get me wrong, Mary," Betty carried on with her explanation. "If there were cash or other items of interest about, then Eleanor wasn't above taking those too. Taking jewels, though, was more about making a statement. Cash can be replaced, but jewelry is much more personal, difficult to replace. That was where I came in. I learned at the orphanage how to pass on items in return for cash. There's only so much honor amongst thieves, so even though we were very careful for Eleanor not to be seen, it wasn't quite so easy for me. It's quite likely the owner knows who fenced them. Rumor is he's got black market connections."

"But if…do we want to know whose pearls they were?" Mary asked again.

Betty hesitated before answering, saying she was fairly certain he was a very dangerous man, yet perhaps forewarned would be forearmed?

"Have any of you heard of a Group Captain George Evans?" She was met with blank stares from all, barring Thelma, whose eyes widened momentarily, though she didn't say anything. "I'm not surprised. He's a senior pilot who sits on the weekly Board of the Accidents Committee for the ATA. Perhaps one of you may have heard of his wife? Virginia Mayes."

Somewhat to her own surprise, Mary made a kind of yelping sound and nearly dropped the remains of her scone.

"I take it you've heard of her?"

"I should say so!" Mary told them between swallows. "She was an up-and-coming actress about seven or eight years ago. You've probably seen at least her biggest film, *Sweet Sunday Sonata*, from thirty-four? I've even met her at a party at my father's manor once, but I think that was after the roles had dried up, sometime in thirty-nine. Rumor was she rubbed some producer up the wrong way and discovered she wasn't as indispensable as she thought she was."

"So you nicked some broad's pearls and it's her husband who's after you," surmised Doris.

Betty was probably about to agree, only Mary spoke first and managed to put the cat firmly amongst the pigeons.

"The husband may have bought the pearls, but for my money, it's his wife who's the power behind the throne."

"Why would you say that?" Penny asked, a moment before Ruth could.

"Forget what you may have seen of her on the screen. I've forgotten more film stars than I can name, but I'll always remember her. Or I should say, I'll always remember her eyes. If the eyes are truly the windows to the soul, then Virginia Mayes would be a vision of hell!"

Chapter Twelve

Crack! Group Captain Evans ducked just in time as the third vase his wife had thrown smashed against the wall.

"I told you, George, don't disturb me until you've found my pearls!" Virginia yelled at him, looking around the drawing room for more ammunition and reluctantly settling upon a cushion this time.

Virginia Mayes was very, very fond of possessions, and having taken the opportunity to rid herself of the two vases her hideous mother-in-law had given them for a wedding present, plus a small, inconsequential one, was a little reluctant to use anything else breakable. With the exception of the vases, everything in the room had been *acquired* on her order. Being a movie star (she refused to accept she was an ex) does not necessarily convert to having taste. Colors and styles clashed with abandon, though heaven help anyone who voiced any comment to that effect. George sported a small scar above his left eye from where she'd punched him when he'd once voiced his opinion of her decorating skills.

Risking a peek from behind the stand-up piano he'd taken refuge behind, George ducked quickly to avoid the flying cushion. The risk of being hurt was very slight and her aim wasn't the best, as it clipped a lampshade on its way past, and with some wobbling, the lamp settled on top of the broken vase.

"For God's sake, woman!" he shouted, allowing his forehead to poke above the piano. "Let me get a word in without throwing anything else!" When no further missiles were immediately forthcoming, he risked getting off his knees and to his feet. On the other side of the room stood his wife, another cushion clutched, undoubtedly ready to be launched if she didn't like what he had to say. "As I was saying, I haven't found your pearls yet. But—" he added quickly as she drew back her hand, "I believe I know who fenced them."

There were times he wondered if life would have been less complicated if he'd married his second cousin as his mother had wanted. Even with only a year gone, she'd have at least been pregnant by now! Mind you, when he thought back to how some of her sisters and brothers looked, perhaps there'd been enough interbreeding in that part of the family already.

A cushion bounced off his head, reminding him he had a slightly mad wife waiting upon him. "Sorry, dear," he said automatically. "Yes, I put out feelers to certain, ahem, contacts I have in London's seedier realms, as I felt certain whoever was behind the theft would have also wanted to get rid of it and quickly, and London's the best place to do that."

"And have you tracked down this person yet?" Virginia's voice dripped in ice, but all her besotted husband could see was the ruby redness of her lips.

"My sweet," he tried reasoning with her, "these things take time. The cream of England, and probably the world, knows your pearls. They won't be the easiest of things to fence."

"So," Virginia purred, slinking nearer and nearer until she slithered down next to him on a red satin couch, "what you're saying is you're no nearer to recovering my pearls? And they're very likely in the hands of some lowlife pond scum, probably to be broken up forever!"

Group Captain by rank he may have been, but he'd only got there through family connections, and even those can only get you so far. His superiors had rapidly discovered the limits of his intellect, and after they'd stopped wondering how he'd managed to attain a commission, let alone so high a rank, he'd been shunted sideways into as unimportant a role as they could find, liaison to the Air Transport Auxiliary. Unwittingly, they'd allowed his nefarious ambitions to run a black market empire to flourish, or so he believed.

"It won't come to that," he hurried to assure her. "I promise you. I have my best men on it night and day."

"In that case, Georgy," Virginia began, causing goose bumps to ripple up his spine. She hadn't called him by that nickname since their brief courtship! "Don't you have better things to do than waste time talking to me? Don't you think you should be getting an update from your *best* men?"

Springing to his feet in his eagerness to please her, George Evans hesitated, his lips hovering over his wife's forehead. Wisely, he decided her hair-trigger temper wouldn't take too kindly to an attempt to kiss her, and he sidled out of the room on his mission.

Of course her weak-willed husband hadn't tried to kiss her—she'd put a stop to that nonsense, amongst other unpleasant activities, as soon as she could. He had no idea she'd married him solely to make use of his contacts. Over the last few months, she'd taken advantage of the many absences caused by his RAF work, which even he couldn't avoid, to take control of his small but lucrative black market racket. He actually believed he was still the one in control. Honestly, if she'd known he was so easy to manipulate, she wouldn't have bothered to marry him!

Picking up the phone, Virginia dialed the number so familiar to her of late and waited, impatiently, for an answer.

"Miss Mayes," stated a male voice.

Good. No smart comebacks, she thought. It looks like they've finally accepted me as their true boss. "The fool's just left the office. Obey what he tells you to do but come back to me first if anything actually comes of it. Understood?"

"Yes, Miss Mayes," came the same reply, and the voice sensibly waited for any further instructions.

"One more thing. Put Miss Tuttle on the line and then continue with your own investigations. I want those pearls back as soon as possible. Remember," she told him, "there's a big reward in this for you, if you get them back within the next month. Otherwise I'll be looking for a new right-hand man. Do we understand each other?"

Chapter Thirteen

Come Friday morning and everyone had gathered in the kitchen ready for their big day. Toast had been eaten and tea had been drunk. To no one's great surprise, Doris still didn't much care for it.

"Still not as good as coffee."

Penny looked at the clock and then glanced back toward the stairs. "Has anyone seen Betty this morning?"

"I'm in the room next to her, and I haven't heard a thing," offered up Doris.

"Well, if she's not here soon, we'll be late for work," Mary stated. "Wait here," she told them, getting to her feet. "I'll go and see where she is."

Standing outside Betty's bedroom door, Mary laid her head against the wood, and when she couldn't hear anything from within, raised her hand and knocked. "Betty! It's Mary. Are you okay?" She waited and when she got no response, announced, "I hope you're presentable. I'm coming in," before she opened the door just wide enough so she could poke her head around.

She wasn't totally surprised to see her friend in bed, but the lack of color in her face and the way she was clutching the blanket to her chin sent a shiver up her spine, and in two quick strides she was sat down beside her. "Betty?" She laid a hand on her friend's

115

forehead and was distressed to find it cold and clammy. "You're not well. Why didn't you let us know?"

A weak smile was all she got, but with a visible effort, Betty dragged herself up in the bed. As Mary helped her sit a bit more upright, she gave her friend a small smile.

"Sorry, I'm not feeling too good, a bit lightheaded. Would you please tell Jane?" she asked, her voice sounding weak to Mary. "I think maybe I've a little delayed shock after yesterday."

"Would you like one of us to stay home with you?" Mary asked, concerned.

Betty shook her head, then looked like she wished she hadn't. "No, I'll be okay as soon as I can get rid of this headache. I'll be fine for Monday."

Mary stood over her friend, a look of contemplation upon her face before she made her decision. "If that's what you want. I'll just get a cold flannel for your forehead and bring up some water before we go. Try and get some more sleep. Okay?"

****

"You're sure she'll be fine?" Penny asked for what seemed the umpteenth time as the three of them strode through the gates of the airfield after showing their passes.

"I'm sure she will," Mary assured her. "Personally, I'd have been surprised if she made it in today. Considering what happened yesterday, she got off lightly. Anyway, does anyone know where Flight Captain Howell is?" she asked.

Doris tapped her on the shoulder and pointed in the direction of the ops hut and the figure of a woman in ATA uniform striding their way. For someone who appeared barely taller than five feet in her flying boots, Jane Howell radiated authority. The three women snapped to as near an approximation of military attention as they could without realizing they'd done so. With her chip-bag hat at a jaunty angle on her head, piercing blue eyes matching her uniform jacket, she was every inch a commander, and despite the pressing need Mary felt to tell her about Betty, a little voice inside told her it would be wise not to speak first.

Standing before them, hands upon her hips, First Officer Howell contradicted their expectations by gracing them with a smile. "I'm glad I've caught you three before you got to the mess. I need to make an urgent request of you all." She seemed to notice the three's deportment for the first time. "For God's sake, ladies, relax," she added, smiling warmly and setting the three of them at their ease. Observing them more closely, she realized, "Betty's not with you! I take it she's feeling under the weather after yesterday's excitement? Can't say I'm surprised."

"That's right, ma'am," Mary confirmed. "It's my opinion she's got a mild concussion, but she did ask me to let you know she expects to be back on Monday."

"Thank you. Mary, isn't it? Oh, and by the way, less of the 'ma'am,' too. I like to keep things informal here as much as possible, so unless there's some senior RAF bod around, or I need to give you a bollocking, let's keep it to first-name terms. I'm Jane, as I'm sure you know, and I know the rest of your names. Now, where was I?"

"You were going to make a request of us?" Penny said helpfully.

"Thank you, yes, Penny, this request. I know all

three of you were due for more familiarization flights of the local area today." She paused for affirmative nods and then continued, "We have to put those off. I can't go into details, because I don't know them, but there's a big flap on, and we need to get as many Spitfires to the squadrons in our area that need resupply, and we need to get them out by Monday."

Jane paused to allow her pilots to take on board what she'd just told them. Apart from some gulping, all she could see was a little apprehension in their eyes, quite understandable, outweighed by excitement. She glanced at her watch and then invited them to the mess so they could grab a cup of tea.

Ten minutes later, a large pot of tea stewing in front of them, Jane resumed her briefing. "Now, this will be a rather unusual delivery. Firstly, I don't believe that any of you have flown a Spit before?" The excitement blazed a little stronger in their eyes at the thought of flying the world's most potent fighter aircraft for the first time.

"Hmm...needs must. You've got your Ferry Pilot's Notes on you?" They all took their little A6 booklets out of their bags to show her they did. "That's good. Now, listen closely. The Spitfire's quite different to the Harvard, as I'm sure you all realize. One's a trainer and the other's, well, a Spitfire. Read and re-read the notes on the Spit until the moment you strap one on, then read them again. Take special care on how to lower the undercart. You'll be surprised how many pilots, men and women, who've flown only a fixed undercarriage kite can retract it upon take-off but then forget to lower it again. It's rather embarrassing and can sting a little."

If she'd hoped to lighten the tension with her little

joke, she was reasonably successful. Though she got no laugh-out-loud guffaws, at least all three smiled to show they appreciated her remark.

"I'm sorry I've got to throw you in at the deep end, but it's all hands to the pumps for the next three days. I need you for Saturday and Sunday as well. It's nearly nine-twenty," she told them. "Go and get suited up, then wait by the Anson outside the ops hut. That's your taxi to the factory where you'll pick up the Spits. Again, use the time on the taxi to read up the notes because, and I hate this as much as you, there are no radios on the aircraft you're going to fly." This announcement was met with only silent acceptance, for which Jane was glad, there being nothing she could do about that situation. "As none of you have flown to RAF Manston before, I've arranged for one of their pilots to lead you in. He's aware of the lack of radios, and though you'd normally navigate by maps and dead reckoning, follow him as closely as you can. Don't exceed a cruising speed of two hundred fifty mph— that's important because these are brand-new aircraft, remember. When you get to Manston, report to the Operations Room and turn in your Delivery Chit. As soon as you're all finished, the taxi will take you back to pick up another batch for the same station so, as much as you can, look out the cockpit and take notes of visual references, as you'll be on your own for the next flight. I suggest you all fly in formation, if possible. There'll be a total of four deliveries each to make, so it's going to be a long old day."

Jane got to her feet, and her pilots hastily did the same. "I won't pretend this is going to be easy, but I doubt if you'll have a more important few days for a

119

while. Don't forget your Flight Authorization Cards, and pick up your sandwiches and a thermos of tea each and get changed. You take off in fifteen minutes. Report to me when you get back of the evening, and…good luck."

With a quick shake of each of their hands, Jane left the three rather shell-shocked girls to their thoughts. They were interrupted by the cook's mate, the somewhat disturbing Ralph, depositing three thermoses and three brown paper bags of sandwiches on the table between them.

"Best of luck, ladies," he said before turning to make his way back to the kitchen, and adding just before he opened the door, "See you later, Doris."

"Is it me, or is there something creepy about that guy?" Doris asked with a shudder.

"He is an annoying little oik," remarked Mary. "Don't let yourself be caught alone with him."

Doris suppressed a shudder. "Don't worry. I have no intention of letting that happen."

Penny got to her feet and took a thermos and sandwich pack from the table. "Much as I'd like to stay and tear that git apart, I think we'd better make tracks if we're going to catch our taxi. It won't make a good impression if we're late for our first job."

****

Come half past five, Doris and Mary were waiting at Manston for Penny to land the last Spitfire of the day. Both were lying on their fronts under the wings of the planes they'd just landed and only the knowledge that they had to keep awake long enough for the Anson to pick them up was keeping their eyes open.

A cough of a Merlin engine cried in the twilight,

and they perked up. After a few seconds, they picked out the expected plane. The first three trips had been routine, if you can call all three of them wishing they'd had more time to study up on the correct boost setting and flap position, and the multitude of other tasks that were required for taking off, flying, and landing their Spitfires—plus, on the first flight anyway, trying to watch where they were going so they could navigate themselves after that. There were no problems with the planes, and the RAF boys on the ground had been delighted to receive them in one piece.

On this last flight, they'd all had reason to curse the lack of radios, as from just over halfway, the plane Penny was flying showed signs of struggling to keep up with the other two. Doris and Mary had throttled back, then back again, until they were all doing just over two hundred mph. Through various gestures they'd realized, and chatted about it on the ground after they'd landed, that this was all the power Penny could coax out of her mount. Both of them had wanted to stay with her, to try their best to encourage and nurse their friend through to the RAF base, but Penny had gestured they should fly on. So, reluctantly and with the awareness of their orders to fly on even if one of them developed a problem (a dictate verbally battered into them during the briefing at the factory in Southampton), they had throttled up and, because of their worry for their friend, had each made somewhat dodgy landings.

Upon landing, they had decided to hell with those orders. If they had the chance to fly in formation after this weekend and one of them had a problem, they'd stay in formation. Friendship meant a great deal, even more so in wartime.

Hurrying to their feet, they anxiously watched as Penny leveled the wings at the last moment and put the Spitfire down dead center of the runway, throttled back, and at the end of the runway did a neat left turn and parked her mount nicely alongside the pair her friends had brought in. Doris barely waited for the plane to come to a halt, beating the ground crew to putting the chocks under the main wheels by a heartbeat as she jumped up onto the wing and helped Penny shove the cockpit canopy back.

"Hey, slowcoach!" she greeted cheerily, trying to mask her relief to see her friend had made it down okay. "Been taking a sightseeing tour?"

It took a few moments for Penny to reach up and take off her flying helmet and then she slumped back in her seat, the exhaustion plain to see in her eyes. "If I ever run across the bugger who certified this aircraft fit to fly, I'll kick him where it hurts!"

Mary had by now caught up with Doris and was perched on the other wing in time to hear what her friend had said, nearly falling off with laughter as a result.

The sergeant in charge of the ground crew had reached them by now and was waiting impatiently for the ladies to vacate the aircraft. "If you've quite finished, I'd like to get this plane turned around—and," he added, scratching his chin, "what the hell kept you, luv? Your friends got here over ten minutes ago."

With help from both Doris and Mary, Penny wearily heaved herself out of the seat, flung her legs through the small hinged door and out onto the port wing. She sat on the trailing edge and slid to the ground, where Mary had rushed around to help in case she needed steadying; she did. However, she still found the energy to fix the insensitive RAF NCO with her best steely gaze.

"Herr Sergeant," she began, and behind her, two other ranks did their best to hide the wide smiles that sprang to their faces, whilst Doris and Mary didn't bother. "First, I'm not your *luv*, and second, the only place this bloody aircraft is going is to engineering."

Though obviously rankled, the sergeant wasn't sure if he had any authority over the women, so he satisfied himself with trying to return Penny's gaze. After thirty seconds, a bead of sweat appeared on his brow and he gave up the uneven contest. "Why would I do that? It's fresh off the line."

"I don't care a monkey's where it's come from!" Penny yelled, building up a head of steam. "I couldn't get enough power out of the bloody thing to go above two hundred miles per hour. By the time I got down, she was coughing all over the place—you must have heard it—and the undercart was also slow to lower. So if I were you, I'd check the plugs and the hydraulic system, to start with. Now," she told him, eye to chin and waving her Flight Authorization Card under his nose, "if you'll excuse me, I'm going to hand in my Delivery Chit to Ops and will be telling them exactly what I've just told you. Come on, girls."

With her friends either side of her, and hoping that her legs didn't buckle beneath her, Penny strode off to the ops hut, sharing a conspiratorial wink with the perplexed erks as they passed.

****

Penny realized she'd fallen asleep in the back of their taxi only when Mary shook her awake and mimed that they were a few minutes from touchdown. Sluggishly, she did up her seatbelt, a vague memory about a chish-and-fips supper mixing with her waving her Flight Authorization card under the senior engineering officer's nose when she'd told him to get the last Spitfire fixed. At least that little document let her essentially wave a finger in any RAF bod's way when she needed to. After that last flight, she had *really* needed to! With a good too many bumps, the Anson finally settled onto the grass runway at Hamble and taxied over to the flight line hut, where an anxious-looking Jane Howell stood waiting for them. Ground crew hurried up to the idling twin-engined aircraft, hefted the chocks under the main wheels, and opened the cabin door.

"Good, you're all back," she said as she lent a hand to each of them as they slowly exited the taxi.

"And just about in one piece," mumbled Penny, her legs shaking slightly as she set course for the hut.

Jane took her arm as she passed and walked with her. "I've just been on the phone with the Engineering Officer at Manston, and he asked me to pass on his apologies to you. You're quite right about that last aircraft you flew being a—I believe he phrased it 'bag-of-nails,' and when you're next down his way, he'd like to take you out to lunch."

Doris and Mary joined the two of them as they started up the steps to the hut, just in time to hear what Jane had passed on to Penny. "Was he that stuck-up stick insect?" Doris wanted to know.

"That's the one," Mary agreed, holding open the door for Jane and Penny to go through.

Penny flopped down into a seat and looked up at

the three of them with heavy eyes. "So long as it's at the Ritz, he's got a deal. Now, will someone help me out of this lot? I don't think I've the energy to do it by myself."

"For what it's worth," Jane said, leaning against the door, "you've all done a fantastic job today."

"No chance of a raise?" asked Doris, flashing a weary smile.

Jane shook her head and looked contrite. "Sorry. Not even taking into consideration you'll be doing the same tomorrow and Sunday. The only good news I've got is that you'll have Monday off."

Doris started to strip off her suit. "Better go and get those fish and chips, then."

Chapter Fourteen

"I never thought I'd be so glad to see the end of a Sunday," Penny said, flopping onto her back on the floor of the flight line hut and pushing her flying helmet off the top of her head.

From her position slouched in a chair, Doris gathered the energy to reply, "Amen to that, sister," before closing her eyes.

At that moment the door crashed open, and following in its wake came a young lady dressed in a knee-length bottle-green woolen coat and stout black shoes. Her red hair was tied back in a short ponytail. "Sorry to interrupt, but has anyone seen someone called Dorothy... I'm sorry, I can't recall her surname, but she's supposed to have fixed me up with some accommodation."

Somewhat to the new arrival's surprise, the room's occupants burst out laughing.

"Did I say something funny?"

Penny recovered first and heaved herself from off the wall where she'd been leaning. "Don't worry about us," she began, undoing her Sidcot suit and whipping off her own flying helmet. "We've had a tough few days, and you said the perfect thing to release the tension."

Their new acquaintance now had a hugely puzzled expression upon her pretty face. She dumped her kitbag on the floor before sitting down upon it and stretching out her left leg with a grimace. "It's been a long day for me too," she commented. "Could someone explain what I said that would cause all this laughter?"

"Allow me," Penny continued, beginning to strip out of her flying suit. "Dorothy is a bit of a legend, though perhaps 'enigma' would be a better description. None of us here has ever set eyes upon her even though she's supposed to be the admin officer whose duties include arranging accommodation. Actually, I did see her, but only once."

"So who sorted out all your billets?" the redhead quite reasonably asked.

Doris propped herself up on an elbow and stared up. "For that we—Doris Winter here, by the way—have Miss Penny Blake"—she nodded at the lady who had been talking to the newcomer—"to thank. Oh, and the scruffy one who's still laughing is Mary Whitworth-Baines, but don't take her personally. I think she's finding a funny-bone she didn't know she possessed."

"Hey!" Mary objected, choking down her laughter upon hearing what her friend had just said. "I am funny! I mean, I do have a funny-bone. And I'm not scruffy!"

Doris reached up to pat her on the knee. "As you say, honey."

"That's all very well," complained their new companion, who still hadn't introduced herself, "but where does that leave me?"

At that moment, the door reopened and a beaming Jane burst through, a bottle of pale ale in each hand. Striding over to the table, she took a bottle opener out of her pocket, opened up both bottles, and poured the contents into four mugs. "It's not quite the Champagne you all deserve, but it's all I could get hold of at short notice."

"Ahem," coughed the newcomer, who'd sprung to her feet unnoticed in the kerfuffle of their boss's entrance. "Ma'am. Mechanic Shirley Tuttle reporting for duty," and followed it up with a salute that nobody recognized.

As if noticing her for the first time, which was quite likely, seeing as she'd entered with all the subtlety and quiet purpose of a heavy bomber, Jane swiveled her head and perused the newcomer. "Yes, Tuttle." Then she added, "I wasn't expecting you until tomorrow. You're early."

"Yes, ma'am. I didn't have anything else to do, so I decided I may as well turn up now. Only thing is," she continued, "I can't find someone called Dorothy who's supposed to set me up with somewhere to get my head down."

At hearing this, Jane let out a more restrained chuckle than her three colleagues. "You wouldn't, at least not today."

"Or ever," put in Doris, earning herself a look of reproach from Jane and a thumbs-up from behind their boss's back from Penny.

"That's as may be," Shirley said, "but what am I supposed to do tonight?"

"Everyone decent?" a male voice asked after knocking on the door.

"Hang on, Lawrence!" yelled Penny. "Give us five minutes. Come on, girls." She took one of Doris's hands and tried to haul her off the floor. "The quicker we get changed, the quicker we can get home. That's right, Boss?" she asked Jane.

"Very true," Jane agreed. "You're all off tomorrow, as I promised."

"Quickly as you can," Jane told the three of them before turning to address Shirley.

"The gentleman outside the door is Third Officer Herbert Lawrence," she explained, "and he may be the answer to your troubles. He boards with his aunt, who runs the local newspaper, and their cottage is just down the way from where these three miscreants live with Betty, my Operations Officer. If memory serves right, I believe his aunt has a room to spare."

"Can't see that being a problem myself," piped up Lawrence from outside.

"Who're you calling miscreants?" Mary wanted to know from where she sat on the floor, kicking her boots off whilst at the same time buttoning up her tunic.

"You three," Jane said, giving Mary's foot a gentle prod. "Enough talking, more changing. Now, Shirley, there should be some ale left in one of those bottles, so why don't you help yourself." She picked up her own mug and raised it to where Penny, Doris, and Mary were in various states of dress. "I'd like to thank the three of you, as well as the rest of the girls who've already packed up, for your extremely hard work over the last three days." She then hiccupped and put her mug down. "Perhaps not the best idea for me to have any more to drink. I've already gone through likely two bottles myself. Anyway, after you've changed, let Lawrence in for a minute, and once he's changed, the four of you can get off. Shirley, I'll see you at eight in the morning over in Ops. The three of you, again, good work and I'll see you on Tuesday."

****

"Come in," Lawrence said to Shirley over his shoulder as he opened the door to his aunt's cottage. He took a look at his watch as his companion set her kitbag down in the hall. "It's half five now, so my aunt Ruth should be home shortly."

"You're sure she won't mind?" Shirley was hanging back and hadn't even closed the door.

"Mind a new person to natter to? Not likely." He grinned. "And for heaven's sake, come in and shut the door."

With a final glance behind her, Shirley gently closed the door and allowed herself to take a look around. Lime green wallpaper covered the hall walls, with an oval mirror center stage and a barometer in place above a small round table.

"Come on through to the kitchen," Lawrence invited, leading the way and heading over to fill up the kettle. "We may as well have a cup of tea whilst we wait."

As the kettle came to the boil, a key turned in the front door and in came Ruth, closely followed by Bobby trotting along at her heels. He promptly ran straight into Shirley's kitbag, which knocked him back onto his rump where he sat with a slightly dazed look upon his face.

"Lawrence!" Ruth called whilst nudging the bag against the wall with her foot. "I wish you wouldn't leave your things lying around. Poor Bobby ran straight into your kitbag," she added, kneeling down and rubbing the dog's nose. Upon getting to her feet, Ruth turned and was confronted by a very sheepish-looking Lawrence and a tall redheaded young woman who was trying and utterly failing to hide behind him.

"And who do we have here?" Ruth asked in a curious though not unkindly voice.

In spite of giving off the appearance of someone who wouldn't say boo to a goose, Shirley rapidly showed that appearances could be deceiving as she then stepped from behind Lawrence and held out a hand. "Don't blame Lawrence, Mrs. Stone. It's my fault, my bag. My name's Shirley Tuttle. I've been posted to the airfield but turned up a day early. Seems no one was expecting me, so I'd no place to stay, and then this boss lady turns up, everyone drinks a load of ale, and Lawrence there invites me to come and stay at your place, and...and...and here I am," she finished, somewhat out of breath.

Ruth considered herself a good reader of human nature, and sure enough, when she subjected this young woman to a hard stare, Shirley turned slightly away, yet just about kept her eyes upon Ruth. Here was someone with a secret or a secret agenda, but as she'd barely managed to keep her attention upon her, the likelihood was it was something she didn't want the burden of. However, things were going to get interesting.

Ruth slipped her shoes off, put on her slippers, and padded into the kitchen. "Thanks, love," she said as Lawrence handed her a cup of tea, then grimaced a little. Her nephew was many things, and she was willing to bet he was more than the civilian taxi driver he claimed to be, but he'd never be a professional tea-maker.

Shuddering, she put down the cup as soon as she considered it polite, then gestured for Shirley to take her seat. "Let me guess. Jane Howell also thought it'd be a good idea."

Shirley retook her seat. "Something like that," she admitted, shrugging her shoulders and drinking her own tea without the same distaste Ruth displayed.

"No Dorothy?"

Lawrence laughed. "What do you think, Aunty?"

Ruth allowed herself a smile and shook her head. "Has anyone actually seen this woman? We are certain she exists?"

"I'm not sure what to make of that," Shirley said, eying the two of them. "That was the reaction of the girls back at camp, too. Am I missing something?"

"A bit of an in-joke actually," Lawrence said but didn't bother providing any further explanation.

Though she'd rather not have anyone else in her house, Ruth could see it'd be the best for everyone, at least in the short term, if this girl did stay with her. She had a spare room, albeit one not bigger than an oversized box room, big enough to take the single bed and small wardrobe it contained, but only just. Though of the same basic design as Betty's, her cottage was slightly smaller and without the converted attic, so with Shirley she'd be at her limit. Plus, her internal radar was still bleeping an alert that something with this girl wasn't right, and the newspaper reporter inside her wanted to know what.

Her mind made up, she held out her hand. "Welcome to Riverview Cottage, Shirley."

****

"Who wanted the cod?" Doris asked, holding out a steaming newspaper-wrapped package.

"Here," said Betty, holding out her hands.

"Plaice?"

"Me," announced Penny and Mary.

"Which leaves me with the Roe," finished Doris.

"Thanks for this," Betty said, putting a bottle of vinegar on the table and then settling back into her seat in the front parlor and opening up her package. "Ah," she uttered, her eyes rolling back as she put her face right into the package to inhale the delicious aroma.

"I told you," Penny said between mouthfuls, "having a millionairess in the house is useful."

Betty promptly splattered Mary with a mouthful of half-eaten chips.

"I beg your pardon!" Then she noticed her food-dashed friend, and a blush spread rapidly up her neck right to the tip of her nose. "Oh, my! I'm so sorry, Mary."

Waving off her friend's concern, Mary put her fish and chips down on the table and got to her feet. "Don't worry, Betty. Your face was a picture," and she went into the kitchen to clean herself up.

"Doris, is there something you'd care to tell me?" Betty asked.

Finishing her mouthful before answering, Doris took the cap off one of the bottles of Guinness on the table and took a long draft directly from the bottle. "Oh, that's so good," she said licking her lips in pleasure and using a fork to push the vinegar bottle farther away from her.

"Doris!" prompted Betty, getting a little impatient.

"Okay, okay!" Doris laughed, putting down her bottle and opening up one for each of her friends. "Long story cut short, as I'm hungry. I married, not to my parents' approval, and now get ten thousand dollars a year."

"Don't forget the apartment on Central Perk," added Mary who, cleaned up, retook her seat and started to tuck in once more.

"That's Central Park," Penny corrected.

"That's, um, not bad," Betty agreed, though she did notice Doris wasn't smiling as much as she had before.

"That was a hell of a few days, girls," Doris was saying when Betty tuned back in. "Hell, if I'd known it'd be like this, maybe I'd have stayed home and satisfied myself with walks through Central Park and dinner at Sardi's each day. They used to serve lobster to make you cry! Mind you..." She paused, placing the last of her supper into her mouth and licking her lips. "Now I've found this, I ain't gonna swap." Having finished her own supper, she leaned over and speared a couple of chips from Penny's.

"Oi! If you keep on wolfing down fish and chip suppers like this, you won't fit through their door!"

"As if," Doris argued. "First—and this is open to debate, ladies—this'll be a once-a-week treat from me. Any objections?" Unsurprisingly, there were none. "Secondly, I've the kind of constitution where no matter what I eat, I never put on any weight. Did I already mention this?"

"I hate you, Doris. Did I mention that?" joked Penny, quickly moving the remains of her chips out of the range of Doris's encroaching fork.

"Me too," agreed Mary, finishing off her Guinness. "Anyone want another?' she asked, getting to her feet and making a move toward the back door.

Betty had been given the Monday off as well, as she'd been in the ops hut coordinating things on the Saturday and Sunday to help out, so she said, "Why not?" She was usually a white wine girl, but she could get used to Guinness, she decided, plus, if the various posters were right, the black stuff was good for her. "If you can manage it, you may as well bring in one for each of us."

As Mary opened the back door, there came a knock at the front.

"I'll get it," volunteered Penny.

A minute later, she ushered Ruth, Lawrence, and a redheaded woman Betty didn't recognize into the front parlor. At seeing her quizzical look, Penny made the introductions. "Shirley Tuttle, newly arrived mechanic, meet Betty Palmer, Ops officer, landlady, and all-round good egg."

"Pleased to meet you, Miss Palmer," Shirley said, holding out her hand.

"Call me Betty. Everyone does," she replied. "So does this mean Ruth's putting you up?"

"Couldn't turn out a waif, could I?" Ruth shrugged, smiling.

"To what do we owe the visit, Ruth?" asked Mary, placing four bottles of Guinness on the table. "I think we've another few bottles out the back," she added.

"No reason," Ruth admitted, and then, when she noticed Shirley had gone to help Mary bring in the other bottles, she added, "though if none of you have anything planned for tomorrow, how'd you all like to come in to the newspaper office? Walter thinks he's found something out."

As she finished talking, Mary and Shirley walked back in. "Where do you want these?"

"On the table, thanks," Mary told her.

"Look, before we settle in, could someone give me

directions to the nearest phone box? I promised to give my parents a call as soon as I settled in," Shirley said.

****

"No. No one knows who I am, Miss Mayes. Yes, I'm certain. No, I'm afraid I haven't had a chance to get Miss Palmer alone yet. I did hear them speaking as I came into her front room just now, something about some bloke called Walter who's got something to tell them tomorrow. Yes, I'm going to see if I can join them, and I'll phone you as soon as I know something. Yes, ma'am, of course. You know I know how much I owe you, so no, I won't let you down."

Putting the phone back on the receiver and pushing the button to get her unused coins back, Shirley rested her head on the cool glass of the phone box and wondered, not for the first time, what she'd got herself into.

Chapter Fifteen

"Who was that, my love?" asked George Evans, slightly concerned to hear a tremor in his voice.

He blew out a large cloud of blueish smoke, partially to get rid of the rancid taste in his mouth and partially so he could observe his wife with little chance of being seen. Virginia hated cigar smoke, and he was surprised she hadn't banned him from smoking in her presence. His beautiful Georgian chair, of which he had been so proud when he'd first set up the office, no longer held as much attraction for him. Certainly it didn't seem as comfortable as it once was.

"Ha!"

As she'd ignored his question, he blew another cloud of smoke, peered over the top of his half-moon specs, and tried to keep the expression on his face as neutral as possible. The least little thing was liable to set her off these days, plus the sight of her taking calls on his phone whilst lounging back on the chaise longue was enough to make his teeth itch.

"George!" Virginia snapped, her eyes blazing under the frown gracing her normally beautiful face, a face she denied him the pleasure of kissing, a situation which showed no signs of changing. Perhaps he'd have to look elsewhere for his fun. Memories of that girl he saw in *Full Swing* at the Palace Theatre last night came to mind—before a pen narrowly missed his left ear. He flinched, and the new scar above his left eye, where Virginia had bounced the heel of a Van-Dal shoe off him the other night, throbbed.

"George! Wake the hell up," his wife yelled at him again.

With a wry smile he saw she'd installed a single bed in the corner of the office, currently hidden away behind a pair of, admittedly, tasteful red velvet curtains.

"Yes, my dear," he replied, deciding to be as neutral as possible until he found out how she was going to display her power over him this time.

"That was Shirley reporting back."

"Please tell me she has some good news," he demanded, thinking he could do with some.

"Nothing yet, though she is now living next door to this Palmer woman."

"Pah!" George spat through his cigar. "Ralph, Shirley, Charlie Chaplin, what does it matter? None of them seem able to find that bloody thermos flask." The words were out of his mouth before he could stop them.

The predatory look on Virginia's face told him all he needed to know, and George actually tried to take a step backward, a little difficult to perform whilst seated, he found.

"Oh, don't worry about young Shirley. You may not have met her, but shall we say she has a very big incentive to do exactly as I instruct."

Used to being obeyed, George forgot his new place and, getting to his feet, pulled down his RAF jacket until it hung straight and went to lean over his wife until the tip of his cigar was mere inches from her immaculately made-up face. Mistake—big mistake—as in one swift movement, she swept up her left hand and knocked his cigar flying, the backdraft from her hand's movement nearly taking his nose off.

"What have I told you about smoking near me? Never do that again! Do you hear me?"

Spittle flew from her lips and landed upon the lenses of his spectacles. This time he did step back, until he found himself back in his seat where he slumped and tried to get his heartbeat under control. He mustn't give away just how genuinely frightened he was of his wife.

Upon hearing what and, more to the point, how she'd spoken, George Evans decided for the sake of self-preservation to seal his lips. He may have worn the uniform of a Group Captain; that didn't mean he was a brave man. The wrong side of fifty, he'd used family connections to avoid going into the Army when the First World War broke out. By the middle of 1917, he'd run out of excuses and joined the Royal Flying Corps. With a combination of luck, caginess, and bribery, he managed to gain a ground post coordinating training on Salisbury Plain. Though boring, it kept him alive, and with his father's influence, plus a doctor on a short leash to certify he wasn't fit for service in France, a string of promotions came his way. Upon the formation of the Royal Air Force in April 1918, he was made a Flight Lieutenant, a rank he kept when the war ended. Finding the peacetime RAF was a great place for a single gentleman, as he saw himself, he stayed. Though he had an unspectacular career, his father, as an influential member of the House of Lords, was able to push a few promotions his son's way, until things stalled at Group Captain. His friendly doctor continued to be useful in various ways, whether he wanted to or not, including keeping him in the RAF. As he was, or had been, making too much money from his black market scams, which would have been much more difficult to pull off in civie street, he found the anonymity of the Forces was a great place to hide.

Taking a deep breath and nearly choking on his cigar smoke as a result, George pasted what he hoped was a winning smile on his face.

"If you're going to choke, George," his wife told him, turning away and picking up the phone, "then at least have the good taste to do it anywhere but in my presence. If I didn't want your name, I'd divorce you," she added with disdain before turning her back on him.

As it didn't look like he was going to get anywhere by trying to schmooze her, he poured a large glass of whisky and lit a new cigar. Settling back in his seat, he watched as his wife drummed her fingers whilst she waited for whomever she'd rung to answer.

"Bramble. Where the devil are you?… We've got a client who's ready to pay through the nose… Yes, yes, the usual cut… Of course in cash. You think I'm stupid enough to put my name to something this hot?… Next Monday… That'll be fine."

Without realizing he was speaking out loud, George repeated the name he'd just heard until it came to him and he jumped to his feet. "Bramble! Casey Bramble?"

Before he knew it, Virginia was nose to nose with him. "And where do you know my friendly doctor from?"

The fierce expression upon her face and the words she'd said made him forget his trepidation at confronting her. "Your friendly doctor?"

"So where do you know Bramble from, then, George?" she repeated, drawing up a chair and sitting next to him, a move that made him wish he had a friendly lion to pet. "Last I checked, he was mine. Not exactly friendly, but certainly my in-my-pocket doctor."

He weighed his answer to avoid saying the wrong thing or giving anything else away. Satisfied he wasn't likely to add to his collection of scars, he told her, "He was my fag at school. A little thwacking with a cricket bat goes a long way to setting you up with a useful oick for life."

"And this…oick…does what for you, my love?"

If he hadn't been so put off by actually hearing his beautiful wife calling him *my love*, perhaps he'd have noticed the words were at odds with the intense stare she was treating him to. Imagine the look a lion gives a zebra before inviting it to lunch. But he didn't, and so fell into her eyes and proceeded to spill his deepest, darkest secret and therefore put himself even more at her mercy. His distraction wasn't helped by Virginia tickling him under one of his chins.

"Oh, pretty much anything I say, my darling."

He'd become so quickly hypnotized by his wife actually paying attention to him he didn't notice she was jotting down notes on a pad she'd balanced on her knee.

"Such as…"

"Such as…putting poison in a certain thermos flask." Her pencil snapped, but he never noticed, as she pecked him on the cheek to distract him.

"So," she said in a voice as calm yet as full of menace as a sleeping snake, "our good Doctor Bramble's been naughty, eh?"

"He never meant to kill her," he heard his mouth saying. His heart was distracted by the continued ministrations his wife was paying to his neglected ego, so that it wasn't aware what his mouth was now giving away. "It was only to make her ill enough so she could be persuaded to tell us what had happened to your pearls. But we never got the chance. She died virtually as soon as she managed to land the blasted plane."

Virginia sat back in her seat and it took a full minute before George realized she'd ceased her ministrations.

"I can see I'm going to have to have a serious talk with the good doctor when I next see him."

George blinked and shook himself in an effort to bring certain organs back into alignment with his brain. "Um…where do you know him from, Virginia?"

Perhaps it was the realization she was never going to get her pearls back, or perhaps it was the phone ringing. Either way, something must have distracted her, as otherwise she'd never have told him her biggest secret, something so big it could put her away for a very long time if the information got into the wrong ears.

"He's on a board of doctors who decide if men are fit for the draft. There are men who're prepared to pay a lot of money to avoid going into the armed forces, and I mean a *lot* of money." She then seemed to come to her senses, her predatory smile made a reappearance, and much to George's annoyance, she turned her full attention to the phone.

She obviously recognized the voice on the other end, and from grasping, her smile morphed into one he hated even more, one of greed. It was the same smile he'd fallen in love with when he'd first set eyes upon her, though he'd been too much in love to tell the difference then between adoration and what it actually was.

"Oh, very well," Virginia was saying, her free hand giving away her anxiety by tapping against her thigh. "It's not ideal, but I'll speak to him. George," she addressed him, not troubling to disguise her impatience, "don't you have some place else you can be?"

In truth, there were many places he'd rather be, and many other people he'd rather be around, but if this was a chance to learn anything about his wife's draft-dodging scheme, he wasn't going to pass up the chance. "Not at this time," he answered, and much to her obvious annoyance, he got up, topped up his drink, and settled back down into his seat.

A low growl emanating from deep down in her throat was cut off as whomever she was waiting for came on the other end of the phone.

"Hugo. What do you want?" There were a few beats whilst someone with a rather effeminate-sounding voice spoke, though not loud enough for George to hear what was being said. "No! We've already agreed a fee, a time, and a place, and none of this is renegotiable. You will hand over the four hundred pounds in used, untraceable five-pound notes to my contact. You will follow the instructions my good doctor will give you, and you will not, I repeat *not*, speak of this to anyone, nor deviate from the instructions you will receive upon attending the appointment. If you fail to abide by any of this, then your next appointment will be with the coroner at the most rundown hospital I can find. Do you understand? Good day to you too, then." She carefully placed the handset back in its cradle, emptied her drink, and slid back onto her chaise longue muttering to herself, "To think I gave up films for this."

Without realizing he was saying the words, George Evans put his foot very much in his mouth. "Perhaps the money's better than the films."

Turning only her head, Virginia fixed her husband with a stare to make paper peel off the walls. "That's the only reason I'm still here. It's certainly not for you."

Chapter Sixteen

"I do love that David Niven," Betty sighed, hugging her arms around herself in an effort to keep warm.

Thelma, striding arm in arm with her friend, playfully squeezed her arm and let out a gust of breath into the cold night air, watching delightedly as the mist dissipated before her. "Oh, come on, I know it's been a wonderful day, but British or not, he can't hold a candle to Ronald Coleman."

"Are you still on about *The Prisoner of Zenda*?" Betty laughed. "How many years ago was that? As swashbucklers go, it's swashed its buckle, but wasn't David so handsome in his RAF uniform? And such an inspiring story! I had no idea the Spitfire was one man's brainchild!"

"Yes," Thelma agreed, chuckling slightly at her friend's enthusiasm before she became somber. "Such a pity he died before seeing how his creation saved the country."

Betty shivered and looked up at the glinting moonlight. "Such a beautiful night, Thelma, but so cold after the warmth of the train."

Thelma glanced up at the clear sky. "Bomber's moon," she muttered, quickening their pace.

"Come on, it's not far to my place. Do you want to stay the night?" Betty asked. "It's getting a little late, and you're more than welcome, so long as you don't mind bedding down on the sofa."

"That'd be nice, thank you," Thelma replied. "Do you think Doris will be disappointed she couldn't see the film?"

"Definitely," Betty replied without having to think about it. "It was very good of her to tell us where her tickets were when she realized she wouldn't be able to make it back from Coltishall tonight."

"Yes, and lucky for us Jane gave us the afternoon off, or else we'd never have made it into the West End in time."

"Why do you think *The First of the Few* is only being shown in Leicester Square as yet?" Betty asked, blowing onto her free hand and, for the umpteenth time that night, cursing herself for forgetting her gloves.

"Who knows?" Thelma shrugged. "Our good luck, I guess...even if David Niven isn't anywhere as dishy as Ronald Coleman," she added, with a twinkle in her eye.

"Oh, don't let's start that again," Betty countered with a gentle dig of an elbow in her friend's side.

"If you'd be honest enough to agree that Ronald's far dishier than David Niven, there won't be a problem," Thelma teased, nudging Betty in return.

Pushing open the gate, she'd barely put her key in the front door when Mary pulled it open. "So," she said, not even giving her friends a chance to hang their coats up, "how was the film?"

"Gorgeous," declared Betty, leaning down to take off her shoes and sliding on her slippers over her stockinged feet.

"Ignore her," Thelma advised, laughing. "She's in

lust with David Niven."

Betty turned a fetching shade of red and placed her cold hands on her cheeks in an effort to both warm them up and bring down her obvious embarrassment, failing slightly on both counts. "Probably not the word I'd have chosen," she said as Mary joined Thelma in laughing out loud at their friend's predicament. "However, I wouldn't turn him down if he asked me to dinner."

"My dear," Mary said, laying a hand upon Betty's back when she'd recovered her breath, "a few years ago, I'd have been delighted to have introduced you, but I believe he's a little too big a star now."

This little declaration temporarily brought conversation to a halt broken only when Penny sneezed violently as she came down the stairs, tumbling into Thelma at the foot as she did so.

"Phew. Thanks for that," she said regaining her balance and tightening the cord on her dressing gown.

"That's okay," Thelma told her, surreptitiously dabbing at her cheek when Penny wasn't looking.

"Now, what's all this about David Niven? I thought Leslie Howard was the star of the film. Doesn't he play R. J. Mitchell? He seems rather yummy!"

****

"Look," Jane said to Penny a few days later, "you're sick, that's obvious…"

She was interrupted by Penny doing her best to blow out the windows by sneezing.

"As I was saying, you're ill, and no matter that you're qualified to fly Class Four aircraft, I can pull in Rita."

Her initial answer was another fit of sneezing.

M. W. Arnold

"That's it," Jane decided. "Take yourself off home. I'll send someone for Rita, and I'll just have to put up with her black looks."

"No, please don't," Penny pleaded, wiping her nose again and snuffling in through her nose for all she was worth. "I can do it, I promise. It's only a sniffle."

Jane eyed her colleague with ill-disguised skepticism. For her part, Penny did her best to look like she wasn't dying on her feet. Reaching forward, Jane placed the back of her hand against Penny's forehead, counted to five, and then a look of relief came upon her face.

"Well, at least you don't have a temperature." She took a step back and one more time studied her friend before coming to a decision. "I know how much a badge of honor thing it is to deliver an aircraft even under the most difficult of circumstances, but I don't want any heroics. Understood?"

Penny took a few moments before answering, going through her thoughts. She'd felt this sniffle coming on for almost a week. However, when she'd woken up this morning, or more truthfully woken up the whole house with a tremendous sneezing bout, the sniffle had become a full-blown cold. Nothing short of being grounded by the station doctor would've stopped her reporting for duty that morning though. She'd always been excellent at hiding when she was ill. This was her first chance to fly a Mosquito bomber!

"Quite understood," Penny replied, tightening her silk headscarf and picking up her traveling case. "Don't worry, I won't let you down."

As the Anson taxi piloted by Lawrence took off, Penny overcompensated from the co-pilot's seat by

148

waving too enthusiastically. Jane shook her head and muttered, "If this comes back to bite me…"

Prophetic words, as it turned out.

****

"Well," declared Lawrence after he taxied up and turned off the engines as near as he could get to the sleek, gleaming, yet deadly effective bomber, unable to keep a note of envy from his voice, "that must be her."

Full of cold or not, Penny wasn't going to waste time at this point. "You think?" She gathered up her bag, replaced her scarf, and hauled herself out of the seat. Opening the cabin door, she turned and raised a hand. "See you later, Lawrence."

Her pilot's notes were up to the job, and within twenty minutes, Penny had taken off and set course for RAF Marham in Norfolk. She enjoyed familiarizing herself with the nuances of her new toy. For a few seconds, she was tempted to disobey rules, open up the throttles, and see what she could really do. Common sense won, unfortunately.

As she neared the general area of her destination, Penny increased her lookout. The nearer she got to the coast, the greater the danger from any roaming German aircraft. Her destination was a well-camouflaged operational airfield she hadn't been to before, so it had been agreed with its station commander she'd be met about ten miles southwest of the station. No model had been specified, so she was on the lookout for another Mosquito. At roughly the specified time, she arrived at the meeting point to find the skies empty. She proceeded to circle, all the while scanning the sky. After a few minutes, something glinted in her rearview mirror and a single-seat fighter flashed past, of a model that her fleeting glance didn't recognize.

"Oh, bugger!" she swore, sneezed, threw the throttles wide open, and dived for a bank of cloud. Glancing in the mirror, she could see what had to be the enemy fighter following her, so she jinked to port and then starboard, and still the enemy was on her tail. By now, she was sweating profusely and questioning her decision to soldier through today; it may have been the last bad decision she ever made.

Even with the throttles open as far as she could push them, she wasn't pulling away from her adversary, though she also didn't think he was gaining. However, Penny could see her fuel was getting low. This trip being intended only as a ferry flight, she hadn't had full tanks to begin with, so she didn't know for how long she could keep this up. Pulling up pre-war memories of aerobatics in her own sweet biplane, she threw the Mosquito into a barrel roll, following it up with a split-S, and then dove for a gap in the cloud. Sparing a second to check her mirror, she felt her heart jump as her nemesis wasn't there. As she broke through the cloud, below her she caught a glimpse of an airfield and, with no other thought in her mind, dove with all the speed she could muster for what was the landing strip, waggling her wings as she leveled out at what could be only fifty feet above ground, hoping to make the airfield defenses aware of her danger. She quickly scanned the sky—nothing behind, nothing to her left— however, on her right wing was the mystery aircraft. Her heart missed a beat and then, when it made no move to shoot at her, she risked a closer look, and that was when she noticed the RAF roundels on its fuselage. Its pilot was waving at her and had pushed up his goggles, whilst pointing at the airfield below and motioning she should land.

Five minutes later, Penny had taxied in behind the strange plane that had nearly caused her to have an early heart attack. After following her pilot's notes to make certain everything was shut down in the correct order, she pushed her now sweat-soaked headscarf off her forehead to hang loosely around her neck and popped the hatch to let in the cool air of a September day. In its place, the head of a grinning pilot popped up. It took her a second to recognize him as the pilot whose aircraft had just caused her so much trouble. She promptly blew her top before he had a chance to speak.

Her intentions were spoiled by her sneezing fit and only after she'd blown her nose three times was she able to speak...well, yell, "What the bloody hell do you think you're playing at? You nearly gave me a heart attack!" The pilot opened his mouth to reply, but Penny hadn't finished yet. "And what were you bloody well flying?"

"Delighted to make your acquaintance," he said, popping her a salute and wiping a few wisps of brown hair from his eyes as he did so, showing no signs of being affronted by the outburst from his airfield's guest.

With the wind slightly taken from her sails, Penny allowed herself to take his hand as she clambered out of her aircraft and took a look around. The cloud she'd dived into had begun to settle over the airfield and gave the impression of being in for a long stay. Her transport arrangements might have to be changed. Only as she allowed her attention to turn back to the other pilot did she realize she still had hold of his hand. For his part, he had a very engaging smile upon his face and looked as if he'd be happy to hold her hand for as long as he could.

"Mm…Squadron Leader?" she began, hoping he'd supply who he was so she could request her hand back.

"Alsop, Thomas Alsop, at your service. And you are?"

For the first time in a good long while, Penny's brain went on a go-slow, probably because of his hand still holding hers, as well as from the way the light seemed to twinkle in his eyes as he gazed at her. Finally she managed to answer, "Penny Blake, er, Third Officer Penny Blake, that is. Could I have my hand back, please?" she finally managed to ask, stifling a sniffle.

Standing face to face in front of the Mosquito, Penny found herself unable to tear her gaze from that of the squadron leader. Peering into his piercing blue eyes, she couldn't say anything more, as her mouth refused to cooperate and let forth any sound. However, she saw her handsome adversary had also now been struck dumb. Fortunately, the standoff was interrupted by a motorbike and its passenger screaming to a halt before them; unfortunately, the passenger was a rather irate Group Captain.

"Bugger," muttered Thomas Alsop, not bothering to keep his voice down, "It's Forbes."

A diminutive, portly man heaved himself, with some difficulty, off the bike. With the aid of a too-short, darkened walking stick, stooping as he walked, he hobbled over to where the two waited.

Ignoring Penny and not even bothering to grace her with a glance, he came to a halt before Alsop and looked up his nose, being too short to look down it, at him. After making his junior officer wait a full minute, the Squadron Leader straightened up slightly and brought his arm up into what could pass as a salute.

"Would you care to explain the shenanigans we've just witnessed, Alsop?"

"This is partially my fault, Group Captain," Penny volunteered, even though she hadn't been asked.

Not that it made much difference, as the officious little man didn't even bother to acknowledge someone else had addressed him. "I'll be dealing with you shortly, young man."

Penny, annoyed, was about to tap him on the shoulder, when she saw Alsop shake his head ever so slightly before answering, "Sorry about that, sir. I think what we had was a…a misunderstanding. Third Officer Blake here didn't recognize my Mustang and thought I was an enemy aircraft, so naturally, she took evasive action, and it took me a while to catch her up so she could see I was one of the good guys."

Finally, the fact that there was another person present in the conversation, said person being female, got through the station commander's skull. He turned slowly on the spot until he was facing Penny, who stood running a hand through her unruly brown hair, not bothering to keep a smirk from her face.

"Hello, Group Captain," she said, holding out a hand which the RAF officer, his mouth hanging open like a landlocked goldfish, ignored. "What he said. I think it's what Miss Marple would describe as a case of mistaken identity. I was told to expect a welcoming committee and thought it would be, well, a Mosquito. I've never seen a Mustang before."

"And I did kind of take her by surprise," restated Alsop, coming around to stand next to Penny. "She hadn't seen me, and I couldn't resist bouncing her."

Penny dug an elbow not too subtly into his ribs upon hearing this.

"Oww!"

"That's on you. I reacted as best I could when this idiot appeared on my six." She took a step away from those eyes, from him, glared and, for good measure, included his commanding officer. "Plus, in case you have both forgotten, the aircraft we deliver don't have working radios. So who's the idiot now?"

Group Captain Forbes opened his mouth, and Penny could almost hear him choke down the rebuke he was automatically going to bark out. However, he also wasn't the kind of man who liked not having the last word.

"That's as may be, young…harrumph, Miss Blake, but I shall be having words with your commanding officer about your behavior." After taking a hopefully calming breath, he told her, "You'd better go and hand in your Delivery Chit and get yourself back to base."

Alsop jumped in. "I don't think that's going to be possible, sir."

"Why not?" snapped Forbes, having to crane his neck as the Squadron Leader had deliberately taken a step toward his senior officer.

Waving a hand to encircle the general area, Penny also waited for the penny to drop.

However, it appeared that this officious little man needed things spelled out for him.

"The weather, sir," clarified Alsop. "We're blanketed with low cloud, and from the look of things, I'd be willing to bet it's in for the night. There's no way the ATA taxi can pick her up in this muck."

"He's right," Penny agreed, turning up the neck of her pullover against the gathering cold, something keeping her from mentioning about catching a train.

It appeared the Group Captain had reached the end of his patience. Either that or he too was anxious to get in out of the cold. "You're probably right, Alsop." He then flicked a hand very—in Penny's opinion—rudely in her direction, saying, "I suggest you notify Blake's commanding officer and then make arrangements for some accommodation for her. Dismissed."

Not bothering to return the salute his officer gave him, Forbes hobbled off to his waiting motorbike and started to berate the unlucky driver before heaving his bulk onto the rear, and then they were gone in a cloud of smoke.

Left alone, Alsop turned his back on his departing senior officer and gave Penny his full attention.

Penny replied with a violent sneezing bout she'd been holding in and finally managed to get out, "Well, Squadron Leader Thomas Alsop, know anywhere a girl can get a drink?"

Chapter Seventeen

The incoming drone was their first warning time was getting short. When the Anson came into view, lining up for final approach to the runway, both turned away and gazed once more into each other's eyes, wishing for anything to put off the forthcoming parting of ways.

"I know it's been said by much more important people than myself, but I hate the war." Penny sniffed into the shoulder of Thomas Alsop's greatcoat, her arms hanging limply by her side in abject misery.

Thomas kissed the top of her head and drew his arms tighter around her waist, watching as the Anson taxied ever closer to where the two of them stood at the base of the control tower. "I don't suppose this Lawrence chap would be open to a bribe? I don't have much money, but I do have a sister who's single."

Whether he meant it as a joke or not, Penny didn't know, but it did serve to defuse the tension somewhat. She snorted a laugh and pinched his bottom. "That's a terrible thing to say, even if it's true! And no, I don't think he'd pretend the plane's unserviceable, not even for me."

"Oh-ho!" Thomas tilted his head back slightly so he could look down into Penny's sorrowful eyes. "Are you telling me I've a rival? I spent all that money in the mess last night for no reason!"

Penny stood on tiptoes so she could tenderly brush her lips against his, an action that brought back happy, very happy memories of saying good night at the door of her room the previous evening. "Don't be silly, Tom. It may be a while since I've had a boyfriend…"

"So I'm your boyfriend, eh?"

Penny, suddenly a little shy, buried her head into his shoulder once more, too nervous to look at him when she tentatively answered, "If you want to be."

Thomas relaxed his hands a little and looked down at her, the intensity of his gaze enough to make her breath catch in her throat. "More than anything, yes, I'd love to be your boyfriend."

If she was going to say anything, two things prevented it. The first was Thomas, not worrying about her cold, catching her lips in a kiss that would have rivaled anything in a Hollywood movie. The other, and by far the least welcome, was the Anson gunning its engines a mere fifteen feet away as it came to a halt, nearly blowing them off their feet.

****

Half an hour into the flight back to Hamble, Penny still hadn't picked up on Lawrence's silent hint to spill the beans, giving him no option but to actually ask.

"So who was the pilot your lips were glued to?"

Penny canted her head a little to look at Lawrence from her place in the co-pilot's seat and then behind her to make doubly sure they were alone in the aircraft before replying. Ah, well, at least it'd pass the time.

"There's not really much to tell," she began, and when his only reply was a raised eyebrow, she sighed and reluctantly elaborated. "His name's Thomas Alsop, and he's a Flight Commander on one of the Mosquito squadrons."

"All rather dry," Lawrence decided, earning himself a clip around the ear for his trouble. "It certainly didn't look like he was giving you a lecture on throttle settings."

"Carry on like that, my friend, and we'll see if you remember how to use your parachute," she told him, adding her best evil grin together with a quick sneeze.

"No need for that." He smiled, and then asked, "How about putting some of that built-up tension to use in opening the thermos and pouring us a cup of tea?"

"Speaking of a thermos," Penny said whilst unscrewing and then digging out a spare cup, "any news from Walter?"

Lawrence nodded and took a sip of sweet tea before answering. "Turns out he was overly optimistic," he revealed. "The note he left for Ruth said he thought he might be able to find something out from a friend about the doctor who certified Betty's sister's death. It turned out to be a waste of time. The man he knew had actually left for home a month ago."

"Dead end, then," agreed Penny as she drank her own tea.

"True. However, after Doris found out what had happened, she said she may have better luck herself. I think she felt sorry for Walter, as she told him he could come to London with her when she goes."

"Fingers crossed," Penny said, picking up a cheese sandwich.

"Enough diversions. I'm still waiting to hear about you and the good squadron bod."

As they still had a while to go, Penny decided she might as well get it over with and tell her friend what happened.

"So by the time we'd finished arguing over who was in the wrong—not me, in case you were wondering—we'd finished dinner and were on our second beer. After that, we talked about where we'd come from and what we'd done before the war. A little moonlight walk around the peritrack, very romantic—we couldn't see a thing because of the fog—and by the time we got back, we'd fallen for each other."

Lawrence turned his head to check he wasn't being made fun of. "Just like that?"

"Just like that."

He sighed and turned his attention back to his flying. "Sounds like a little slice of heaven," was all he said until they landed.

Lawrence dropped her off outside the flight line hut, then taxied over to the refueling point. Stretching her arms above her head to ease the cramps from her muscles, Penny looked around the airfield. All looked normal. Even the craters left from the sneak attack by the two enemy fighters a few weeks ago were hard to distinguish. Her friends and colleagues all appeared to be out on deliveries, as upon opening the hut's door, the cupboard was bare, apart from Jane Howell, who was casually—perhaps too casually—leaning against a table.

Penny sneezed her greetings.

"Good morning, Penny," Jane opened with, nursing a cup of steaming tea in her hands. "Everything all right after yesterday's little adventure?"

Putting down her overnight bag, Penny failed to stifle a yawn. "I think so," she ventured cautiously. "Everyone made me feel very welcome."

Jane raised an eyebrow. "*Everyone?*" she laid heavy emphasis on this word.

Beginning to see where Jane was going, Penny contemplated putting on a face of contrition, but as she didn't think she'd done anything wrong, decided not to bother. This didn't mean she didn't know to whom she was referring. "I suppose you're talking about some officious little Group Captain?"

"Never having met the man…" Jane started with a smile, but Penny couldn't resist putting in her thre'pence worth.

"Lucky you."

"Anyway, I've had a phone call from a certain Group Captain Forbes, who's a little, shall we say, upset about some flying you did yesterday."

Though she'd guessed what was coming, to actually hear the words out loud was quite another, and without giving it a moment's prior thought, Penny set out her case for the defense. "I know I performed some maneuvers we aren't supposed to know, let alone do, but I really thought I had some Jerry on my tail. I'd never seen a Mustang before and did everything I could think of to save myself. Thomas…er, Squadron Leader Alsop, that is, even admitted to bouncing me, the Mosquito that is, for a bit of fun. So you see, I didn't do anything wrong." She signed off her statement with a tremendous sneezing fit.

Jane passed her a clean handkerchief and waited for the explosions to subside before answering, meanwhile patting her consolingly on the shoulder. "Don't worry about anything, Penny. It's all resolved, or so far as he's concerned it is. He wanted me to sack you."

"What!" exclaimed Penny, unable to hide her sense of indignity.

"Woah, steady on there and let me finish."

Penny sat down on the nearest seat and deliberately took a few deep breaths. When Jane was satisfied she wasn't about to blow up again, she carried on from where she'd been interrupted.

"Which, of course, I'm not going to do. Then he wanted you grounded, forever, which," she placed her hand over Penny's mouth to forestall another outburst, "I'm also not going to do. Anyway, to get rid of him, I told him I was grounding you for a week. In a way, that's true, but," Jane reapplied her hand as soon as she saw Penny about to open her mouth again, "actually I'm putting you on the sick roster for a week until you get rid of that cold."

"I can still fly," Penny protested in a kind of mumble.

Jane shook her head. "I know you can, but you're not going to. Think of it this way," she added hastily. "So long as you fly, anyone you're around is likely to pick up your cold. It's all very commendable wanting to carry on, but I can't risk losing any of my pilots to illness, let alone any operational pilots at squadrons you may infect on deliveries. Does that make sense?" she asked Penny.

Obviously reluctant, Penny slowly nodded her head, tried not to feel guilty about kissing Thomas, though he had told her he didn't care about catching anything, and then undid her scarf and placed it on top of her bag. "I know you're right. That doesn't mean I like it, though."

Jane smiled and took a seat next to her. "That's

good. I hoped you wouldn't like it."

After another sneeze, during which Jane edged her seat a little farther away, Penny managed to ask through her nose, "This *grounding*, it won't go on my record, will it?"

"Not at all," Jane assured her. "It's only a phantom one to get rid of that nitwit. You being on the sick roster, however, that's non-negotiable. As soon as you've changed, you're to make your way home and hole up in your bedroom for at least the next five days. Are we understood?"

Penny dragged herself to her feet and made her way over to her locker. The order to go and put her feet up seemed to have made her actually feel ill for perhaps the first time. Taking note of this, Jane decided to test out her theory and, at the same time, perhaps make Penny feel a little better.

"You should know that I had another call directly after the first one. A certain Squadron Leader Alsop. Turns out he'd heard what his Group Captain had to say and wanted to set the record straight—his words—as to what actually happened."

Penny had stopped to listen with her sweater half over her head. "Oh. What did he say?"

"Backed you up completely, plus, he was very complimentary of your evasive maneuvers."

To hide the blush that was spreading up her neck, Penny pretended to be having trouble in getting her sweater over her head. Jane, feeling a little mischievous, reached over and yanked hard upward.

"He also wanted to make sure you're still on for that date you promised him as soon as he has a free weekend."

Now divested of her sweater, Penny didn't know where to look, so resolved her embarrassment by exploding into another fit of sneezes.

****

The sound of laughter woke Penny from a particularly lovely dream involving a moonlight walk along the Seine, followed by, for reasons that were starting to rapidly recede, the back of Thomas Alsop's head flying in a plane over the Alps into a beautiful sunset. Typical, she thought, running her hands through her hair, making it more messy than usual. Just when things are getting interesting, I wake up.

Making her way downstairs gingerly, though as quickly as she could, as she could feel a bout of sneezing coming on, she only just managed to get both feet on the ground floor before, sure enough, all hell erupted from her nose and mouth. If nothing else, it brought everyone running into the hall, where they found her doubled over. She felt like she'd pulled a muscle in her side after the final enormous sneeze.

"What the hell was all that about, babe?" demanded Doris, wrapping an arm around her friend. "Come on, if you're not going to blow up again, let's get you into the lounge."

As Doris hobbled awkwardly with Penny and helped her lie down on the sofa, Betty told her she was going to make her a hot water bottle.

"Honestly," Mary was saying as she went to sit on the floor by Penny's head, "we had no idea you were here. Why didn't you say something? We'd have kept you company."

Penny smiled weakly down at her, as Doris decided it would be much more comfortable for Penny to use

163

her lap as a pillow. "Thanks, Doris, I think. I went to bed as soon as I got back and only woke up a few minutes ago, otherwise I would've."

"That was probably my braying out loud," apologized Doris, stroking her friend's hair out of her eyes. "Sorry about that."

"Don't worry about it," Penny told her, reaching up and clasping the American's hand. "If I'd have slept any longer, I'd feel bloody awful in the morning, so you've done me a favor."

Betty came scuttling in from the kitchen and, before Penny could argue, lifted up Penny's feet and put the bottle beneath her bedsock-clad feet. "Better?"

Though she hadn't been cold, Penny wriggled her toes against the heat and immediately felt her eyelids begin to drop. "I wouldn't sit there too long, Doris," she warned, looking up at her friend's smiling face. "I don't snore, but I have been known to drool in my sleep."

"Oh yuck," said Betty, taking a seat and grinning over at Penny.

In an effort to keep herself awake, Penny did her best to focus on what had brought her downstairs. She shuffled her bottom up a little so her head was leaning more on Doris's shoulder than on her lap, whilst Doris wrapped her arm around her waist for support. "So what was the cause of all the hilarity?"

A very timid knock on the door frame caused all four women to look up. Only the head of Walter, Ruth's assistant reporter, showed around the corner.

"Um. That'd be my fault," his head replied.

"And that would be because of...?" Penny asked, trying and failing to sit up a little more.

"Well," he began, shoving a hand through his hair.

He was interrupted by a rapping at the front door, and Walter, apparently glad of any excuse not to continue with his story, let out a quick, "I'll get it!" and promptly did so.

"Only me!" trilled Ruth. She hung up her coat and made for the lounge and then, when Walter didn't follow her in, turned and grabbed him by the hand. When they got to the door, he dug his heels in. "Walter! What on earth's the matter?"

"I think that's my fault," Penny decided after looking around at her friends' faces and then at where she could just about see one of Walter's eyes. "Walter, you can come in. It's only a dressing gown. I'm sure you've seen more flesh on display at the theatre."

Though he allowed himself to be dragged into the room, his reluctance was obvious, and Doris could swear she heard him say as he pulled out a chair and sat down, "Never been."

Doris looked directly into his eyes and told him, "I'll take you," then became acutely aware of the stares of the other women. Walter was rapidly doing a beetroot impression.

Penny waited for something else to happen or for someone else to speak, but it became apparent everyone else was waiting to see what either Doris or Walter would do next. As both seemed incapable of speech at present, she repeated the question she'd asked before Ruth turned up. "So, Walter," she began, and when he continued to stare open-mouthed at Doris, turned to Ruth instead. "Ruth, I know you weren't here, but something tells me I'll get more out of you than I will out of those two."

"Is this about what Walter was up to today?" Ruth

asked the room at large and got nods all around. "Fine, here's what happened. I got into work this morning to find a note from Walter, pushed through the letter box, waiting for me. Apparently, he had a friend who worked in one of the admin offices at Guys Hospital and thought he could find out where the doctor was who signed Eleanor's death certificate."

"And what went wrong?" Penny asked.

Mary and Betty both burst out laughing again, causing Walter to resume his beetroot impression and Doris to throw him a look of sympathy. Ruth, just about maintaining her composure, opened her mouth to answer. However, she too then succumbed, forcing Walter to overcome his silence.

"I got into London and then realized I didn't know the doctor's name."

Penny answered with a couple of sneezes, banging her head against Doris's elbow as her head shot forward and back again, but for Walter's sake she kept as straight a face as she could. "It could happen to anyone, Walter. Don't worry about it. So what did you do? Did you call Betty up and ask her?"

Betty immediately gathered herself and stopped laughing. "He did, but I couldn't remember either."

"So what happened next?" Penny wanted to know.

Walter filled in the details. "I took a train back home and went to work, where Ruth told me off for being a bit of a fool, and then we came around here about an hour ago."

Penny gingerly laid her head back against Doris's shoulder and looked over at Betty. "And…" she prompted.

"And," replied Betty, reaching down to pick up a

cardboard box that was beside her seat, "as I didn't recall, I had to go searching, and that's what made me remember this box," she finished, laying a hand reverently upon the lid of the unopened box.

Mary, as if slightly afraid of the answer, asked in a whisper, "Are these your sister's effects?"

Wiping away a solitary tear rolling down her cheek, Betty nodded.

"Why's the certificate in there?" Ruth asked, the reporter in her showing.

"Because," Betty replied, "after I'd arranged for her burial, I couldn't bear to look at anything to do with her. It's too painful."

Ruth leaned forward. "Do you want me to look?" she offered.

After a moment, Betty shook her head. "No, I'll have to open it some time, so now's as good a time as any."

Matching deed to words, Betty took a deep breath and, at the same time, put the box on the floor before her and took off the lid. Fortuitously, the death certificate lay open on top of other knickknacks. Reaching down and ignoring everything else, she took it out, replaced the lid, and smoothed the document out on her lap.

"Well," asked Mary after Betty didn't immediately answer, "what's the name?"

After another few seconds, Betty finally looked up and told them.

"Doctor Bramble."

Chapter Eighteen

In The Victory, Shirley and Ralph both nursed a half pint of Tennants bitter, Ralph by choice. Shirley—well, she really didn't care what she drank at that moment. She kept throwing glances toward the entrance in case her colleagues from the ATA came through the door. This would have caused her no end of problems, though in another way it would certainly get everything out in the open.

She looked over to where Ralph was slouched forward, one hand nursing his glass, the other propping up his chin. He was certainly no gentleman, as she'd had to buy her own drink, and she was now wondering why on earth he'd asked her to meet him here after work.

Ralph had been one of the gate guards that morning, and under the pretense of double-checking her ID as part of an exercise, he'd pulled her to one side and told her he worked for Virginia Mayes and he needed to talk to her that evening. Apart from ordering himself a drink, he hadn't uttered a word.

Enough prevaricating. "Ralph!" she snapped, slapping a hand down next to his glass hard enough to make it jump slightly. "What do you want?"

"Right," he mumbled, taking a long sup from his glass before putting it down, sitting back into the bench seat, and looking at her through haunted eyes. "Sorry.

Find I need a pint or two in me guts after having anything to do with Miss Mayes."

This unexpected declaration reinforced the impression Shirley had of the woman who'd sent her here, and she couldn't suppress the shudder that shook her body.

Ralph noticed. "She has the same effect on me as well, luv."

In spite of the words, Shirley noticed the lack of sympathy in his voice. "So what's she got over you?" Reckoning as they were in roughly the same boat, she wasn't likely to get in trouble for asking. At the very least, he'd tell her to mind her own business.

Ralph lifted his pint once more before answering. "Nothing I know of, though I wouldn't want to put her to the test. She makes the Group Captain look like a pussycat."

"Who's the Group Captain?" Shirley asked, puzzled. "I've only dealt with Virginia."

Letting out a resigned laugh, Ralph let the side of his mouth curl up. "He's the git she's married to and who used to run the black market racket in their part of London. I ended up doing little jobs for him. That's how he got his mitts on me. I tried not to have anything to do with his missus, nasty little witch, but now she runs the business..." He didn't have to say anything else as a shudder coursed its way through his body again. He then turned an eye on Shirley. "What's her worship got over you? Must be something nasty, as I can't see why else a nice girl like you would be doing her bidding."

If he hadn't accompanied this with a lecherous wink, Shirley would've been flattered, albeit only a

169

little. Though she had a low opinion of her own self-worth, even she thought she could do better than a lowlife like Ralph. She certainly didn't have any intention of telling him anywhere near the truth. Confiding in the wrong person—and you couldn't get any more wrong than Virginia, she'd found to her dismay—could be costly.

She settled for simply refusing to tell him.

"Sorry. Let's just say she knows something about me I'd rather keep quiet."

He wasn't best pleased with her refusal to divulge, and she wished she'd never asked, now.

"So why did you bother to ask me, if you weren't going to spill?" There was a definite hint of anger there.

"Because you told me you wanted to talk, and we hadn't exchanged a word before then." As he wasn't looking ready to relax, she shrugged. "I didn't expect you to tell me anything. So what was it you wanted to talk about?"

He eyed her, patently, to see if she was taking the mickey, and fortuitously decided she wasn't, as he picked up his pint again and drained it. "You've been asked to keep an eye on this Betty Palmer." He paused whilst she nodded. "That's to see if she's still got this bloody thermos flask his nibs wants back." Another statement rather than a question, and again Shirley nodded. "Has either of them asked you to keep an eye out for anything else?"

"No, just that." Shirley contemplated what he'd said for a minute and decided the pair of them hardly passed for the world's best spies. Should she confide in him that she'd barely been inside Betty's house, let alone been able to search for the thermos? Probably not, as he didn't strike her as the most stable of men.

Ralph shook his head and got to his feet before replying. "Doesn't it seem strange they've got the two of us looking for the same thing? Seems a bit like overkill to me, and that means only one thing. Whatever the importance of this thermos, there's a good chance whoever has it holds a lot of power in their hands. Well," he said, shoving a flat cap hard down on his head so the peak shadowed his eyes, "see you tomorrow." He then strode out of the pub without a backward glance.

Leaving her barely touched drink alone, Shirley got to her feet and pulled on her coat. Settling her scarf around her head, she strode out after Ralph, muttering, "And a whole heap more of trouble."

She promptly stumbled into Lawrence and let out an "Oof." Tripping backward, she would've fallen if he hadn't caught hold of her arms in time.

"Sorry about that," he told her as he settled her back on a more even keel.

"That's okay," she assured him, and then a thought struck her. "Hang on. Didn't you say you were going around to Betty's? What're you doing here?"

What he told her was rather surprising.

"Keeping an eye on Ralph there." He gestured toward the airfield. "And now, on you."

Shirley went to remove his hands from her arms, but she found herself unable to do so. "Lawrence, I'd like you to let me go. Please," she added when he showed no signs of doing so and indeed, tightened his grip slightly.

"Not just yet," he told her and then, when she tried to take a step back, fear now showing in her eyes, added, "but don't worry, I'm not going to hurt you." He looked around and found they were still alone. "I've got something I need to tell you, and it has to be at Betty's, so please come along with me."

****

"Betty!" Lawrence called as he strode into her lounge just behind Mary, who'd let him in. "We're here!"

"Bring her in," came the low reply, and Lawrence gently guided Shirley into sitting on the sofa alongside Penny, who greeted her with the usual sneeze.

"Sorry about that," she said, wiping her nose, "but believe it or not, I am getting better." She grinned.

"Bless you," Shirley told her, despite being totally unprepared for what was about to happen. Lawrence had refused to reveal anything on the way to the house, and as he'd also refused to release hold of her arm or hand, she'd had little choice but to come along. Now she was getting the impression no one else in the room knew exactly what was about to happen either.

Betty sat back in her chair nursing the ubiquitous cup of tea. Next to Penny were Mary and Ruth, whilst in the other seat was Doris. A young man Shirley hadn't seen before was at her feet, one of his hands casually resting on the cushion with one of Doris's lying across his. Both were making a supreme effort at pretending not to be aware of this.

Under the impression she'd been brought in as the next best thing to a prisoner, Shirley decided to test her theory. "Lawrence, you were about to do your Hercule Poirot impression?"

"Miss Marple, surely," Penny interjected before she could stop herself.

"Why don't you just let him get on with it," advised Ruth.

"Thank you," said Lawrence, taking up a bottle of Guinness from the sideboard where he'd left it before going to collect Shirley. "Shirley, as Ruth says, please keep quiet." He waited a few seconds to make certain she obeyed, and when he was satisfied, nodded and leant against the door frame. "As Ruth will attest, my name is Herbert Lawrence, and I am a pilot, but I am also a detective sergeant in the Special Branch."

"Don't even think about it," Penny advised, her hand gripping Shirley's arm in a vise-like grip the instant Lawrence's words were out.

Lawrence noticed, yet simply nodded an acknowledgement to Penny before continuing. "I was sent here to find a connection between the death of Eleanor Palmer and a draft-dodging racket that's going on in London."

Betty's attention was immediately drawn to what he'd just said, and she leant forward to ask, "What kind of connection, Lawrence? And"—she turned her head toward Shirley—"what's she got to do with this?"

"I'm coming to that, Betty. Now, everyone." He stood up straight to address the room, and all could see the authority ripple from every pore as he spoke. "What I'm about to tell you is something I'm not supposed to divulge, but you'll all figure it out soon anyway, as I go on, and I can tell there'll be a time when I'll need your help. My sources—and no, you can't ask what they are—tell me the doctor who's involved in the racket is also the same one who's responsible for your sister's death, Betty."

This statement had the effect of silencing his

audience so completely you'd have thought the King had walked into the room. Penny still had Shirley's arm gripped tightly, whilst Doris and Walter were now openly holding hands, though both had their attention riveted on Lawrence. Mary had passed her bottle of Guinness to Betty, who forgot her normal insistence upon a glass and took a long pull before flopping back in her chair.

Shirley broke the silence. "And where do I come into this?"

Lawrence came and stood over her, then knelt down on one knee to show that he wasn't a threat.

"I think you've firsthand knowledge of this doctor," he stated.

"Why would Shirley know Doctor Bramble?" Doris asked, causing Lawrence to turn his head and consequently lose his balance as he turned to stare over at her.

Recovering to sit on the floor, he asked Doris, "How do you know he's called Bramble?"

"It's on the death certificate," Mary supplied.

"Ah," Lawrence murmured, wiping his brow. "For a minute, I thought we had a leak."

"But again, what's Shirley got to do with this?"

"Shirley?" Lawrence turned to face her and asked, not unkindly, "Do you want to tell them this, or should I?"

Bobby, who in typical doggy fashion was lying at Ruth's feet, nose to tail and snoring gently, his fluffy ears twitching every now and then, opened one eye at Shirley, and the warm feeling the sight engendered gave her the courage to speak. She took a deep breath and addressed Lawrence. "No, I want to tell everyone why and how I ended up this way."

Lawrence nodded and settled back with the others and waited for Shirley to compose herself before she started.

"My father-in-law's a Catholic minister up north," she began. "My mother-in-law can only be described as ruled by him, and he's definitely one who doesn't believe in sparing the rod. When my husband, their son, was reported missing earlier this year..."

At hearing these words, Betty started to heave herself out of her chair, but Shirley noticed and motioned that she should sit back down, which, after a moment's hesitation and after glancing at Ruth, she did.

"...I went for a walk as soon as the telegram came, and when I got back home, I found the front door bolted and my clothes bundled inside an old suitcase. Eventually, after I'd banged on the door enough, he opened long enough to tell me he'd allowed me to stay as long as he had because his wife had told him the child I was carrying was their son's. He said he'd never believed that but felt it had been his Christian duty. He finished by telling me I was no child of his and that he never wanted to see me again. He then slammed the door in my face."

Pausing to catch her breath, Shirley accepted with thanks the Guinness Penny passed to her. Her nerves were ragged and her mouth was dry.

"He didn't even care I was two months pregnant. So with little chance of any help from anybody in that town—his word was gospel—I took a train into London and...found someone who could help with my...situation."

"By 'situation,' " Ruth couldn't help but interrupt,

"I take it you mean you wanted to find someone who'd perform an abortion?"

"Yes," Shirley stated with conviction, and when still no one showed signs of condemning her to the seven circles of hell, waited a short while to allow her heart rate to settle down to normal. "Obviously, I didn't know anyone, but I was in such a state, by the time I'd spent twenty hours wandering around the East End without sleeping, that I started asking the most dodgy characters I'd normally run away from if I saw them. I don't know if you'd call it lucky, certainly not with the way things have panned out, but I'd just about given up and was wondering what I was going to do when I felt a tap on my shoulder. The next thing I know, I'm being led down some back alley."

"Not the smartest thing to do," Mary commented, and Shirley could only shrug in agreement. "So what happened?"

"The best thing to say is that the doctor wasn't a butcher. It still left me wondering what I was going to do. I had nowhere to stay, and no job. Things weren't looking good. Then in came this lady, someone who dressed like she could've been walking down a red carpet. She said she could use me, and after paying the doctor, I had hardly any money left, so I didn't have much choice but to agree. She took me to a cheap hotel, got me something to eat, and told me to wait there until I heard from her. The next day, she was back, still dressed to the nines. She didn't threaten me, and I never saw any kind of weapon, but that look, that expression, was enough to let me know I had to do whatever she said or it'd likely be the last thing I'd ever do."

"This was Virginia Mayes?" asked Lawrence.

Shirley nodded. "Though I didn't find out her name until after I'd left London."

"Hold on a second," said Doris, not noticing the pained expression upon Walter's face, as she tightened her already strong grip on the fingers of his hand. "Are you telling me the...the person who's behind...behind everything"—she swept the room with her free hand—"is some movie star?"

"Movie star?" Penny sneezed. "The name's vaguely familiar. Is that where I've heard it? Not that I could tell you anything she's been in," she added for everyone's information.

Lawrence smiled and filled in a few blanks. "I'm not surprised. She hasn't done anything for a few years, and word is she managed to piss off every producer in England, and now no one'll employ her. But this doesn't stop her swanning around all the parties and places she can get into like she was still in movies."

"So how's she making her money now?" Betty asked.

Penny blew her nose. "Let me guess—she's the brains behind this draft-dodging racket you mentioned, and this doctor has something to do with it too."

"Well," Lawrence said, "she certainly is now."

"Are you telling me," Betty broke in, "she's the person responsible for the death of my sister?"

Shirley sat back, quite glad of the break in her monolog, and took in the bits and pieces of information now flying about, learning this and that to add to what she'd already figured out. Things were sounding more and more like an Agatha Christie mystery!

Lawrence, a little surprisingly, was shaking his head. "Actually, no. We're pretty certain it's her husband who's been the brains there. He's a serving Group Captain, but hardly blessed with the brains God gave him, which is why his wife, this Virginia, has taken over."

"What men are?" piped up Ruth, providing a much-needed moment of comedy relief.

Betty, the only one not to smile at what Ruth had said, promptly broke the moment. "If you know it's this bastard who killed Eleanor, why haven't you arrested him yet? Hell, give me his name and address and a cricket bat. I'll have a word or two with him myself!"

Turning a sympathetic eye to Betty, Lawrence sadly shook his head. "I quite understand, really I do, but you must leave this to the police. Believe me, I want to see someone swing for her too."

It took a few minutes before Betty finally, and very reluctantly, settled back in her seat, everyone taking her silence as the sign they could carry on.

Walter finally managed to extricate his crippled fingers from Doris's grasp. "So have you at least spoken to this Bramble character yet?"

Lawrence shook his head. "You wouldn't believe what a slippery customer he is. He doesn't seem to practice, or at least not under that name, and all our efforts to track him down have failed. He doesn't sign anything under the name of Bramble, but all the signatures look, according to our handwriting experts at least, like they've been done by the same person. We've even tried, ahem, shaking down a few of the Group Captain's people, but they just clam up, as do those we bring in who we believe have false exemption certificates. For some reason, they all seem so much more afraid of his wife than of what the police can do to them," he added wistfully. "Shirley," he prodded, "I think it's time you continued."

Shirley prepared herself. "As you've probably all guessed, this Bramble is also the one who performed my abortion, not the best decision I've ever had to make." She stopped to wipe a tear from beneath her eye and saw she wasn't the only one, as both Ruth and Penny were blowing their noses. Of course, Penny was getting over a cold, so Shirley couldn't be entirely certain. "Anyway, Virginia told me I would pay my debt by coming here and finding out if Betty had any evidence that could be traced back to her—or her husband, I guess. She's also obsessed with finding some pearls..." Betty snorted, and Doris suppressed a chuckle. However, as Shirley didn't know why, she carried on from where she'd left off. "...some pearls a Hollywood producer gave her. If I couldn't find either of those, then I was just supposed to keep an eye on you, Betty, and—if I got the chance—search your house."

Betty asked, "So why are you telling us all this now?"

"Apart from the fact that Lawrence here already knows all this"—she raised an eyebrow at him to check and got a firm nod by return—"I can't do it. Yes, I'm afraid of her and have no doubt if she knew I was speaking to you all and she could get hold of me, that I'd be dead, but this isn't me. The baby really was my husband's, and if he weren't...dead, I wouldn't be in this pickle, but I am. He'd want me to be the honest person I, well, used to be. If you all want Lawrence to take me in and you'd never speak to me again, then I'll quite understand. I don't deserve to have any friends," she finished, her voice full of misery.

Betty, ever so slowly, got to her feet and came to stand next to a trembling Shirley. She regarded the younger woman for a short while and then wrapped her in her arms and told her, so everyone in the room could hear, "You're among friends now, Shirley."

"And I've an idea about how to track down this doctor," piped up Doris, an expression of extreme malice on her face. "He's so going to regret messing with any of my friends!"

Chapter Nineteen

After Ruth and Lawrence had taken an emotionally exhausted Shirley back home, at Betty's insistence, the room had become quiet, everyone lost in their own thoughts at the weight of what they'd heard that evening. Mary had fallen back on the age-old British custom of "if in doubt, make a pot of tea." Of everyone in the room, the most serene was Penny.

"Mary," Betty said, heaving herself to her feet, "give Penny there a nudge. She'd be much better off in bed."

Mary took a dozy Penny upstairs, pausing only for a quick sneeze on the landing. There was a knock at the door, and Betty went to answer. It was Thelma. She hadn't seen her for a few days, which usually meant something was in the wind. Stepping back, she let her in.

"Well, this is a surprise."

"For me too." Thelma's eyes were downcast, hiding something, the reason she was there so late. True, The Victory, where she had a room, was only a short walk away, but once the day's work was over, she tended to keep to herself.

Betty turned to go back into the lounge, then came to a stop when she realized Thelma hadn't followed. "You don't need permission, you know."

Thelma still hadn't raised her eyes, let alone moved

her feet once Betty had closed the door. "I've something I have to tell you, something that after you hear it, you may not want anything more to do with me."

Betty raised an eyebrow. "Well, it seems to be my day for announcements." Thelma opened her mouth, but Betty didn't give her a chance to ask why. "I'll fill you in later. In the meantime, come in and take the weight off your feet. There's some rabbit pie left, if you're hungry?"

A glance toward the kitchen, together with a very audible grumble of her stomach, gave Thelma away.

"I think that's a yes." Betty chuckled. "Doris, if you could tear yourself away from Walter for a minute, could you get a plate of pie and a glass of elderflower wine for Thelma? We can wait until you've eaten," she finished as Thelma followed Doris into the kitchen.

Ten minutes later, everyone had retaken their seats whilst Thelma, burping softly, perched herself on the edge of the sofa, wringing her hands nonstop. Only after she'd sat for a few minutes and not spoken a word did Betty decide enough was enough and prompted her, "Please, Thelma, tell us what you came to say."

****

October 1941 - Luton Airfield

The four-ton lorry misfired as it backed up to the kitchen, and Thelma felt her heart miss a beat. For the umpteenth time, she wondered why she'd gotten involved in this racket. True, she'd been looking for a way to make money, real money, ever since her father ran out on her mother and her at the outbreak of war, leaving her the sole bread winner, but she'd never thought about turning her hand to anything illegal; then a stranger had introduced himself in the mess a few nights ago.

He'd been behind her in the queue and then followed her to the table, where he took his seat and simply stared. That was all: he'd just stared. Then he said, "I've been watching you, Miss Aston. You board at the cheapest place in town. You never go out. Your only relation is a housebound mother to whom most of your wages are sent. You, Miss Aston, are looking for…a way out."

She hadn't been able to stop herself from asking, "A way out of what?" By now, he had her full attention. He was an inconspicuous fellow, smartly dressed in a tailored suit, and with short, dark brown, slicked-back hair, and he had the unmistakable air of the military about him. Which branch, she didn't know and didn't care, as it mattered little whether he'd lucked out on speaking to her at a particularly low moment or he'd really done his homework, as he had her down to a tea.

"What do you want, Mister…?"

"George," he'd said, holding out a well-manicured hand. "George will do."

"Very well, George," Thelma replied, looking around to see if anyone else was watching or listening in. "What do you want?"

George *Whoever* finished his coffee and regarded her before answering, "Straight to the point, Miss Aston. I like that." If he'd been hoping to get some kind of reaction, he wore a good enough mask not to let it show when he didn't get it. "Very well, what do I want? I want two sides of beef, four pork shoulders, and a list of other goods I have in my pocket, and I will pick them up on Friday."

Thelma would have laughed, though as this stranger had read out the items as if they were any other shopping list, she'd not believed it appropriate. "And why should I give these to you? Can you give me any reason I shouldn't call the police right now?"

After a look around the crowded mess hall, George simply pushed a fat brown envelope across the table to her.

Having seen enough films to have a fair idea what it contained, Thelma whisked it under the edge of the table, opened it, and had to stifle a gasp of amazement. The envelope contained enough pound notes to feed her and her mother for the next six months. After getting her breath back, she carefully pushed the envelope back across to him. "And what would I have to do?" she demanded.

George pushed the envelope back and, placing one of her hands on top of it, patted it lightly but firmly before settling back. "For that? Nothing. Consider it a *welcome to the family* gift, and that's just a sample of what you could earn. Just think, you'll never have to worry about your mother again."

Thelma *was* thinking about her mother, and she carefully slipped the envelope of cash into her bag. "Same question," she told him.

"To business, then," he said, allowing a smile a snake would've been proud of to grace his lips. "I believe you're the station mess manager, and I would like you to arrange for those items to go missing."

"Missing," she'd repeated, knowing he knew exactly what she did and taking it to mean he had been watching her closely and this meeting was the result of much careful planning.

"Missing," he'd confirmed. "Let me put it like this. I know who you obtain your supplies from. All you have to do is obtain more cuts of meat and so on from them than the station has ordered, make certain there's no one but you around when they're delivered, and I'll do the rest. I'll even show you how to, um, 'cook the books,' I believe the saying is, so that you're covered. In return, those envelopes will keep coming."

****

September 1942 - Hamble

Finally, after taking some steadying breaths, Thelma raised her head and finished. "That's how things got started, how I got into the black market."

After a few beats of silence, Doris broke the tension in the room, "Wow! Am I glad Lawrence isn't around!"

Thelma managed a couple of chuckles before sobering up again as Betty asked, "All very...interesting, shall we say, but why would I never want anything to do with you? I am a little concerned for your freedom, but I still don't see the connection."

"Well, so long as no one's about to run off for the police, I'll elaborate. You see, after a few months, I got greedy. I started to think I could skim a little off the top for myself, even though the money he paid me was good—very good, to be honest. That's when I found I was out of my depth. I thought he was just some wide boy, all bark but no bite. I was wrong."

"Why? What happened?" asked Mary when Betty looked incapable of asking.

"He found out. Of course he would. Then he decided to give me a little warning."

"What kind of warning?" Doris wanted to know,

185

patting her seat for Walter to take. She sat down on a cushion at his feet, resting her arm on his knee once more, oblivious to the stares she got from her friends.

This must have been the bit which Thelma had been dreading, as she started to rock back and forth, silent. Betty got up from her seat and told Mary to shove over so they could all sit together and both hold onto Thelma's hands, to give Thelma the courage to carry on with her story.

"I now know why your sister was wearing your flying suit, Betty, and I should have noticed something was wrong. You don't go up much, so it's much cleaner than ours, and her hair was slightly different to how you normally wear yours, but that was the only difference between yourselves. I can't blame the ground crew. It should have been me going up, only when I recognized one of George's henchmen dressed as ground crew and realized something was wrong, I turned tail. However, someone else was there, someone who'd been in his car once when he came to check up on me, some doctor."

The only sign Betty gave of the tension she was feeling was when she squeezed Thelma's hands tightly enough for her to wince. "You think his name might be Bramble?"

Thelma nodded, ignoring the pain in her fingers. "Yes, that's it. I only overheard his name the once and did my best to forget it, but that's it."

"And then?" Betty prodded. "After you'd seen him?"

"I saw him take something out of a black case, a small glass phial, I believe, and tip it into a thermos. Then he ran over to the Moth and climbed into the front seat. Betty, whatever was in that flask was meant for me, I'm sure of it. Whether he meant to kill me or only to make me ill, ill enough to make me behave, he mucked up and killed your sister."

****

After hearing the end of Thelma's story, Betty didn't say a word to her, merely got to her feet, put on her coat, and left the house by the front door. A minute later, Mary pulled on her coat and hurried out too, saying in her wake, "I'll go keep an eye on her."

When the door had slammed shut again, Thelma slumped into her seat and let out the breath she hadn't known she'd been holding. "It's been a hell of an evening," she said to no one in particular.

Doris took it upon herself to reply. "Well, I think she's handling things a lot better than I would. Hell, if I were her, chances are I'd have slapped at least two faces tonight and maybe added a few kicked shins into the bargain as well!"

Thelma turned a confused expression upon Doris. "What happened earlier? What did I miss?"

"First things first," Doris said. "There's something I need to clear up. Are you still involved in the black market, Thelma?"

"And we want the truth. Remember what I do for a living," added Walter, taking a small notepad out of his trousers' back pocket for emphasis.

"I know," she assured him and then turned to look Doris in the eye, in the hope she'd believe her. "Doris, I can assure you I am no longer in the black market. I got out right after everything with Betty's sister, and at the same time I arranged for my transfer here. I haven't seen either of those men since."

After a quick whispered conversation with Walter,

M. W. Arnold

Doris visibly relaxed. "Make sure Betty knows. That's important, or she'll never trust you again."

****

"Betty!" Mary shouted after her stumbling friend, and again, "Betty! Wait up!" until she'd caught up with her a few strides later.

Betty hadn't got far, in fact, barely twenty yards, and was crouched down next to a tree overhanging the river, its branches trailing in the water and creating strange patterns as it swept past. Mary stooped next to her and looked down to where Betty appeared to be staring blankly at the water as it swept past. After failing to see anything of interest for a few minutes, she was forced to conclude Betty wasn't really looking at anything, so she placed a hand on her shoulder and squeezed.

"Betty, are you okay, love?"

Betty's eyes, normally so full of life, were as dull as they must have been in the days and weeks immediately after the death of her sister. Mary, of course, didn't know this for sure, but she was as empathetic as they came. Not knowing what else she could do, she wrapped her arms around her friend and just held her tightly. Her body reacted to the tears that were coursing silently down Betty's cheeks by shedding tears in sympathy as the two clung to each other, bathed in the moonlight.

A drone of engines overhead drew Mary's eyes, and over Betty's shoulder she could just make out the dark outlines of a bomber raid setting out for, presumably, Germany. With her arms still around her friend, Mary offered up a silent prayer for the brave crew's safety. Going out night after night and getting

188

shot at by forces they mostly never saw took a certain type of bravery she admired beyond anything she knew. She hadn't had the opportunity to deliver a bomber, not yet having qualified for that class of aircraft, though she knew Penny had delivered Mosquitoes and had told her that one of the ground staff had let slip that the chances of a bomber crew getting through a tour of around thirty operations were slim, very slim. The thought was enough to make her shudder, something which Betty must have mistaken for a shiver of cold.

Wiping a hand across her eyes, Betty gently removed Mary's arms from around her. "I'm sorry," she said with a sniff. "Are you cold?"

Suppressing a chuckle, as she didn't think it would be appropriate, Mary answered, "No, just thinking about something."

Betty tilted her head up to the sky and the bomber stream still passing overhead. "I think I can guess. 'Brave' hardly begins to describe them, does it."

"No. I'd hope, if it ever came to it, I could have as much courage."

Both women stood and watched for the half hour it took for the bombers to pass overhead, not moving until the last had disappeared from sight and the drone had died away into the night air.

"Good luck, boys," both women said at the same time, then smiled at each other at the utterance.

"Now," Betty began, linking an arm through one of Mary's and, to her relief, heading back toward home, "suppose you tell me why you followed me?"

Thankful the darkness hid her face, Mary sorted through her thoughts before settling upon, "I was worried about you. The way you rushed out after what

Thelma told us… Are you all right?"

The way Betty hesitated slightly in her stride made it clear Mary had been right to follow her friend. "I will be," she stated. "At this moment, though, not really. What Thelma admitted was a shock, and that's why I needed to get away for a bit, on my own."

Mary blushed and, again, was glad of the night's camouflage. "Sorry about that."

Betty squeezed Mary's arm. "No, company's good."

"What are you going to do, or say?" Mary asked.

"I'm not sure," Betty finally admitted, her hand upon the garden gate. "I've had time to think, and I can't blame Thelma. She chose a quick and what she thought easy way to make money, albeit for a good reason. It wasn't her fault my sister was killed. Both were in the wrong place at the wrong time."

Mary kissed Betty on the cheek and then opened the gate and took her friend's hand. "Come on in from the cold. They're all going to be worried about us."

Chapter Twenty

"How do you think things are between those two?" Mary asked Doris with concern, pointing toward where Betty and Thelma sat with their heads bent close together, deep in conversation.

Doris shrugged her shoulders. "Well, they haven't killed each other, so far, so fingers crossed they'll be all right. They're both sensible broads," she added before turning her eyes back to the sky, scanning for the taxi plane. She looked at her watch, shook her head, and voiced her concerns to Mary. "Where d'you think they've got to?"

Mary glanced at her watch and did her best to hide her own concern. It was just past four in the afternoon, so light wasn't a problem yet, and the plane was only about fifteen minutes overdue. The big issue was that the fog had started to come down early off the Solent, and already the visibility was down to about a mile and would, within the hour if she were any judge, be pushing landing visibility limits. At least they should be safe from any sneak raiders, she thought.

Lawrence had been due to land at spot-on four, and he was usually punctual to the minute. She was convinced a pool was operating on the time he landed and she suspected him of having a small scam going. Twenty minutes past, now, and her heart was beginning to sink. Thelma and Betty strolled over, and the sight of them arm in arm, considering what had happened, would normally be heartening, yet even this couldn't bring a smile to the ladies' faces at present.

"They're late," Thelma said—rather unnecessarily, Mary felt, and had to bite her tongue from saying something nobody needed to hear.

Doris, though, wasn't so backward in coming forward and treated the two women to a death stare. Mary, noticing and not wanting her friend to say anything untoward, pinched her bum, which had the desired effect.

Lying at their feet was Bobby. The spaniel's ears were flat to the ground, his paws either side of his head, though his big brown eyes were wide open. Betty reached down and scratched the top of his head, for something to occupy her hands, and sighed. The dog nuzzled into the fuss, and then his head jerked up and he jumped to his feet and started to bark, gaining everyone's attention. Bobby made to dart toward the landing field, and Doris managed to grab his collar just in time. With no way to break free, he contented himself with barking his head off.

Bobby's fame after warning everyone of the previous air raid had not only earned him free rein over the base, but enough tidbits that Ruth had started to mutter about putting him on a diet. Now alerted that something was coming, all eyes turned to the sky, scanning for Nazi raiders, determined not to be caught napping again. After another thirty-odd seconds, the steady drone of what everyone recognized as the Cheetah engines of an Avro Anson were heard.

Doris picked Bobby up in her arms, no easy task as he was still barking and squirming away, desperate to be the first to greet the incoming aircraft. Sure enough, appearing low out of the fog, came the Anson. She winced as the undercarriage clipped the tip of a tree, followed by a rather bumpier than normal landing. A short while later, the plane came to a halt in front of the flight line hut where they were waiting, the relieved ground crew running up to join them.

By the time the door was flung open, Doris and Mary were at the front of a queue of people waiting to greet and, perhaps in Thelma's case, berate them.

Sure enough, as soon as Penny jumped down to the ground, closely followed by Lawrence, Thelma had pushed her way to a place between them.

"Just where the hell did you two get to? We may call this a taxi service, but that doesn't mean to say you can just stooge around the sky for as long as you like!" Her brief tirade over, she wrapped them both in a huge hug. "And if you ever pull anything like that again, I'll ground the pair of you for a month!"

With all the paperwork finally signed, Lawrence sat with his head bowed in a battered wooden chair, Penny mirroring him. Bobby was lying in her lap, happiness leeching from every hair of his furry body. Penny didn't even seem aware she was stroking him.

"So," Mary began, sitting down on the wooden boards, "what happened?"

Lawrence glanced at Penny, and when it became clear she was too tired to speak, answered, "Worst weather I've seen in ages. We nearly didn't take off, and if we were RAF, they wouldn't have let us. Then we couldn't see where Hamble was, because of the fog, so we had to stooge around, hoping there'd be a break in the cloud that would let us see where we were. We got lucky and had the break we needed. I know we were a little low coming in..."

"A little low!" laughed Betty, as she came over with Thelma and Mary. "The ground crew have only just finished picking twigs out of the undercarriage."

"If it helps, I know the tree I hit. I can always put them back," Lawrence volunteered.

The joke had the effect of relaxing everyone, and even Bobby seemed to be shaking with laughter, though that could have been the result of everyone deciding to rub his stomach at the same time.

****

"Have you called it a day yet?" Doris asked Ruth, opening the door of the *Hamble Gazette* enough to let her head through and winking at Walter, who promptly knocked a glass of water over his desk.

An exasperated cry of, "Walter!" came from Ruth, as the hapless reporter hurried to stop the flow before it hit the floor. Ruth rose to let Doris in. She raised an eyebrow at the crowd of Betty, Thelma, Penny, Mary, and Lawrence accompanying her. Lawrence and Penny had dark circles under their eyes. Any questions she may have had were banished from her thoughts as Bobby barreled into the office in a state of high excitement, tail wagging twenty to a dozen. A brief chase ensued until Ruth cornered him and hoisted him up into her arms. "What's got into you, then?"

"Ignore him, Ruth," Doris advised. "He thinks he's the hero of the moment again."

Ruth promptly stepped outside and turned her eyes to the sky, by now virtually totally obscured by the fog. "I didn't hear an air raid warning," she exclaimed, still futilely searching the sky. "Been stuck at my desk all day. Did anyone get hurt?"

Thelma stepped away from where Penny and Lawrence had both settled down on a low wall.

Gesturing over her shoulder at the seated pair, Thelma laid a hand on Ruth's shoulder, reaching in to fuss Bobby again, causing him to almost wriggle out of his mistress's arms. "Those two had a, shall we say, fretful journey back, and had us all more than a bit worried. Bobby picked up their aircraft coming in before anyone else heard or saw a thing. It set a lot of worried minds to rest, I can assure you."

Ruth looked down at the bundle of fur in her arms and placed a hand on his stomach. "Hmm. I guess he's had a few more treats. Young man," she addressed her dog, waving a finger at his nose, "if you get any fatter, you won't fit in your basket!"

Bobby showed his appreciation of this by licking her finger, in case it held more food, and wagging his tail more furiously than ever.

"Yes, I'm very proud of you, again," she told him. "It would be nice if you spent the odd day here with me, though, instead of scrounging for food up at the airfield."

Mary joined the two of them, Doris having gone over to Walter's desk to help him clear up his latest mess. "Oh, don't, Ruth. Everyone loves having him around, especially in case we need those early warning ears of his."

Giving up holding him any longer, Ruth set Bobby down, and he immediately went and sat down next to Penny and laid his head on Lawrence's lap.

"To what do I owe this visit, then?" she asked Thelma.

"Doris," called Thelma, nearly causing Doris to fall off Walter's desk, where she'd been in the act of leaning in to steal a kiss, "if you could put Walter down for a second, come and explain what you've just told us. Betty!" she said over her shoulder. "You'd better come over too."

Once the sign on the door had been turned to Closed and Walter had made and brought over cups of tea, including those for Penny and Lawrence, who claimed they were too tired to move. Once everyone had taken a seat, including Doris, who settled back on the edge of Walter's desk, Thelma asked Doris to explain her idea.

"I was thinking, whilst we were waiting for those two to get back, about tracking down this Bramble guy. I mean, there can't be many doctors with that name in England, can there? If even Lawrence's enquiries can't track his whereabouts down, and the General Medical Council—I think that's what you called it—can't help, then he's obviously gone underground."

Ruth had gone into newspaper editor mode. "All very interesting, but if even the Special Branch can't track him down, what makes you think you can help?"

Doris treated everyone to her best predatory grin. "Oh, don't let this sweet demeanor put you off. I lived in Brooklyn, New York, the only place my husband and I could afford, and where, well…if you didn't go out in pairs, you simply didn't go out." Cue everyone's eyelashes heading toward their foreheads. "I've a friend I went to school with who's on the books of the US Embassy's Press Office. Let's say he owes me a favor or two."

"So you think he may be able to help with finding

this bloke?" Ruth asked.

Doris shrugged. "I think he's our best bet. Who knows what the police will find, but if we want to do something, fellow Marples, then we need a contact in the black market. Forget all this crap of us Yanks having everything we could want. That may still be true back home, but here, though the embassy will eat better than most, if they want a little extra, I'm sure they'd use the black market the same as you and me. To do that, they'd need someone who would have those contacts, and Eddie would be that man."

Walter, looking more than a little concerned, asked, "And how do you know he's here?"

"Got a letter from him the other week, telling me he was over and asking if we can meet up. It's okay," she said reassuringly, upon seeing a frown appear on his forehead. "He's just a friend. Anyway," she carried on from where she'd left off, "wherever he's gone, he's always been the person to go to if you need something. He may only have been here a short time, but I'd bet my last dollar he already knows how to get anything he wants, and that means he knows people."

"And you want to go and talk to him. Right?" Ruth asked. "You can't ask him over the phone?"

Doris shook her head. "Besides wanting to catch up with a *friend*"—she emphasized the word for Walter's sake—"this isn't the kind of thing you ask over the phone."

****

As they walked down Piccadilly the next day, the Ritz in their sights, Walter squeezed Doris's hand, barely containing his excitement. "I can't believe Jane gave you the day off. What did you tell her?"

M. W. Arnold

Doris pulled her coat tighter around her shoulders and shrugged. "Not me. Betty and Thelma went to see her after we'd been to fill you and Ruth in, and they just said she'd given her okay."

Walter stopped suddenly, making Doris halt as well. "How much do you think they told her?"

"No idea," she admitted. "Either way, we're here now."

"Come on," she said, pulling his hand, "or we'll be late, and you don't want to miss afternoon tea at the Ritz, I've been led to believe."

****

"I'm Eddie Winters," said a thin rake of a man as he got to his feet. His messy black hair was badly in need of a cut. Doris happily received a kiss on her cheek, whilst Walter, a little reluctantly, shook Eddie's hand as he continued, "Doris, so good to see you again. Shame it's in the middle of a war zone. And Walter, Doris tells me you're a newspaper man?"

Taking back his seat, Walter studied this man, only the second American he'd ever met. What was it about this race? Were they all born with an excess of personality?

"Not sure if what you call a newspaper man's the same as what I actually do. I'm merely a reporter on a local newspaper," he told him.

"Doesn't really matter what I think, Walter," Eddie said, turning serious, "so long as what we discuss today doesn't make any of the papers, no matter how small. I had to pull in a lot of favors to get this post, and I'm not going to lose it for anyone," he added with a wry smile.

"I had a feeling you'd say something like that," Walter said, holding open his suit jacket. "See, no

198

notepads, not even a pencil. Believe me, and you should appreciate this, it feels like I've gone out naked."

This being his first time at the Ritz, Walter could feel his eyes bulging in shock. It was difficult to believe a war was on, to look around. It appeared most of England's upper class was still able to take high tea, and even though he knew that eating out was off the ration, it obviously made a big difference where that was. His only quibble was that Doris had told him she was paying. He'd been brought up to believe a woman shouldn't pay when they went out. However, what he earned at the paper barely allowed him to spring to the odd beer and cinema outing, let alone what this place would cost. She'd told him about her status as a millionaire, and he was determined to work on his feelings, as he found her irresistible.

The irresistible American nudged him in the ribs. "Walter, you can stop being polite now. We've caught up, and it's time to pay attention."

"Right, okay," he agreed, glad that this coincided with the appearance of the afternoon tea. "Bugger me!" he exclaimed after the waitress had made her exit.

"This dame's worth paying a service charge for, my friend," Eddie told him.

If this was what this spread was in wartime London, what would it be like in peacetime? Walter didn't know what extra the service charge got you, but there were cucumber sandwiches, next to smoked salmon. Egg and watercress shared another tier with cheddar cheese, and those were only the sandwiches he could see. On another tier were both plain and raisin scones, with little pots of clotted cream and strawberry jam. His first thought was to check that he wasn't dribbling and drooling. Across the table, Doris was placing a few sandwiches and a scone on her plate, whilst Eddie was pouring tea for them both.

Accepting the pot, Walter poured himself a cup, added a dash of milk, and took a sip. Earl Grey—not his favorite, but he'd put up with it. Once everyone had filled their plates and taken their first few bites, Doris dabbed a serviette to her lips. "Thanks for meeting us, Eddie. I need to ask you a favor."

"Go ahead, babe. You've more than a few favors to pull in," he offered.

Doris took another sip of tea before answering. "I need you to find a doctor who's working on the black market, specifically to do with draft dodging. The name's Bramble."

Eddie leant back in his chair and devoured a cucumber sandwich before answering. "It's not much to go on, though the field should help. Any first name? What does he look like?"

"Sorry, that's it," Doris said apologetically, trying to think why they hadn't asked Shirley or Thelma for a description and pondering that Miss Marple wouldn't have made the same mistake, "but I can't emphasize how important this is—literally a matter of life and death."

"More specifically, death," Walter felt inclined to add.

"And how soon do you need this information?" Eddie asked.

"Yesterday," stated Doris plainly.

Chapter Twenty-One

The sound of laughter rang clear as a bell through the open window of Betty's lounge.

"Could that be them?" Ruth asked the room in general, twitching the curtain aside as quickly as she could.

The unmistakable timbre of Doris's voice shouting, "I never said you had two left feet!" at the top of her voice gave them their answer.

"I'll go and put on the kettle and warm up some stew," volunteered Mary.

"Achoo!" put in Penny. "Sorry. Wasn't expecting that one," she added, blowing her nose before settling back under a blanket on the sofa.

The sound of a key in the front door perked everyone's ears up, and their eyes nearly went out on stalks when Doris and Walter tumbled through. One of Doris's arms was draped around Walter's waist, one of his around her shoulders, and both their faces were decidedly flushed. Upon closer inspection, Walter's face was marked with kiss outlines that perfectly matched Doris's shade of lipstick.

Mary came in behind them with a tray of cups and the teapot. "Excuse me," she said, pushing gently past the two and placing it on the table in front of Penny. Upon seeing the state of the newcomers, she promptly flopped down onto the sofa, barely missing her friend's feet. "Oh, my God! Well, I guess that explains the laughter."

This prompted Doris and Walter to start laughing again, and Doris grabbed Walter's face between her hands and planted a huge, wet kiss upon his face before pulling away and taking a seat.

At this point, Betty and Ruth gave up trying to keep straight faces, and before long the whole room seemed to radiate happiness. Eventually, everyone managed to settle, and Mary handed the two newcomers a cup each. "Still not as good as coffee," Doris announced to no one's particular surprise, scrunching up a little so Walter could perch on the edge of her seat.

"So we can assume the two of you are a couple now," decided Betty, barely waiting for the two to exchange knowing looks and lean their foreheads together. "Would you care to tell us what happened in London? Did you have any luck?"

"I managed to persuade this beautiful lady to step out with me," Walter said and managed to duck in time to avoid the cushion Penny threw at his head.

"I think we'd all surmised that," Ruth told him, though as her lips were twitching at the edges, everyone knew she wasn't really annoyed. Indeed, she reached across and patted his knee.

"What can I say?" Doris chipped in, replacing Ruth's hand with her own. "We went dancing and he swept me off my feet, my badly bruised feet."

"Hey!"

Doris pecked his cheek. "He can be very persuasive when he wants to be."

"Aw," issued from Betty's lips, "now I don't mean

to toss water onto a fire, but we'll celebrate this later. Can you tell us what happened? Did you meet your friend, Doris?"

Everyone could see that Doris had to tear her attention away from Walter before she was able to answer.

"Yes, of course. Sorry, Betty," she apologized. "We were able to see Eddie."

"And was he able to help?"

"I hope so. We had a talk, and we gave him all the information we had. If we could get his first name, that'd help, but as we don't have it"—she shrugged resignedly—"he couldn't make any promises. I gave him your work phone number, Ruth. I hope that's all right?"

"Not a problem with me," Ruth told them. "I hadn't thought of that. I suppose that was your idea, Walter?" She held up a hand. "Don't worry, you did right."

Mary got up to answer a knock on the door, bringing in two more members of their group, Lawrence and Shirley.

"Hi, Aunt Ruth, everyone," announced Lawrence, whilst Shirley, still in awe at being included and having friends, waved shyly back.

"You'll have to bring in a couple of chairs from the kitchen," Mary advised.

"So what have we missed?" Lawrence asked after the two had found places to put their chairs.

Doris filled him in and then waited for the policeman to take in the little information and comment. "You're right," he agreed. "It's not much for him to go on. Do you think he'll have any luck?"

"If anyone can do it, Eddie can," Doris told the room.

"I might know something that could help," Shirley said, actually raising her hand like she was at school. This had the good effect of everyone noticing she'd spoken, as only Lawrence, who sat next to her, had actually heard her at first. She repeated a little louder, causing Betty to lean forward.

"What've you got?"

Shirley coughed to clear her throat, slightly nervous because everyone's attention was on her. "If we had this doctor's first name, it'd help to track him down, right? And even the police don't know his full name?"

Lawrence shook his head. "I checked with my bosses, and they can't find a Doctor Bramble anywhere, so it could be an alias. If so, then that makes it even more difficult to find the bugger, especially with manpower as it is."

Ruth stopped tapping her finger on her teeth to ask a question. "So even if you can get hold of this person, it wouldn't be the end of this dodge?"

Lawrence treated the room at large to his best grin, and Doris nodded, impressed. "Let's just say, if we can get our clutches on him, I think he could be persuaded to give up some names pretty quickly."

"How do you think you could help?" she asked Shirley.

"Could I see Eleanor's death certificate, please, Betty?" she asked, shrinking into her seat in case Betty shouted at her. It'd take a while before she would get used to having people she could trust again.

Without waiting to ask why, Betty hurried upstairs,

and there were the sounds of rummaging and cupboard doors being banged. Then, slightly out of breath, she was back and thrusting the certificate into Shirley's hands.

Patience had never been one of Doris's attributes, and when the only difference in Shirley was that her brows furrowed, Walter had to keep a firm grip on Doris's hands to stop her from interrupting. "Give her time."

Finally, Shirley got to her feet and went to kneel beside Betty, placing the certificate on her lap. "Look." She pointed to the signature. "Would you agree that this looks like a C?" Betty moved the certificate close to the end of her nose for a closer look and nodded. "In that case, it'd tally with a name I heard being called whilst I was waiting for...you know what. I think his first name is Casey. Or at least that's what he could be going under."

By way of answering, Betty dropped to her knees and hugged Shirley, who a little nervously wrapped her arms around Betty and hugged her back.

Penny threw her legs onto Mary's lap, sniffed, and said, "I know you'll pass that on to your lads, Lawrence, but Doris, do you think you could let your friend know that name tonight?"

By way of an answer, Doris got to her feet. "Not a problem. He's a press man. They never sleep. Bobby!" She slapped her hand against her hip, and Bobby raised an ear to show she had his attention. "Come on, walkies!"

The W word had the normal effect. With a lot of scratching of his ear and stretching, Bobby trotted over.

"Good boy," Doris praised him and held out her

hand to Walter.

"Oh, no, you don't," Ruth piped up. "I need to have a word with this young man. You go and make that call, and you, my lad, go upstairs and wash that lipstick off your face."

****

Left temporarily alone, Lawrence had insisted upon accompanying Doris to the phone box. With everyone else pootling around in the kitchen, Betty took down her sister's reframed picture from the mantelpiece.

"I haven't forgotten you," she whispered, having taken a quick look around to see if she could be overheard. "Never. We'll get them, Ele, I promise. We'll find who murdered you." She brought the picture up and pressed it to her lips.

"Ahem."

Betty wiped her eyes dry and looked around. Standing in the open doorway, unsure whether she should turn around or come in, was Shirley. The poor thing was wringing her hands together and kept glancing over her shoulder. Betty beckoned her in.

"I'm sorry," Shirley told her, taking a seat near the window, as far from Betty as she could in the otherwise empty room. "I didn't mean to disturb you."

"That's okay," Betty said, glancing once more at the photo before putting it back in its place.

Shirley's eyes followed Betty's to the frame. "That's your sister, then."

Betty nodded, but words wouldn't come to her throat.

"I wanted to say, Betty…" Shirley started, but was interrupted as Betty got to her feet and came and sat beside her.

"If you were going to apologize again, then please don't. There's no need, and I won't hear of it. You were in an impossible situation, and you came clean to us before any harm was done. That says a lot about you."

"Am I disturbing anything?" Ruth asked, hovering in the door, a perennial cup of tea in her hands.

Shirley spoke first. "No, Ruth, of course not." Then she surprised them all by calling out for Mary and Walter to come and join them.

"You hollered?" Mary enquired, as they both took a seat.

"Yes, there's one more thing I forgot to mention earlier, and as I don't want to have any more skeletons in the closet..." She trailed off and had to collect her nerves again, as everyone had shuffled forward in their seats as she spoke.

"Carry on," Betty told her gently and smiled in encouragement.

Taking heart from Betty's words, Shirley cleared her throat. "Before Lawrence ran me down tonight, I'd been in The Victory with...Ralph Johnson. He wanted to know if I'd been asked to look out for anything else, besides the thermos, or to try and get any other information out of you, Betty." After a few moments for everyone to take in what she'd just told them, Shirley added, "But there wasn't anything more, and all that's in the past."

"Does he know you've, well, changed sides?" asked Ruth.

"No," Shirley replied, "or, I should say, not yet."

"Hmm." Ruth sipped her tea whilst thinking and then looked up at Shirley, a gleam in her eye. "That could work in our favor. If you think you can do it, you could be our little double agent!"

****

"Did you hear something?" Doris asked, gripping Lawrence's arm whilst turning her head to look behind them.

"Do you really think we're being followed?" Lawrence asked, wishing—and not for the first time—that he could use a torch.

Doris nodded and then, remembering that he wouldn't be able to see her, told him, "I may be paranoid, but I can think of one person who's got reason to be watching us."

"Ralph Johnson." He filled in the blank.

"Exactly." A thought then struck her. "Isn't there anything we can do about him? You know, lock up the bugger and throw away the key? That type of thing?"

Lawrence laughed before replying. "Now, wouldn't that be nice. Unfortunately, we're the good guys, so no matter how nice it'd be to throw him in the nick, we still need a reason. Until he does something stupid, which from what I've seen of him around the airfield shouldn't be difficult. Meanwhile, we'll just have to be careful."

"Ralph!" Doris took Lawrence by surprise by shouting at the top of her voice. "We know what you're up to, so do us all a favor and keep the hell away from us!"

By now, they'd reached the gate to Betty's cottage, and not only was Lawrence digging a finger in his ear but Doris's outburst had drawn everyone out of the cottage.

"What the hell was all that about?" asked Penny, her eyes staring out into the dark in wonder.

Coming through the gate, by the time they reached the small crowd, Doris's face had gone a nice shade of red. Fortunately for her, the darkness of the night hid her embarrassment. "Yes, er, um, sorry about that, everyone. I didn't mean to get you out into the cold."

"All very well," Ruth said, "but why did you yell? You scared the living daylights out of us!"

Lawrence took pity upon her and taking hold of her shoulders propelled her into the house. He waited until everyone had come back in before answering. "It's nothing. She got a little spooked, and I think just yelled something out to make her feel a bit better."

But Doris wasn't having that, and now she'd recovered somewhat from her embarrassment, spoke up. "That's kind of true, but it really did feel like someone was watching us, and Ralph was the only one who came to mind."

Both Ruth and Betty went to take a look up and down the river bank and when satisfied nothing and no one was in sight, made sure the front door was locked behind them.

No one saw Ralph peek out from behind a large oak tree, his eyes nervously searching left and right before slinking off into the night.

Chapter Twenty-Two

It'd been a full ten minutes since Mary had seen the ground. She'd reversed course twice, but it hadn't made a difference. Being able to see what was below you was a lot easier when the view didn't resemble a blanket of cotton wool.

Looking over the side of the open cockpit of her Miles Magister, her frustration grew as every now and then she caught a fleeting glimpse of green or brown—no blue yet or she'd be over the sea and definitely in deep trouble. More than a glimpse would be nice. Though the drone of her engine was reassuring, the state of her fuel gauge was worrying.

What had started as a relaxing training flight toward the end of the day was rapidly turning into a bad idea. If she crashed, not only would Jane be onto her case, but she'd heard that crashing could sting. If she'd have known about this change in weather, she wouldn't have taken off. Met hadn't anything on the board, so off she'd gone, and now she was wondering if she'd get down in one piece. Glancing down at her attire, Mary regretted now taking off in her regulation skirt rather than slacks or her flying suit, having been taken in by the warm weather. She wasn't a prude, but she didn't relish bailing out and coming down to earth showing her stockings and rather large silk knickers (made from parachute silk she'd been given by an RAF airman hoping to curry favor at one of her deliveries) to all and sundry.

Five minutes later, with her fuel gauge hovering over the red line and her anxiety mounting, she caught a sudden break in the weather and a fleeting glimpse of what looked like an airfield below her. Despite her misgivings about diving through cloud, she had a split second to make a decision before she lost her chance, and she took it. With her eyes locked on the break, she turned and dove, wisps of cloud flashing by. As she entered the break, she held her breath, praying it would last. A few seconds later, her luck held and she was through. Looking around, she didn't recognize any landmarks, so with dwindling fuel and no other choice, she set the nose of her plane toward the runway she could make out and, despite noting a red flare bursting off her port beam, thirty seconds later had landed. Breathing a sigh of relief, she taxied over to where some C47 transport aircraft were parked.

As she switched off the engine, a Jeep screeched up and, to her surprise, two American officers hopped out.

"What the hell d'you think you're playing at, bud?" yelled the first to reach her plane. "Didn't you hear us telling you we're closed?"

Though she knew there wasn't anything they could do to her, Mary took a few minutes longer than she'd normally allow for her post-flight checks, as her nerves were still jangling from the stress of the near miss she'd had, and she wanted the extra time to calm down. When she was ready, she stood up, and with her personal bag clutched to her side, climbed out of the cockpit. Forgetting who was watching, not that she had much choice anyway, she showed a pair of shapely stocking-clad legs to her audience who, judging by the way their eyes bulged, were dumbstruck by the unexpected show.

"Holy cow!" exclaimed the one who was still behind the steering wheel, taking off his cap to wipe his forehead. "It's a goddamn dame!"

Deciding it'd be best if she took the high ground straight away, Mary fixed first one, then the other, with her best winning smile. "I should think so too, gentlemen. These stockings were hard enough to come by, and one wouldn't wish to waste them."

"Don't just stand there gaping, Pete," shouted the one in the Jeep. "Help the lady down."

Mary didn't let Pete have the chance, as she'd decided she wanted to keep them off balance for a while longer, so she jumped down off the wing before this Pete could get to her. It helped that both were good-looking. Both still had tans, too, which told her they hadn't been in England long.

The one called Pete, looking much friendlier now he saw he was greeting a female pilot, held out his hand. "Pleased to meet you, ma'am. First Lieutenant Pete Gabrowski at your service." He jabbed his thumb over his shoulder. "The big mouth there's Second Lieutenant Donald Westheath."

Mary shook his hand. "Pleased to meet you, Pete. I'm Mary Whitworth-Baines, Third Officer in the ATA."

They'd now been joined by Donald. "Call me Don, please," he began and then looked over the Miles Magister she'd just landed. "Pardon me for asking, but what's the ATA, and what're you doing here? The station commander's in a right snit and shooed us out to find out what's going on."

Mary explained the purpose of the ATA was to transport aircraft to units but was interrupted by Pete before she could elaborate.

"Sorry to interrupt," he began, again touching an imaginary forelock, "but we're a transport squadron, and I'm pretty sure we aren't waiting upon anything like this," he ended, slapping a hand on the wing.

"I'm sure you're not," she agreed, whilst removing his hand from the wing, "and believe me, it's only the weather's fault I had to land here at all."

"D'you mind my asking what you were doing up in this crap anyway?" Donald asked. "As far as I know, everything below Birmingham's grounded."

Mary pasted a sheepish expression upon her face. "In my defense, I'll be having words with our Met officer when I get back. Clear skies, my foot!"

This little joke served to break any remaining ice. "Come on," Pete told her. "I don't think you've a chance in hell of getting off today, so let's get you something to eat and fix you up with a bunk for the night."

****

"What d'you mean, you fly with no radio?" Donald asked, not believing what he'd just heard.

They were now in the mess of what she'd had explained to her was the 62nd Troop Carrier Group at a station called RAF Keevil, only recently arrived from some place called South Carolina. They'd swiftly squared things with the station commander who, also an American, had proved very hospitable once she'd explained how she came to be there. He had made certain she was comfortable for the night and had even told her he'd call up Hamble and let her people know where she was.

Mary savored the slice of steak she'd just put in her mouth before answering. What she'd heard about American bases from her friends was proving true. Very kind and friendly people—and as for the food! Not quite the quality that the Savoy, the Ritz, or other top London eateries could still provide, but not far off it, and the quantity was such she thought she'd need to change into slacks to fly back tomorrow.

Opening her eyes as the steak slithered down her throat, lubricated with copious quantities of gravy, she noticed the table where she sat had gathered quite a crowd, all men, something Pete, who sat directly to her left, didn't look very happy about. However, she'd been asked a question and so, whilst cutting off another thick slice of steak, turned her head to her right to answer.

"Quite normal, believe it or not. We've no radio and, when we're flying, say, Spitfires, no ammunition either."

A general shaking of heads accompanied this statement, and someone from the crowd piped up, "Y'all fly pursuit planes?" in a tone of voice that indicated he didn't believe her.

"If you mean fighters, of course we do. I personally think they don't arm them in case we take it into our heads to go and win the war on our own," she threw back, determined to keep the conversation tone light. Then she clarified more seriously once everyone had had a little chuckle. "Seriously, though, we fly everything the RAF uses, to anywhere in the United Kingdom."

"And it's an all-women unit?" asked one pilot.

Mary shook her head. "By no means. There're quite a few women, don't ask me for an exact number, but the majority are men. However, at my base, we're all women, bar one man who flies our taxi aircraft."

"Hot damn!" swore Donald. "How do I get a transfer?"

That cracked everyone up, though the mood became more serious when the station commander appeared in their midst.

"There you are, Mary," he said, pulling up a chair from another table behind her and straddling a leg either side. "I wanted to let you know I've spoken to your boss—Jane, I believe she said her name was. Sounded like a very nice broad," he added, "who thanked me for letting her know where you were. She was very relieved to hear you were in one piece and said that, assuming the weather's okay tomorrow, you're to be back at base by ten. She also said she'd be very interested to know how you ended up in Wiltshire."

"Thank you, sir," she told him, blushing. Then, as she hadn't had the chance when she'd first met him, "I'd like to thank you for your hospitality, sir..."

"Call me Frank," he told her, smiling.

"Frank," she said, noting how many of those gathered around the table were nudging each other. "I mean it, you've all been very kind to me, and the food, well, what can I say? It's been a while since I've eaten this well."

"I'm sure the cooks will be very happy to hear that. Now," he said, "if you'll excuse me, duty calls. As for the rest of you guys..." He stood surveying his men. "Haven't you seen a woman in uniform before? Stop crowding her and find something else to do."

Once everyone dispersed except Pete and Donald, Mary relaxed a little more and finished her meal in peace. Pushing her plate forward, she let out a long sigh. "Gentlemen, please indeed pass my compliments to the chefs. I don't think I could eat another sausage."

Donald got to his feet and returned a few minutes later with a large dish of chocolate ice cream. "I don't know about a sausage, Mary, but I hope you've room to force this down."

Mary tugged at the waistband of her skirt. "I think I've about half an inch to play with. I'll give it a go." So saying, she took up her spoon and dug in. The ice cream was delicious, and she had to make a deliberate effort not to wolf it down as quickly as she could. Once she'd finished and had collapsed back into her seat, she toyed with the cup of coffee in front of her.

Pete broke the silence. "So how did you come to drop into our laps?"

"Lucky," she told them, "very lucky. If there hadn't been a hole in the clouds, I'd likely have dropped, literally, into your laps when I ran out of fuel, and that would only have been another five or so minutes."

"I'm not being funny," he continued, "but couldn't you navigate back to base?"

Mary knew what she was about to tell him would be yet another surprise. The truth often was. "Couldn't. We're not taught to fly by instruments. It's a map and number one eyeball."

As she'd expected, both Pete and Donald, the only occupants left at the table, were wide-eyed in amazement. "You mean you don't know how to blind

216

fly?" asked Pete, needing her to confirm what she'd said.

"Afraid not."

"And you still managed to get down in one piece? Mary," Pete said, "that's a hell of a piece of flying."

Donald appeared equally as eager to talk flying, perhaps more so if she read the way he was leaning toward her as he spoke. "Would you like a go on our Link Trainer?"

The word "trainer" got her attention, though she had no idea what he was talking about and asked him to explain.

"It's basically a flight simulator we have here."

"Flight simulator?" Mary had heard of them but had never seen one.

"Think of a tiny plane that doesn't fly but sits in a room and mimics the actions of a plane without going out of the room it's in."

"Sounds very useful," Mary agreed, "but how can that help me with flying on instruments?"

Pete jumped ahead of his friend. "Ah, this is the clever bit. It's got a hood that goes over the cockpit area so you can't see outside, and you have to fly by using the instruments only."

Now they really had her attention. Even more so when Pete brought out a pen and started to explain some pointers whilst drawing and scribbling on the white linen tablecloth.

"There're some things you must remember when you lose visibility. The first—don't shoot the messenger—is to straighten up. No one really flies into cloud, mist, or fog, as the first thing you'd want to do is to look for a way around. Also, try and always

217

remember the last spot height on your map, then add a safe margin, turn through one-eighty degrees, and descend as smoothly and steadily as you can. All the time you're doing this, think. Keep thinking, as you must remain alert."

"Anything else?" Mary prodded, hoping they'd be offering her a stint in this trainer. Her hands were literally itching to get hold of it.

"Well, yes," Donald said a little hesitatingly, "but you're not going to like it."

"Go on."

"If there's still no visibility at your safe break-off height and you're running on fumes, point the nose to the sky, climb fast, and bail out."

Once more, Mary looked down at what she was wearing. "I'm glad I was able to land, or else you lot would have had quite a sight as I floated down."

"Ahem," Donald cleared his throat and began, "I for one wouldn't have min—"

He was promptly cut off by Pete. "I don't think there's a need for you to finish up, Don."

Deciding that young Donald had suffered enough, Mary patted him on the arm and asked the question she'd been dying to get out since he'd first mentioned the simulator.

"So, Pete, is it too late to have a go on this thing?"

Pete treated her to a wide grin. "As it happens, I know the guy who's in charge of it, and he could be persuaded to open up the room."

"Something tells me he isn't too far away," she speculated.

Pete dug a hand in his pocket and held up a key.

****

Upon touching down at Hamble around nine thirty the next morning, Mary wasn't one bit surprised to see Jane waiting for her as she taxied in. "Damn. Looks like I'm in trouble."

"What was that?" came the query from the front seat, closely followed by, "Ouch. That hurt, Mary!"

"Sorry, Pete," she apologized, "I always seem to hit that hole, but I think your sore back could be the least of our worries."

Five minutes later, Mary and Pete had climbed down and, at least in Mary's case, were waiting somewhat nervously for Jane Howell to finish striding up to where they stood next to the aircraft.

"You amaze me, Miss Whitworth-Baines. Not only do you decide it's a great idea to take off for a training flight at four thirty in the afternoon, when you know how quickly the weather can close in around here, you get yourself stuck at a strange base, and you manage to come back home with one more crew than the aircraft took off with! All in all, congratulations on a most remarkable sortie." She turned her attention to the young man in an unfamiliar flying suit who stood to one side of Mary, struggling to keep an amused expression off his face. "And just who are you?"

Pete quickly pulled out his cap from within his suit, put it on at what could only be described as a jaunty angle, and threw her a quick salute, which Jane didn't trouble to return, not that this seemed to bother him. "First Lieutenant Pete Gabrowski, ma'am."

Not to be put off by his obvious American charms, Jane placed both hands on her hips and asked, "And to what do we owe the pleasure of your company, First Lieutenant Pete Gabrowski?"

Further conversation was deemed impossible by the roar of a low flying C47 transport passing by overhead and proceeding to land, then to taxi in the group's direction. Noting its USAAF markings, Jane noticed many station personnel were watching, either never having seen that type of aircraft before or, more likely, never having seen an American-crewed plane up close before.

"Friends of yours, First Lieutenant?" she asked, before they all had to cover their ears. Pete just had time to grin and give the thumbs up before the twin-engined aircraft pulled to a stop and finally powered down on the far side of Mary's Magister.

"I'm sorry for the surprise, boss." Jane noted her deference to rank, rather than the usual first name she preferred no matter the situation. "Pete and his friend Donald, who's waving at us from the C47, were very good to me when I had to put down at Keevil, and as they don't have anything on today, they wanted to see where we are."

"See where we are?" Jane spluttered, her cheeks getting red.

Mary had noticed this and hurried on, trying to head off Jane taking out her anger on her American friends.

"Sorry. They honestly were curious, as they'd never seen an all-female flying unit before, but they won't stay long."

"And the C47?" Jane wanted to know.

"That I don't think you'll mind," Mary told her, risking a smile. When she wasn't immediately answered, she looked up at where Donald still stood in the open doorway and nodded her head. Pete trotted over to his friend, reached up to accept a large silver-colored drum, and staggered back to where Jane and Mary were waiting.

"One gallon of raspberry ripple, ma'am. With the compliments of our commanding officer, Frank Burrows. He's the guy you talked to about Mary yesterday evening, in case you don't remember," he added.

Mary was certain she saw a blush begin to creep up Jane's cheeks and decided it wasn't a good idea to risk her temper again by asking if a certain soft-voiced American commander was to blame.

"And I've another twenty gallons on board for you, ma'am," Donald yelled, nudging another couple of drums into the doorway.

Pete put his drum down at his feet and addressed Jane, who seemed to have been struck temporarily dumb. "Ma'am. Think of this as a gesture of appreciation, appreciation of a remarkable show of airmanship by Mary here in getting down safely yesterday. Plus, she was a credit to the ATA whilst we hosted her. We're a long way from home, and she entertained us yesterday evening with some great stories that meant, for the first time since we've been here, we didn't feel homesick."

Jane took a few moments to take stock of what Pete had said and to notice that some of the ground crew were eagerly engaged in unloading the drums of ice cream. To give her some thinking time, she called over the mess manager. "Make sure every drum—and I mean *every* drum—gets to the kitchens. Also, inform the quartermaster that none of these drums are to be opened until I say so. I shall hold both of you responsible. Understood?"

Mary could swear that the sergeant's mumbled, "Yes, ma'am," was very reluctant, but Jane let him trot away to supervise the unloading.

She now turned back to where Mary and Pete were watching her. "Mary, ordinarily, I'd give you a right rollicking…" She paused when she saw the confused expression upon Pete's face. "That means I'd yell at her," she informed him. When he nodded, she turned her attention back to Mary. "However, as you seem to have made some good friends, and in the spirit of enhancing good relations between our two countries, Pete"—she held out her hand to him to shake—"I gladly accept your commander's kind gift. Please let him know that I shall be calling him later this afternoon to thank him personally. It's been a long time, a very long time, since a lot of people here have had ice cream, so this will make a very welcome change over spotted dick. Again, my thanks."

"Spotted dick?" Pete asked Mary.

"Don't ask," she advised, as Jane treated the two to a smile and then headed over toward the kitchen block.

"So," Mary began, "how long can you stay?"

"Not long, to be honest," he replied, shaking his head. "Despite what I said, this literally is a flying trip to deliver the ice cream."

"Pity," Mary said and quickly ran into the flight line hut before trudging dejectedly back. "You can't even meet any of my friends. Looks like they're all out on deliveries."

The melancholy mood was happily interrupted by a loud woofing. Bounding over toward them from the direction of the main gate was Bobby, who only stopped barking when he slid to a halt at Mary's feet. Dropping to a knee, she gave him a welcoming fuss behind the ears.

"Who's this, then?" Pete asked, joining her.

"This is our early warning system."

"Your what?" he asked, laughing at both her answer and the dog, who'd flopped down onto his back for a tummy rub.

"That's what we all call him," Mary said. "He's a friend's and is actually called Bobby, but a few weeks ago his barking alerted us to a Nazi hit-and-run raid that we'd had no warning of. Ever since, he's had the run of the station and as many tidbits as he can eat."

"Do you think he likes chocolate fudge ice cream?" Pete asked.

Chapter Twenty-Three

The Grand Rover wasn't the place a gentleman such as Group Captain George Evans normally frequented. He suppressed a shudder as he looked around, then checked that the Webley revolver he had secreted in his overcoat pocket was still there. As it wasn't quite eleven in the morning, there were only a few people present, making it easier to keep an eye out for unwanted interlopers.

As the door opened and another person who wasn't the one he was expecting came in and made for the bar, the Group Captain watched the barman spit in a pint glass and proceed to polish it as if this were a scene in a cheap film. He pushed his own glass of what was supposed to be whisky a little farther away from him and checked his watch once more. The doctor was late, again. If he didn't turn up today, then he'd have to risk going to his lodgings himself. Not that he wanted to, as those were in an even more insalubrious location than this public house.

It had turned half past and he was doing up the last of his coat buttons against the rainy late September weather when the door to the pub crashed open and in stumbled the doctor.

"Sorry, sorry," he stammered, nearly knocking over multiple chairs in his haste to get to where Evans stood, his back to the wall. "Blame the underground.

Another thing that's not as good as pre-war."

Now he'd finally arrived, Evans unbuttoned his coat and sat back down. He still didn't touch his drink, and neither did he offer to buy one for the doctor. "Never mind the state of the underground, Bramble. Sit down and listen."

Bramble opened his mouth to argue but then saw the expression upon his compatriot's face and decided against it. Instead he took his seat and waited.

"To business," Evans began, pulling a small black notebook out of a pocket. "I've heard certain bovine gentlemen have been sniffing around, asking questions about me…and about you, Doctor."

"About me?" Bramble let out a nervous laugh that did nothing to hide his growing anxiety. "What would they want me for?"

The laughter that came from Evans was nothing like Bramble's. It was laughter that would have the dead shaking in their bones. Bramble hadn't heard it from the Group Captain in a while—in fact, not since the man's wife had taken over his enterprises—and he'd hoped never to hear it again.

"What would they want with you?" Evans echoed. "Are you joking? Let me see… My sources tell me you're under investigation in relation to my wife's draft-dodging scheme, and then there's the little matter of you poisoning that girl at Luton. Would you like me to go on? I'm sure I can come up with something else."

The doctor had taken out a handkerchief to mop his brow as Evans spoke and was now wondering if he should have followed his first instinct upon waking that morning—to try to make a run for it.

"Now, if I was you, I'd be looking at arranging a

safe passage to America. It'd be much easier for you to hide there than in England. The longer you're here, the greater danger we're both in, and, my dear doctor, this is entirely of your own making."

"Mine?" the doctor exclaimed incredulously whilst wondering if his mind was being read, but he didn't get anything else out as Evans immediately raised his voice.

"Yes, your own. I knew how desperate you were for money as soon as I saw you at the Savoy. You always have been, since school. You had no qualms about slipping a mickey finn into that girl's thermos, but no, you had to bugger that up. Then you got yourself caught up in my dear Virginia's scheme. I suppose she caught whiff of your hunger for money too?"

Doctor Bramble could only sit there with his mouth hanging open.

"Well, the time's come to make sure there are no loose ends, at least so far as that dead girl's concerned. The time has come for you to think, and think hard, as both our lives may well depend upon it at some point. Are there any loose ends to tie up?"

As he finished, Evans made sure the doctor caught sight of his revolver by deliberately flicking his coat to one side, then raised his eyebrows in an unmistakable gesture; he should think very carefully before opening his mouth.

Gulping, the doctor held up a hand to tick off on his fingers. "Firstly, I took the coroner out for dinner, and by the end of the night he was in agreement that there were no suspicious circumstances to warrant an autopsy. If he ever decided to change his mind, certain incriminating photographs would reach the papers, ones I'm certain his wife wouldn't care for."

"Devious," Evans admitted, "and the whereabouts of these pictures?"

Subservience was the trick to Bramble's survival at present. "They're safe, that's all you need to know, and no, he doesn't know anything about you."

Evans sat back, briefly considered his doctor, and decided so long as this coroner didn't know him, he could dismiss the photos. Of course, if proof came to him this was any different, it would be a completely different matter. "Go on."

Before Bramble had a chance to reply, the door of the pub banged open and the sight of the two people who'd made such a dramatic entrance made his breath catch in his throat. Resplendent in sparkling white boots and a flowing brown fur coat that trailed behind her as she strode toward them from the closing doors, was Virginia. Her face looked as if she were chewing a bee. Close behind her strode one of Evans' ex-enforcers. He went by the name of Big John, though his given name was Winston. As he had hands the size of shovels, everyone was happy to let him be called whatever he wanted.

With a signal to the barman, Virginia took a seat next to her husband whilst Big John persuaded the few other patrons present they had other places to be and then locked the door behind them. The barman, who hurried over with a large gin and tonic for her while Evans silently hoped he'd cleaned this glass by the usual method, backed quickly away out of earshot.

"So this is where you ran off to, George." She smiled sweetly at her husband, who suppressed a shudder. She then turned to the doctor. "My dear doctor, I'm so glad to see you. I've wanted to have a friendly chat with you for a while. You're not drinking?" she queried upon looking down at the table. "We can't have that. Winston," she addressed her minder, "please go and get the good doctor a whisky." George absently noted she was the first person he'd ever heard call the man by his given name and escape with all fingers in one piece.

Once the whisky had been placed in front of the doctor, the minder once more returned to his post.

"Now, back to business. First, thank you for confirming that the coroner won't be a problem."

"How the hell did you know that?" George blurted out.

His wife turned a smile as sweet as a praying mantis upon him. "You may have picked a seat where no one can sneak up on you, but, dearest"—she pointed above his head—"you really must make sure there are no open windows above your head."

Evans slumped back into his seat and, not for the first time, wished he could leave this cesspit of a pub. One glance at the minder by the door was all he needed to persuade him such an attempt would be a pointless exercise.

"Now that's sorted, Doctor, are you able to confirm any and all evidence of your complicity in Eleanor Palmer's death has been removed?" She didn't have long to wait, judging by the wonderful pale color his face went. "I assume that means no. Fill me in."

"As you know, we still need to get hold of the thermos flask," he started and, upon noting her begin to tap furiously on the table, nervously cleared his throat.

228

"Which I know you're working on. However, I wasn't able to obtain the personal effects they removed from the body. There were too many people around. I'd only just managed to get back on base and to the aircraft before they called another doctor. As it happened, I had to explain the parachute and flight suit when I got there."

"And what did you say?" Virginia asked, taking a sip of her drink. She pulled a face and pushed the glass to join her husband's.

"I told them, and this took quite a bit of persuasion," he added, though Virginia only raised an eyebrow, as if she thought he was trying to big up his story, "that she'd agreed to take me up for a ride. When she started to feel ill, she told me I'd have to jump, as she didn't think she'd be able to make it down in one piece."

"And they believed that?" George Evans asked.

The doctor shrugged his shoulders. "She couldn't contradict my story."

"So you're telling me no one's been able to check there's nothing that could incriminate either you or us in this death?"

Her husband, sensing a growing storm, backed his chair as far away from the doctor as possible, and just in the nick of time. Virginia raised an eyebrow toward Big John who, in a surprisingly short space of time, was behind the doctor. The ominous sound of cracking knuckles filled the room and, a moment later, the doctor found himself hoisted up by his lapels until he was nose to broken nose with the minder.

Virginia stood and came up beside the pair. Her voice could have cut glass. "A few things, my dear doctor. As my husband mentioned, certain elements are trying to track you down. They are also after my husband and me. Have no doubts—if we go down, you will go down too, and we will all hang. You will put yourself at our disposal, at the end of the phone. You will not try to leave this country—I heard that too—and finally, we have another, er, customer, so I suggest you come with me. We have business."

She got to her feet and tapped her minder on the elbow, the farthest up she could reach. "I don't think you need to exercise your muscles today after all, does he, Doctor?" Bramble furiously shook his head. "In that case, goodbye for now, George. Enjoy your drink. We'll see you later. Oh, before I forget, call up Ralph and tell him to get his finger out."

With that, Virginia left the bar, her minions close behind. George, forgetting what he'd seen earlier, picked up his glass and downed his whisky. As he opened the door to leave, the barman came out from behind his bar. "She's scary," he said with a shudder.

Evans stopped briefly and turned to face him. "You have no idea."

Chapter Twenty-Four

"I never thought this was something I'd say during a war, but can we never let Bobby eat ice cream again?" Ruth pleaded, wafting her notebook in front of her face.

Lying at her feet, Bobby cracked open one eye and promptly belched again. The waft of chocolate fudge ice cream mixed with dog breath swept all before it, and everyone in the office either held their noses or joined Ruth in frantically trying to clear the air.

"For God's sake," Ruth said, crunching up a piece of paper and throwing it at Walter, who was leaning on his desk, "open the bloody door."

Walter glanced outside. "But it's raining cats and dogs!"

"I don't care if it's tipping tigers and wolves," she countered.

Being nearest to the source of the gas attack, Ruth didn't waste any more oxygen on speaking.

"Who knew such a smell could come from such a little dog!" stated Ruth as she joined Walter in poking her head outside.

The rain was indeed crashing down, and together with the mist that came up from the river, it was a typical miserable autumn afternoon. The drone of an aircraft raised everyone's heads to the sky, or in Bobby's case, a right ear. Walter, with a hand shielding his face somewhat, first caught sight of the Anson as it flitted in and out of the angry sky.

"That'll be Lawrence bringing the girls back, I expect," he uttered, before wiping his forehead.

Bobby proceeded to fire off a double-barreled attack, then let out a snort of what could only be satisfaction and rolled onto his back.

"If you think I'm coming anywhere near your tummy, Bobby," Walter managed to get out between gasps for fresh air, "you've another think coming." He considered stepping outside no matter how wet he got but instead took a look at his watch. "It's nearly five, Ruth. What do you say about calling it an early night?"

His boss looked back toward where Bobby's legs were pin-wheeling, chasing rabbits in his dreams as he gave the occasional whimper. Ruth smiled at the sight before her furry friend let off a rearward gas attack of epic proportions that not only had her and Walter both stepping outside but also woke the dog.

Gasping and coughing, Ruth clung to the door frame. "If I ever get my hands on those Yanks, I'll bloody well kill them!"

Walter had their coats ready in a flash. For his part, Bobby cocked an ear, unwilling to get up unless something was in it for him.

Ruth and Walter looked at each other, and Ruth grinned. "Rock, paper, scissors to decide who goes back in and puts his leash on?"

Walter sighed and prepared himself to lose. For a game that was supposed to be based on random chance, his boss had a remarkable record against him. At times, he'd even thought she could read his mind. In the best traditions of the game, he faced off against her, fist closed before pumping it up and down three times. A few seconds later, Ruth's paper having beaten his rock, Walter was trying to clip Bobby's leash to the dog's collar before his breath ran out. Barely in time, the two, at least in Bobby's case, trotted out of the office, and Ruth locked it behind him. The phone chose that moment to ring.

Keeping hold of Bobby's leash, Walter raised an eyebrow that hinted, "You're the boss, and you should answer it." Her wry smile told him she knew he was right, and she took out her keys.

"Hold the door, will you?" she asked as she stepped back in and rushed to her desk before the phone stopped.

She picked it up. "*Hamble Gazette*, Ruth Stone, editor. How can I help you?"

The next thing Walter knew, Ruth's eyebrows had shot up and she scrambled for a pen and paper before crouching over the phone, inadvertently preventing him from hearing what was being said. Bobby tugged at his leash, not happy with getting wet for no reason, making for the warmth of the office. "No. Stay here, Bobby. We'll be on our way shortly."

Two minutes later, Ruth put the phone down. She then carefully folded the paper she'd been writing on and put it in her bag before joining Walter and taking Bobby's leash from him.

"Mind if I ask who that was?"

Ruth shook her head. "That was Doris's friend Eddie. He's managed to track down the doctor!"

****

"Come on, Ralph!" Ruth almost snapped at the airman who was still stubbornly refusing to let her onto base. "You know who I am."

233

Ralph pushed the cap on his head back until he had it set at what was decidedly not a regulation angle. "Of course I know who you are, Mrs. Stone, but that doesn't mean you can just walk onto the airfield for no reason."

"I have my reasons," Ruth squeezed out from between clenched teeth.

"Which is?" prompted Ralph, toying menacingly with the Lee-Enfield rifle he was carrying.

The standoff was ended by the fortuitous arrival of Thelma, who'd been passing, had noticed the confrontation, and made a hurried detour.

"What seems to be the problem, Johnson?" she asked.

Though she didn't officially have direct authority over him, Ralph reluctantly drew himself to something approaching attention. Ruth and Thelma noticed he'd quickly glanced toward the guardroom to make sure no one who could really get him into trouble was about to come out. "This civilian wants to come on base but refuses to tell me why."

Thelma adopted a tone that would have brooked no argument from Winston Churchill, let alone some lowly aircraftsman with a very dodgy nature. "No arguments, Johnson. I'll take responsibility for Mrs. Stone. Whilst she's on camp, I shall keep her in my presence. Come on, Ruth," she finished and linked an arm through one of Ruth's before marching her around the gate and past an open-mouthed Ralph Johnson. She had to give a little tug on Bobby's leash as he stopped and cocked his leg against the butt of Ralph's rifle where it rested upon the ground.

The two of them waited until they'd gone around a corner and were out of sight of the guardroom before clutching each other.

"And then when Bobby cocked his leg! I thought I'd burst there and then." Thelma bent down to where Bobby was scratching behind an ear. "You cheeky little thing, I could kiss you!"

Ruth hurriedly clutched her friend under the arm and heaved her to her feet, saying, "I wouldn't do that if I were you. He's still burping, amongst other bodily functions, thanks to the ice cream, and let's say ice cream and dog breath is not a very nice mixture. Actually, that's part of the reason Walter and I shut up early tonight."

Thelma contented herself with patting the dog on the head.

Ruth recalled why she was there. "I need to speak with Betty. Before I left the office, I took a call from Eddie Winters. He had some information I need to get to her, and it can't wait."

Immediately turning serious, Thelma grabbed Ruth's hand and led her toward the ops hut. "What're we waiting for?"

They had a short while to wait as, despite Thelma immediately going up to Betty and pointing at Ruth with some urgency, Ruth couldn't make out what was said as she stayed by the open doorway. Everyone who had an interest in what she had to say was in the room. Nevertheless, Betty waved her away.

"She'll be with us in a few minutes," Thelma told her when she was back by her side. "She wants to get everyone booked back in, and then we're all finished for the day."

"I've been thinking," Ruth said, keeping her voice low so those who didn't need to know passed them in safe ignorance. "We need to make sure Shirley knows about this too. Depending upon what everyone agrees after I've told you all what I've learned, maybe we can persuade her to pass on some misinformation to him that can get to whoever he works for. What do you think?"

Thelma didn't need to think twice. "Leave it to me. I'll go and speak to her," and matched actions to words by striding out of the hut.

"Hi, Ruth, whatcha doing here?"

The dulcet tones came from their favorite American as she dumped her bag and parachute at Ruth's feet. Shortly after, she was joined by Penny and Mary, who followed suit.

"I'll tell you when we're someplace a little less crowded, Doris. Why don't the three of you get changed, and Thelma and I will meet you outside the mess as soon as possible. She's just gone to see if she can get Shirley."

"Who's gone to get who?" asked Lawrence, absently dumping his kit at his feet, narrowly missing Bobby's front paws, who barked his displeasure at him before settling on an ear scratch by way of an apology.

****

Half an hour later, everyone (Thelma had pulled seniority in Engineering and dragged Shirley off the Anson she'd been working on) had decamped to Ruth's place. Though a little more crowded than Betty's, Ruth insisted they'd all eaten and drunk enough of Betty's produce and she should take a turn. As not everyone could fit comfortably into her front room or kitchen, and as the rain had finally died off, Ruth told everyone to grab a chair and take it out to the back garden. When the chairs ran out, she popped upstairs and came back with a couple of tartan blankets and laid them upon the ground for those who didn't have a chair.

Ruth had just sat down herself when from the front door, there came a loud hammering.

"I'll get it," said Lawrence, heaving himself to his feet. Less than a minute later, he was back, and trailing in his wake was Walter.

"Sorry, Ruth. I wanted to see what you'd found out," he said, standing in the rear doorway.

Ruth got to her feet. "I'm so sorry, Walter. I was so anxious to get to Betty that I forgot to tell you to come along. Forgive me?"

Seeing how contrite she was, Walter bent down to kiss her cheek. "You're forgiven. I was fortunate to see you all walking down here."

"Never mind all that," piped up Doris, beaming up at Walter, then patting the blanket beside her. "Park your keister here, honey."

Walter's face lit up, and he needed no second invitation. Doris promptly leaned against his shoulder and linked her fingers through his, and in a very short space of time he was relaxing into his beautiful foreign girlfriend's arms. Penny winked at the couple, catching Doris's eye.

Ruth quickly checked everyone had a glass of her favorite elderflower wine in their hands. "Right, I think I'd better get on with things whilst the rain holds out. As you all know, I had a call from Doris's friend Eddie a short while ago and wanted to get you all together before I told you what he had to say. Word on the street says the doctor worked for a Group Captain George Evans."

"Worked?"

"Hold on, Penny," Ruth said, "I'm getting there. Yes, he used to work for this Group Captain, and I'm perfectly aware it's the same name as the one you used to…we'll say 'work for,' Thelma." She proceeded before Thelma could get embarrassed or anyone else could ask something else. "Anyway, Eddie told me he'd had a bit of luck when he was at an embassy party. He overheard one, in his words, 'dressed-to-the-nines young Englishman' boasting to a small group of how he'd beaten the draft. Eddie took a chance, as he had no reason to believe it could be anything to do with the doctor we're interested in, and held up an FBI ID."

"Eddie's always liked being prepared," Doris told everyone.

"Yes. So he pulled him aside and got him to admit the name of the doctor in exchange for a promise he wouldn't tell the British police. He confirmed the name was Bramble and also that he'd handed over the money to a very stuck-up woman who only told him to call her Virginia."

"She used her real first name?" Lawrence exclaimed, shaking his head. "Despite everything, she's still an amateur."

"A rather stupid one, at that," added Mary.

"Did he get anything else out of him?" Penny wanted to know.

Ruth aimed a primal grin at Lawrence. "He didn't try to get him to elaborate, as he didn't want to arouse any suspicions. However, the chap who was going to take the medical for him was there too, when the meet took place. He was told that was so he could practice his signature for the forms. I have no idea if that's the usual practice. Lawrence?"

He took a sip of the good wine before answering. "To be honest, I don't know, but it doesn't sound usual for the two to meet. That could indicate something, but I'm not sure what." He shrugged his shoulders. "Anything else, Ruth?"

"Just the one. Apparently, the toff wanted to get some kind of insurance in case something went wrong. He said the whole thing was quite dangerous, considering the minders this Virginia surrounds herself with, actually. So he waited outside once they'd finished with him and followed the doctor. From what he said, the doctor was bundled into a waiting car and dropped off at some place in Belgravia."

"He's staying at Evans' apartment," Lawrence said, clapping his hands.

"Sounds more like he's being kept prisoner," suggested Doris. "Ruth?"

"Only that as they got out of the car, this chap in an RAF uniform came out of the apartment block, followed by a snazzy-looking dame. They started to argue before he was able to roll down the window on his car to hear, so he didn't get everything. What he did hear was Virginia stating this would be the last time they used the doctor."

"Hmm. Sounds like they're definitely panicking," Lawrence speculated.

"Do you think they're going to disappear?" Betty wanted to know, leaning forward in her chair, glass in hand long forgotten.

"Very possible," Lawrence agreed after giving it some thought for a few minutes. "It's also very likely the doctor will disappear too."

The contemplative silence was broken by the sound of Betty's glass breaking in her hand, closely followed by her loud yelp of pain.

Chapter Twenty-Five

Ruth took the rabbit pie out of the oven and immediately wished she'd had a bigger rabbit.

Penny looked over her shoulder. "I don't think that'll be enough for everyone."

"No kidding!" added Doris as she folded up a blanket. A grin broke out and she snapped her fingers before checking her watch. "Tell you what, why don't I pop down to the chip shop and get a load in. Then everyone can have a bit of everything, a kind of picnic!"

"So much for only once a week," Penny joked. Doris poked out her tongue in reply. Mary came into the kitchen, an arm around Betty's shoulders, and immediately the conversation swung from how they were going to solve the problem of feeding everyone. Ruth and Thelma got to their feet from where they'd been sitting at the kitchen table and hurried over.

"How's your hand?" Thelma asked, her voice full of concern.

Betty held up her bandaged left hand and smiled self-consciously. "Stings a bit, but that's what you get for being stupid."

Thelma drew Betty into a hug and told her, firmly but gently, "No, you aren't stupid. Impulsive, perhaps. Your mind heard that Bramble may get punished before you could get hold of him and, well, that happened."

"Listen to her, honey," Doris added as she folded the last blanket. "You want revenge, and we all understand that. I'm sure if Lawrence were here instead of phoning his bosses, he'd agree."

"Exactly," Ruth said, remembering she needed to put the pie back in the oven. "You're certain she doesn't need any stitches, Mary?"

Mary laid a hand gently over Betty's bandaged one, causing her to wince slightly. "No, none of the cuts are deep enough, and there's no glass in there, either. I'll change the bandage in the morning, but she'll be fine before you know it."

Betty leant her head on Mary's shoulder and smiled over at her friends, making sure to include Walter and Shirley, who'd just come inside after picking up the pieces of glass, in Walter's case, and after pulling some carrots from the back plot, in Shirley's. "Thanks, Mary, and thanks to everyone for understanding."

"So," piped up Doris, "give me half an hour, and I'll be back with as much fish and chips as I can carry."

Walter tapped Shirley, who was looking a little like a rabbit in the headlights again, "Why don't you give her a hand?"

"Great idea!" Doris beamed and, not giving her a chance to say no, grabbed hold of her hand. "Come on, love, we're on fish 'n' chip detail."

With Doris and Shirley out of the way, Walter was put on carrot preparation duty whilst Ruth, Penny, Mary, and Thelma all but carried Betty into the lounge, insisting that she take it easy.

"Look who we ran into!" yelled Doris shortly after, as she let herself in through the back door, shoving a loaded-down Lawrence ahead of her, his arms piled high with steaming packets of fish 'n' chips.

"They ran me down before I could escape mule duty," he jokingly moaned as he, Doris, and Shirley placed packet after packet onto the kitchen table. He noticed Betty poking her head around the doorway. "Hey, Betty! How's the hand?"

"Mary's done a very good job. I'll be fine," she assured him before she was gently ushered back into the lounge.

Ruth stared at the mountain of food in front of her. "Just how many people do you think need feeding?" she asked Doris in amazement.

"I think there're nine of us," she answered, doing a quick tot up.

Penny picked up and held a delicious smelling pack to her nose. "You'll have to forgive our Doris," she advised Ruth. "She's got a fixation on English fish 'n' chips. We keep telling her that she'll soon stop fitting in a cockpit if she keeps on wolfing this down."

"She'd be gorgeous, however," Walter surprised himself by saying, wrapping his arms around Doris from the rear and then looking sheepish at being so forward.

Doris laughed and snuggled back into his hug, "I think I've been very good for you, Walter." She then surprised everyone by leaning up toward his ear and, not troubling to keep her voice down, told him, "You've certainly been very good for me. I didn't think I'd find anyone so kind and caring again after I lost my Donald."

Walter turned her around and drew her into a hug so full of love that the rest of the household all found reasons to leave the two alone for a while.

They decided the rabbit pie would be just as good warmed up tomorrow, so shortly afterward, comfortable on the blankets now laid down in Ruth's lounge and various cushions scattered around, everyone was enjoying an excellent fish supper.

"You'll have to tell me how much I owe you for this, Doris. It is supposed to be my turn for supper," Ruth told her between chips.

Doris waved her request aside, and everyone just about understood what she answered, her mouth being crammed with cod and chips. "If you can't share what you've got, what's the point of being a millionaire?" The reply prompted Walter to cough what he'd been eating into his hand.

"You're a what?" he managed to splutter out on the third attempt.

Doris kissed him on his cheek. "I'll fill you in sometime, honey."

****

Supper took a long while to finish, partially because Doris had insisted upon buying everyone large portions and no one wanted to waste a morsel, but also because it had put everyone in a good mood and no one felt like going home. With some light orchestra music playing on the radio and everyone sitting or lying where they'd eaten, empty newspaper wrappings in their hands, Lawrence spoke up.

"Let me fill you in with what happened when I spoke to my superiors," he volunteered, moving his cushion into a slightly more comfortable place before looking over at Shirley. "Shirley, this concerns you, so listen closely."

These words had everyone, not just Shirley, sitting up a little straighter.

"My bosses are quite happy for everything to continue as they are. With the information your friend provided, Doris—don't worry, I made certain they know it's a reliable source and has to remain anonymous—we can pick up the doctor any time we want and we could charge them all with various black market offenses as well as the draft-dodging scheme. Nevertheless, we still need evidence so we can charge them with Eleanor's death too." He looked over at Betty, as she needed to hear what he was about to say. "That's very important to us, okay?" Betty just stared back, and after a short while, he took that for a yes. "I discussed a plan I've been formulating for a while, but it all depends upon the answer you give me to a question I have to ask you, Betty."

"Ask away," Betty told him, putting down her wine glass.

"Shirley's told us that Ralph's been told to keep an eye out for Eleanor's thermos flask, right?" Shirley nodded. "Betty, is that thermos in the box of things they gave you after they released what was found on her body? Sorry, I really don't mean to upset you," he added quickly as Betty wiped a tear away.

She got to her feet, favoring her right hand to lever herself out of her chair. "I'll go and get the box everything's in," she offered. "I can't remember what's in there."

Before anyone else could say anything, Shirley hopped to her feet too and declared, "I'll come with you, Betty. You never know who could be out there."

"If you mean Ralph," Betty asked, steel flashing in

245

her eyes, "I could take him with one hand tied behind my back."

****

"I told you I didn't need a chaperone," Betty said for the second time in as many minutes to Shirley as she pushed open the gate to her cottage.

"And I told you I wasn't listening," Shirley told her, newfound confidence clear in her voice as she waited for Betty to open the front door.

"Fine," huffed Betty. "You may as well come in. I'll only be a minute."

Betty had barely disappeared around the top of the landing when Ralph appeared, all clad in black, from around the side of the cottage.

"Shirley," he whispered, his head twisting back and forth, trying to check that no one was sneaking up at him.

"Bugger!" she couldn't help but cry out.

"Anything wrong?" Betty shouted down the stairs, though fortunately she didn't come down in person.

Glaring at Ralph who had hunkered down behind a large potted plant beside the door, Shirley thought quickly. She cleared her throat with a couple of coughs. "Just a bat that nearly flew into my hair," she shouted back.

"They can be a little curious. Down in a second!"

After listening closely for as long as she dared, Shirley, remembering the blackout, pulled the door closed before she turned back to Ralph and hissed, "What are you doing here?"

After turning around to check the coast was clear once more, he leaned in to say, "I've been watching this house for a while. His Lordship"—he spat on the ground, much to Shirley's disgust—"and her majesty are getting more than a little twitchy. They're dropping hints it could be bad for my health if I don't find that bloody flask thing. I'd been thinking about breaking in, but with her lodgers being pilots, I can't be sure when they'll be out. Then I saw the two of you, and here we are."

Shirley felt her stomach lurch with nerves. She needed to get rid of him, and quick. "Look, I may have news for you, but you'll have to wait until tomorrow. I'll meet you in the mess for lunch. Okay?"

As time was short before Betty must come back downstairs, Shirley made up his mind for him. "Do you need a hand, Betty?" she shouted, pushing the door slightly open and then quickly turning to Ralph again. "I'll see you tomorrow. Now bugger off!"

****

Following Betty back into Ruth's lounge five minutes later, Shirley laid the box at Betty's feet and then turned to where Lawrence was chatting with Penny.

"Lawrence, I've had an idea," Shirley said at the same moment he turned to look at her. "Betty, is the thermos in the box?"

"Hold on," she replied, bending down to rummage, then quickly straightened up. In her hands was a small, blue thermos flask.

"Great! Lawrence, you said I'd have some part in a plan you had? Let me run mine by you first, and then you tell me if it's the same thing." Lawrence gestured for her to go ahead. "How about I tell Ralph the thermos has been found and it's being sent up to London—we can work out train times later—for testing

247

for poison?"

Lawrence was unable to hold in his grin. "As near as dammit, Shirley." He sat back and considered her. "You've come far in a short space of time. Well done."

Penny took the flask from Betty's hands and turned it this way and that before asking her, "Has this thing been tested?"

Her friend shook her head. "No, having a toxicology test done never entered my mind. I just knew it wasn't an accident."

"I'm sorry," Penny said, kneeling beside Betty. "We keep upsetting you."

Betty sniffed, wiped her nose, and then fixed a smile on her face before replying. "That's all right. All this talk's just bringing everything back, but..." She looked around at everyone's concerned faces. "It's good, it really is. If all this gets justice for Eleanor, it'll be worth it."

Penny sat back on her heels, a little relieved, and not even being aware she was doing it, unscrewed the thermos's cap and took a sniff. She lurched back, wrinkling her nose, "Curdled coffee, nothing else."

"You were expecting what?" Doris asked, her brow furrowing in thought, and then her head snapped back. "Almonds! You were expecting to smell almonds! Take that, Miss Marple."

"Only thing is I didn't smell them." Penny smiled.

"Ah, well." Doris sighed. "Guess I shouldn't give up the day job."

"I've no idea what you two are on about," Lawrence muttered, shaking his head. "Let's get back to Shirley's plan. Shirley, would I be right in saying you're hoping Virginia's people will try anything to get this flask back?"

Looking around the room, she took a deep breath and nodded decisively. "Yes. From the threats Ralph's implied since I arrived, not to mention what Virginia herself said before sending me here, I'm sure she would do anything to get that flask. Maybe it could be used as leverage against Evans."

"Impressive logic! I think you missed your calling, Shirley. You should've been a policeman. If they take the bait, it'll be pretty good evidence that Bramble and, by association, Evans and Virginia are responsible for Eleanor's death." Shirley felt a blush spread up her cheeks and was spared having to answer as Lawrence noted, "So you'd need to make sure they know when and where they can get hold of the flask, plus a volunteer to carry it there and make sure it's taken."

"No! You can't do that!"

As Shirley thought, Mary had sounded her objections. She had been right that her new friend had feelings for the policeman. Not knowing quite how to answer, she was grateful when Lawrence went and sat down next to her. Perhaps he hadn't been blind to the little things Mary had said and done after all.

"Don't be angry at Shirley, please." He made a move to take Mary's hand and then, slowly and obviously to someone who was watching as closely as Shirley was, reluctantly put his hand back in his lap. "This is exactly what I was going to suggest to Shirley myself. It's what my bosses and I have been discussing. If she hadn't brought it up, I would have."

It took a while for the frown on Mary's face to slide away. Perhaps the miserable expression upon her face meant she had remembered the double-agent role

Shirley was playing. Either way, she eventually smiled over at her, and for Shirley that was enough.

Lawrence, as if proving not all men were dumb Neanderthal morons, picked up on the clear communication between the two women. "Good. In that case, let's get this over with. I'll go up on Monday. No point dragging this out. Will that give you enough time to arrange things, Shirley?"

"Which brings me to what happened whilst you were grabbing that box, Betty."

"So I *did* hear another voice," Betty said, finishing off her wine and then holding up her empty glass for a refill, which Penny promptly provided. "Thank you, Penny."

"We were followed by Ralph," she stated, noting that no one was very much surprised. She hurried on, "There wasn't any threat to either of us," she added assuredly, "but he was very anxious. I know I was getting ahead of things, Lawrence, but I told him I'd have news for him tomorrow. I didn't go too far?"

"Fine by me." He shrugged. "You can tell him you've a friend who's taking the thermos into London for testing. I don't know what time I'll leave, off the top of my head, but tell him I'll aim to be in for about ten in the morning at Waterloo on Monday. Good enough?"

"Good enough," Shirley echoed.

Chapter Twenty-Six

Jane had joined Thelma and Penny for a quick lunch of chicken soup and bread and butter, and had been chattering away for five minutes without Thelma hearing a word she'd said.

Jane elbowed Thelma in the ribs, and her tea promptly sloshed over the edge of her cup. "Hey, are you listening to me?"

Reluctantly, Thelma turned her attention to Jane. Timing is everything in life, and though she'd normally be happy to talk with Jane, Shirley had walked in five minutes ago, taken a seat where she could see the entrance, and presently sat stirring her spoon around and around in her soup, nervously waiting for Ralph to turn up. Judging by the way she jumped at every excessive noise, it was just as well she didn't know she was being watched.

Unfortunately, in thinking this, she hadn't answered Jane, and when she refocused, Jane had taken to staring at what had taken Thelma's attention.

"Is there something wrong with Shirley?"

Having now landed herself in a dilemma, Thelma had to think quickly. The longer she took, the more chance of her boss and friend taking it upon herself to go and speak with Shirley. Sod's law would decree that Ralph would then turn up, and they didn't want to have to go through this rigmarole again. She'd have to tell

Jane something.

"Hold on a second, please," she asked.

"If you're not interested in what I've got to tell you, Thelma, I won't..." Jane started, before she noticed the pleading expression upon her friend's face and sat back down. After another moment, she asked, "Is there something you want to tell me?"

Thelma quickly checked Shirley was still on her own before answering. "Want to tell you? No. Need to tell you...yes, and I really, really hope you'll understand that I can't tell you everything. I can," she quickly added at seeing Jane open her mouth, no doubt to object, "however, assure you, as much as I can, and I hope that'll be enough, that nothing going on will prevent deliveries or hurt anyone."

Whilst Jane tried to make sense of what Thelma asked, Ralph entered, collected his soup and tea, and made his way over to where Shirley, who'd noticed his entrance, was sitting up a little straighter.

Somewhat reluctantly, Jane agreed. "All right, as a friend, I trust you. I can't say I'm happy about it. After all, I am supposed to be in charge, and that usually means I know everything that's going on," she added wryly.

"I understand," Thelma said with a weak smile. "I'd be the same in your place, but please understand I can't tell you everything, as it's not my place to." She sighed and gave herself some thinking time by looking around the mess. Chicken soup day was popular even though wartime chicken soup never warmed up quite as well as the pre-war stuff. "Did Betty ever talk to you about how her sister died?"

Jane shook her head. "I never knew she had a

sister. What happened?"

"That's for Betty to tell you—should she choose to." Thelma shook her head. "All I'll say is that she died by mistake, and a bunch of us have ended up helping Special Branch in trying to track down her murderer."

There, that would have to do, Thelma decided, already worried she'd said too much. Though she trusted Jane, and she was sure Betty did as well, she hoped Betty would understand when she told her about it later. With hindsight, they all should have guessed Jane would eventually get wind of something.

Jane glanced as Ralph leant in toward Shirley. "I suppose that's something to do with this?" She jerked her head imperceptibly toward where the two sat.

Thelma nodded. "Yes. Look, come over to Betty's tonight, and by then I'll have had time to talk to her and we can fill you in."

Jane asked, raising a single eyebrow, "How many are in this gang, then?"

Thelma raised her spoon to her lips and drank some of her rapidly cooling soup. "Come around about seven, and all shall be revealed."

****

"I'm here. What do you have?" Ralph spat out without preamble and proceeded to shovel his soup down his throat without waiting for an answer.

Shirley didn't bother to keep the look of disgust from her face; she'd seen pigs with better table manners. Her stomach fluttered. She looked up straight into the eyes of Thelma. The briefest of nods from her friend was all it took to settle her nerves.

"I told you I had something for you, something that

will put you, hopefully us, into that pair's good books. That's why I'm going to tell you, and then you can tell them."

He placed down his spoon and drank his tea in one long gulp. "Depends what you've got for me," he told her, his head canted to the side, questioning.

Remembering the evil grins she'd seen both Doris and Ruth use, Shirley did her best to mimic them, and when Ralph didn't burst out laughing, assumed she'd got it about right. "I know where this thermos flask those two are so eager to get hold of will be tomorrow."

"Palmer found it, then," he observed.

"Yes. You know," she added, trying to get an answer to something that had been bothering her for a while, "I've always wondered why either you or someone else in their organization didn't just break in and ransack Betty Palmer's cottage. I don't think it would have taken long to find it."

Here Ralph did let out a quiet chuckle. "They don't pay me enough to risk a spell in prison for something I know nothing about. Just yelling at me to try and get hold of some poxy flask had me alarm bells ringing. Something anyone wants so bad can't be good news for anyone else."

Shirley nodded, genuinely understanding what he meant. "And why haven't they done anything themselves?"

A little more of the old, less likeable Ralph was in his snort. "Those two? Ha. One," he said, raising a finger, "neither of those buggers would want to get their own hands dirty, and secondly, they don't know anyone like me outsides of London to do the job."

Shirley sat back, slightly stunned. "You mean

they're that stupid? They haven't tried to get anyone to do the job in all this time?"

"I know," Ralph said, a little cheerier. "Talk about thick as two short planks. I can't believe it either, but if neither of thems thought of it, I'm not going to suggest it meself. So this information you mentioned, getting back to the reason we're here, what is it?"

"Tell them if they want the thermos, it'll be on the train arriving from Southampton at ten Monday morning. It'll be carried in a brown paper package by a man with a copy of the *Hamble Gazette* under his arm and a small brown suitcase in his other hand, and he'll be wearing the uniform of the ATA."

"I think even the thickest muscle couldn't miss him. Nice touch about the uniform," he added.

"Makes him easy to spot, so long as they know what to look for."

"That's their lookout," Ralph added, finishing his soup.

What she'd told Ralph had stunned him, and here she was, virtually a complete stranger, giving him the opportunity to get back in with the Group Captain and his odious wife. He had to know she'd presented him with a chance to take all the credit. She could see he'd immediately figured that out and was now trying to work out why.

She pre-empted him. "Never you mind the why. Suffice it to say I don't like having anything to do with you or them. So long as you agree to say we got the information together, that'll do me. Agreed?"

"I'd better go and phone this in," he said getting to his feet. He then turned, and she could see conflict upon his face before he surprised her by saying in parting,

"Thank you."

****

Satisfied all with Shirley had gone well, Thelma suggested Jane and she should take a walk outside. The weather was bracing, with a quick breeze blowing off the Solent, bringing with it the annoying cry of seagulls. As they walked toward the flight line, Jane surprised her by taking her by the arm, and when Thelma turned her head to look at her, she would have sworn she could see stars dancing in her friend's eyes. Something had got her very excited, and Thelma didn't think it had anything to do with what she'd just learned.

"Do you remember that American commander I had to deal with after Mary decided to have an overnight stay at their base?"

"I do seem to recall you telling me you'd spoken to him a few times, yes," Thelma answered, not trying to keep a smile from her face.

Jane didn't seem to notice she was being teased. "He called last night and asked me out to dinner!"

If she could have done a little dance of joy, Thelma suspected that was exactly what Jane would be doing now. "Well, well, that's very interesting. When's he coming over?"

Any answer was immediately rendered moot by the roar of powerful aero engines overhead, and they both involuntarily ducked as a C47 roared across the field. All eyes were immediately drawn upward as they watched the aircraft take up a vector to land. Both noticed at the same time it had American markings, and they broke into a run toward the flight line hut.

"Did you know we were expecting Yanks today?" Jane asked as they came to a stop and waited for the

256

transport's engines to run down and stop. Thelma shook her head as Betty strode out with a huge grin.

"I was wondering if I'd see you shortly, boss," she said, winking at Thelma. "When you arrange a date, you arrange a date!"

Neither Jane nor Thelma had long to wait for the answer to this as the engines finally stopped and, a few seconds later, the rear doors were thrown open and a head was stuck out.

"Hey, ladies! Do either of you know where I can find a Jane Howell?"

****

Thelma turned to where Betty stood beaming at Jane and Frank as they happily ignored all and sundry, their two heads close together as they discussed who knew what. "And how long did you know about that, then?"

"I don't know what you mean," Betty replied, a look of innocence upon her face that wouldn't fool anyone.

"I mean, and well you know it," Thelma said, playing along, "about how long you've known a certain Yank colonel was coming?"

Betty shrugged happily. "Only a few minutes. He came on the RT requesting permission to land, asking if we could keep it quiet from Jane."

Thelma slapped her friend on the back and grinned too. "It's lucky we happened to be coming along then."

"That bit was," she agreed. "However, he also told me that if we didn't give him permission to land, he'd feather an engine and declare an emergency so we'd have to let him land anyway."

Thelma looked over her shoulder and saw another

American climbing down the ladder and setting up, of all things, a deckchair under one of the wings. Beside it, he opened and put down a bottle of Coke and, adjusting a cap over his eyes, settled in to wait for his boss's return.

Nursing a cup of builder's-strength tea, Betty restarted the paperwork she'd been in the middle of before Jane's date had interrupted her. However, she didn't manage to get far, as she could feel Thelma staring at her from where she'd leant up against the wall. "Penny for them?"

When Betty merely nodded her agreement, Thelma said, "Did anything happen to you after your sister took your flying suit and pass?"

"Well, I told them she'd flown a lot pre-war and had missed it so much she wanted to get up to see if she'd lost her touch."

"And the enquiry believed that?" asked Thelma.

Betty shrugged and took a sip of tea. "They didn't kick me out, though I did get a warning about my future conduct."

Next thing they knew, the door banged open and Bobby appeared, swinging from the door handle before trying to bark whilst he still had the knob between his teeth. He promptly dropped to the floor where, after giving himself a quick shake, he started toward Thelma, wagging his tail, a very pleased look upon his furry face.

"That's a new trick, boy," remarked Betty, leaning down to ruffle him behind the ears.

"A dog of many talents," Thelma agreed, pleased she wouldn't have to voice her opinion of the enquiry's findings. She didn't think she'd have been so lenient.

Chapter Twenty-Seven

Penny opened the front door, spot on seven, to reveal Thelma and a strange-looking Jane.

"You'll have to forgive Jane, here," began Thelma as she followed her through the door. "She's had a rather traumatic afternoon."

Deciding as they were now off duty she could risk teasing her boss, Penny showed them through to the lounge. "Yes, Betty was saying there'd been a *flying* visit of sorts this afternoon."

"Oh, ha-de-ha!" replied Jane, rather po-faced.

"Stop teasing her," Betty advised as she came down the stairs. "I suspect Jane's a little more interested in what's going on than talking about her love life. We can get that information out of her later," she added with a twinkle in her eye. "Tea?"

"You need to ask?"

"Doris?" Betty raised her voice so it could be heard in the kitchen. "Put the kettle on, please, and bring in the pot when it's ready. Jane and Thelma have just arrived."

"No problems!" came back the reply.

Jane took a seat in the middle of the sofa and indicated that Betty and Thelma should take their places next to her. Mary barged past just as Penny came in. "Hi, Jane," she said by way of greeting. "Forgive me for not staying, but I'm going around to Ruth's."

"Lawrence wouldn't be there by any chance?" teased Penny, waggling her eyebrows.

Mary refused to rise to the bait, waving her goodbyes.

It appeared Jane wasn't in the mood to beat about the bush. "Thelma says you've something to tell me, Betty, something she assures me does not interfere with our operations. That's right, isn't it, Betty?"

Penny put down a magazine and spoke up. "If there's anyone you should be annoyed at, Jane, it's us. Doris and I had the idea to find out what happened to Betty's sister, and it kind of snowballed from there. We both fancied ourselves as Miss Marples."

Jane turned to look at Penny with a most confused expression upon her face. "But I understood she died in an accident."

Penny glanced at Betty to make certain it was okay to continue. "That's what the death certificate said, only Betty never believed it, and we've since found out there's a very good chance she was actually poisoned."

"Poisoned! Why would anyone want to murder her?" asked Jane, her voice rising as she flopped back into her seat.

Betty and Thelma looked at each other before Thelma answered, "Can I just say that, on behalf of us both, there are certain things in our pasts that we'd prefer to keep there." Jane had put on a face that quite clearly said she'd like to hear more, but before she could speak, Thelma read her mind. "I know you want to know details, Jane. I would if I were you, but please believe me again nothing we've done and nothing we're doing should have any effect on our duties. If it does, and I believe I speak for Betty too..." Betty nodded her agreement. "We'll let you know as soon as possible."

Jane got to her feet and paced around the lounge for a little while, every now and then opening her mouth, but nothing came out until she finally sat back down and drank her tea. "How many of you are involved in this, whatever you're doing, then?"

"Everyone in this house and over at Ruth's, too," Betty informed her.

"I suppose this explains why Herbert Lawrence asked me for Monday off?"

Penny coughed. "There's something about Lawrence you should know, but it's for him to tell you, I'm afraid."

For the first time since she'd entered the house, Jane smiled. "I expect you're referring to him being a member of Special Branch?"

"How did you know?" asked Thelma, nearly spilling her tea.

"You don't think they'd be allowed to place anyone on my base without my knowing about it, do you?"

****

"What're you doing here, Mary?" Ruth asked as she answered her door.

Mary looked sheepish. "Jane came around to be filled in, and I wanted to get away."

The sound of a male voice laughing from the direction of the kitchen made her head swivel.

"Or could it have something to do with our friendly policeman?" Ruth asked, though Mary had already started to make her way toward the sound.

Lawrence and Shirley sat at the table, halfway through the rabbit pie Ruth had prepared the other day, and both stopped what they'd been talking about as soon as Mary entered the room.

"Mary!" Shirley put down her knife and fork and rushed around the table to greet her friend, rattling off rapidly, "Is everything all right? Penny told me Jane was coming around tonight to be told everything. Has she been around? What happened?" She stopped to catch her breath.

Mary held up her hands. "Sit back down and finish your tea," she told the excitable girl, joining them at the table, as did Ruth. "I don't know. I left before anything was said."

"She's very understanding," Lawrence added, putting down his fork. "I'm sure it'll be all right."

"And by now she probably knows as much as she needs to know," stated Shirley, quite enjoying herself despite the seriousness of the situation. "What did the boss have to say when you asked her for Monday off?"

"It wasn't a day I was due to have off, so I had to pretend an aunt had been rushed into hospital for appendicitis. She wasn't happy but agreed so long as I worked the next day I was due off." He rubbed at his chin. "Mind you, she possibly knows by now it's a white lie."

"So everything's set up for Monday, then?" Ruth asked.

Lawrence nodded as he sat back. "And if for some reason they don't manage to get the thermos off me, not that I'm going to put up much of a fight—"

They were interrupted by Mary's gasp. Lawrence asked, "Are you all right, Mary?" while Ruth and Shirley shared a look that agreed how typical it was for a man to miss an obvious sign. Mary gave a rather painful-looking grimace instead of answering, and Lawrence missed that too.

"Then I'll take it on to Scotland Yard for testing. Obviously we'd need to do that at some point, so we wouldn't be wasting it."

"Um…what do you mean by 'not put up much of a fight'?" Mary stammered out.

This unexpected question actually caused Lawrence to pause and re-evaluate the pained expression she was aiming at him, though still without realizing its full meaning. Eventually Lawrence re-discovered what his tongue was for. "Don't worry. All I'll do is let them do a snatch-and-grab on the platform. I don't doubt that's where they'll do it, as it'll have so many people milling around it's confusion personified," he declared.

If he hoped to put Mary's mind to rest, he'd failed, and judging by the looks on both Ruth and Shirley's faces, hers wasn't the only one.

****

It hadn't been the most auspicious of starts to the day.

He'd got to the station only to turn back, as he'd forgotten the thermos, the very reason for his journey. Subsequently, he'd nearly missed his train and had barely managed to jump on before it pulled out. It hadn't boded well for the rest of the day.

He'd been about to alight as it pulled into Waterloo when he'd had a mild panic attack. The newspaper— he'd forgotten the bloody newspaper! He couldn't reasonably purloin or pass off any other paper as the *Hamble Gazette*. It had an illustration of the river Hamble flowing into the Solent emblazoned across the banner, which looked like no other. Then his hand brushed against his jacket pocket and, hey, presto, tightly folded exactly as he'd left it the previous evening, the last edition. Sending a silent thanks to Ruth for persuading him to pack it away, he put his service hat on, picked up his bag, and joined everyone else on the platform.

Lawrence looked up at the station clock and just had time to note it was only slightly after ten when—it happened. An enormous jarring force in his ribs took his breath away, forcing him to his knees, closely followed by something hard and wooden being swiped across the back of his head. As stars sprang to life in front of his eyes, his last thought as he collapsed to the floor unconscious was, "That could have been less painful."

"Mister. Mister!"

Something was shaking his arm, together with a ringing in his ears. His head was pounding, and his left ear was wet. Something was shaking his shoulder, and other voices were joining in the chorus urging him to open his eyes.

"That's right, sir, just open your eyes for me. You're going to be okay."

This voice was softer, sweeter than the first, which had also sounded so much younger. The new voice had a quiet authority that got through to his fuzzy brain cells. He cranked an eye open. At first, he thought he could see the wings of a dove, albeit rather blurry, so he forced the other eye open, and gradually things came into focus. The voice belonged to a white-hatted nurse who was mopping his brow and head with a rag and a bucket of water someone had placed beside her. At least that explained the wet ear.

He let out a groan and struggled to get his hands beneath him. "Easy there, young man," the nurse told him, whilst getting to her knees and putting her hands beneath his arms. "You took quite a whack to the head."

At last Lawrence was able to sit up—and then wished he hadn't, as the drummers inside his head decided to increase their tempo and volume, and his stomach gave a lurch he could have done without. He put his hands to his head once more and screwed his eyes shut. Helpful hands heaved him to his feet and sat him on a wooden bench. Someone asked him, "Could you manage a cuppa, luv?" The British cup of tea. If only everything could be fixed with such a simple solution.

Peering through the slit of one eye, keeping the other closed, Lawrence saw he now sat between the nurse and a beat constable. Accepting the tea, which was proffered by an elderly lady dressed in the gray-blue uniform of the WVS, he raised it to his mouth, took a long sip, and then had a sugar rush to rival that of Bobby on ice cream. "Thank you," he croaked out, and she beamed at him and stood back, making sure he drank it all.

"Feeling any better?" the policeman asked.

After taking a moment to cautiously move his head from side to side, he felt able to reply, "I think so, yes."

"Did they do much damage?" he heard the policeman ask of the nurse.

"You were lucky," she replied, addressing her comments to both Lawrence and the policeman. "There'll be a good-sized bump, and that headache you've got isn't going to go away any time soon. But you'll be all right."

"Thanks for everything, Nurse," Lawrence said gratefully. "Sorry to have been a trouble."

"Phish," she admonished him. "Don't be silly. It's not like you meant to get turned over." She got to her feet, handed him the cold, damp rag, thanked the WVS lady for the bucket, and turned toward the policeman one last time. "Well, I don't think there's anything else I can do here, so if you're all right, Mister…"

He held out a hand. "Lawrence, just Lawrence, miss. Thank you again for everything you've done for me."

As soon as she was out of sight, Lawrence gritted his teeth and faced his colleague. "I'm sure you have a lot of questions you'd like to ask, Constable, but I'm just going to take something out of my inner pocket to show you first. Okay?"

Despite feeling less than at his best, he needed to gain this man's trust, if only for a short time. The policeman stood up and took a few steps back to put some distance between the two. "Go ahead."

Acknowledging the man's professionalism, Lawrence used his left hand to take his warrant card out of his inside left top pocket and held it open so the constable could see.

Once he'd finished reading it, the constable sat down and took off his helmet. A shrewd look in his eye was backed up by his words. "I'm guessing that whatever happened here was part of some operation?"

Before answering, Lawrence checked around, and the flask in its brown paper bag was, indeed, gone. He smiled and clapped a hand upon the constable's shoulder, wincing at the pain it cost him. "I can't tell you much, only that the pain is worth it. Now," he said, suppressing a groan, "I need to report in."

"Whoa there, sir," the constable said, making a quick grab for one of Lawrence's arms as he wobbled slightly. "Perhaps you'd better take it easy for a while."

After a moment or two, Lawrence felt the slight dizziness subside, and he was able to hold his colleague's gaze without feeling like a lie-down was needed. "I appreciate your concern, Constable. If it'll make you feel better, you can walk with me to Scotland Yard, to make certain I don't get run over."

Chapter Twenty-Eight

"Jane looked a bit distracted, don't you think?" queried Penny.

A cup of builder's-strength tea before the first taxi aircraft took off for the day had become a ritual for the girls of The Old Lockkeeper's Cottage. As Lawrence had never quite mastered a smooth take-off yet, they all, including Doris, agreed having something to bolster their backbones was well in order.

"From what I hear, she had a very good time with her Yank," put in Mary.

"Hey!" Doris protested.

"Don't be like that," Mary soothed. "As far as we're concerned, you're *the* Yank, or at least *our* Yank."

For reasons she didn't bother to explain, this seemed to satisfy their American friend, and she settled back, with her customary grimace, to finish her tea and wait for Lawrence to sign for the aircraft.

"So what happened?" Penny asked.

"I'm not sure I should tell you," responded Mary. "If you hadn't fallen asleep—and by God, you snore—you'd have found out for yourself."

Penny put her head to one side, pouted, and did her best to look affronted at her friend's accusation. "I do not snore!"

"Yes, you do," remarked Betty, as she followed

Lawrence out to where the three pilots lounged on their parachute packs. "In fact," she added, with a sly wink Penny couldn't see, "we've toyed with the idea of asking if you and Mary would change rooms."

"Change rooms...but I love my little room." Penny then finished with, "I'm not that bad, am I?"

"Not that bad?" Doris queried, picking up and joining in. "We've had Messerschmitts and Heinkels dropping messages asking if we can turn the noise down as they can't get to sleep!"

"Don't you think that's a bit..." Penny started to protest when the *penny dropped*. "Oh, very funny," she said, crossing her arms and pouting.

Betty sat beside her and nudged her gently. "Don't take it to heart, Penny. You know we're only teasing. However," she added, "you do snore. Even Jane was surprised."

The urge to find out what had gone on between Jane and her American friend won over the desire to carry on sulking. "Well, come on, then, fill me in. Jane and the Yank?"

She didn't get an immediate reply and was about to ask again when Doris and Mary scrambled to their feet and took to staring at the space above her head. With a sense of foreboding, Penny pasted what she hoped was her friendliest smile on her face, slowly got to her feet as well, and turned around.

"You were saying, Third Officer Blake?"

Penny wiped a bead of sweat from her forehead. "Ah, yes, sorry about that, boss."

Jane took a look at the clock above Betty's desk and surveyed the nervous crowd around her, all except Lawrence and Betty, who seemed to be very much enjoying things. "Lawrence, don't you think it's time you were off? We don't want to keep anyone waiting," she added, all the time not taking her eyes from a nervous Penny.

"Yes, ma'am," Lawrence agreed, hoisting his parachute over his shoulder and striding toward where the ground crew had started up the engines of the Anson.

As Mary and Doris made to follow him, Jane tapped Penny on the shoulder and motioned for her to wait.

"So what trouble's Penny gotten herself into?" Shirley asked, as she stood by the steps of the Anson.

Doris couldn't hide her grin, and even Mary was struggling to stop from laughing. "She didn't check her six before asking about Jane's love life," Doris explained.

Shortly after, and much to everyone's surprise, Penny strode up to the plane as if she didn't have a care in the world.

"Going on what Doris just told me," Shirley said, a wide smile upon her face, "I've no idea why you're grinning. I was half expecting to hear you say Jane had grounded you!"

"*Moi*?" Penny placed a hand upon her chest. "Ground her best pilot? Of course not. She just wanted to share—in confidence, girls—what a good time she had with her new American friend."

If anything was going to pique their interest, this was it, and everyone, including Lawrence, pricked up their ears.

****

Lawrence, who'd arrived extra early to make up for

his jaunt to London the previous day and had only the remnants of a headache left, was glad of the excuse to put off the flight for a few more minutes.

He'd arrived back at his aunt's cottage late yesterday afternoon with, exactly as the nurse had promised, a splitting headache and a very sore rib or two. Fortunately, there had been no one else at home, so he'd some privacy. Upon removing his shirt to examine what he expected to be just some bruising to his chest, he was surprised to see the marks left by what could only be a set of brass knuckles!

A long twenty minutes later, he pushed open the door of the *Hamble Gazette*, to be greeted by his aunt Ruth. Her welcome tailed off as she noticed the grimace on his face as he stepped into the office, a hand clutching his ribs.

"Someone looks like they've been in the wars, forgive the bad pun," remarked Ruth. Laying down her pen, she moved around the desk toward where Lawrence was now leaning against Walter's desk.

He managed a self-effacing smile. "Let's just say things didn't quite go like I'd planned."

Ruth reached to pull him into a hug, but as soon as she squeezed even a little, he winced, evidently in some pain.

Walter reappeared with a half bottle of whisky, poured a good measure into a glass, and placed it in Lawrence's hands. "Here, get that down you."

Lawrence knocked the drink back in one and then let his head drop.

"Someone needed that," Ruth said, with a hint of a smile, and then showed Lawrence to her seat. "Have you had anything to eat today?"

As always seemed to be the case, Lawrence's stomach growled.

"I guess that's a no," she said, opening a drawer in her desk and pushing her pack of cheese sandwiches toward him. "Here. If you can eat, you're welcome to them."

After wolfing one down, Lawrence let out a sigh. "Suppose I'd better tell you what happened." He settled himself a little more comfortably in the chair before filling them in. "I guess I was hoping I wouldn't get roughed up so much," he admitted. "Knuckle dusters hurt a bit."

Ruth's hands flew to her mouth. "Knuckle dusters!"

Lawrence shrugged. "My own fault. Too many comics when I was younger. Guess I couldn't resist acting the hero. My ribs took a pounding, but I don't think anything's broken."

"Some bloody hero," Ruth scolded. "More like a bloody fool, but at least you got the job done."

"Funnily enough, that's what my bosses told me, too," he mumbled.

"You know who's going to yell her head off at you? Mary. She's going to give you hell," remarked Walter.

"Mary? Why'd she give me hell?"

Ruth laughed and threw her hands in the air. "Men! I often wonder how you lot managed to wind up running the world when you know so little about emotions. Honestly, Herbert." She used his given name to make certain she had his full attention. "I thought you were a policeman."

Lawrence merely stood there, dumbfounded.

"You can't tell me you didn't notice how concerned she was at what you were planning." Ruth shook her head in disbelief.

****

Lawrence was snapped out of his reverie by Mary tapping him on his shoulder. "I think Jane would like it very much if we took off," she advised him, pulling his earphone away from his head and pointing to his side of the aircraft where their boss stood pointing at her watch.

"Ah," he began, settling his headphones back correctly. "Perhaps you're right."

A few minutes later, a weird silence amongst the racket descended upon the Anson as first Mary sneaked a glance at Lawrence and, upon being caught, snapped her head back around to study the fields below. Whereupon Lawrence's head gradually swiveled to look over at Mary, and when she caught him, he'd find the instruments tremendously interesting.

Behind them and thoroughly enjoying the game of head tennis, Penny and Doris were betting on who'd get neck ache first.

"See you later, ladies," Lawrence shouted from the open window of the Anson once they'd landed outside Southampton.

Doris couldn't wait any longer, though. "Come on, Mary." She prodded her with her bag.

"Come on, what?" Mary asked back, although they all knew she knew what Doris meant.

"You and Lawrence. You do know he's got the hots for you?"

The rapid spread of a blush from her neck to the tips of her ears was enough of an answer. "If I, as you say, do something about it, will you two stop teasing me?" she asked.

Doris and Penny looked at each other, back to their friend, then back to each other before turning and answering as one, "Not a chance!"

****

"Should I not have invited myself over?" Tom Alsop asked as Penny, for what was the umpteenth time that evening, stifled a yawn.

She took a draft from her wine glass and reached over the table for his hand. "No, of course not." She tried again upon realizing how that had come out. "I really am, despite appearances to the contrary, delighted to see you, Tom."

"I suppose it's my own fault, turning up like this and dragging you all the way to Southampton for dinner."

Determined to prove she wasn't as tired as she knew her body to be, Penny looked over at Tom. He really did suit the uniform, she thought, fighting the urge to reach over and stroke his slicked-back hair. "You absolutely should have," she assured him again. "After the busy day we've had, this is just what I need to take my mind off things."

"Even if you'll be even more tired tomorrow because of it?"

She squeezed his hand. "Even if I'm absolutely, totally, completely exhausted beyond belief tomorrow."

"That's good to hear," he replied, "very good to hear. Though I'm now feeling incredibly guilty about it."

"You are? But why? I know I'm likely to fall asleep in my soup…"

The knowing smile on Tom's face caused Penny to laugh, and she started to relax for the first time since Tom had shown up in his Austin 8. Tom drove the way he flew, if her memory of how he flung that Mustang around was correct—slightly manic. They were fortunate there were few cars on the roads these days, or at least on the back roads Tom took.

After delivering two Spitfires and an Oxford Airspeed that day, she'd been quite ready to turn in for an early night when the toot of a car horn had caused her to raise her head as she came down the steps of the flight line hut. She found herself staring into Thomas Alsop's piercing eyes, and, at least for those few moments, her weariness had faded away. She'd never changed out of her flying suit and into her day uniform so quickly. Not having seen him for a few weeks, she hadn't taken much persuasion to accept his dinner invitation. If only the weariness she felt would go away for an hour or two.

She held up her glass. "A toast, Tom, with congratulations on your DFC!"

"You do know I'm in deep trouble at the squadron because I told them I'd changed my plans?" he told her, taking a sup of his drink.

"Oh, how so?" Penny asked, as their tomato soup was placed before them.

Tom laid his napkin across his lap, and for a few moments, all that could be heard was the slurping of soup. "I had told them we'd have a squadron party to celebrate tonight, but instead of a long drive back to the base followed by a night of drink, I told them I'd rather see you."

Though secretly delighted to be chosen over his

squadron, Penny did feel slightly guilty about his choice and told him so.

"You really shouldn't feel that way," he chided her, pushing his soup bowl away. "Look at it like this. I'd a choice between a bunch of hairy-assed louts, or the very pleasant prospect of an evening spent with a very, very beautiful lady. It wasn't hard to make the right decision," he added with a smile.

"As you put it like that," she told him, once more reaching for his hand and this time, quite daringly, bringing his fingers to her lips, "I shall do my best to stay awake."

"And I shall do my best to be worthy of your staying awake," Tom echoed.

The next few hours were spent in comfortable relaxation in front of a roaring fire before it came time for Tom to drive Penny back to Hamble. Penny was pretty stiff, even more tired, but both of these were overridden by how happy she felt. "This has been a lovely evening, Tom. I hope it won't be too long before we see each other again."

Not caring who could be watching them, Tom took her in his arms and stroked his fingers tenderly down the side of her face before leaning in to kiss her full red lips with a passion that inflamed them both. He looked down into her eyes and saw his feelings mirrored there. "I don't think I could take it if I didn't see you again before long. Ever since you dropped into my life, I've not been able to think of much else. I have to see you, and a lot more often, if you'll forgive the terrible grammar."

Penny threw her arms around his neck and hugged him to her body. "Oh, Tom, that's both the most romantic thing anyone's ever said to me, and also the corniest! Plus, you are right, the grammar was awful."

"I can accept that." Tom laughed, kissing her on the neck in a way that made any other thoughts temporarily float off into the ether. "And I'll do my very best to keep my promise."

She took his head between her hands and looked him in the eye, deadly serious for once. "You do that, or you'll have me to answer to."

Chapter Twenty-Nine

The wine glass smashed above George Evans' head. Virginia then picked up the bottle of Burgundy and took aim. Whether to save the bottle or himself, he wasn't sure, George popped his head up from behind his old desk and shouted at his enraged wife, "Not that bottle!"

Much to his surprise, the bottle was placed to rest next to the Group Captain's best brandy. The Napoléon, he was pleased to note, didn't appear to be in any danger of taking flying lessons either.

In probably the riskiest maneuver of his military career, a singularly unexceptional endeavor thus far, George Evans crept as bravely as he didn't feel around to the unprotected side of the desk. The expression in her eyes he took for indecision. A mistake.

"Why on earth did you get a forensics report on that damned flask?" she demanded, waving a few typed pieces of paper in his face.

So, more like disbelief.

"What the hell made you do such a thing, George? I was under the impression the purpose of going to all the trouble obtaining the thing was to destroy it. Ralph actually did something right, and what's the first thing you do, you let it out of your hands again because you apparently wanted to get a..." She flipped over a page and read out, "Toxik... Totix... Tosix..."

"Toxicology report," George supplied.

The expression "if looks could kill" should have been invented for Virginia Mayes. "George, do you have any of the sense you were born with? Do you trust who you gave it to? And I would advise you to have the right answer. Big John is at the other end of this phone," she warned, taking up the receiver and putting a finger into the dial.

Truth was, curiosity had led him to have it tested—he wanted to see if Bramble had been stupid enough to leave a fingerprint on it, and he had. Now he only had to think of how to explain handing it over to an old friend of his in the Royal College of Medicine.

He decided to start with some other good news. He took another sip of brandy. "First, as you can see, it confirms the presence of strychnine…"

"I can read that for myself," his wife replied through clenched teeth.

"…but more importantly, our good doctor was stupid enough to leave his fingerprints on it." He sat back, expecting to enjoy the praise of his wife, and was, thusly, very disappointed.

"And how do you know that?"

George gulped and plucked up his courage. There were certain people in his pay he trusted to keep secret—his contact in Marylebone Police Station in this case, though he'd be surprised if she didn't know who had done the deed soon. She had access to the ledgers which detailed all payments, after all. Still, no point in volunteering any names unless he had to. "Someone in our pay," he decided to say to placate her, "checked it for me."

When all she did was to wait for him to carry on,

Evans knew his guess had been right.

"You do know that Bramble will now do anything to prevent the flask from falling into the authorities' hands?"

"Of course I do," she snapped. "I would also hope he knows his next trip would be in a wooden box if he crossed me."

Evans gulped. It sounded like she'd already thought through her options for dealing with the doctor. Just by looking at Virginia, he had little doubt that if push came to shove, the same justice would be dealt out to him as well.

"And who," she began as she picked up a letter opener and began pushing back her cuticles with it, "did you get the report from?"

George Evans didn't miss the meaning of the gesture, though he was surprised she hadn't found the name herself yet. "He's an old boy from my RAF training days. Let's just say we were close and he knows how to keep his mouth shut."

Virginia flicked the letter opener sharply up so the point was aimed at her husband's chin. "Let's hope so. Which reminds me, where is that bloody flask?"

"Bugger, knew I'd forgot something," Evans exclaimed, making a dart for the door as the letter opener whizzed past his ear.

A few moments later, she'd placed the forensics report in the safe and put the key on its chain back around her neck. There was a knock at the door, and Big John strode into the office, instantly making everything seem a little bit smaller.

"How's our guest today?" she asked. "I assume he isn't giving you any trouble?"

Big John twirled his bowler hat round and round between fingers the size of sausages with all the dexterity of a professional juggler. In a surprisingly high voice that never ceased to amaze her, agreed, "He wouldn't dare to try," adding a toothless grin for good measure.

Satisfied the doctor was safely locked up and behaving himself, she dismissed her minder and picked up the phone. After waiting an interminable number of seconds, she was through to the mess at Hamble airfield and pretended to be the mother of Ralph Johnson.

"At last!" she shouted down the phone. "If I was a suspicious person, I'd think you've been avoiding me. If you've kept me from dinner, I'll have your guts for garters! Now, listen and listen very closely. First, I am appreciative of the information you provided—we got the flask. Yes, yes, I do appreciate how much difficulty you had finding it, though I am curious how you came to come by it, so do fill me in."

For the next few minutes, Virginia felt her temper rising as Ralph's explanations became more and more unbelievable, until she finally interrupted, "Stop right there, Johnson. I think I've heard enough fiction just now to fill a library! Reading between the lines, answer me yes or no—was it Shirley Tuttle who told you where the flask would be?" The stunned silence from the other end of the phone was all she needed to hear. "Why didn't you just say so in the first place? In that case, tell her I'm disappointed not to have heard about this from her myself. Pass on this message...*nobody* resigns from my employ!"

Chapter Thirty

"Shirley!" Ralph hissed.

Her head inside the cowling of the Cheetah engine, Shirley waved a hand vaguely behind her, barely managing to keep a grip on the spanner she was holding, as it nearly slipped from her greasy hand. She continued to ignore him.

He glanced around to see if anyone were watching and was relieved they were pretty much alone in the maintenance hangar. There were a couple of other mechanics working on the undercarriage of a Tiger Moth, and their shift manager was in the office, bent over paperwork.

Since he'd reported in to Virginia Mayes, he'd been building up the courage for this day. Ms. Mayes had been very firm on making the point that no one escaped her service, and he believed her. If he'd been afraid of his Lordship, then it went double as far as Virginia was concerned. Undoubtedly she now knew all he'd done whilst in the sole service of her husband, so she now held the sword over his head; he had no doubt she wouldn't hesitate to wield it at the slightest provocation. It brought on an attack of the shudders merely thinking about it.

The queasy feeling caused his stomach to contract, and for a second, he thought he'd be sick. He'd been trying to catch Shirley at home, or on her way in to work, or anywhere, for the last week, but whenever he'd seen her she'd been accompanied by one of her friends. Even when he'd caught her eye, she'd given a single, nearly imperceptible shake of her head and went back to ignoring him. That's what had brought him to the hangar. He'd been unable to convey he'd passed on Virginia's message to Shirley, and he knew the longer it took to confirm, the angrier she'd get, and no one would be happy. She may have managed to take over the organization, but she was far from stable; he wasn't stupid enough to say it out loud though.

"Shirley! For cripes' sake, put down that bloody spanner and stop ignoring me," he hissed a little louder. Stealthily, he made his way up onto a platform she'd built out of two boxes and a plank so she could reach the top of the engine.

If she'd been hoping he'd go away if she ignored him, it must have finally got through to her, now he was actually standing at her shoulder, that she couldn't ignore him any longer. Carefully extracting her head from the cowling, Shirley turned to face Ralph, who was waiting impatiently. To emphasize she was ready to defend herself if it came to it, she stood with the grubby spanner tapping gently against her thigh.

"What is it?" she asked, not bothering with any manners.

It'd take a lot more than a snapped question to upset Ralph, especially with a despotic harlot pushing him to this conversation. The sooner he got her message across, the better for everyone, especially him. He had, though, noted the spanner and so took the sensible precaution of stepping back out of range if she decided to take a swing at him. Or it would've been sensible if he'd remembered he stood on a makeshift platform and not the ground.

With a squeal that reminded Shirley of what one of Betty's rabbits made when grabbed by the scruff of its neck, she watched as Ralph tumbled backward to land with a heavy thump on his back on the hangar floor. It appeared he wasn't one of the strong and silent types, though. He let out an ear-piercing yell and proceeded to writhe around as if he'd fallen into a thorn bush from ten feet, rather than onto a concrete floor from about three feet.

She jumped down, landing beside him, dropping the spanner to the floor with a loud clang that brought an immediate yell of, "Tuttle! What the bloody hell have you done now?" followed by the crash of the sergeant's office door as he charged toward them. He was brought up short by the sight of Shirley kneeling on the floor with one of her hands behind Ralph's head.

"Sorry, Boss," she began, looking at the hand she'd placed behind his head and upon finding no blood, wiped it on her overalls to remove the hair oil which, with the grease, wasn't a nice combination. "Ralph, here, fell off my platform."

In the tradition of managers everywhere, hers simply stood over the fallen airman, glaring at him with no sympathy anywhere upon his face. "And what the bloody hell were you doing in my hangar in the first place, Johnson?" he barked. Shirley noticed he'd watched her quick examination. That, together with the way Johnson was squirming around and the self-pitying look on his face, must have told him that no real harm had been done.

Shirley got to her feet without offering a hand to

Ralph and took a seat on her bench, doing her best to hide her enjoyment of Ralph's uncomfortable predicament. She knew she'd been avoiding talking to him since she'd passed on her information. They both knew, and she hadn't been blind to how much she'd annoyed him by refusing to talk to him. Each night, she'd made a point of walking home with one of her friends, and when she'd gotten to Ruth's, she'd stayed in. As she'd lately gotten into the habit of taking a walk along the riverfront, her change of behavior hadn't gone unnoticed.

****

"Not going down The Victory tonight, then, Shirley?" Ruth had asked when for the second night running, she'd politely turned down the invitation from Ruth and Lawrence. "The other girls are coming," Ruth had added, in the hope this would persuade her, but to no avail.

Whenever she was around those she counted as her friends, she still couldn't help but take a back seat. Part of the reason was her natural shyness, which she worked hard to hide, but mostly she felt she didn't deserve such good people as friends, especially as she'd come with the intention of spying on one of them. No matter how much Betty kept assuring her she had nothing to forgive, Shirley still found that hard to accept.

Nevertheless, it appeared she had been accepted, so she felt everyone deserved to know her fears. She took a deep breath and asked both Ruth and Lawrence to take a seat, which both did, after exchanging knowing looks.

"What's wrong?" Lawrence asked, letting his

police head take the lead. "Is something worrying you?"

"Ralph," Shirley came right out with. Both Lawrence and Ruth nodded their heads as if that was the name they were expecting to hear.

"What's he done this time?" Ruth enquired.

Now she'd started, Shirley started to feel a little silly. After all, she didn't have anything else to go on but a bad feeling whenever Johnson was around. "Nothing really, or, actually," she amended, "it's just since I passed on the information about Betty's thermos, he's been trying to get me alone and..." She stopped, feeling silly again, until prompted to go on by Lawrence.

Moving over to sit beside her, Lawrence took one of her hands and pulled her into a comforting embrace. "I think we need to find out what he wants. Do you think you can do that?" he asked her.

After thinking things over for a minute or two and taking note of the encouraging looks her two friends were giving her, she answered, "Yes, yes, I can," she declared, her chin jutting in defiance. "I'll speak to him."

"Brave girl," Lawrence told her, giving her a final hug before getting to his feet to go and stand beside his aunt.

"If that's all sorted, then I suggest we not keep the others waiting," Ruth told her, taking Shirley by the hand.

Allowing herself a smile, Shirley squeezed Ruth's hand and cheekily asked her, "So, what's with *Herbert* then?" earning herself a playful swat to the bottom from said Herbert.

****

"How's your back?" Shirley asked Ralph as they limped, at least in his case, out of the hangar and back toward the mess.

"Why should you care?" he grumped back, wincing as he tripped over a stone.

Shirley shrugged. "I don't. I was being polite."

"After ignoring me for the best part of a week, you're being polite. Don't make me laugh."

Fighting the urge to trip him up, Shirley looked up and noticed Betty waving at her from a window in her ops hut. She waved back, tempted to let Ralph go back to work on his own, except that her boss had ordered her to, in his own words, "See this bugger back to the kitchens!."

Digging her heels in as they came to the rear entrance of the kitchens, Shirley shoved a hand against his chest. "Why've you been trying to get hold of me then?"

Wincing again, Ralph treated her to his best glare and was slightly put off when she didn't move. "Fine, I've a little message for you from her nibbs."

"Virginia?"

"You know anyone else who thinks she owns you?" Ralph shot back.

Though she'd managed to keep her feelings to herself when Ralph had eyed her up, Shirley couldn't keep in her distaste, mixed with more than a little fear, of Virginia Mayes. Suppressing a shudder, she asked, "What does she want? Wasn't she happy with the information? She got the thermos she wanted."

Sensing her growing nervousness, Ralph bared his teeth. "Oh, she was happy all right. Happy enough to tell me to let you know no one walks out on her. She'll have another job for you at some point."

Upon hearing this, Shirley felt her knees begin to wobble, and if she hadn't sat down immediately on the kerb, she'd have fallen down.

Ralph merely stood over her, unable to resist gloating. "You seriously didn't think you only had to do this one thing and your debt would be paid?" He could see from the way she looked up at him, eyes haunted, hands all a-tremble, that's exactly what she'd thought. "You did! You actually thought all you had to do was one job. Christ almighty, what train did you come in on? No, love, there's no way out."

Determinedly, she blinked back tears. No way was she going to cry in front of this little twerp. Shirley looked up at Ralph laughing his head off. "But she can't do that. I...I did what she wanted, found where that bloody thermos flask was for her! She didn't say anything about doing anything else!" She swiped an arm across her face, smearing it with grease at the same time, a big part of her wishing she still had the spanner.

If he was still in pain, he didn't show it as he bent down until his face was at her level. Where the knife came from he started waving in front of her face she didn't know. "There are other ways to get out of her clutches," he spoke into her ear. "I haven't killed anyone, yet, but there's always a first time. I don't think of meself as a violent man, but you've been annoying enough that I could change me mind."

What happened next took Shirley completely by surprise. In a blur of blue, Betty came charging at the two of them, waving a piece of two-by-four she'd picked up from somewhere. From what she shrieked, she must have heard what he'd said.

"Not on my bloody watch you won't, you little bastard!" and launched herself at him as if she could fly.

The two of them went down in a whirl of arms and legs, interspersed with unintelligible yells and curses. Before Shirley even had the chance to think, let alone move, there came a terrible, piercing scream and Ralph stood over the twitching body of Betty, who lay at his feet with a knife sticking out of her stomach.

Chapter Thirty-One

"It's all my fault!"

Since they'd arrived at the airfield medical center, it had been all anyone had been able to get out of Shirley. The poor girl was in such a state no one was even sure if she knew what she was saying anymore. One thing Jane and Thelma were certain of was she'd kept her head long enough to call for help even before Ralph disappeared, plus she hadn't made what would likely have been a fatal mistake in pulling the blade out. She'd left the knife in Betty's stomach and wrapped the rag she had tucked into her pocket around the knife, keeping her hands there until help came. Not the cleanest of bandages, but it had served its purpose until the medics arrived.

All the time this was going on, Betty had stayed conscious and, apart from when she'd been stabbed, hadn't let a sound pass her lips, though sweat had poured from her brow. The medics had had to prise Shirley's bloodied hands away from Betty's wound. By the time they'd made her ready to move to the medical center, word had got around the airfield, and it took a little pushing and yelling from Thelma, with Jane hot on her heels, to get through the gathered crowd.

"It's all my fault!" Shirley muttered again, staring at her blood-covered hands and then, totally ignoring their state, placed them on both sides of her head and started to sob.

Jane and Thelma, sitting on either side of the miserable mechanic, with Betty being tended to by the station doctor in another room, didn't know what they could do to ease her distress. After being assured by the medics Betty would live, the ambulance had delivered her to the doctor with Jane, Thelma, and Shirley hot on its heels. They'd nothing to do now but to be told what had happened and to wait for the door to open. At first, they'd tried to persuade Shirley to clean the blood off her hands, but that had only distressed her all the more, so they'd settled her down on the bench between them to wait.

After half an hour of waiting, Shirley dropped off to sleep. Only being propped between the two of them prevented her from falling off the bench.

"She can't half snore!" commented Thelma after about ten minutes.

They were the first words either had uttered since Shirley's last outburst, and the tension in the room eased slightly. Jane leaned forward a little to stare at Shirley's face, checking she was still asleep. She was rewarded with a loud snort.

"Phew! I wonder if her husband was deaf?"

"A bit hard of hearing," was Shirley's unexpected reply, startling the two of them.

Jane recovered first. "Sorry, we were just trying to break the, well, not silence."

Shirley sniffed and, unthinking, wiped her nose with her hand, smearing blood on that one part of her face that had previously been clean. "No word yet?"

"Not yet," Jane answered and then, realizing Shirley had said something coherent for the first time in a while, ventured, "How about we get you cleaned up a bit?"

Shirley looked at her hands, dawning horror upon her face before she visibly pulled herself together and replied, admittedly in a very shaky voice, "Probably a good idea." She then allowed Thelma to guide her to a wash basin in the corner.

With one white towel already turned a vivid scarlet, Shirley and Thelma were about to repeat the process with the remaining towel when the door they'd been staring at earlier opened and out came the station doctor. His apron was smeared with blood, but he had a tired yet satisfied expression on his face.

Jane was the first to find her voice. "Doctor, will she be all right?"

The doctor turned to face her, slumped down onto a wooden seat, and picked up the phone on the desk before answering. He held his finger over the dial and told them, "She's stable. I don't think she's in any danger, but I'm going to transfer her to the South Hants Hospital to be certain. She needs x-rays and will need more surgery…"

"More surgery!" Shirley couldn't help but shout, her face turning pale.

Upon seeing who had spoken, the doctor replaced the receiver and brought a genuine smile to his face as he looked over at her. "And you must be Ms. Tuttle?" Shirley nodded, some color returning to her face upon noting the doctor didn't appear to be in a hurry. "Well, I would shake your hand, but," he glanced down at his own, "I've only just washed up. To answer your question, yes, she's going to need more surgery. I removed the knife, cleaned the wound, and stitched her up, but she needs to be checked over by a better-equipped facility to make certain there's no more internal damage." Upon seeing Shirley going white again, he got to his feet and, ignoring the blood that was still on her hands and face, leaned in to kiss her on the forehead. "I'm playing it safe, Ms. Tuttle, that's all. However, I can safely say you did a very commendable job with your first aid. I was very impressed." He released her hands and made his way back to pick up the phone's receiver. "Now I really must arrange for our patient to be taken to hospital."

Whilst the doctor was calling the hospital and the MT flight to arrange for the station ambulance to take Betty in, Thelma turned back to the business of finishing Shirley's clean-up. Five minutes later, a pale and unconscious Betty was carried into the waiting ambulance.

****

"There's a Moth coming in to land now," Thelma mumbled, putting down her binoculars and picking up another cold cup of tea, making a face upon taking a slurp. Fortunately, there were only three pilots still out, and two of them were likely to be in the Tiger Moth that was now on finals. Picking up her binoculars again, she trained her eyes on it, took them away, and rubbed her eyes. What she thought she'd seen couldn't be right. "Thank heavens Jane's not around to see this," she muttered to herself as she made her way over to the flight line hut.

"Just as well Jane's not around for what?" said a voice at her side, belonging to said Jane.

Thelma wryly shook her head. "If you haven't seen, boss, you'll soon find out."

"It's not got anything to do with this rather unusual Moth taxiing in, is it?"

As they came to a halt beside the hut, Thelma shoved her hands into her pockets. "I assume you were watching for them too, then?"

Jane shrugged her shoulders. "Sod's law would choose today for Doris and Penny to be late back."

"You heard Mary's stuck at Upavon?"

"Not a lot we can do about that." Jane shrugged.

"Do you think we should call and tell her what's happened?" Thelma asked, whipping her hat off so it wouldn't get blown away by the wash from the biplane as it pulled up.

"No point!" Jane shouted to be heard. "Now," she said, rubbing her hands together, "let's go and see what these reprobates have to say for themselves."

To say the scene at the biplane was chaotic would have been an understatement. It had pulled to a stop only a bare twenty feet from where they stood, so it took a very short while to get to it, and when they did, if they hadn't seen it themselves, they likely wouldn't have believed it.

By now unstrapped, Penny was standing up in the rear cockpit, all quite normal so far. However, the scene in the front was quite another, which, being viewed via binoculars, wasn't what either Jane or Thelma had been able to quite make out.

"Who's next?" shouted Doris, waving a fist.

For a few moments, both Jane and Thelma could only stand there, mouths hanging open in disbelief at the sight before them. A foot encased in plaster was sticking out of the front cockpit. This foot belonged to Doris, who was actually sitting on the lap of Lawrence.

The twin-seat biplane had brought in an extra passenger!

Joining Penny, Jane climbed up onto the lower wing and helped Doris to carefully ease herself off Lawrence's lap. With the aid of Thelma, they had her leaning a hand on the fuselage whilst balancing on her good foot.

"Here you go," Lawrence said. "She'll need that." He passed a crutch from beside him to Jane, who passed it on to Doris.

Jane decided the time had come for questions. The trouble was, she didn't really know where to begin. Looking at her waiting companions, she sensibly decided the matter of Betty could wait until she got to the bottom of what had happened here. She started by giving them an opening and hoped they'd tell her what had occurred without her needing to press.

"Who'd care to begin? Doris?"

Now she could see her pilot, Jane could see she'd taken more damage than a broken foot. There were numerous small cuts and abrasions on her face and hands, too. Doris herself, though, appeared to be in quite high spirits as she waggled her injured foot in the air.

"I had an argument with a hill," she began, "and lost. You should see the state of the other guy!" Her statement ended with a burst of laughter before she flopped down onto her bottom, where she continued to laugh.

Jane turned to Penny and raised an eyebrow. At least Penny had some sense about her, it seemed. "It's true," she said, settling down and pulling Doris into a sitting position. "Doris got caught in some low cloud and flew into a hill. The plane's a wreck, the undercarriage got ripped right off, I was told, but Doris here got lucky, if that's the word, as apart from the cuts she only broke her foot."

At hearing this, both Jane and Thelma regarded the seated and still giggling Doris with much more sympathy. "And the giggling?" Thelma enquired.

"That'll be the morphine," Lawrence supplied, taking out a packet of cigarettes and passing them around—only Jane took one—before lighting up. "The hospital wanted to keep her in, but she insisted upon coming back here, so that's why they dosed her up."

"Dacka-dacka-dacka." Doris began shooting an imaginary machine-gun into the air. She found this so hilarious she collapsed back into a prone position despite Lawrence's best efforts to keep her upright.

"Do you mind if we get her home, boss?" Penny asked.

Jane perused Doris who, though she looked a bit of a mess, didn't look like a few more minutes would do her much harm. "Before you go, do you want to tell me how come the three of you ended up in this predicament?"

Lawrence looked up. "Well, I'd gone to pick up Penny, here, but we then found out about Doris and what a fuss she was kicking up and decided to fly over and see what we could do."

"And this was your solution?" Thelma asked, though she was fighting hard to keep a smile from her face.

Penny and Lawrence both looked at each other before, at the same time, shrugging. "I know it's not strictly according to regulations," Penny began, earning herself a raised eyebrow from Jane and Thelma, "and I'm sorry about that, but we couldn't leave her there, and it did work, no harm done."

After a few minutes, Jane let out a bark of laughter and planted an arm around Penny's shoulders. "Honestly, if I'd known how much trouble you and your friends would cause me, I'd have sent you to join the Wrens!"

Penny had the good grace to look a little sheepish. "I'm sure Doris didn't plan on flying into a hill."

Jane was quick to reassure her. "Don't get me wrong, I couldn't be happier that she's alive."

"Ooh! Me too!" yelled Doris, obviously having overheard part of the conversation, and then sat up to give, unbidden, her own singularly personal version of events. "I was proceeding on a northwesterly heading when it got all black and I couldn't see a dicky-bird, let alone a tickerty-boo. Next thing I know, this whacking great hill-type thing popped up out of nowhere and started bashing up me and my kite." She reached down to rap her knuckles on her cast. "You wait until I get this off, and I'll kick its fanny!" She then flopped back again and fell fast asleep.

The other four, after listening to their drugged-up friend, could only stand there until Lawrence piped up, "I guess that about sums it up. We picked her up, and here we are."

Thelma bent down and with Lawrence's help heaved Doris to her feet and into a chair Jane had dragged outside, all without waking her. "Do you think we should get this idiot home before she does herself any further harm, Jane?"

Jane shook her head. "Before you do, there's

something you all should know. Right, Thelma?"

Thelma looked at both Penny and Lawrence before agreeing.

Jane continued, "There's no easy way to say this. About an hour ago, Betty was attacked and stabbed by Ralph Johnson."

Anything else she was going to add was drowned out by a torrent of startled questions from Penny and Lawrence, which all amounted to the same thing: Was she alive? What had happened to Johnson?

As things turned out, she was able to tell them that though Betty would now be at South Hants Hospital for at least a day or so, the base doctor was quite certain she'd make a full recovery. Okay, so he hadn't said exactly those words, but she chose to embellish a little, as they'd had a hard day, too. So far as the whereabouts of Ralph Johnson were concerned, she was about to admit she had no idea when she was interrupted by one of the flight line staff poking a head out and telling her she had an urgent phone call. A very short minute later, she was back and had acquired a grin a shark would envy.

"As it turns out, the cat's come to the mice."

At the questioning looks the others threw her way, Jane tried again. "That was the guardhouse. Johnson's handed himself in."

Lawrence clapped his hands together. "Excellent. If you'll excuse me, ladies, I have a job to do."

"Hang on, hang on, hang on," Doris slurred from where she was now held up by only Thelma, Lawrence having forgotten he was supposed to be holding her up when he'd heard the news about Johnson. "What was that about Betty…Betty! What's happened to my mate

Betty?" Doris demanded, trying to push herself to her feet and instead falling backward onto the grass once more.

Chapter Thirty-Two

Lawrence had barely taken his seat across from where Ralph sat when he became aware of raised female voices rapidly approaching the guardroom.

With a sense of foreboding, he got to his feet, snapped to Johnson, "Don't move a bloody muscle," and went toward the office's door.

There were two small rooms in use as cells, and apart from a toilet, that was about all the hut had, so he'd shooed the commander of the guard out and commandeered his office so he could interrogate Ralph Johnson in relative privacy. To do so, he'd needed to show the guard commander his Special Branch Warrant card, as the commander had been rather confused as to why an ATA pilot would want to see someone who'd just confessed to murder. The poor man was now slouched outside with his men, trying to resolve what was going on, and he'd had to swear him to secrecy as to his real identity. If Johnson thought he'd actually killed Betty, then he could use the threat of the hangman's noose to get any information he wanted.

He hadn't even had a chance to introduce himself before he'd been interrupted. With the intention of yelling at whoever was making all the noise and of getting them out of his hair, he slammed the office door shut, shaking it to its hinges. However, when he opened the door that led to the outside world, what he was presented with was a spectacle to rival any farce he'd ever seen on stage.

"Is that bastard in there?" Doris was yelling, her crutch waving in the air, narrowly missing both Penny and Jane's heads. Thelma, having had to go back to work, was safe from the unfolding confusion. "Let me at the swine! I'll get a confession for you, Herbert!" she yelled upon catching sight of a flummoxed Lawrence.

The drugged-up American then made a determined lurch in his direction, catching her two friends by surprise as she wrenched her arms out of their clutches. She was fine for the first step, though after this her body remembered it had a broken foot, whereupon when she went to pick up said broken foot, it refused to obey. She promptly tumbled face first into the grass beside the guardroom. It didn't stop her demanding at the top of her voice, "Open that door, Herbert, and I'll shove this crutch so far up his…"

"Doris!" Penny snapped, struggling to keep a grin off her face, leaning down with Jane to help up their very vocal friend and to sit her on a bench.

"Do me a favor, Penny," Jane asked as she stood back up and made her way over to where Lawrence and the guard force were watching the carry-on with open mouths, "and keep a hold of her, will you? I need to speak with Lawrence, here."

"I'm ready!" interrupted Doris again, at the top of her lungs. She then raised her head, ignoring the patch of grass that was stuck to her left temple, and spotted Lawrence again. "Herbert, old chap, you play good cop, I'll play bad cop. You Brits know what I mean?" she added, looking around at her audience. "We'll soon have him singing like a canary!"

Jane took Lawrence by the elbow and led him past the guards, treating them to her best stare to encourage them to get back to work, and back into the guardroom. Shutting the door behind her, which barely muffled Doris's continued shouts and yells of suggestions, some of which were even possible, she collapsed into a seat, closely followed by an equally hassled-looking Lawrence.

"I assume you didn't know she knew your real first name?" she said, effectively easing the tension.

Lawrence shook his head. "That, I didn't. I may have to speak to my aunt about this later and"—he jerked a thumb over his shoulder—"with Doris. That's if she remembers all this tomorrow."

"Good point," she agreed and then became serious. "So, Johnson?"

"In there." Lawrence pointed at the door to her left. "I was about to have a chat with him when our friendly Yank interrupted things."

"She seems determined to confront him," Jane agreed. "I know she's still high on the morphine, but after you left, she couldn't focus on anything else once she'd heard about Betty, and Penny and I couldn't persuade her to get in the wagon we'd arranged to take her home. She insisted we walk her here. I'm sorry," she added. "I had no idea she'd react like this."

"That's all right," Lawrence assured her and then lowered his voice. "Who knows, maybe we can make use of her if he decides to be awkward. The stupid bugger thinks he killed Betty."

"Really! Hmm, well that could work in our favor," Jane agreed with a feral grin.

"We'll see." Lawrence nodded. "Now, if you'll

302

excuse me, I'm going to have a chat with Johnson. Oh, so you know, I've called my bosses in London, and they know everything that's happened today. Until they come to take him in for more questioning, we'll be keeping him here. I personally don't think he knows much of use, but seeing as I'm going to let him think he's killed Betty, if he does know something, I'm sure he'll cough it up, hoping to save his neck."

"Not much of a neck to save," muttered Jane. "Right. You go and get him. I'll be outside. I don't think it's a good idea to bring Doris in, but I also don't think she'll agree to go home until she knows more. Mind you," she decided to say after a moment's pause to think, "the same goes for me and Penny."

With that, Jane got to her feet. The glance she cast at the door behind which Ralph Johnson waited could have blown it to smithereens. Determination settled in her expression, she went back outside.

"You got him ready for me?" Lawrence heard before the door closed. It made him smile.

Opening the door, the first thing he noticed was that Ralph's attention was immediately drawn to the space directly behind him and he had a sense of satisfaction bloom inside his chest. Obviously he'd heard at least some of what Doris had been yelling. Good, he thought. Something else that would tip the culprit off balance.

"What's all the noise about? Who's that yelling?" Ralph demanded as soon as Lawrence shut the door. "And why are you here?"

Careful to maintain a neutral expression on his face, Lawrence took a seat in front of where Ralph was handcuffed to the desk, then slapped his hand down on the top, *hard*. An empty cup jumped clean off the table and shattered on the floor. Pens and pencils went scurrying after it. Finally, he took his warrant card out of a pocket and laid it, face up for Ralph to see, in front of him.

Now that his prisoner was clear as to whom he was talking, Lawrence began. "I suggest you remember that you're here to answer questions, Johnson, not to ask them. Now, why did you kill Betty Palmer? Why make the jump from third-rate gangster"—no harm in winding the little oick up, he thought, more likely to let things slip like that—"to murderer?"

It appeared his choice of words had their desired effect. When Ralph opened his mouth to answer, at first nothing came out. What closely followed was a string of incoherent letters that failed to make any sense. Lawrence then had the added satisfaction of seeing him attempt to wipe away the beads of sweat that had formed on his forehead, but as he was unable to move either of his hands, Lawrence having taken the precaution of handcuffing both, his frustration only increased. Lawrence stirred the pot a little more.

"Nothing to say for yourself?"

An internal conflict was going on inside what passed for Ralph's brain as the seriousness of his situation became apparent to him. Lawrence believed accusing him of murder had had the desired effect. The Special Branch officer could see, from the way Johnson's shoulders slumped, he'd now get whatever he needed out of him.

"I didn't mean to kill her."

The words, when they finally came, were barely audible, so Lawrence made him say them again. He'd take every little bit of power over his prisoner he could get.

"I didn't mean to kill her," Ralph Johnson repeated louder.

Lawrence let a minute's silence work for him before answering. "If you didn't mean to kill Betty Palmer"—he repeated his friend's name to enforce his control of the prisoner—"why did you have a knife in your hand? Were you threatening Miss Tuttle?"

Tears had begun to leak from Ralph's eyes, and when he finally brought his head up from where he'd been staring at the floor, Lawrence saw a broken man.

"I wouldn't have hurt her," Ralph pleaded. "I was only threatening her because Virginia Mayes wanted me to."

"And why did she want that?"

Ralph sniffed. "So she'd know she was still owned by her."

Lawrence allowed himself an inward smile. This was enough information for him. Neither Ralph nor Virginia Mayes knew Shirley had switched sides. "And you'd be prepared to put that down in a statement?"

"Yes, yes, anything you want," Ralph agreed with desperation in his voice.

"Good," Lawrence replied. "Now, let's see what we can do to keep that noose from around your neck, eh?"

Lawrence had the satisfaction of seeing Ralph's pupils widen and his throat gulp audibly. The bait was taken.

"Suppose you write down everything you know about Virginia Mayes and George Evans' little empire, and don't miss anything out. I also want to know what happened to the thermos flask. I've a personal interest in that," he told Ralph, rubbing his head and glaring at him.

The look he shot Ralph had the desired effect again. "Um...I'm sorry about that. Virginia sent some people I don't know after you, and I think they must've decided to have some fun when they found out you were a copper."

"When I meet them, I'll see about having a little fun of my own," Lawrence promised. "Now, I'm going to get us some tea. Here's pen and paper," he told Ralph, pushing the items across the desk to him and then getting up to undo his right hand. "You make yourself busy with the statement, and I'll be right back. Don't think of doing anything stupid. The door's open, and I'll be able to see everything you do," he added, pointing to a kettle directly in line of sight with the office.

"Something you should know. The Group Captain had a...I think they called it a forensics report done on the thermos. It's in a safe in their Belgravia flat," Ralph volunteered.

Lawrence nodded to show he'd heard as he reached the door. He turned back and in perfect imitation of film police everywhere, held up a couple of fingers. "Oh, just a few more things I'd like to know." Ralph's head snapped up from where he'd been bent over the piece of paper. "First, why did you stab Betty?"

"I didn't mean to!" His answer burst out in a plea. "She launched herself at me, and when we went down, it just happened. I swear—I swear to God!—that I never meant to do it."

"Write it down, exactly as you've told me."

Ralph nodded and went to put pen to paper again.

"One other thing. Why's Virginia so interested in Betty and that damn thermos flask?" This was what Lawrence had wanted to know from the start but had waited for the right moment to bring it up.

Ralph's face developed a fresh sheet of panic, and he made a visible effort to bring it under control. Lawrence helpfully put a fist above his own head and made a face as if he were being hung, to encourage him. He hurried to try and explain. "I don't know everything," was the first thing out of his mouth, "but from what I've overheard, they're trying to cover up the death of someone called Eleanor Palmer."

"Betty's sister?"

Ralph shrugged. "Must be. Anyway, I think they're trying to make sure there's no evidence that could lead them to this doctor bloke they've also got their fingers into. I think they must believe Betty has something of her sister's that could lead back to them."

"Apart from the thermos?"

"Apart from the thermos," Ralph agreed.

"Interesting," Lawrence said to himself, whilst making certain that Ralph could hear him. "So there could be something else of Eleanor's in the effects she's got at her house."

"I guess so," Ralph decided to say, when Lawrence didn't say anything further straight away.

"You get on with writing up everything you've just told me, Ralph, and I'll get us that tea."

After watching Ralph write for a few seconds, Lawrence strode over to the kettle, filled it up from the tap, placed it on top of the guardroom's Hexy burner, and leant back against the sink to wait for it to boil. Tea made—builder's strength, naturally—he picked up both cups and carried them back into the office, where Ralph had just placed down his pen.

"There you go," he told him. "Drink up, and I'll take a look at what you've written."

Lawrence, keeping an eye on his prisoner, as he still had a hand uncuffed, picked up the paper and began to read. By the time Ralph had somehow drunk his piping hot tea, Lawrence had finished reading. "That'll do," he told him. "Now, date and sign it at the bottom."

Ralph did as he was told and pushed the statement back to Lawrence.

Lawrence stood and took out the keys to his handcuffs. "I'm not going to have any trouble now, am I?"

By now totally beaten, Ralph bowed his head and shook it before stating, "No, sir."

"Good," Lawrence replied, and a few moments later Ralph, with both hands cuffed behind his back, was being led out into the main office space and toward the cells. "Right. You're going to kick your heels in here for the while. I'm going to be calling Scotland Yard to see if we can get you picked up today. If not, you'll be here for the night." So saying, he turned the key that was in the lock of the left-hand cell and opened it.

The door to the guardroom crashed open and in stormed Doris. Hot on her heels were Jane and Penny, with Penny having her arms wrapped around the American in an attempt to slow her progress. Despite having inches on her, Penny was being dragged forward by her slight friend, though, if Lawrence was reading things right, it didn't appear Penny was putting all her effort into trying to stop her. This made him turn his attention briefly to the door, and as he'd thought, it hadn't been forced open, but merely had battered back against the frame, which made all the noise. Finally, Jane wasn't attempting to stop Doris or help Penny, so this looked like they were using their friend's drugged-up state for their own means. Although Ralph had indeed cooperated, Lawrence decided he still deserved some payback for what he'd done to Betty.

This was exactly what Doris had in mind as, with fire blazing in her eyes, she launched herself at the stock-still Ralph. "You murdering scumbag!" she opened with. "If you lay another finger on any of my friends, it'll be the last thing you ever do!"

Lawrence wondered if perhaps she wasn't as drugged as she appeared. She sounded much more coherent all of a sudden. This impression was pretty much confirmed when he shot a glance at Jane, who winked at him.

In the meantime, Doris had marched up until she was nose-to-chin with Ralph. Lawrence was a little disappointed to note Ralph looked much more scared of the diminutive American than he had of him. Before he could decide what to do and how far he should let them go, Doris took matters into her own hands—literally.

She turned her back, and he saw Ralph begin to relax. This was a mistake, as the next thing he knew Doris had gripped her crutch with both her hands and brought it around in a complete circle to connect with Ralph Johnson's nether region. Johnson promptly let out an anguished squeak and collapsed to the floor, writhing and moaning.

Doris had a look of immense satisfaction on her face and then seemed to remember she was supposed to be high on morphine. She took a renewed hold of her crutch and, with an exaggerated show of swaying back and forth, waved it slowly over her head once more. "Who's next? Come on, I'll take you all on!"

Clearly stifling a laugh each, both Jane and Penny caught hold of her by the shoulders. "Come on, Doris," coaxed Jane, "let's get you back home."

"New York! You're going to take me back to New York? That's mighty kind of you," she drawled, bowing her head and nearly falling over for real.

With very little effort, both women took their friend back outside, Lawrence mouthing to them, "I'll be out in a second." Shutting the door after them, he went to heave Ralph back to his feet.

"Come on, you. You'll be all right."

Ralph very gingerly got to his feet and, with tears in his eyes, looked over Lawrence's shoulder to make certain he wasn't going to be attacked again. "You can't let her do that! I'm your prisoner," he added, somewhat sulkily.

While Ralph was still distracted by his pain, Lawrence undid the handcuffs and pushed him into the cell, adding, as he slammed the door shut, "I didn't see a thing."

As Lawrence closed the guardroom door, Ralph found his voice again. Lawrence was glad the closed door muffled his disgusting language. Outside, Penny and Jane sat on the grass verge, on either side of Doris, and all three, much to the bemusement of the men on guard who hadn't seen what occurred inside, were laughing their heads off. He crouched down before

310

them and addressed Doris.

"I take it you don't feel so woozy anymore?"

Doris shook her head and then looked like she regretted it, though it didn't stop her from laughing again. "Not so much, Herbert," she said, earning herself more laughter from her friends and a pained look from him, "though my foot's rather sore."

Lawrence held out his hands to help her to her feet. "Come on, then. I'm sure Jane can rustle up some transport from somewhere to get you home."

"Did you tell him Betty isn't dead?" Jane wanted to know.

Lawrence turned his best feral grin on his friends and shook his head. "Must have slipped my mind. He can stew on it for a while."

Chapter Thirty-Three

Virginia Mayes' normally perfectly coifed hair was below her usual standard. This was the first thing to strike George Evans as he strode into what had been his office that bright October morning.

"Aren't you supposed to have left by now?" she muttered at him before picking up the sugar tongs and adding two cubes to her tea and stirring it. The silver spoon clattered against the side of the cup, evidence of her agitation.

The strain of running the black market rackets was taking their toll on her. He knew he'd have a hard time explaining things to St. Peter if he got to the pearly gates, especially his part in the demise of that Eleanor Palmer character. Suppressing a shudder, he nearly spilled his tea. He was realistic enough to know what would happen to him if he got caught. He didn't think Virginia was as wise. Each evening, she still got dressed up to the nines and went out to the Ritz or some other club usually full of his old cohorts, as if she didn't have a care in the world. Evans let his gaze slide over to the safe, the safe he knew his wife believed he no longer had a key for and which contained secrets he didn't know about. He'd learned, in his long career of breaking the law, to keep copies of anything that could be used against you, especially keys. Over the last week, he'd used his free time in the evenings, when his wife was out enjoying herself, to good effect and had painstakingly copied, not trusting the job to anyone else, all the paperwork in the safe. All ledgers and accounts books and even the forensics report had been copied and were stored in a safe deposit box to which he had the only key safely on a chain around his neck.

Those few in the organization who still felt a modicum of loyalty to him and, to his lessening satisfaction, still called him "My Lord," had been keeping him informed on how close the police were getting. It didn't make very comforting listening. He was under no illusions how the RAF would feel if, and when, it came out that he was party to murder. If he was to avoid the noose, he'd need every advantage he could get. If only he could get a look at that damn Betty Palmer's house!

He realized he hadn't answered his wife. As she was reading an accounts book, he made a show of slurping from his teacup, something he knew annoyed her. "I told my staff not to expect me before ten this morning. Plenty of time to get to the tube station."

Knowing this was likely to irk his wife, as she liked having him around as much as he enjoyed her company these days, Evans drank down the last of his tea and took up his service cap.

As he'd thought, she threw her pen down and settled back into his old seat. Another tress fell out of her hairdo as she looked across at him. This was when he noticed she had developed a tick over her left eye. She really was feeling the strain. He decided to see if she'd let slip the state of her conscription-evasion business. He was also curious as to what had happened to the doctor. The man was implicated too deeply in everything, and Evans would feel better if he knew what had happened to him. He hadn't seen nor spoken to Bramble in weeks.

"So, Virginia," he began in what he thought of as his best loving yet persuasive tones, "still finding uses for our doctor?"

The fact she ignored her loose hair and answered him straight away without sniping back at him was enough to confirm to Evans just how distracted she was. He nearly—nearly—felt sorry for her.

"Don't you worry about him, George," she advised. "The good doctor's not going anywhere."

"Still finding uses for him, then?" he asked her, placing his cap on his head and settling it at a jaunty angle he mistakenly believed the ladies liked.

From the way Virginia didn't reply straight away, he knew she was weighing up how much to tell him, and what.

"Let's just say," she began slowly, "he's on a break whilst I let things settle down for a while."

Evans waited for her to elaborate, and when she didn't, he picked up his gas mask case, threw her a quick salute, and turned around to leave the room. To his surprise, she had one more thing to say to him before he closed the door.

"George, my dear," she said with all the subtlety and gentleness of a shark circling its prey, "if you could see your way to finding out if there's any more evidence against either us or the doctor at that woman's house, then do so."

Evans shut the door without answering. His marriage was dead; how long would this business arrangement last?

314

****

Somewhat to his surprise, an opportunity to satisfy his wife's request presented itself when he'd been at his desk for only a couple of hours. The first thing he'd done when he got in was to secretly enjoy the cup of strong camp coffee his secretary always made him. It seemed to be the only drink she knew how to make, and somehow it seemed right. He never used one of his favorite silver spoons, however; he believed it would dissolve in the liquid as he stirred.

While he was trying to force down a canteen rock cake—more rock than cake these days, he thought, chuckling at his own little joke—he picked up the latest incident report to come across his desk. He'd choked down the piece of cake and was washing it down with the dregs of his coffee when he noticed the airfield where the unfortunate pilot was based…Hamble.

Coughing, he opened the report and began to read. Five minutes later, he'd found out a Doris Winter—one of those Yanks they had to put up with, he mused silently—had run into a hill and written off an Avro Anson. The report said she'd run into unexpected low cloud. The pilot had the luck of the devil, though, and apart from a broken foot and various cuts and bruises, she'd live to fly again. Procedure, of course, meant a Court of Inquiry would have to be called to investigate the incident. He sat back with a smile of content on his face for the first time in ages.

Someone was watching over George Evans, and a plan began to form in his mind. He would be, as a senior pilot, sitting on the upcoming weekly board of the Accidents Committee for the ATA, something which he'd cried off, citing various illnesses, previous appointments, and any other amount of ridiculous excuses, for most of the last six months. If he could wrangle a reason to go down to Hamble, perhaps he'd get an opportunity to find out where Betty Palmer lived and take a quick look around her place. Perhaps the time had come to take a risk.

Getting to his feet, Evans locked the door to his office, closed the blinds, and sat back down. Opening the bottom drawer to his desk, he took out a Webley revolver, cracked it open, and then loaded it with its six cartridges.

"Just in case I need it," he told himself grimly.

Chapter Thirty-Four

Betty had no memory of what had happened. Only
when Lawrence turned up in the afternoon, to relate the
same details Shirley had told her, did she believe it. All
the while he talked, Nurse Baxter held her hand, doing
her best to keep her calm and, for the most part, she'd
succeeded. There'd been a bit of an argument when
Betty had wanted to take a look at her wound and the
nurse had, quite rightly, refused. It would not have been
a pretty sight. The surgeons had had to tidy up the
emergency surgery performed by Hamble's doctor, as
well as go in and check for any further damage. The
nurse had patiently explained this over and over until
Betty finally understood and calmed down.

Betty had always hated hospitals, and being stuck
in one didn't do her temper any good. Despite the
kindness of the nurse, her mood improved only when
Ruth and Shirley visited on the day after the incident.

****

"Bobby!" Betty laughed as the spaniel bounded in,
towing his owner behind him like a miniature furry
tugboat. "What are you doing here, boy?"

Ruth reached with her hand and slowly, hesitantly,
Shirley appeared from behind her. How she'd managed
to hide was anyone's guess, but the girl was a nervous
wreck. Her eyes were red raw from crying, and when
Betty looked at her fingers, all the nails on the hand

Ruth was holding had been bitten down to the fingertips. She didn't approach the bed, even when Bobby jumped up to lie down beside Betty, presenting his tummy for a scratch.

"It's all right, Shirley," Betty coaxed as gently as she could, motioning with one hand, which wasn't easy, as her other hand was being licked to death by an over-excited Bobby. "Please, come here and sit next to me." She patted the bedside as Ruth sat down in the only chair.

Betty had to pat the bed a number of times before Shirley released her tight grip on Ruth's hand and, ever so slowly, sank onto the bed. Even then she had her eyes fixed upon Bobby. Betty reached out, gently took Shirley's jaw in her hand, and raised her head so she locked eyes with Betty.

"Why so sad?" Betty asked, reaching up to wipe the tears from Shirley's eyes.

It was too much, and Shirley broke down in floods of tears. They had to wait a good few minutes before she could get her breath back enough to speak. "Oh, Betty, how can you bear to have me around?"

"What on earth do you mean?" Betty asked, honestly confused.

Shirley wiped her eyes on the sleeve of her cardigan and then looked over at Ruth. "And you, Ruth, look at what I've done to you, too!"

Ruth looked confused. "I don't understand. What did you do to me?" Neither she nor Betty could make any sense of what their friend was saying.

Taking out a handkerchief, Ruth passed it to Shirley, who noisily blew her nose, causing Bobby to raise his head and snort.

"It's my fault Lawrence was hurt," Shirley stated, before trumpeting again.

"What are you on about, girl?" Ruth snapped her fingers and laughed. "Don't be silly. He laughed it off quick enough, and it'll take much more than that to get through his thick head."

"But it's my fault!" she insisted.

"You're being irrational," Ruth scolded her now more firmly. "He's fine," she told her again, "and if you don't believe me, he'll tell you himself. I don't like to see him hurt," she revealed, "but there are worse things happening at the moment in this world."

Somewhat reluctantly, Shirley slowly shook her head before turning back to Betty. "But it is my fault you're in here," she told her miserably.

Betty squeezed Shirley's hand. "You're being daft. If what I've been told is right, I'm the one who jumped at Ralph. No one forced me."

"Yes, but if I hadn't been talking to him, he wouldn't have pulled a knife on me," argued Shirley.

"Look," said Betty, trying to find a way to placate her young friend. "I'm going to be fine. The doctors told me the knife missed anything vital. I'll be sore for a few weeks, but that's all."

"But you were stabbed!"

"And I'll be fine," she assured her again. Betty then thought of something to help make Shirley feel a little better. "I had a word with Lawrence, and what he was able to get out of Ralph will prove very useful in bringing down this Virginia's black market scam and, with luck, will help get justice for my sister. So no more tears, do you hear me?"

Shirley wiped her eyes again before finally

allowing herself a small smile.

"That's better," Ruth said and then noticed a nurse lurking, obviously wanting to come over.

Betty saw her too. "Hi, Grace. These are my friends Ruth and Shirley."

Grace was nothing if not diplomatic as Ruth willingly held out a hand to shake but Shirley could only manage another weak smile before blowing her nose once more. "And who's this?" she asked, tucking the clipboard she'd been carrying under an arm to reach down and give Bobby a quick stroke.

"Meet Bobby," introduced Ruth, as her dog rolled over onto his back to present his tummy in his signature move.

"Well, hello, you," Grace said and then added, taking a quick look around the ward, "Watch out for Sister. She doesn't allow dogs on the ward."

****

The nurse hurried up to Betty's bedside, skirts flying and face all red. The smile on her face, though, betrayed she was only pretending to be annoyed. Sister Henry was watching her, arms folded and a strict frown upon her face, from her desk at the head of the ward.

"Betty," she began in a low voice and then, more loudly for the benefit of her superior, "Miss Palmer, I know you're anxious to get home, as are we all to get you there." She made certain Sister couldn't see the wink she gave Betty. "But do you have to have the dog on your bed? Animals aren't allowed in hospital."

Bobby, as though understanding he was the subject being discussed, raised his head from Betty's lap and cocked an ear up at the friendly nurse.

"You tell Sister Henry, there, we'll be gone as soon

as my friends get here." Betty shifted around in her bed until she could see around the nurse to where Sister Henry, obviously having heard Betty's words, appeared to be debating with herself whether she should come and exercise her authority or not. What Betty said next made the nurse choke down laughter and Sister Henry go red. "Honestly, Sister Modesty Henry, you were just the same when we were girls. Because one puppy gives you a nip on the finger is no reason to hate all dogs."

Nurse Grace Baxter was by now struggling to stop herself from giggling, and Betty paused, not wishing to get this kind girl into trouble with her superior. The girl couldn't be much over eighteen or nineteen, and she'd been so patient with her ever since Betty had woken up, confused and in pain.

****

Near the Sister's desk at the other end of the ward, a posse of Betty's friends, all with huge smiles upon their faces, entered with as much finesse as a herd of elephants. At the forefront was Ruth, who held a lead without a dog.

"I knew I shouldn't have let you off the leash," she scolded Bobby who, totally contrite, woofed his apologies, turned around and around on the bed, and promptly settled with his head between his paws.

Next to reach her bedside was Mary, who leant over Betty's bed and kissed her before giving her a brief hug. "Honestly, I get stuck in the middle of Salisbury Plain for one night, one flipping night, and everything happens at once! I'll bet you set it up like this," she turned and mock-accused Penny and Doris as the two slowly followed her in.

"You wish," retorted Doris as she hobbled toward

Betty. "Some Miss Marples we are, eh? We fuss around, and all our Betty has to do is launch herself like Superman at Ralph, and he sings like a bird! That'd make some show on Broadway, I'll tell you!"

Betty folded away her sheets and lifted her nightdress so the others could see the dressing. "Are you forgetting the little matter of my getting stabbed?"

Knowing her friend wasn't really upset, Doris took the seat next to her bed. "It'll take a lot more than that to kill you off." She became more serious. "I'm really, really happy you're going to be okay, though. You've been so kind to this Yankee in King Arthur's Court."

"What's Mark Twain got to do with anything?" asked Lawrence, a puzzled expression on his face as he hurried into the ward to join them.

"Nothing." Doris hurriedly waved away his question, suspiciously wiping a hand quickly across her eyes whilst pasting a beam on her face. "You've got some transport?" she asked to cover up any awkward questions anyone might decide to ask.

Lawrence jangled a bunch of keys. "Jane gave me the keys to her own Jeep, and you know how much she loves her new little toy. Shirley's keeping an eye on it whilst we're here."

"Tell me about it," agreed Penny. "I still don't know how her boyfriend arranged it, but since it turned up, she hasn't let anyone else near it."

"Aw. Who's teacher's favorite, then," Mary teased, quickly moving out of the way of a swat Lawrence aimed her way.

"If that's the case," Nurse Baxter jumped in, "I think we'd better get your paperwork finished so you can get out of here." She looked around. "I think it would be very good for Sister's blood pressure if we get both you and Bobby out of here."

At hearing his name mentioned, Bobby cracked open an eye and, upon seeing a lack of food, closed it again as not being worth any more of his attention.

"Thank heavens!" cried Betty. "I can't wait to get back to work."

Nurse Baxter wagged a finger at her patient. "I'm afraid you can't, or at least not yet. You know you've got to give it a week, as the doctor already told you."

Betty folded her arms and huffed. "I was hoping you'd forgotten about that."

The nurse waved a piece of paper in her face. "Sorry. It's all here in black and white."

Bobby nearly took things into his own paws, as Nurse Baxter hadn't taken enough care in watching where she was waving the paper. It collided with his nose—whereupon, before anyone could stop him, he snapped his jaws firmly upon it.

"Bobby! No, let go! There's a good boy," instructed Ruth, taking a hold of the paper, upon which Bobby, by now fully awake, commenced his favorite game of tug-of-war. Being paper, the game didn't last very long, and in a moment, Bobby was contentedly shredding Betty's discharge papers into tiny pieces.

Mary grinned at the look of horror upon the nurse's face. "Tell you what. We'll help Betty get dressed while you go and get another copy filled out."

Half an hour later, Betty was back home, propped up in bed and feeling like the world was against her.

"I'm not sick!" she protested as Penny and Mary fussed around doing their best to make her comfortable but in actuality merely irritating her. Ruth had gone back to work, whilst Lawrence had taken the Jeep back to Jane, with Shirley insisting she too should be getting back. "Honestly. I've been cooped up in that damn hospital for what seems like forever, and the last thing I want to do is to spend any more time in bed!"

Penny and Mary both leaned in on either side of their friend and gave her a kiss on each cheek before Penny told her, "Humor us, just for today."

Their patient eyed up her good-humored nurses and eventually let out a resigned sigh, settling back into the pillows. "Oh, very well, but," she made sure they took note of her tone, "only for today. Tomorrow, I get up."

Her two friends looked at each other before agreeing. "Deal. Now, we've got to get back to base. Planes to deliver, you know how it is. Is there anything we can do for you before we go?"

Betty thought for a moment before deciding. "You can get me my copy of *The Body in the Library*."

Penny's face fell. "But I haven't finished it yet."

"You shouldn't have started it yet," Betty retorted. "I've only just bought it."

With the Miss Marple in her hands, Betty took a sip of water from the glass the women had placed beside her and settled down once more to read.

"Don't you dare tell me who did it," Penny warned before waving her a goodbye.

As the front door slammed, Betty waited a few minutes before calling out, "Doris!"

The American popped her head around the corner a few moments later. "You hollered?"

Betty grinned. "Care for an outing?"

A while later, Walter looked up from his copy and let out, "Well, bugger me!" promptly earning himself a firm rebuke from his boss.

"Walter! How many times have I told you to watch your language?"

He had the grace to look somewhat rebuked as he got to his feet to let into the newspaper office two visitors Ruth hadn't noticed. The clunk, clunk of Doris's crutches on the wooden floor as she entered made her sit up and take notice.

"Betty! Doris! What are you doing here?" she said as she hurried around her desk to settle both of them into seats. "Surely you should both be at home, taking it easy!"

Betty and Doris exchanged grins as they sat down.

"I think we've both had enough of lying around for a while," Doris volunteered, receiving a nod of agreement from her companion. "Besides, for once, I've been led here by Betty, not the other way around."

"So where's Bobby, then?" Betty asked, looking around the office.

Ruth laughed. "Where do you think? He stayed in the Jeep when Lawrence dropped us off. I suspect he's doing the rounds at the airfield."

"He is our mascot, after all," Doris said with a grin.

Walter reappeared, having made a pot of tea. "Cure of all that ails you," he said, chuckling as he put down the tray and proceeded to pour before pecking Doris on the cheek and retaking his seat.

"It's not champagne, but it'll do," Doris decreed.

"So what are we celebrating?" asked Ruth.

"If what Lawrence has told me is correct, with some luck, Eleanor's murderer will be brought to justice," Betty told them.

Chapter Thirty-Five

"Come in," Jane called and laid down the pencil she'd been whittling away at on her desk.

Into her office came Doris's broken foot, closely followed by the rest of the American, until she stood before Jane's desk. Though still unable to fly because of the cast, Doris hadn't let that slow her down too much. In the last week, she'd not only ignored the doctor's orders to rest up, while both Thelma and Jane herself had tried without much success to talk her into staying away from the airfield, but had taken it upon herself to join the airfield's unofficial mascot, Bobby, in watching each and every plane movement in and out. To say she was restless would be putting it mildly, as the engineering staff could attest to.

The Monday after Betty got home, Doris had joined Penny and Mary in going in to work. She'd diverted into the guardroom, as the barrier rose to let them in, and had caught them up at the ops hut five minutes later in a foul temper. Nobody had thought to tell her the police had arrived over the weekend and carted Ralph Johnson off to London. Everyone had a good laugh when she told them she'd wanted a *talk* with him; no one was in any doubt what she meant. Mary had commented he'd be better off with the worst of London's police than to risk Doris's wrath.

So when she settled in the chair before Jane's desk,

her boss wasn't surprised to see she was wiping oil from her hands.

"Sorry about the mess," Doris told her, indicating the overalls she was wearing. Judging by the state of them, she'd had a very mucky time of late, something she confirmed a moment later with, "Had a fight with a bottle of oil."

"Never mind," Jane said, adding, "Just try not to touch anything."

"Sure," Doris agreed, treating her to a toothsome smile on her grease-and-oil-smudged face. "So what can I do for you?"

Jane cleared her throat before picking up a letter. "I'm afraid we're going to have a visitor tomorrow morning. You know there has to be an investigation into that Anson you crashed the other week?"

Doris nodded. "Not surprised. I've been waiting for this."

"I'm sure it's only a formality," Jane informed her. "Mind you, it is a bit odd."

"Why?" Doris asked.

"Well, we've had accidents before. That's to be expected with flying, let alone what we do."

"So why's it odd?" Doris asked again.

"First," began Jane, "when you take the weather into factor, it should be pretty much open and shut, pilot not at fault."

Doris nodded again. "Tell me about it. The sooner we all get instrument training completed, the better. Perhaps if I'd been through the course, I'd have been able to avoid that bloody hill!"

"Perhaps," Jane agreed. "That's one thing. As for the other, I wasn't expecting you to have to appear before the Board of the Accidents Committee yourself. It's not the full committee that's coming, just some Group Captain. Though what he expects to learn, I don't know." Jane hesitated. "I have to ask you this. There isn't anything you've left out of your report that could have an effect on things, is there?"

Doris momentarily bristled before she remembered that though Jane was her friend she was also in charge and so, occasionally, had to ask awkward questions. She took a moment to calm herself before answering formally, "No, Jane, I've left nothing out. Everything happened exactly as is written down."

Jane smiled and settled back into her seat, then pulled out a desk drawer and took out a bottle of whisky and two glasses. She poured two shots, pushing one across to her friend and raising the other in toast. "Thanks for understanding. Now, before I let you go back to harassing my mechanics, let's have a toast. Don't get to your feet," she added quickly, as Doris made to stand up.

"What are we drinking to, then?" Doris asked with a grin, picking up her own glass.

"To getting rid of our unwanted visitor as soon as possible. Goodbye, Group Captain Evans." She threw back her drink.

Across the desk, Doris, who'd raised her glass to her lips as Jane had begun her toast, spluttered her drink everywhere.

****

Mary climbed out of the Tiger Moth, and the argument that had started when they'd clambered in at Duxford after finishing the day's delivery of Spitfires carried on.

Penny was already out of the front cockpit and waiting for her friend when she slid off the wing. "I am not getting engaged to Tom!"

"Then why's he flying in tomorrow afternoon? And why's Thelma only assigned you two deliveries in the morning? You'll be back in plenty of time for him."

"How do you know what I'm down to do tomorrow?" Penny queried, taking off her flying helmet and laying it on the wing next to her flying bag. "We never know what we're doing until the morning. You know that."

Mary appeared to be a little flustered and fumbled as she tried to undo her helmet. "Well, um, I couldn't help listening in when you were talking to him yesterday in the ops hut, and you sounded so...loved up."

Penny hesitated, slinging her bag over her shoulder, and threw a look at Mary, who shifted from foot to foot as if she had been caught with her hand in the biscuit jar. "Or something like that," she stammered and then, upon looking up and seeing the grin spreading upon her friend's face, burst out laughing. "Will you stop winding me up!" Mary play-punched her friend on the shoulder. "You know I'm only jealous."

Penny flung an arm around Mary's shoulders. "I don't know why you'd be jealous of me. I'm not the one with a boyfriend on site."

Mary's cheeks promptly took on a nice healthy rouge tinge. "I have no idea what you're on about. I haven't been on a date since we arrived." She suddenly stopped dead. "Which is a very depressing thought, now I say it out loud."

"Oh, come on." Penny gave her a hug. "It's not my

fault you haven't asked out Lawrence." She added, when Mary pouted, "Or more patently, he hasn't asked you out. And don't give me any more stares. We've all seen how the two of you look at each other, so it's hardly anyone's fault but your own selves if neither of you have actually done something about it."

"It's that obvious?"

This time Penny kissed her friend on the cheek. "To everyone...and I mean *everyone*."

What might have happened next was interrupted by the sight of a rather angry-looking Jane actually running across from her office directly toward them. Behind her was a stumbling, hopping Doris, who was alternately waving a hand at them and then nearly tripping herself up, her plaster-encased foot not making it easy for her to keep pace on the uneven ground.

"Blake! Baines!" she yelled at the top of her voice, causing both pilots to come to a halt in surprise. Jane never used surnames unless someone was in trouble, and judging by the volume at which she'd shouted and the pace at which she was approaching, both of them were in for a rocket.

Mary momentarily glanced over her shoulder and wondered if she had time to get over to the Tiger Moth, start it up, and take off before Jane got to them. As if reading her mind, Penny grabbed her hand and shook her head. "Not enough time."

With mounting apprehension, Penny and Mary watched and waited as Jane skidded to a halt in front of them, sending small clumps of grass showering over both girls' flying boots. After gulping in lungfuls of air, she planted both hands on her hips and did her best to stare at both of them at the same time. When she finally had enough oxygen to speak, both wished she hadn't.

"And when were the two of you planning on telling me Group Captain Evans was involved in Eleanor's death?"

"Ah," said Penny, trying not to look Jane in the eye.

"Bugger," added Mary with feeling, which didn't answer their boss's question either.

"Goddamn," puffed Doris as she finally caught up and leant on Jane's shoulder to catch her breath. Realizing what she was doing, she hobbled across to lean on Penny instead, hoping her boss wouldn't see the oil stain before she had time to disappear.

"Indeed," Jane commented, planting herself full in front of the three of them. When no one seemed ready to explain, she pursued with, "Evans. Explanation, ladies. Is this part of what Betty told me *wouldn't* affect the running of my station?"

All three looked at each other before Penny opened her mouth. "Well, could be."

"Only 'could be'?" Jane questioned, raising an annoyed eyebrow.

"Can we change our plea?" asked Doris.

"This isn't a court, Doris. This isn't even a democracy," Jane told her sternly. "Anything that happens which could affect the smooth running of this airfield is *my* business. Do you three understand this? Now, Miss Marples, perhaps you could tell me just what he's up to? Why's he coming here tomorrow?"

Mary did her best not to look too annoyed at being included in Jane's Miss Marple analogy. "What have we missed? Sorry, Jane, but if you told us that, perhaps it'd help," she offered.

The three saw Jane's body un-tense slightly as she realized they were missing some information. She proceeded to fill them in on what she'd told Doris.

"I'm with you, Jane," Penny said. "We've had accidents before, and there's never been a reason for one of the Incident Team to come. The only thing I can think of—jump in if you don't agree," she told her friends, "is that it's something to do with Betty's sister. From what Shirley's said and what Lawrence has let slip after speaking with Ralph, he's looking for anything linking him to Eleanor's death. We think he's getting desperate."

After she'd finished explaining her thoughts, Penny stood back, and with Mary and Doris also watching, Jane began pacing back and forth in front of the three, obviously processing what she'd just been told. Eventually, she stopped pacing and looked at her watch, then turned her gaze first to the sky and then to the flight line before finally settling on the three women in front of her.

"Do you believe he could do anything to upset flying?" she asked, all business.

The three girls looked from one to the other, then to a skeptical and obviously worried Jane, and finally back to each other one last time. Doris answered this time. "We can't promise you that, Jane. None of us thinks he will, but we can't be sure what he has planned, so we have to be ready for him. Mind you, the clever money's on his aim being at Betty's house."

"What does Lawrence say?" Jane wanted to know.

"Where is he?" asked Mary, causing her companions to smirk slightly. The sooner the two of them sorted out their feelings, the better.

Doris flopped to the ground as Jane replied, "He's due back from London later, so I doubt if he knows yet."

Doris looked up at everyone. "I don't know about you lot, but how about we all check in and sign off for the day? Then we can all reconvene at Betty's place later. I'm sure she'll want to hear all about this."

Everyone nodded their agreement, and Doris held up a hand.

"Fish and chips for ten?"

****

Betty sat in her favorite chair, a bottle of the proverbial Guinness at her feet, and stared at the huge piece of plaice on her plate, together with an equally large portion of chips. "I'm never going to eat all this," she muttered. "Pass the vinegar, someone."

Walter, from where he had perched between Doris's feet on the settee, shuffled across to pass her the bottle.

"Thank you, Walter," she said as she liberally sprinkled her plate in enough vinegar to float the Titanic before holding the container up for anyone else to take. Doris wrinkled her nose in distaste.

"Cheers," Lawrence told her as he got up off the floor long enough to pluck it from her hand and then sat down again.

Next to him, Mary shyly took the bottle off him, their fingers touching before they sprang apart, as if some dastardly deed had just been performed. Mary almost dropped the bottle in her haste.

Of all people, Ruth spoke up, though everyone else in the room was grinning at their antics. "For God's sake, you two, if you like each other, say so!" However, upon seeing the embarrassment on Mary's face and what looked like shock on Lawrence's, she calmed herself down, took a few extra breaths, and put down her plate before trying again. "What I mean is, life can be cheap at the moment. We never know how much time we're going to have, so if you two like each other as much as the rest of us believe you do, then talk and see where that takes you. Okay?"

Lawrence looked back and forth between his aunt and the bright-green eyes of the blonde bombshell beside him and made a decision. Slowly, gently, he reached out and took Mary's hand.

"What do you say?" he said, just loud enough for everyone else in the room to hear. "When all this is over, we go to dinner? Talk…and stuff?"

The room erupted in laughter, interspersed with clapping. Doris felt the need to make sure Mary understood something. "By 'all this,' he doesn't mean the war, sweetie."

"I know," Mary told her and proceeded to try to eat with her one free hand, reluctant to let go of Lawrence's now she had it.

Jane, balanced on the arm of Betty's chair, held up her glass of carrot wine—a recent attempt of Ruth's that only she seemed able to stomach, hit the side with her fork, and waited for the various conversations to settle down.

"Thank you. Now we've settled the most pressing matter of the evening," she began, to more laughter, "there's the little matter of tomorrow." Jane noticed Betty open her mouth to speak, but she pre-empted her. She placed her free hand on her friend's arm and directed at her a look of deepest sympathy, intermingled with compassion, as she shook her head. "I'm sorry, Betty. I know what this means to you, believe me, but no matter what you think or say, you are not coming in to work tomorrow."

"But the doctor only said I should take it easy," Betty argued, "and I won't get in the way."

"It's got nothing to do with that," Jane told her, keeping her grip firm. When she was unable to quantify that statement, especially under Betty's hard glare, she admitted, "All right. I don't want you to get hurt. You've almost managed to get yourself killed once, and I want you safe, here, in your home. No arguments! That's an order," Jane told her and softened the impact by smiling. "And you know how often I order anyone around."

Seeing she'd been outmaneuvered, Betty, ever so reluctantly, nodded once and set about tearing her fish apart.

Jane turned her eyes upon the rest of the group. "Now, we need to discuss tomorrow. I'll be arranging the schedule, with Thelma's assistance, of course." She acknowledged Thelma, who, her mouth stuffed with chips, could only give her a greasy grin. "All the deliveries we have to make will be taken care of by our other pilots. In fact, I've already called a few back from their day off. They weren't happy, but that's my problem. You'd all want to be there, even if it means cutting corners in the deliveries and"—she held up a hand as Penny and Mary opened their mouths to protest—"though I know none of you would be so unprofessional, let's say I've taken the decision out of your hands. Agreed?"

"Very much so," said Mary on Penny's behalf,

making certain to keep eye contact with Jane so she understood they would never have acted in any way but professionally.

"This means, Penny and Mary, you'll have to be in disguise." She flashed them both an evil smile. "As it happens, the kitchens need a ton of potatoes peeled, so that'll keep you pair busy. I've had a word with the mess manager, and not only is he more than happy to have the pair of you sit outside, where you should be able to see everything going on, together with a couple of Lawrence's men to keep you in check, but he's got some overalls for you to wear." Both Mary and Penny groaned and shook their heads. "Doris, you may as well park yourself with me until Evans gets here—that's supposed to be around ten a.m.—as he'll undoubtedly want to talk to you, even if only to carry on his pretense in being here." Jane now turned her attention to Lawrence. "I gather you tried to get yourself assigned to fly Evans in?"

"True." He scowled, swallowing a chip. "The bugger's piloting himself. Still, we'll have about a dozen of my lads waiting in the flight line hut, as well as those two peeling with this two, just in case, as I doubt he'll come alone."

Shirley raised her hand and actually waited for Jane to look over at her before speaking up. "You think he's really coming here to search for anything linking him to Betty's sister?" She waited for both Jane and Lawrence to nod before she carried on. "If he's so desperate, won't that make him, well, more dangerous?"

"I think there's a good chance he won't be on his own," Lawrence repeated, after a moment's thought, "and yes, that makes him all the more dangerous, which is why we'll all have to be at our most vigilant. Now, before we all get back to our tea, thank you again, Doris." He picked up his Guinness and raised it in her direction. "I've one more bit of news for you. Whatever happens, this all ends tomorrow. Whilst we deal with Evans, and whoever he brings with him, my colleagues will be picking up his wife and any of her cohorts we can get our hands on. With what we've put together from our own investigation, tied in with what we got out of Johnson and what you lot filled in, we've got an ironclad case against the lot of them."

Betty stopped her assault on her fish to look up, her eyes wide. "So Evans is going down for the murder of my sister?"

Lawrence looked at her, and his face showed nothing but confidence in what he was saying. "Thanks to Shirley," who blushed at the mention of her name, "gaining Johnson's confidence, we know where the forensics report on Eleanor's thermos should be, and that together with what I expect we'll find in the doctor's bag to tie him to whatever poison he used, I fully expect this to be enough. Plus, I suspect he'll sing like a bird to try and save his neck from the noose. Don't worry, Betty, we'll get Eleanor justice."

After allowing everyone a few minutes to digest things, he turned serious. "However, I don't want any of you to put yourselves in harm's way tomorrow. That is not your job. Leave that to the police. You'll be introduced to our men tomorrow morning. If you see anything happening, scream, blow a whistle, yell—I don't care, just make a noise. Remember what I said earlier and treat the Group Captain like a cornered fox.

At some point, I expect him to try and make a break for this house, but don't worry, Betty. I'll have men stationed outside, hidden away, so you'll be all right. Now, I suggest everyone eats up and has an early night. I want you all to have your wits about you tomorrow."

Chapter Thirty-Six

Betty had taken out the box of Eleanor's effects and was sitting on her bed, removing each item, one at a time, and carefully examining each, making doubly sure she hadn't missed anything that could help put away Doctor Bramble and the Group Captain. If it'd help with putting his wife in jail too, then so much the better. However, with the others due to be up and about in an hour to make it in to work, so far all she'd found were memories of happier times.

She held up the scarf Eleanor had been wearing when she'd been killed, and it brought back the memory of when she'd given it to her for her last birthday, their last birthday. Sitting in a pub in the East End of London, Eleanor had pretended to use it as a face mask, saying no one could recognize her if she wound it around her face for her next job. Betty had held her tongue about trying to get her to change her preferred employment, well aware such a change would affect her income; her arguments for it never got her anywhere anyway. Sighing, Betty laid the scarf reverently beside the pillow on her bed. It held no interest for the police, now it looked like things were coming to a head. She'd keep it close to her heart.

There wasn't much in the box. Nevertheless, she'd been up before six going through it. The scarf joined a pair of woolen socks, her own flying suit—which she'd never used since—and a woolen pullover on her bed. Betty picked up the box to make certain she'd not missed anything. Empty. Taking up the flying suit once more, Betty went through the pockets until she found what she was looking for, her sister's wallet. A smile flickered across her face as she recalled the first time Eleanor had showed it to her, explaining that in her line of work, carrying a handbag about wasn't practicable. Inside was five pounds in money, a cinema ticket stub from over a year ago, a small brass key, and a folded picture of the two of them, a picture from happier times that could only now exist in memory. Unfolding it, she smoothed it out as best she could before making her way slowly, much slower than normal, down to her lounge and placing it next to the picture of Eleanor she had on her mantelpiece.

This was where Doris found her an hour later, leaning on the mantelpiece and staring at the picture.

"Betty," she asked tentatively, touching her on the arm, and then standing back to give her time to acknowledge her presence.

Doris was surprised to see a smile on her friend's face when she finally turned around, a smile laced with memories and sadness. "I'm fine," she answered. "Really!"

Shaking her head, Doris looked around to check they were alone. "No, you're not. How can you be? But you will be, and we'll all help you. Won't we, ladies?"

Unseen by Betty, Penny and Mary had crept into the room, Penny nursing a cup of tea and Mary munching on a slice of toast. "Of course we will," agreed Penny, whilst Mary nodded between bites of toast.

Betty slowly got to her feet and held out her arms. "Come here, you lot. Give me a hug, and then you'd better get off to base. Best not to keep Jane and Lawrence waiting today."

Who knew how long the hug would've lasted if there hadn't been a knock on the door, closely accompanied by a loud bark.

When the door was opened, Ruth, Lawrence, Shirley, and an ever-excited Bobby were waiting.

"Everyone ready?" asked a grim-faced Lawrence.

Mary, Penny, and Doris all looked at each other, then turned and nodded as one, determination written on each of their faces.

"As we'll ever be," Mary agreed with a forced smile, touching Lawrence on an arm in passing.

"Bring it on!" Doris announced, waving a crutch in the air and sending the lampshade flying.

****

The time had just passed twelve thirty, and Mary threw what she reckoned to be her umpteen-thousandth potato into the tin tub in front of her before picking up yet another spud and waving it menacingly in Penny's direction. "Remind me to stamp on Doris's bad foot the next time she mentions fish and chips."

Equally disgruntled, Penny took yet another urgent glance up into the blue, cloud-speckled skies. Apart from the usual seagulls and a Miles Magister stooging around, the skies were empty. "What do you think's keeping the swine?"

"You've got me," mumbled Mary, starting to peel.

"Don't suppose you've an idea what he'll be flying?"

"Tom told me he'd be using an old Hurricane,"

answered Penny, her eyes glazing over.

Mary threw her half-peeled potato at her friend, who nimbly fielded it and sent it straight back. "Not your boyfriend!"

"Sorry," Penny apologized. "Just trying to take my mind off the boredom."

Mary surveyed the two sacks of potatoes still to go, then switched back to the bath in front of them. "Do you think Bert's using us? I mean surely we've already peeled enough of these damn things for today. If he tells us to start another sack, do you know what I'll tell him to do? I'll tell him he should st…"

Whatever Mary had been about to say was lost in the sudden roar of what they both recognized to be a Merlin engine as a Hurricane fighter swept low overhead before performing a tight turn and settling into finals for their landing strip.

"Tom!" cried Penny happily, springing to her feet. Behind her a Miles Magister, somewhat less gracefully, staggered around a turn and took up a holding pattern as the Hurricane commenced its landing.

"Or perhaps that's Tom," Mary suggested, getting to her feet and receiving a potato to the head from Penny for daring to even joke about her boyfriend's flying abilities.

Both tore off their aprons at the same time, faces a mixture of anticipation and, though neither said it out loud, fear as what they'd talked about the previous evening began to unfold.

Still in the overalls they'd been wearing whilst performing their kitchen duties, both trotted off toward Jane's office, happily ignoring the shouts from the cook behind them. The Hurricane had now landed and was taxiing toward the flight line hut. As they arrived at the ops hut, Penny skidded to a halt, torn between rushing over to greet Tom or doing as they'd agreed and joining Jane and Doris. As the Group Captain wouldn't have been expecting to be met by anyone in fatigues, she reluctantly joined up with Mary as she held open the door for her.

"Sorry," Penny said, shrugging her shoulders as she closed the door behind her. "Impatient, I guess."

The door burst back open and in rushed a slightly breathless Thelma. "There you are! I've been looking for you. You've left a rather irate cook, I must say." Penny and Mary both looked rather annoyed before they noticed Thelma's grin. "I told him he knew why you were there, and if he didn't like it, he could peel his own potatoes."

Further conversation was halted as Doris and Jane appeared from Jane's office. "You two," she said, pointing at Penny and Mary, "go with Thelma and keep out of the way. Remember what Lawrence told us last night? We've plenty of police around to watch over things."

"But he's never seen us before," argued Penny, reluctant to miss out on anything.

Jane took a look out the window as the pilot of the Hurricane clambered out and unhitched his parachute pack. "I'm not going to tell you again. Both of you, go with Thelma. You'll be safe with her, but hurry. That Magister will land shortly, and I want you both hidden away before Evans checks in. Understood?" Her posture and tone left no room for argument.

As Jane turned to go back to her office, Doris in silent flow behind her, apart from the clump, clump of

343

her crutches, Penny called her back, "Um…what about Tom?"

"Tom? Tom who?" Jane asked, turning around.

"Tom Alsop," supplied Doris. "You know, Penny's boyfriend. The Mosquito pilot." She winked at Penny, who'd gone a nice shade of red.

"That's what I came to tell you," Thelma broke in, somewhat exasperated. "That Hurricane, it's flown by a Squadron Leader Thomas Alsop. I believe you know him, Penny?"

Penny immediately grabbed Thelma by the hand and pulled her toward the door. "What are we keeping him waiting for, then? Let's go. See you later!" And she was out the door, towing a rather alarmed-looking Thelma behind her, before anyone could stop her.

"See you in a bit," echoed Mary.

****

Someone knocked at Jane's office door, and before she'd completed calling out, "Come in," the door opened and in came two men.

"Flight Captain Jane Howell, I presume," said the taller of the two.

From the uniform of an RAF Group Captain, Jane knew she was now face to face with the man who not only took delight in running black market operations but was at least partially responsible for the death of her friend's sister. Clenching her teeth, as the alternative would be to stand up and punch him in the face, she set her best smile in stone, stood from her desk, and held out her hand.

"Group Captain Evans," she said, noting with no little satisfaction that he winced as she gave him her strongest handshake. My God, the man's a wimp, she thought. "Please, have a seat." She sat back down and indicated the two empty chairs in front of her desk. "This is Third Officer Doris Winter," she introduced. "I thought it would save time if she were present. And who is this?" she asked of the man who'd come in with him and who had the look of someone who very much wanted to be anywhere but where he was.

Almost as if he didn't matter, Evans wagged a finger over his shoulder. "This? This is my personal doctor. He travels everywhere with me. I have a...a condition on which he is an expert."

"And his name is?" asked Doris when Evans made no effort to elaborate.

"Bramble," Evans supplied, his attention never wavering from Jane. "Casey Bramble."

Hoping Evans hadn't seen the way her eyes nearly sprang out of their sockets, and to take his attention away from Jane, whose mouth had dropped open, Doris decided to play the brash American to the hilt.

"So, Mr. Evans," she began, aware that calling him by a civilian title would be bound to get on his nerves, "why exactly are you here? We've had accidents before and never had a member of the board turn up." Doris sat back and folded her arms in a deliberate show of belligerence.

Her plan worked, as Evans shot to his feet, his hands automatically making sure his hat was on straight, and planted himself directly in front of where Doris sat. By doing so, he had his back to Jane, who now recovered herself and took a moment to make her face blank. For his place, the doctor merely looked like he could wish himself anywhere but where he was.

"Firstly, Ms. Winter," Evans began, hands planted

on both hips and a very unhealthy shade of red shooting up his neck, "since when did you stop saluting a superior officer when he walks into a room?"

Doris had to prevent herself from rubbing her hands together in delight. Here was someone she'd love to come up against across a poker table, all his emotions right on the surface. It'd be like taking candy from a baby! A quick look up at Evans, who stood in front of her glaring down from under his hat, persuaded her to teach him another lesson. Honestly, she'd have liked to kick him in the nether regions, but until she could perhaps persuade Lawrence to leave her alone with him, a verbal brow beating would have to do.

Not bothering to change her position, Doris glanced up totally unconcernedly at him. "Actually, we never salute. We're a civilian organization, as I'm sure you know, so if you're waiting for a salute, I hope you're a patient man."

Jane quickly turned a barking laugh into a cough. "Doris," she said sharply, not that her friend took her tone personally, "that will do. Group Captain, please take a seat. I'm sure this won't take long, as I know you've got better things to do with your time."

Reluctantly, he did indeed turn around and take back his seat before replying, "That I have."

"So just why are you here? As my colleague pointed out, this isn't usual procedure."

His eyes flicked toward the door, confirming what Jane had just said. "That's true. Actually, I can deliver the outcome of the investigation right now." Both Jane and Doris instinctively leaned forward upon hearing this. "I decided to come here because I wanted to meet the person who managed to walk away from that crash.

346

From what I can see of the pilot," he said, turning his head to Doris, who promptly winked at him, "she's as outspoken as any other Yank—but," he added quickly, as Doris had been about to interrupt him, "after also visiting the crash site and taking into account the weather at the time, she must be one hell of a pilot. So the verdict is Pilot Not at Fault. Also, a commendation will go on Ms. Winter's record in recognition of her exceptional flying which avoided her getting killed. Congratulations, Winter," he added, standing once again and holding out a hand.

Doris hesitated only long enough to remember she had a part to play before getting to her feet and making the swiftest of handshakes.

Somewhat surprised at this news, Jane took a few moments to recover. "Well, if that's all, thank you. We won't keep you any longer. However," she then said, upon remembering there had to be an ulterior motive for his presence and suggesting he should fly out wasn't the best of ideas, "if you don't have to be off straight away, would you like a tour of the airfield?"

Jane didn't fail to notice the greedy expression upon his face at hearing her words, and he fell upon her suggestion, as if he'd been fumbling for a reason to hang around. "What an excellent idea, Jane. May I call you Jane?" he asked, and though she'd rather have had her wisdom teeth pulled out by a mass murderer without anesthetic than continue to play the gracious host, Jane forced a smile onto her face and nodded; gracious host she would be.

A minute later, they were all back outside, and as an added bonus, the weather was as good as an English October could make it; it wasn't raining.

Pulling on his greatcoat, Evans asked Jane, "Do you mind if my doctor has a wander around on his own? I'm sure our conversation will bore him to pieces."

Jane agreed. They needed a reason to separate them. Once they were walking across the grass, it didn't take long before Evans dismissed him.

"Meet me at the guardroom in an hour, Bramble," he told him dismissively.

"Yes, sir. Have a good time, sir," Bramble replied, his voice filled with a mixture of sarcasm and obsequiousness, the first words he'd spoken in their presence, before striding off.

After five minutes, Doris made her excuses and left Jane to have the dubious honor of escorting Evans around. Looking toward the flight line hut, she could see Penny sat on the edge of the decking with her arm linked through one of Tom's. Mary, though, saw her waving at them, and after speaking briefly to the two of them, she started trotting across toward her. Before she'd gone more than a few yards, Lawrence and another man in overalls joined them.

"What happened?" Lawrence asked without preamble.

Doris filled him in, together with her assumption that the doctor was on a mission he'd been set by the Group Captain, though exactly what, she didn't know.

"Where's he headed?" Lawrence asked.

"Last I saw him," Doris replied, "he was walking in the direction of the guardroom."

"Do you think we should warn Betty?" Penny asked, having finally joined them, Tom in tow.

Lawrence barely had to think about it. "Go and

phone her, Doris."

However, Doris shook her head. "Can't. She's not on the phone."

"Bloody hell," he swore. "How long since you last saw him?" his voice rising with anxiety.

"Probably about ten minutes now," she told him dejectedly. Then she had a thought. "I could call Ruth. She's much closer to Betty's than us and could be there in a few minutes."

He didn't have to think about it before answering. "No. If we're right and he is going to her house…"

"I can't think where else he'd be going," Mary interrupted.

Lawrence carried on as if he'd never stopped. "…then I think we have to assume he's armed. I will not risk Ruth or Walter getting hurt for anything. She is alone, isn't she?"

Penny, Doris, and Mary all looked at each other before Penny replied, "Not quite. Ruth didn't like her being left alone, so she dropped off Bobby before work."

"Hold on, hold on." Penny grabbed Lawrence and forced him to look at her. "I thought you'd stationed men outside her place?"

Chapter Thirty-Seven

Doctor Bramble couldn't believe his luck! Not only had the woman in charge of the airfield allowed him to go off without an escort, but when he pretended to be there to examine Betty Palmer's wounds, the gate guard had been only too happy to provide him with directions to her cottage. That solved the problem of finding the house with no street signs about.

Though he'd arrived with Evans, Bramble was taking his orders from the odious Virginia, orders which, if he needed to follow to the letter, were against his instincts, let alone his Hippocratic Oath. He patted his pocket. The weight of the item it held weighed down not only the pocket but his conscience too, and he cursed the day he'd got involved with the black market. Having a gambling habit had led to his reuniting with Evans and, by consequence, his wife. A little blackmail from them both had led him into this mess! He couldn't believe how stupid he'd been. Evans had told him that to have his debts to the casino paid off, all he had to do was slip a little poison, not enough to kill, only enough to make her ill, into a pilot's flask before a flight. How he'd come to put too much in was beyond him. However, what's done was done, and he had to live with her death on his conscience. Since then, they'd both used him for their own reasons, and now, here he was, a doctor, sworn to do no harm, about to break into a house, ransack it for who knew what and, if it came to it, shoot another innocent woman.

If he had the courage, he'd throw the revolver in his pocket away, only Evans had told him he'd kill him himself if he lost it, it being his own personal one. That was the only thing that stopped him from throwing it into the river. He let out a bitter laugh. If only Evans knew he'd sent a coward into battle for him!

****

Left at home, Betty was not a happy bunny as she headed toward the kitchen. Her first thought had been to disobey Jane's "advice" and sneak onto base. She wanted to see this Group Captain Evans who was responsible for the death of her sister. If she had the chance, perhaps she'd be able to have a one-to-one "chat" with him, though that was more wishful thinking than anything else. The knowledge Jane was right in making her stay at home didn't make her feel any better. In fact, her wound chose that moment to start throbbing, reminding her she'd already paid a price too close to the ultimate.

Bobby trailed behind, close to her heels, as ever on the lookout for any tidbits of food. Betty reached down, gingerly holding her hand to her side, and fussed him behind the ears.

"Sorry, boy, you're not the only one who wishes they were someplace else." The dog whimpered in agreement and lay down at her feet with his head between his paws, doe-brown eyes staring up at Betty.

When Ruth had called around earlier, she'd insisted upon leaving Bobby with her, "Just in case." She told Betty that with the dog there, she'd feel better about leaving her alone briefly, until she could get back from making sure Walter knew what to do. Betty had told her not to bother, but Ruth had insisted. Walter could hold the office for her today.

Taking her cup of tea with her, plus a plate of biscuits she knew she'd have to share with her doggy companion, Betty made her way into the lounge. She settled, with a groan she didn't mind letting out as there wasn't anyone around to make a fuss of her, into her favorite chair.

The clock on the mantelpiece struck two, and the Home Service was just starting up with some "For the Schools" program. Betty could feel her eyelids getting heavy. Her empty cup was on the floor, and Bobby had settled on her lap. Honestly, was her last thought before she started to snooze, if this kept up, Ruth would be expecting her to chip in for his license.

Sometime after, she was startled awake by Bobby suddenly jumping off her lap. Heaving herself out of the chair, she looked down at the spaniel. He'd taken up a post right next to her legs, his hackles were up, and his teeth were bared. A low growl was issuing from his throat, and he was focused on the lounge doorway. Betty looked up straight into the eyes of Doctor Bramble.

"Please don't do anything stupid, Miss Palmer."

Perhaps he should have addressed Bobby too, as the dog launched himself, jaws agape, at the doctor. Moving swifter than she'd have thought he possibly could, Bramble brought the butt of the pistol he was holding crashing down on the head of the brave dog, who crashed to the floor in a heap, blood immediately appearing through the fur on his head.

"Bobby!" Betty cried and fell to her knees to cradle

the fallen dog in her arms. She looked up into what she could now quite clearly see were the desperate eyes of the man before her, and though angry tears threatened to blind her, she shouted up at him, "Who are you? What do you want?"

"My name is Doctor Bramble, Betty Palmer, and believe it or not, I am very sorry we are meeting like this," he told her, taking a few steps back into the hall to put some space between them. "Now, leave the dog alone and sit back down, as I have a few questions to ask, and then things can get back to normal, at least for you."

Betty, after satisfying herself that Bobby was still breathing, laid his head down onto the rug and then, keeping a very close watch on her captor, sat back down in her chair.

Once there, and whilst keeping one eye on Bobby, she narrowed her eyes. "Normal? And what makes you think things can get back to normal...Doctor? I know you killed Eleanor." Though held at gunpoint, Betty had the satisfaction of seeing him flinch, and she knew, despite being the unarmed one, she actually held the advantage. Now she needed a way to take it. She briefly had time to wonder what had happened to Lawrence's men.

The gun in his hand actually wobbled before the doctor regained control. "I am honestly sorry about your sister, Miss Palmer. I didn't intend to kill her."

If it hadn't been her own lounge, Betty would have spat at him. Sincere apology or not, he wasn't going to get her forgiveness. "I don't care. You killed her, and if it's the last thing I do, I'll see you swing for her murder!"

353

M. W. Arnold

The venom in her words made Bramble take a step back before he recovered a little composure. "That may be, but before then, I've been instructed to find out if you have anything which would prove what happened."

A whimper from the floor distracted Betty, and ignoring the order to leave him, she knelt to check Bobby was still breathing. Believing she'd come to no harm, at least until the doctor had got his answers, she dropped to her knees, dragged a handkerchief from the pocket of her skirt, and tied it around Bobby's head, tying a knot under his chin. Then and only then, once satisfied the bleeding had been stemmed as much as possible, did she retake her seat.

She was about to open her mouth when she noticed the top of a red head bob up from the corner of her eye at the front window. Looking directly at Bramble, she saw no sign he'd noticed anything, and so to distract him, she decided actually answering his question with the truth would serve her purpose; plus it didn't reveal anything. "Nothing," she said, "I've found nothing."

"And I'm supposed to believe you?"

Betty risked a quick glance at the window, nothing. Where were those policemen Lawrence had promised? She got to her feet and started to walk toward Bramble, carefully skirting the unconscious dog. "What have I got to gain from lying to you? But if you don't believe me, come through to the kitchen. I brought down the box of her things this morning. It's on the kitchen table, and you can look for yourself. Then you can get the hell out of my house, preferably by the same back door I presume you came in. I don't want scum like you using my front door," she growled as she came to stand right before him, the muzzle of the revolver actually pressed

354

against her stomach.

Taken by surprise, Bramble again took a few hasty steps back toward the kitchen, keeping his gun leveled at Betty, who allowed a grin on her face yet chastised herself not to get carried away. "Very well." He stepped backward, with Betty never more than two steps before him. "But no tricks, Palmer. I will shoot you."

She gave him a single nod of her head and skirted around to the other side of the kitchen table, until she was by the kettle. Holding it up, she caught the back door creeping open and the face of Shirley appeared around it. "Tea?"

"Why not," Bramble said. He made the mistake of taking a seat at the table, only then pulling the cardboard box containing Eleanor's effects toward him.

With the kettle boiling, Betty moved slowly around the room until she was by the cooker. With Bramble's attention focused on taking each item from the box and scrutinizing each carefully, Betty silently took a grip of the object she'd spotted as she sidled across the room. By now, Shirley was only a few feet behind Bramble, who still had his head bent over the box. If the pistol weren't still pointed in her direction, Betty would have been tempted to try something. However, she wasn't stupid, though with Shirley creeping step by step closer and closer, her friend could, if she was as brave as she hoped, provide her with a distraction.

Betty noticed Bramble's head turn as Shirley accidentally stepped on the only cracked stone in the kitchen floor, making an unexpected noise. Not knowing what else to do and now out of time, Betty yelled, at the top of her voice, "Walkies!"

Bramble stood up, or rather tried to as he banged

his thighs against the table, causing him to crash back down into his seat. Shirley yelled like a banshee and dived toward him as Betty hefted the item she'd gripped. With all her might, Betty brought the cast iron saucepan down toward Bramble's head, catching him a glancing blow.

A moment later, Shirley got up somewhat painfully from the floor. Her dive had done no more than end up with her hands around the doctor's knees. "Is he…is he dead?" she asked.

Shaking slightly, Betty put the implement down and reached across to the doctor's neck where it had smashed into the table. "He'll be okay," she replied.

Further conversation was interrupted by a hammering at the front door, accompanied by the voice of Lawrence yelling, "Betty! Are you okay? Let me in!" Bobby made a very shaky-legged appearance from the lounge, attempting to bark his support, but what came out was more of a whimper as he shook his head, splattering blood across the kitchen floor.

Shaking slightly in shock from what had just occurred, Betty told Shirley, "You get the door. I'll take care of Bobby."

****

Jane had never been as bored in her life, nor as proud of her self-control. Group Captain Evans, besides being responsible for the murder of her friend's sister, was also the most self-centered, pretentious git she'd ever had the misfortune to meet in her life. At one point, he'd even suggested she address him as "His Lordship." At this ludicrous proposition, she had laughed out loud and not bothered to try hiding it. If she wasn't one hundred percent certain he would be arrested very soon, she might not have dared, but it had felt so good, a kind of release, and so she'd enjoyed it. When he'd asked, his face a picture of amazement, why she'd laughed, she hadn't bothered answering but merely strolled on.

The incident had also confirmed her first opinion of the man; he had the brains of a goldfish. How he'd risen so far in the RAF she had no idea, though she could now understand why some animals ate their young.

Whilst Evans was peering into the open door of one of the station's Ansons, Jane looked at her watch— a quarter past two and the longest hour of her life was nearly up, thank God. She looked over toward the ops hut and, as arranged, Thelma gave her the thumbs up from the window and waved the receiver of a telephone in the air; Lawrence had the doctor under arrest!

"Come on, Group Captain," she said, tapping him on his shoulder, "it's time we got back to my office. Your doctor will be waiting for us."

As Jane proceeded to stride off, Evans had no choice but to follow. She glanced over her shoulder to make sure he was.

"Very well," he said as he caught up with her after a few steps. "I think I've seen enough," he added just as they reached the hut.

Thelma stood at the open door, waiting for the two of them. Jane stepped aside for him to go in before her, Evans throwing her a simpering smile in thanks as he did, which slipped off his face as he saw what was waiting for him.

As he passed Thelma, she began, "Welcome, your Lordship," bowing before breaking into laughter. "I'm sorry, Jane," she managed to get out. "I can't keep it up, even for this clod."

Behind her, and unseen by Evans until he'd entered the room, were two uniformed policemen and two of Lawrence's detective colleagues. "Group Captain Evans," stated the larger of the two detectives whilst stepping forward and holding out a pair of handcuffs, "you are under arrest on suspicion of the murder of Eleanor Palmer, blackmail, and multiple black market activities. You do not have to say anything but anything you do say will be taken down and may be given in evidence."

"Don't tell my wife!" Evans surprised everyone by shouting out as the cuffs snapped shut on his wrists.

In fact, it caused such surprise that the Group Captain was able to break out of the detective's grip and run out the door as fast as his feet would take him. Momentarily stunned, the first person to react was Penny's boyfriend, Tom, who darted out the door after him, Penny close behind, before the police could also come to their senses and follow.

As chases went, it wasn't the longest, as Evans was in his RAF shoes, having changed out of his flying boots when he landed, and was slipping and sliding all over the place on the slick grass. With his bound hands, he obviously wasn't going to get far, and as she ran after him as hard as she could, Penny couldn't help wondering where he thought he was running to. Whilst they'd been waiting for everything to kick off, Penny had taken the opportunity to fill in Tom on most of the facts and what was likely to happen today. Consequently, he was quite fired up, and when he launched himself, he took Evans right behind the knees.

The crack of what Penny suspected was one of the Group Captain's kneecaps as he twisted on his way down could be heard quite readily across the airfield. To make sure, she threw herself onto his chest whilst Tom got himself into a better position to hold him, her knee accidentally grinding into his groin as she did so, which brought her no little satisfaction.

By the time the policemen had caught them up, Tom had hauled a squealing Evans to his feet with one hand and was holding off a fuming Penny with the other.

"Let me at him, Tom," she begged, waving her hands and trying to kick Evans, who was hopping up and down on one leg whilst also scrunching his legs together. "Just give me a minute with him. For Eleanor. Please?"

The larger detective—Frank, Penny believed was his first name—gently but firmly took hold of Penny whilst his smaller colleague, Percy, thanked Tom and took control of Evans.

"Thank you, Squadron Leader," said Percy and marched off his hobbling captive, who was loudly complaining.

"Oww! Watch my bloody knee," Evans was yelling at the detective, who was pointedly ignoring him.

"Can I have a go as well?" asked Mary as she finally caught up with Penny and Tom, who had their arms around each other. She towed a breathless Doris behind her.

Detective Frank smiled as he shook his head and then went around shaking everyone's hands. "Ladies, and gentleman"—he inclined his head toward Tom—

"you all have the thanks of the Metropolitan Police Force, and mine and my colleagues', of course, for everything you've all done to help us bring that bastard to justice. We've got to get back down to London straight away, but I'm sure Lawrence will fill you in on the details in the next few days."

Finally joining the celebrating crowd were Jane and Thelma, arms linked and wide smiles on both their faces. They'd obviously heard everything that had just been said.

Jane spoke as host again. "It's been a pleasure to have you here, Detective. Safe journey, and please look after yourselves," she added, leaning in and shaking him warmly by the hand.

After the detective had caught up with his colleagues, Tom, now holding Penny's hand, turned to the other four beaming ladies and asked, "Is it always this exciting around here?"

Chapter Thirty-Eight

"Remember, remember the fifth of November," sang Penny, badly out of tune and interspersed with many "La-la's," as she didn't recall the rest of the poem.

Doris rolled her eyes and heaved herself out of her chair. It had been two weeks since all the excitement at the airfield and a week since Doris had succeeded in persuading the doctors to take off her cast. True, Jane hadn't cleared her to fly as yet, but merely being able to hobble around without having to use a crutch was good. Heaven, she'd discovered, was being able to scratch her foot whenever she wanted. In fact, Mary and Betty had both had to warn her not to go overboard or she'd draw blood.

Now, she felt like smacking Penny on the bottom with her stick, due to her insistence on singing the same thing over and over again, only she couldn't catch her friend, something Penny was very aware of. Deliriously happy with the way things were going with Tom, she'd taken to breaking out into song at every opportunity, something no one else was happy about. "Please, Pen," Doris begged as her friend led her a merry dance around the kitchen table, "stop singing!"

Penny took pity on Doris after the second turn around the table and pulled out a chair for her panting friend. "I suppose Walter's pleased you can't chase him around either?" she teased as she helped Doris into a chair.

Doris mopped her brow and pouted across the table at her friend. "I'll have you know Walter's been a sweetie, as you well know."

Penny and everyone else who lived at The Old Lockkeepers Cottage did indeed know this. He'd been around each night after work making either—it depended upon whom you asked—a nuisance or a *sweetie* of himself. Doris had never been happier, and though she moaned after he'd gone that he didn't have to come around each night, everyone knew they were only words and she wouldn't have it any other way.

In fact, Betty's cottage seemed to have become the place to be if relationships were involved. Tom had called on the telephone only the other night. The newly installed instrument was something to thank Jane for arranging, though Betty thought her real reason for doing so was to keep a close eye on her favorite three pilots and Betty. The phone call partly explained why Penny was so happy. Mary had spoken with Lawrence a few times as well. He hadn't stopped apologizing for the cock-up with the lack of policemen outside Betty's cottage. Everyone could see she'd be happier when he wasn't so tied up with helping to mop up things in London. Even Jane had spoken to her American boyfriend, despite relentless ribbing, once or twice. Betty had suggested setting up a rota; no one was sure if she was joking.

Mary came into the room, Betty leaning on her arm, though not as much as she had been a week ago. When she'd swung that frying pan at Doctor Bramble's head, she'd put everything she had into it. She may have taken him out, but she'd also burst her stitches at the same time, and as a consequence, she'd been readmitted to hospital, this time with bed rest. She'd been released only three days ago.

"I'm with Doris here, Penny," she teased, sliding into a chair and accepting the proverbial cup of tea, though Penny did pretend to withhold it and pouted a little at her words. "You really can't sing."

****

Ruth held the door open for Walter as he positioned the wheelbarrow at the office entrance and then carried Bobby from his basket next to her desk. In a moment, the dog was lying down, nestled in his blankets, ready for the short walk back home.

"He's looking nearly back to his old self," Walter ventured, picking up the handles.

With the newspaper locked up for the night, Ruth fell into step with Walter. The wheelbarrow squeaked as the two of them walked down the street, waving hello to the few people around in the early evening. They made quite a sight as they made their way toward the river and found it very amusing that everyone wanted to make a fuss of the spaniel. The story of how he'd tried to protect Betty had spread rapidly around town and this, together with the warning he'd provided earlier in the year of the air raid, had cemented his position as the most popular dog in Hamble. Ruth had even fielded a phone call from a national newspaper about him earlier that day.

A short while later, Ruth knocked on Betty's door whilst Walter lifted Bobby out of the barrow and placed him on his paws, holding him by the side for an instant whilst he got his balance.

Betty had hidden her injury from Lawrence and his colleagues whilst they were carting off Bramble. They'd also been happy with Shirley's assurances that she would make certain Bobby got the best attention possible. Once the men had gone, Betty had refused to go to hospital until Bobby had been seen by the local vet, Reginald Dawson. He'd cleaned and stitched up the cut on the dog's head and advised Ruth, whom Shirley had phoned, to try to keep him off his feet for a week, as he was likely to have a concussion. Ruth had, naturally, taken him literally, hence the wheelbarrow, which she was finding increasingly difficult to keep him in.

As if to prove he was no longer an invalid, Bobby, upon catching sight of Shirley as she approached along the riverbank, woofed loudly and bounded the few strides to his new favorite human.

"How's my darling boy, then?" Shirley fussed him, being careful not to dislodge the bandage he still had around his head. In answer, Bobby did his best to lick her to death, only to sit back on his haunches, pulling a face as his tongue found a smear of oil she'd missed on one of her cheeks.

"How come you're not going home?" she asked of Ruth before turning to speak to Walter and finding he was busy, as Doris had answered the door. "No need to ask how you're doing, Walter," she teased before catching hold of Bobby's lead and being led indoors as the spaniel charged through to the kitchen to bury his face in the water bowl Betty kept for him.

With the sounds of happy lapping in the background, Shirley joined Ruth in taking off her coat. "I've those indoor fireworks Betty asked me to bring over," Ruth replied, kissing Shirley on the opposite cheek to the one with the oil on it. "And besides," she added, catching sight of Mary and smiling, "I heard from Lawrence this afternoon. He should be arriving around about seven. Assuming his train isn't delayed."

Mary took a look at the clock on the kitchen wall and let out a squeal of alarm. "Seven! Ruth, you rotter, I've only half an hour to make myself presentable!" And she promptly scrambled up the stairs.

Leaving Shirley sitting on the floor of the kitchen with Bobby's head lolling in her lap, Ruth went into the lounge to join the rest of the household.

With Doris on Walter's lap, Ruth joined Betty and Penny on the sofa. She threw a glance to the ceiling. The sound of Mary crashing around could quite clearly be heard. "I gather this means she and Lawrence are an item?"

"You know," Betty ventured, "I'm not totally certain. They seem keen on each other, but I don't think they've even walked out yet."

"I get the feeling we're going to find out soon, one way or the other," put in Penny.

"So what's Lawrence coming over for? Is he staying for a while, then?" Betty asked.

Ruth shook her head. "I don't really know. He wasn't able to talk for long, though he did say he'd be letting us know what's gone on since they carted those swine back to London."

Bobby appeared in the doorway, cocked his head at everybody, and then disappeared in the direction of the front door. A second later, amid a crescendo of barking, there followed a rapping on the door and Shirley yelling, "I got it!"

"Hey, Bobby!" came Lawrence's voice as the door was opened.

"You're early!" Mary shouted from upstairs as the bathroom door opened and closed.

Lawrence and Shirley came into the lounge. "I'll just get a chair," Lawrence commented, seeing that, with Mary still to make an appearance, there wouldn't be enough seats to go around.

"Better make that two, dear," Ruth advised as he went into the kitchen.

"And be a honey and put the kettle on, too!" Betty followed up.

Having followed his orders, Lawrence heaved in two chairs from around the kitchen table. "That's a fine welcome." He grinned, taking a seat nearest the door whilst he waited for the kettle to boil.

"Stop teasing the man," Penny told them. "Here, take my seat, Lawrence. I'll make the tea."

"Bless you," he replied, kissing her cheek as they passed. Taking her seat, he flopped back into it, stretched out his legs, and let out a weary sigh.

Ruth reached out and took his hand. "Tired?"

He gave her a smile to match his sigh. "How could you tell?"

She tapped the side of her nose. "I'm not the editor of a newspaper for nothing, you know. Though I do want to know why you didn't tell me about this undercover lark."

The slight tension that had started to build in the room, as everyone realized how tired Lawrence was, eased off at the little joke. Nobody envied him having to explain himself to his aunt though. When Penny brought in a tray of tea and biscuits, with Bobby trotting along at her heels, a biscuit between his teeth, everyone fell upon the refreshments with relish.

Lawrence had taken a few sips of tea and bitten into his first biscuit when Mary appeared, shyly silhouetted in the door frame against the sun streaming in through the kitchen windows, in a daffodil yellow summer dress. What words were about to come from his mouth were forgotten as, biscuit still in hand, Lawrence got to his feet and, as if they were the only people in the room, took her in his arms and swept her into a kiss rivaling that of Jane Austin's Mr. Darcy.

After a full two minutes, Betty, not troubling to keep her voice down, leant toward Ruth and placed her hand on her friend's arm, saying, "I suppose we have our answer now."

As the laughter in the room grew, Lawrence and Mary gradually seemed to realize where they were and broke apart. However, they kept their hands clasped together. "I suppose we could have been a little more...discreet," Mary suggested before leading Lawrence back to his seat, pushing him down. she dragged over one of the chairs he'd brought in and sat next to him. "Drink up. You look out on your feet."

"Under the thumb already?" Walter teased, earning himself a swat on the arm from Doris. He kissed her on the forehead. "Some of us like that, love."

"Enough, everyone," suggested Penny. "Lawrence, I think the sooner you fill us in, the sooner you and Mary can get out from under the microscope."

He nodded, finished his biscuit, and took a long, satisfying sup from his cup. "Right, yes, good idea." Lawrence turned to Betty as being obviously the most affected. "Betty, I'm sorry no one's been in contact to let you know what's been happening. That's my fault. I asked my guv'nor to let me come down and fill you in personally. I hope you don't mind. Right, we've spent the last couple of weeks in rounding up as many as we could find of the Evans and Mayes gang. We've probably missed a couple, but no one who'd be of much importance, and I'm sure we'll get them too before long. Mayes will be charged with black marketing, blackmail, and aiding and abetting draft dodging, Evans with black marketing. Shirley?" he looked at her anxious face to find she was holding onto Bobby and hanging upon every word he said. "You've nothing to worry about now. All right? There aren't going to be any charges brought against you, so try to relax and enjoy yourself from now on."

"What about Ralph?" Shirley managed to ask.

Lawrence ran a hand though his hair before answering. "He's going to be put away for quite a while. I don't think you have to worry about him anymore," he added upon noticing the stern expression Betty was shooting at him and letting Shirley know. "Try not to give him another thought, my girl."

"As for Evans and Bramble, both are likely to face the death penalty," he started and then waited for the effect those words had on his friends to calm down. "We've recovered enough evidence to link the doctor to the flask, and as soon as we told him this, he started talking and hasn't stopped. We even found out why we had so much trouble finding him," Lawrence revealed. "The name he'd qualified under was his mother's, and that's why we never found him."

"You mean," Mary interrupted, "he isn't called Bramble?"

Lawrence bent down to kiss her forehead before straightening up. "Actually, yes and no. Yes, his name is Bramble—well, actually, it's Brumble, which he hated, but not as much as he hated his mother's, his mother's *first* name. We now know he's known as Casey Bramble, but he took his exams as Cam or Cameron Bramble."

After a short silence, Betty declared, "Well, can't blame him for that."

"He's given us more than enough additional information to make me confident in saying you'll not be seeing either Evans or Mayes again. I can't say if Bramble will swing, taking into account he's turned King's Evidence, but he'll never cause anyone any harm ever again, Betty," Lawrence finished off.

Whilst Lawrence had been talking, all eyes in the room had been on Betty, and at his last words, Doris heaved herself off Walter's lap, Mary and Penny joined her, and the three knelt on the floor at Betty's feet. Penny held out a handkerchief to their friend, whose tears flowed down her cheeks. "Wipe your face," Penny gently said, and as Betty did so, she took hold of her friend's free hand and started to stroke the back of it. "Are you all right?"

After a few sniffles, Betty smiled down at her friends and from the light that appeared in her eyes as she did so, she looked like the years had rolled off her. Keeping her grip on Penny's hand, she regarded Lawrence with much affection. "Thank you, Lawrence, and everyone. I don't know how I've been so lucky to have such good friends."

Mary got to her knees and planted a kiss that left a red smear on Betty's cheek, quickly joined by ones from Penny, Doris, Ruth, and Shirley, leaving her cheeks looking like an advert for Max Factor.

"I'm not sure how much use we were as Miss Marples," Doris told her, wiping her own tears from her face, "perhaps we'd better stick with being best friends."

"Hear, hear!" said Penny, quickly echoed by Mary and Shirley, and Bobby's bark.

"That leaves two more things, and then, if you're okay with it, Mary, I'd like to take you out for a walk." Mary nodded her head eagerly, not saying a word to hold this up. "Betty, I don't think it'll come to it, but if you want to attend the trial, let me know, and I'll arrange everything."

Betty took her time before answering, and when she did, everyone in the lounge went quiet as a church mouse so as to be able to catch what she said. "I'm not sure, Lawrence. It's a lot to take in. Perhaps you could ask me nearer the time?"

"No problem," he replied.

"And the other thing?"

"Um, yes," Lawrence hesitated, going a fetching shade of red before speaking. This left no one in doubt that what he had to say was potentially awkward. "Both Evans and his wife kept going on about a string of pearls they insist were stolen, and they both seem to think your sister had something to do with it. I am sorry to ask, but as a policeman, I have to. Do you know anything about this?"

By way of an answer, a slightly enigmatic smile appeared on Betty's face and, curiously enough, on Penny, Doris, and Mary's faces too.

Mary took hold of his hand and suggested, "If an

anonymous letter was delivered to you, with an explanation, would that be enough?"

Epilogue

November 1942

"Whose bloody idea was it that indoor fireworks would be fun?" muttered Betty, wiping her forearm across her brow before dipping her scrubbing brush into the soapy water and taking it to the kitchen table once more.

Bonfire night two days ago had gone well. Everyone had enjoyed themselves, despite the last awkward question brought up by Lawrence before he and Mary had disappeared for their long-awaited walk. She hoped he got what he was looking for, both with Mary and the answer to the question he'd asked. She doubted she'd seen the end of the latter, though. In fact, she took a look at the clock. Even though Jane had told her not to come in to work until tomorrow, she felt she could get away with taking a stroll up to the airfield. If she was caught, she could tell Jane she was passing and, whilst she was there, would wait around for her friends and walk back with them.

With one last look at the scorch marks on the table, Betty admitted defeat on that front and rushed, as much as her still aching side would let her, up the stairs to change. Her uniform felt a little tight around her side, but she put that down to last night's rabbit pie. It did feel good to put it on again.

She opened the back door. "Bobby!" In answer to her call, the spaniel rolled off his back and trotted over to sit by her side from where he'd been asleep amongst the carrots. "Good boy," she told him, reaching down to rub his ears, and then, with a pat to her skirt, she led him indoors, locked the back door, and took her hat from its hook by the front door. "Care for a walk?" she asked, fixing his lead to his collar.

Ruth had told Betty that whilst she was still off work, the recovered Bobby would be left with her. This had caused a minor argument resolved by Bobby falling asleep on Bonfire Night on Betty's lap. Still, she did feel rather guilty and hoped over the coming weekend everything, or as many loose ends as were possible, would be tied up and she could hand back this lovely spaniel to his true owner.

At the guardroom, they were greeted by the chaps on duty as returning heroes. Bobby especially seemed to enjoy all the attention. Betty often thought if he were a pudding, he'd be a tart. After they'd finally managed to get away, Betty let Bobby off his leash, and the spaniel promptly rushed off in the direction of the kitchen, his next favorite haunt after the flight line hut.

Betty took a look around; nothing had changed. There'd been no more bombing raids since the one back in September, and now, with November turning out as damp and cold as she'd expected it to…well, "good to be back" didn't come close, even to a windswept airfield. An engine was gunned somewhere above her head, and when she looked up, she just had time to catch a glimpse of a Magister trainer buzzing overhead, a head and arm hanging over the side and waving in her direction. She grinned. She'd recognize that mess of brown hair streaming out from beneath the flying helmet anywhere.

Betty quickly made up her mind and, making certain her hat was on firmly, set off at her best pace toward the hut and the plane her friend was bringing in to land. It'd been too long since she'd been around the excitement of the airfield, and already she was feeling better. The ground crew stood by, ready to lock and chock the plane when Penny brought it to a standstill. As she reached her destination, she was a little surprised to see she wasn't alone. Thelma stood watching, her arm linked with one of Shirley's. The engineer actually looked totally clean, considering she'd had a long day tinkering with the base's planes.

"Betty!" both exclaimed at the same time and hurried to meet her. "So good to see you, but didn't Jane tell you she'd have you strung up if she saw you before tomorrow?" Thelma asked.

Betty tapped the side of her nose, one hand on the top of her hat to prevent it blowing off. "What Jane doesn't know…"

A voice coming from around the corner of the hut made them all jump in alarm. "Won't what? Hurt her?"

All three did a comical turn of heads until they were looking at where Jane was now leaning up against a wooden post. If they thought they, especially Betty, were going to be in trouble, though, the huge smile on Jane's face indicated otherwise.

"Jane!" Betty said in an unnaturally cheerful voice. "We were just talking about you!"

"I heard," she said, ungluing herself from the post and coming over to join them. She gave Betty the eye before settling herself down on the hut's decking and patting it. "Come on, you lot, take a seat here. I've news, but I want to wait until Penny's here."

"Doris and Mary are just finishing off their paperwork," Thelma told them. "Do you want them to hear?"

"Fine with me," Jane replied.

Whilst Thelma stood by to help Betty in case she needed it, Shirley shifted from one foot to the other. "I'll see you later, then," and made to walk away before Jane interrupted her.

"Sit, please, Shirley," she asked. "This affects you, and I promise," Jane added upon noting a look of panic come over Shirley's face, "you'll like it."

Before anything else, Lawrence strode over from the direction of the kitchens, a half-eaten ham sandwich in his hand, with Bobby hard on his heels just waiting for anything to slip from it. "Betty, there you are. I was told you were around." He held up an envelope with the word 'Herbert' typed on it as he got to where she sat. "Do you know anything about this?"

"About what?" she asked, earning herself a look of disbelief from Thelma, who'd known her long enough to know when she had something to hide.

"About this anonymous letter. This letter that has just one rather cryptic line typed inside."

"Which says?" Betty asked, trying not to meet his eyes.

"I quote, 'Pearls equal bricks and mortar,' unquote."

"I have no idea what that's supposed to mean," Betty told him, po-faced.

Lawrence raised an eye, but further discussion was forestalled as Doris and Mary chose that moment to come out of the hut. Thelma quickly told them, "Girls, take a seat. Jane's got some news. We're just waiting for Penny."

Shortly after, all were sat down and Jane stood up, motioning for everyone else to stay where they were.

"Shirley, I'm so glad that you're here. Thelma was down at the guardroom and intercepted a rather lost messenger boy about thirty minutes ago. It seemed he's new to the area and was asking for directions to Ruth's house. Now, as you probably know, Thelma can be quite persuasive, and though it's certainly not normal, she found out why he was after you, and your being here makes this as good a time as any to give you this."

Pulling her to her feet, Jane handed over a telegram to a confused Shirley. In wartime, only one reason came to everyone's minds when they received an official telegram. However, Jane was smiling as she handed it over. The silence was deafening. As she read it, everyone could see her face getting paler and paler until, afraid her legs would collapse from under her, Jane and Thelma, who'd been watching closely, each took her gently by an elbow and eased her down until she was sitting once more.

"What is it?" Doris asked, her voice shaking.

In spite of her very pale demeanor, Shirley was now beaming from ear to ear, and none of them thought they'd seen her happier in the whole time they'd known her. Finally, she managed to tell them what the message said.

"I don't believe it! It's from the War Office. My husband, my Ted, he's alive! He's a prisoner of war in Germany."

"That's wonderful!" she could make out Penny

saying from amongst her friends as they all tried to hug her at once. "Well, not wonderful he's a prisoner, but wonderful he's alive. What happened? Does it say?"

Shirley turned the message over but had to shake her head. "There's nothing else. It does tell me the camp he's in, so at least I can write to him now."

Penny kissed her cheeks and hugged her friend again. "He's alive, that's the main thing. Just hold on to that."

"I will," Shirley agreed, tears of happiness now rolling down her cheeks. "Oh, I will!"

Doris disentangled herself from the happy melee and stood up, clapping her hands. "There's only one way we can celebrate!"

Penny slapped a hand to her head. "Please, don't say it."

"Fish and chips all round!"

The Air Transport Auxiliary Mystery Club has more adventures in store! If you enjoyed *A Wing and a Prayer*, you'll want to look for the next book in the Broken Wings series. Here's a sample:

Wild Blue Yonder

by

M. W. Arnold

Broken Wings, Book 2

Chapter One

May 5th 1943

Shirley Tuttle made another vain attempt to tuck her ponytail back whence it had come, only for the slipstream to hook it from her fingers again.

"Can't you fly a bit slower?" she yelled for what she knew was the third time in the last five minutes.

Adjusting her goggles a little, she gripped the side of the open cockpit even harder.

"Can't you hear the cylinder?" Doris Winter shouted back into her earphones. "Bloody thing's misfiring like crazy!"

Shirley frowned and did her best to concentrate on the note of the engine over the whistle of the wind. She still couldn't hear anything out of the ordinary. Knowing perfectly well Doris would keep them up for as long as the fuel lasted if she couldn't pinpoint the problem she claimed was there, Shirley removed her flying helmet from her left ear, shifted as much as her seat restraints would allow until she could lean forward and slightly out of the cockpit. She made the mistake of looking down and had to make a serious effort to keep her breakfast down. Doing her best to ignore the bitter taste in her throat, she blanked out the racket from the engine as much as possible and focused as if her life depended upon it.

Somewhat to her surprise, she could hear something; barely. So, to make certain she wasn't imagining things, she leaned over the other side, being extra careful not to let her eyes stray toward the ground this time. After a couple of long minutes, Shirley put her flying helmet back on straight, leant back into her seat, not the most comfortable of things, and got her breathing back under control.

Before she'd quite managed to settle, Doris spoke into her ear again. "Well. Could you hear it? The bloody cylinder needs replacing!"

Aware of the risk she'd never hear the end of it if she didn't agree, even though she did, Shirley replied, "You're probably right. I'll replace it—if you manage to get us down in one piece."

She knew she'd said the wrong thing when immediately she'd finished speaking the little trainer was sent into a rapid roll to the right, quickly followed by one to the left.

"You were saying?"

Only once she was certain she'd swallowed the last of her breakfast, again did Shirley answer. "I was saying…you're right, and I'll replace it once we land."

"Thought you'd see it my way," Doris replied, not troubling to hide the smugness from her voice.

"Good-oh," Shirley told her after a few moments, not trusting her stomach not to intervene if she tried a longer sentence.

Shirley did her best to relax into her seat and to do what Doris had encouraged her to do when they'd strapped into the airplane twenty long minutes ago,—to enjoy the flight. As Doris straightened and then turned the plane onto a course to take them back to their home base of RAF Hamble, she tore her eyes from the tiny windshield before her and looked around. The late afternoon May skies were a bright, cheery blue, with only wisps of cloud scattered about. They followed the path of the River Hamble, and she could make out the patchwork of fields and hedgerows in Britain's green and pleasant land. As they came in toward the airfield, they passed over where the bombs had fallen late last year when the airfield had suffered a hit-and-run raid. Even here you could barely discern the craters they'd left. It stirred her spirit to see the country look so relatively normal.

Time heals everything, she thought as Doris advised her to "Stand by. We're coming in to land."

She gripped the lips of the cockpit, tried not to bite her tongue, and whispered a prayer as the undercarriage bumped the uneven grass once and bounced up a little before settling onto terra firma at the second time of asking. Only as they pulled up before the flight line hut and the ground crew dashed under the wings to put chocks under the wheels did she start to breathe a little easier. However, not until the engine finally juddered and stopped did she feel able to release her grip. Undoing the harness, she heaved herself out of the seat and was a little surprised to see she hadn't actually left finger marks.

"Earth to Shirley," Doris said, resting a hand on her forearm. "You all right?"

Sweeping the helmet off her head, Shirley ran her fingers through her red hair and, finding those fingers a little shaky, gave up the idea of retying her ponytail. If her boss called her up for it, she'd let him; or she'd throw up all over his shoes. The odds were slightly in

M. W. Arnold

the latter's favor, she thought, allowing her American friend to give her a hand down. Fighting the urge to drop to her knees and kiss the grass, she gratefully kept a hold of Doris's hand and, with unsteady knees, made her way into the hut.

Waiting for them was the operations officer, Betty Palmer. She held out a steaming cup of tea to a grateful Shirley, who took a long, rejuvenating swallow. Sighing as the sweet brew washed around her mouth, she closed her eyes. "Betty, you are an angel. Where did you conjure up so much sugar?"

Betty tapped the side of her nose. "The cook owes me a favor," she said with an enigmatic wink.

Allowing her legs to collapse under her, Shirley sank into a chair, finding the energy to say, "My nerves thank you and would like to have your children."

Doris flopped down next to where the mechanic was sipping her tea and ruffled her hair. "See, told you you'd survive!"

"Barely," Shirley countered, a smile playing on her lips. "What did I do to deserve those rolls?"

Doris opened her mouth to reply when she became aware of Betty, hands balled on her hips. "Rolls? Something you want to tell me, Doris?"

"Not if I don't have to," Doris muttered, canting her head to one side and trying a set of puppy eyes on her landlady.

Betty patted the American on the head before disappearing into the hut and reappearing with a cup of her own. She took a seat next to her friends. "You weren't trying to put the wind up our Shirley, were you?"

Doris affected a look of such affront both Betty and

4

Shirley burst out laughing, shortly joined by the perpetrator. Once she'd got herself under control, Doris held up her hands. "Oh, all right. I was curious as to how she'd react once we were in the air. Shirley told me as we took off she had thoughts about being a pilot."

Betty's eyebrows darted toward her hairline, "Really?"

Shirley blanched and vigorously shook her head, gulping furiously before she was able to find her voice. "I don't think so. I'm quite happy to keep my feet on the ground."

"Are you certain?" Doris asked, placing a hand over her friend's. "'I really didn't mean to put you off, if it's what you really want to do."

Shirley leant her head on her friend's shoulder and squeezed her hand. "You didn't," she assured her, "not really. I don't think I've the stomach for it."

Betty got to her feet, placed her hands on the small of her back, and stretched before saying to the younger girl, 'Don't dismiss the idea so quickly. We need pilots, and we even train complete novices now."

Doris heaved herself to her feet to follow Betty, though not before saying to Shirley, squeezing her shoulder in encouragement, "Now there's something to think about."

****

"You're sure you haven't heard anything from him?"

Ruth Stone put down the piece she was editing for the next edition of the *Hamble Gazette* and tried to usher up a smile her face didn't feel like finishing. She was very fond of the young pilot who stood anxiously wringing her hands in front of her. Considering the amount of time she'd spent around Ruth's cottage since she'd got together with Ruth's nephew Herbert—or Lawrence as everyone else called him—this was a good thing. Mary Whitworth-Baines had asked her the same question every day for the past two weeks.

"I'm sorry, Mary," Ruth replied, knowing it wasn't the answer either of them wanted to hear. "Believe me, you'll be the first to know if…" She hastened to amend her words as her friend's mouth dropped open. "I mean, when, when he contacts me…if he doesn't write to you first, of course."

Mary whipped off her Air Transport Auxiliary cap and swiped the back of a hand across her brow. The weary expression on her face mirrored the one on Ruth's. "I'm sorry, really I am. It's just I'm so worried about him."

"Me too, honey. Me too."

"It'd help if we only knew where he was, or what he was doing!" Mary sighed, letting her head slump before slowly raising it to look at the older woman. "Special Branch or not, you'd think they'd let him write or something."

"I agree, but obviously not."

"And you're sure he didn't give you any hints where he was going, or how long he'd be away?"

Ruth turned her head to where her assistant and reporter Walter wasn't bothering to hide his curiosity at the conversation. "Make yourself useful and put the kettle on will you, Walter?"

"No problem, Boss," he said, pushing his chair back and stepping over where Bobby, Ruth's cocker spaniel lay on his back, legs twitching as he dreamt.

"Please…" She turned back to Mary, allowing a little exasperation to show. "You ask me the same question every day, and the answers still the same."

Mary was granted a little time before replying, as Walter appeared with the tea. Taking hers with thanks, she took a quick sip, scalding her tongue a little. "I'm sorry, Ruth, really I am. I'll try not to be so troublesome. I just can't stop worrying about him."

Her own nerves betrayed her as Ruth's cup rattled a little when she placed it back on the saucer. "It's all right. I do too." Then, as the thought struck her, she picked up the piece of copy she'd been working on. Passing it to Mary, she said with a grimace, "This may give us both some perspective."

Ten minutes later, Ruth had shut up the newspaper office for the day, and they were making their way back to Riverview Cottage where she lived. Mary was walking arm in arm with her, whilst Bobby trotted along at their heels, stopping every now and then to sniff at the bases of trees and to scare a few foolhardy ducks into the river. The article had obviously given Mary much to think about, exactly as Ruth had hoped. Even Bobby's antics, usually enough to set anyone laughing, were being ignored. She didn't even appear to notice when he scampered around her heels, dropping, picking up, and then dropping again a stick for her to throw. Taking pity upon him, Ruth stooped and threw the stick, hoping it wasn't coated in what it smelled like! As Mary hadn't noticed, Ruth quickly dipped her hands into the river, took out a handkerchief to dry them, and caught up with her friend, who now stood with one hand on the gate of Betty Palmer's cottage where she lodged.

'"Mary?" Ruth whispered, laying a hand gently on her friend's shoulder.

She hadn't meant to shock her with the article, merely make her realize there were bigger issues in the world than their own troubles. Perhaps showing her the piece she'd written on the Luftwaffe air raid on Exeter from the night of the third of May was too much? It wasn't like her own imagination wasn't running away with her sometimes as well.

Obviously she'd known her nephew far longer than Mary, who'd only met him the previous year. However, the two had grown close even in such a short time. Perhaps the relationship had progressed so quickly because of the incident at the airfield last year. Their friend Betty had been stabbed whilst her sister's death was being investigated. At first, Ruth hadn't entirely approved of their lodgers, all members of the Air Transport Auxiliary, setting themselves up as real-life Miss Marples. To say their methods were unusual was to put it mildly. However, together with a hefty dose of luck, they had played their part in bringing the matter to a satisfactory conclusion.

"If I'd known it would have this effect on you, I'd never have written the article." Ruth told her when Mary still hadn't made a move to open the gate. "Really. I don't know why I did. I stupidly wanted to try to get your mind around to the fact there are bigger problems than ours around."

After a minute, Mary blinked and seemed to become aware of where she was. The smile she placed upon her face was distinctly forced, though her voice was warm enough. "It's all right. It has helped to put things into perspective." Her smile became a little more natural. "I'll try to stop bothering you so much." She took her hand off the gate and linked her arm with Ruth's again, and the two set off once more toward Ruth's cottage. "I can't help it," Mary blurted out as the two of them stopped before Ruth's front door. "I think I love him!"

Before Ruth could reply, a telegraph boy, these days nicknamed "the angels of death," stepped out of the shadows and handed her a telegram. All the blood rushed from her head, and even as she reached her hand out to take it, she fell to the ground in a dead faint.

A word about the author...

Mick is a hopeless romantic who was born in England and spent fifteen years roaming around the world in the pay of HM Queen Elisabeth II in the Royal Air Force before putting down roots and realizing how much he missed the travel. This he's replaced somewhat with his writing, including reviewing books and supporting fellow saga and romance authors in promoting their novels.

He's the proud keeper of two Romanian Were-Cats, is mad on the music of Brian Wilson and the Beach Boys, and enjoys the theatre and loving his Manchester-United-supporting wife.

Finally, Mick is a full member of the Romantic Novelists Association. *A Wing and a Prayer* will be his second published novel, and he is very proud to be welcomed into The Rose Garden.

Visit Mick at:
https://www.facebook.com/MWArnoldAuthor
Twitter: mick859
Instagram: mick859